# Paddy Kelly

---

# The American Way

*Dear Patti,*
*Enjoyed meeting you guys, and really enjoyed our chat!*
*Enjoy the read!*
*P. Kelly*

## Fiction4All

# ACKNOWLEDGEMENTS

Before writing this book, I'd never heard of the Lawrence Strike however, after reading Volume IV of Philip S. Foner's thirteen volume achievement, *History of the Labor Movement in the United States,* it was clear that the forty-two pages he devoted to this story weren't nearly enough and the accomplishments of these people in the face of overwhelming odds was of such magnitude that it had to be included in the *Building of Empire* series as a standalone story.

Foner's works should be mandatory to every prospective graduate of History, Law, Sociology and Politics.

My original intention was to write a novel devoted to the Triangle Factory Fire however, my sister sent me a copy of David von Drehle's *Triangle; The Fire That Changed America* and I knew within the first three pages that here was my historical launch point. After reading the beauty and accuracy with which von Drehle captured the 1911 incident and the plethora of awards his book garnered, (pretty much every literary award New Yorkers have to offer which essentially renders all other criticism mute), that the task had been admirably accomplished. Any student of the Triangle episode is obligated to read his book.

Research can be fun but is never easy so many thanks to Anne, Head Librarian at the Law Library, University College, and her more than able staff, The New York Public Library and their staff for all their assistance in the months of trolling through the Congressional Record and all its associated documents.

Thanks to my parents' innate sense of history arising from their socio-economic oppression resulting from the political aftermath and unchecked corporate greed following WWII, which played no small part in our day-to-day family life.

Much appreciation to John Wells Davidson editor, *A Crossroads of Freedom, the 1912 Campaign Speeches.*

Many thanks to Didrik Wenklo who's help in proof reading was invaluable.

I am much indebted to friend and colleague Tim Janos whose technical abilities with a camera and those incomprehensible editing machines allowed such a professionally polished promo video to be produced, now on *You Tube* under *The American Way, Book Trailer*.

Folks at the Lawrence Museum in Lawrence, Mass. deserve a nod for much of the general information on the worker's conditions in the factories of the period and their work records.

Another friend and colleague, David Kehoe, who on more than one occasion made sure I had food in the cupboard, and a few bucks to buy paper to print on, gets a very special thanks for the Foreword.

And last but not least, (cliché but true), my undying gratitude to my fans and supporters of *Operation Underworld* for it is their financial support which allowed me to write *The American Way*. It is my fervent hope that I and other history junkies like myself may continue to bring history to life so that you may identify more closely with the lives of those who came before us.

Hopefully the trend will evolve into tradition.

# Paddy Kelly

## FOREWORD

One of the first things you learn when writing a story about true life is just how unwieldy true life is. Another is how difficult it is to extract the compelling story you know is there and relay it to an audience you want to be sympathetic, while remaining true to the characters, their sense of who they were and the way they emoted through their experience. This task is compounded further when you realize that the good guys don't always win and storylines rarely resolve themselves in a timely and orderly manner. The writer, who discovers a story that does behave itself by coming to a satisfying conclusion, following an exciting climax, is one luck son-of-a-bitch.

Little did, my good friend, Paddy Kelly realize that, in the summer of '61, when his Italian seamstress mother related the stories of the Triangle Factory fire and the New York City garment workers' strikes, that he was one luck son-of-a-bitch.

One element inherent in this story is the fact that the American dream was badly floundering. Good men and women were dying and with them their dream of a better life never having been realized. Additionally, beneath the veneer of respectability of a nation some called 'the greatest on God's earth', the rules of the game were being molded not by men true and just, but by men whose avarice, motivated by greed fueled an unbridled lust for power.

Can we say the same today?

The country was/is still an idea to be proud of, but the question was and is yet to be answered, would She be proud of them?

Although this chapter of American history took place almost exactly 30 years prior to the sinking of the Normandie in New York Harbor, the two stories share profound similarities.

Both involved a large number of immigrants, convoluted but enterprising paths of the main participants, and both dealt with an ongoing struggle by the common man against coordinated government sponsored corruption.

3

Further, the conditions propagated by the dishonest industrialists of both periods is not without severe consequences.

The actions of the dishonest lumber, oil and mineral barons created and contributed to the climate which directly gave rise to the foundation of Organized Crime in America. The founders of Italian and Jewish organized crime came to appreciate that working within the system was a pointless exercise and therefore not a viable option to realize the American Dream. Immigrants such as Lucky Luciano, Meyer Lansky and Albert Anastasia were not inherently evil, they merely realized how to fight back against the likes of William Wood and William Howard Taft. That was to play by the same rules as the industrio-political leaders. It is no coincidence that Luciano's Syndicate was founded, structured and run like a large American corporation.

This was the time when crime truly became the left hand of politics in America.

Interestingly then, as today, both Organized Crime members and big Industrialists saw themselves as merely being 'competitive'. The faces have changed but, in many respects, the complexions remain the same.

The events of this story took place at a time when the Political and Industrial Bosses were learning how to more efficiently mask their treachery, cover their tracks and divert blame. Perhaps more importantly, they became able to consolidate and control large sections of the print media as they do today through electronic media. Interestingly as well, is the Government's reaction to the events of the Lawrence Mill Strike and the Bush Administration's reaction to 9/11, which bear striking similarities.

One was the passing of *The Espionage Act*, a wide ranging piece of legislation, granting authorities dangerously broad powers and prohibiting the interference with military/police operations. This is the bill which helped lay the foundation for the *Patriot Act*, which also dramatically increased the ability of law enforcement agencies' to invade public privacy. Both are woefully open to interpretation. *The Espionage Act* allowed Woodrow Wilson, traditionally remembered for his humanitarianism, to order the arrest and imprisonment of thousands of innocents, including a politician who ran against him, Eugene Debs.

After making a speech in Canton, Ohio, in which he merely criticized The Act, Debs was arrested, tried and sentenced to ten years in the Atlanta Penitentiary. His is but one high profile example of the hundreds of people in the early years of the last century to be arrested and denied the basic human rights which were laid out in the American Constitution, but apparently no longer guaranteed.

Atrocities which were sadly repeated in the early years of this century.

Perhaps the most significant result of the Lawrence Strike is that it gave rise to the time when government officials, in this case President Taft, Governor Foss and Mayor John Scanlon, along with their respective colleagues, were able to test the waters with regards to how much brute force they could employ to suppress the American people and rival political movements.

Both sides, the workers and the government interests, fully realized that this strike, like the others of the era, were political movements, heavily rooted in the ongoing, world-wide, class struggle. The approximately 3% who controlled roughly 97% of the national economy were, for the first time under attack. This period was truly the onset of the Class Wars in America.

Further, Lawrence is a sad and frightening glimpse of how one generation of European immigrants, having become Americans, just half a century earlier, abused and exploited to a scandalous extent, the generation that followed.

One of the primary goals of the novelization of the Lawrence story was to capture the different backgrounds, personalities and temperaments of the strike leaders, strikers, industrialists and politicians and their similar and conflicting rhythms. To this end one of the more useful devices the writer has employed is to write the characters' dialogue in proper English to signal they are speaking their native languages and to write in broken English to indicate when they are not. Chief among these characters are the unsung heroes of the strike, Joe Ettor, Arturo Giovannini and 'Big' Bill Haywood.

# The American Way

Above all *The American Way* is not meant to be a mere historical recounting of the incidents. It is a humanistic account of the characters and their social and political impact on the history of America. As Mr. Kelly points out in the book with his quote from George Bernard Shaw to Upton Sinclair:

*'I have regarded you, not as a novelist, but as an historian. For it is my considered opinion, unshaken at 85, that records of fact are not history. They are only annals, which cannot become historical until the artist-poet-philosopher rescues them from the unintelligible chaos of their actual occurrence and arranges them into works of art.'*

It is also important to point out that the Lawrence action was not a woman's strike, organized and led by women as taught in many Gender classes. The action was led, at great loss and expense, by all the men and all the women of all nationalities of the Industrial Workers of the World, to whom this story actually belongs. It is wrong to twist it into a gender issue. The leadership of the I.W.W. and its members, (some 200 plus of them in the Lawrence chapter), who preached and practiced without exception, across the board equality, led and organized the strike.

As part of the series *Building of Empire: Crime and Politics the Cornerstone of America*, Paddy also demonstrates how, with each successive administration, U.S. citizens have become less and less influential in the selection of their Government and the industrial magnets more and more in possession of that country. The events leading up to and including the 1912 election, and the candidates' abject fear of the I.W.W., were instrumental in this evolution.

The compelling facts surrounding the first 48 state election that was the 1912 presidential race are a cornerstone of present day political evolution. The colorful lives of the three candidates, for example, and the fact that two formally resided in the White House combined with the way in which the political atmosphere was dominated by this new, and extremely controversial, concept of 'Progressivism' are exemplary of which way the country was heading. However, long before the Progressives and their attempt to reign in and tame the industrialists, events surrounding the race for the 'Big Prize' would signal a change in the not so great American tradition, the Wild, Wild, West. Not the fabled Cowboys killing the renegade Indians, which would give rise to America's mythical agrarian past. But the wild West way of thinking that seeped down from politics into business and public life and dictates there is only one rule and that is that there are no rules. The attitude whose dictum is 'Winning isn't everything. It's the only thing!'

The viciousness of the 1912 election was to also set new standards in mudslinging, gerrymandering and the spread of propaganda.

Wilson's election marked only the second time between 1856 and 1932 that a Democrat would be elected and it would be another Roosevelt who would win in '32. With Wilson receiving only a little over 40% of the popular vote, he relied heavily on the support of the newly devised Electoral College, a system that is capable of rendering the popular vote mute.

Unions which were the biggest threat to the existing system enjoyed by industrialists such as Mellon, Carnegie and one of the richest men in the world J.P. Morgan were, for the sake of political expediency, generally branded anarchists. Taft's people, for example, knew where their bread was buttered and vigorously fought for and supported the industrial tycoons and the judicial supremacy.

By 1910 the rifts had widened to chasms and by New Years Day, 1912, the battle lines were well established. Conflict was inevitable all that was needed was the spark to ignite the conscience of a nation.

That spark was to come from the scrap bin beneath a cutter's table on the eight floor of the Triangle Waistcoat factory in Greenwich Village, New York on a clear Saturday afternoon, as the work day was ending. The story was later retold, by a Sicilian seamstress, to her Irish son, in the Summer of 1961.

I hope you will enjoy this story as much as I did.

- David Kehoe,
writer, historia

To the woman who first related the stories of the
New York garment worker's strikes to me.
My mother


And in gratitude to the man who infected me with
his habit of voracious reading, and unbeknownst to himself,
would have made a good Woobly.
My father.

## PROLOGUE

At the turn of the last century, the sprawling forests which used to cover eastern Texas, Louisiana, Mississippi, Alabama, Florida and southern Georgia were sold by the Federal Government to private lumber interests for as little as 12 ½ cents an acre in tracts as large as 87,000 acres. This land was public domain and as such had been earmarked for the building of houses and schools for the poor at a time when whole districts of schools were closing due to lack of funding.

Following the illegal sale of these lands, the lumber companies moved into the towns across the vast southern region, bought the judges, ousted the sheriffs and replaced them with hired gunmen who deputized their own men. Anyone who objected, including former authorities, had only to name their price or be jailed. As the prosperity of the mills grew out of all proportion to the short time it took them to establish themselves, large numbers of bodies were required to man the machines and do the dangerous work.

This problem was solved by jailing any unemployed men or small groups of men passing through the regions. Later a company agent would conveniently show up and offer to pay their 'fines' provided they worked them off. These work periods routinely lasted two to three times the illegal sentences which had been metered out. Voluntary workers seeking refuge from economic depression often found themselves in similar situations.

Pay was usually by 'time check', a piece of paper stamped, "To be cashed at a later date." If cashed prior to that date a 'cashing charge' of up to 50% was added. Paper chits or cardboard discs often served to substitute wages as well and were usually marked "Good for Merchandise Only." Merchandise restricted to what was in The Company stores and which was between 5 and 50% more expensive than the national average. If the worker insisted on being paid cash he was charged a surcharge of up to 30%, on the transaction. It was not unusual for any worker who objected too loudly to quietly vanish.

In early 1911 the only attempt to break up what in essence was legalized slavery, acknowledged on the Federal statute books as 'peonage', of tens of thousands of lumber workers resulted in the mass beatings, torture and execution of **hundreds** of union organizers. This with the full knowledge and endorsement of the Governors of the states involved, as well as, in several cases, President William Howard Taft. A contemporary Federal 'investigation' stated that;

*We found literally every labor law on the statue books being violated. In these communities free speech, free assembly and free press are denied and time and again the employer's agent may be placed in office to do his bidding.*

The report was forwarded to the White House however, no action was taken and these conditions remained in some areas for years after The Great War ended in 1918.

These were not 'isolated incidents' found only in the 'backwards' South. These working conditions were representative of the standard of the unskilled laborer throughout the United States at the time. A time when America established herself as a world leader. A political and military world leader based solely on her industrial might. Industrial might founded on the exploitation of immigrant and domestic labor.

The sole group of individuals who attempted the rescue of these workers were a small group of men and women who, in contrast to the government of the time, were dedicated to the principle that **all** men **are** created equal. A group who left a legacy, which to this day, remains written out of the American history books. They were the soon to be outlawed, (by presidential edict), labor union the Industrial Workers of the World, derogatorily known as the 'Wobblies'.

At the same time as the "Great Lumber Wars" of the South were being waged, during the worst winter on record, against one of the richest men in the world, the understaffed, financially struggling I.W.W. were unexpectedly dragged onto another Battle front . . .

Paddy Kelly

'I have regarded you, not as a novelist,
but as an historian. For it is my
considered opinion, unshaken at 85, that
records of fact are not history. They are
only annals, which cannot become historical
until the artist-poet-philosopher rescues
them from the unintelligible chaos of
their actual occurrence and
arranges them into works of art.'

**- George Bernard Shaw
to Upton Sinclair 5 days after
the bombing of Pearl Harbor.**

# INTRODUCTION

In the Spring of 1911 you could forgive New York City for its unique style of urban aesthetic. That distinct brand of romantic ambience which influenced the great Robert Henri and his collection of newspaper illustrators-turned artists. Henri's Muses?

The swelling skyline, steaming rooftops and hundreds of miles of cracked pavement and uneven cobbles. The endless rows of brownstone walk-ups and tens of thousands of clothes lines of clean laundry flapping like giant doves in the afternoon breeze above the dirty, dank horse shit-strewn streets of the isle of Manhattan. Henri's talented group were the *New York Realists*, later sarcastically dubbed by a cynical Press, "The Ashcan School".

However, New York, like New Yorkers, has a way of absorbing her critics. Tainting them with guilt by association and, much like China and the Chinese have managed to do across the ages, eventually assimilating them into her culture and making them her own. Of course the impressionistic forms perceived through the warm earth tones and subdued colors of the cityscapes The Realists created did nothing to relieve the bitter winters. Winters rivaling anything in Northern Europe which would gradually give way to a heat mounting daily in oppressiveness until mid-Summer when, combined with an asphyxiating humidity, became so murderous as to cause horses to faint, hundreds to die and encourage every insect within the city limits to attempt to outbreed its equatorial cousins.

Contributing to this modern, turn-of-the-century, medieval atmosphere were the babble of scores of foreign languages emanating from the 18,000 immigrants hemorrhaging into 'The City' each month. Immigrants arriving with hopes, dreams and aspirations.

Aspirations which would quickly turn to exasperation, frustration and finally desperation at the overcrowding which already stood between 600 to 800 persons per acre. A fact which the politicians and factory bosses conveniently spun as evidence of the 'Land Of Opportunity'.

Not to put too fine a point on it, but there were more Italians living in the confines of New York then there were in the entire nation of Italy.

Somewhere around 1910 the U.S. population hit 92 million, up from 76 million in 1900. In less than two years America's countable population would be 100 million. One hundred million men, women and children who required food, shelter, clothing and work.

In other words, goods and services.

The contradiction was that in a country founded on immigrant labor more than half its citizens had little or no access to the end products of the results of their labor. Worse yet, sixty to sixty-five percent of America's working population had no access to government.

Add to this social stew the fact that New York City was not only the financial capital of the nation, but there were more factories in the confines of N.Y.C. alone then in the largest most productive woolen center in the world at the time, the state of Massachusetts, and the dramatic events which were about to unfold were understandably justified.

From an industrial perspective, production quotas saw no ceiling in sight and realistically 18,000 warm bodies a month might not be enough fodder for the ever propagating factories.

With the nation's population threatening to spill over the 100 million mark, a 58 hour work week was the standard, providing the company adhered to the law, as 100 hour work weeks were not uncommon. Essentially there were no child labor laws, mandatory hourly wage laws had been stalled in Congress for the last 20 years and there was no overtime pay. Things were, as far as the manufacturing sector were concerned, looking pretty bright.

On the streets of the Lower East Side however, the only future which could be envisioned was one of diminishing hope as the exploitation of immigrant labor, increasingly sanctioned by law, broke new boundaries and climbed to ever greater heights.

The fact that in late 1911 early 1912 one hundred people a day died in U.S. workplaces, the price of a 12 cent loaf of bread varied by as much as a dollar, and there was virtually no government support for the creation of any kind of relief, counseling or immigrant education in the American system, didn't seem to slow anything down. For each one hundred that died every day, including The Lord's Day, five to six hundred got off the boat in New York City alone.

The cornerstone to free enterprise was free labor. Or at least as near to free as you could get it.

So by 1911 those coming into the country were, in a painfully unfolding reality, finding the American Dream a foreign nightmare. This of course meant that the immigrants, would have to learn the hard way. The American way.

An Englishman visiting the Little Big Horn memorial in Montana remarked that Custer's last stand was a 'tragic event'. The father of the Native American family standing next to him offered an alternative viewpoint.

"Depends whether you ate hamburger or buffalo." The heat at the bottom of the Great Melting Pot has always been a helluv'a a lot hotter at the bottom then it is at the top.

So in the Uptown districts of New York, where the heat never reached above room temperature, the ever growing plethora of 'private' clubs for the wealthy, as social diseases do, was rapidly spreading. Throughout these districts of the yet-to-be-christened 'Big Apple' pot-bellied entrepreneurs loitered in exclusive clubs, thumbs neatly tucked under tight fitting braces, sucking on over-sized, over-priced cigars congratulating each other on their business acumen and guile and how they got Manhattan Island from the Indians for a miserly $24 worth of blankets and wampum.

That is until the inevitable happened. They 'civilized' and educated the red man, made him speak their language and were able to get his side of the story.

Turns out he kept records too and not only did the Native Americans who took the chest full of pretty beads and warm blankets, no doubt with a measure of puzzled gratitude, not own Manhattan, as ownership of land wasn't a concept to such an advanced peoples, they didn't even live there. They were only down from the north for a hunting trip. None of which altered the fact that the most civilized of those Indians could never become a member of one of those exclusive 'Members Only' clubs.

The most exclusive and most politically powerful of those private clubs in the United States at the time was Tammany Hall.

The Hall was an interesting institution.

Nearly as old as the United States itself, Tammany didn't control New York politics. It was New York politics. Which was handy for the Democratic Party as the Mayoral seat of N.Y.C. was the quickest way to the Governor's mansion in Albany which, was one of the most direct stepping stones back south to #1600 Pennsylvania Avenue, Washington D.C.

Tammany's unofficial credo was, 'anything for a vote.' and it wasn't just a motto. History duly records they did **anything** to procure votes.

However, Tammany was also interesting because to this day there is no universal consensus on its actual contribution to the people. Was it all bad or was there some good? There can be no question it was corrupt, but can there be such a thing as good corruption? In the mythology of the moral high ground of American idealism, no such animal exists.

To the hundreds of thousands of underprivileged New Yorkers at the turn-of-the-century whose votes were wooed, cajoled and bought by the Bosses with free picnics, a turkey at Christmas or a few quid when the rent was overdue and dad was out of work, corruption was a matter of perception. All the Hall asked in return was a vote. A pencil tick on a piece of paper. For a century and a half The Hall controlled, drove and was New York City politics and nothing short of a disaster could change that.

It was on a Saturday afternoon, out on the dirty streets of the Pig Market, Washington Square Park and Greene Street not much was different, save for the fact that the deadliest work place disaster in three and half centuries of New York City history was only about fifteen minutes away.

In the next forty-five minutes the face of New York politics would be transformed forever. By the next morning, how the nation was perceived abroad would be severely affected and by Monday morning the entire labor history of the United States would be influenced for the next seventy to eighty years and with it, how presidents would conduct their domestic business.

So it was that hundreds of thousands of Europeans, from hundreds of nationalities banded together to break tradition, cross cultural, ethnic and religious boundaries and meld into one to free themselves from the slavery of the turn-of-the-century, 'free' enterprise system.

This unification did not come quite as gradual as industrialists and their cronies in Washington would have liked or as smoothly as some twentieth century filmmakers and historians would have us believe. It occurred in only a few short years, ignited and then spurred on by spontaneously erupting, key events, the political heat of which would weld the determination of a dedicated few into the commitment of hundreds of thousands and then millions.

So, even though it might have been an Olympian challenge to cross Hester Street without getting hit by a horse cart, robbed by a pick pocket or stepping in one of those piles of horse manure, Lower Manhattan had to be forgiven, as The City had only just begun to assume the mantle of a modern day Rome. A crown she wears, to this day a century later, involuntarily, but with unapologetic pride.

Because that's the way it was in March of 1911 in New York City.

'16 tons and what'a ya get? Another day
older and you're deeper in debt.
Saint Peter, don't ya call me
'cause I can't go. I owe my soul
to the company store.'

**- Chorus from the ballad**
*16 Tons*

## CHAPTER ONE

Massachusetts Federal Penitentiary
October 31st, 1920

"Sorry, visiting hours ain't till three. Yaw gonna havet'a wait." The young blond anxiously glanced at the clock. Half past twelve.

"Officer I have a one o'clock deadline! All I need is a few words with one of your prisoners. Five minutes, no more. We can talk through the bars!" She smiled and let her ankle length coat accidently fall open. The elderly guard gave a sympathetic grin.

"Who'a ya here ta see, Sweetheart?" The young woman deciphered through the thick New England accent.

"Bill Haywood."

"The Commie agitator! Nuthin' I ken do fer ya!" The guard turned and shuffled away. "Yaw gonna havet'a wait." The old man vanished as the steel door slammed shut. Resigned to her fate the reporter took a seat on the cold steel bench, lit a cigarette and waited.

Thirty minutes later a younger, shotgun wielding guard showed up and escorted the shivering woman to Block D where a matron was standing by. She was searched, her hand bag taken away, had to sign in and was taken to one of the dozens of abandoned, six foot by ten foot stone cells.

"Haywood! Visitor!" The guard announced as he let the reporter into the cell, locked the iron door behind her and remained to stand sentry outside.

The large man lying on his back, hands behind his head on the metal rack with the flat mattress and pillow didn't even afford the visitor a glance but continued to stare at the dark green, enameled brick wall.

"It's freezing in here! Don't they even give you a blanket?!"

"Red Cross day's first of the month, Sister. Beat it!" The

18

prisoner snapped back.

"Sir, my name is Katherine, Katherine Kennedy, political correspondent for the *New York Times*."

Bill gave an expression of disgust and rolled over on his side.

"Visiting hours are over. Hit the bricks Kid!" Having already escaped the death penalty twice in the last twenty years Haywood was in no mood to humor a young hack with delusions that there might be a third.

"Mr. Haywood my editor has given me permission to . . ."

"To interview Big Bill Haywood before he goes to the gallows so's you can increase circulation and reel in the big bucks! That it? If you're lucky maybe you'll even get a Pulitzer nomination."

"Yeah! Hell'll freeze over before we see a woman get the Pulitzer!" The reporter quipped as she removed an envelope from her overcoat pocket and offered it to the prisoner.

"Mr. Haywood, about an hour ago our New York office received this wire from our Moscow correspondent via Berlin and London." Haywood couldn't be bothered.

"Guard! Show this lady out. Beat it kid. I need my beauty rest." The guard began to unlock the cell door.

"Sir, it has to do with Jack Reed." Haywood didn't move. "At least read the god-damned thing, you obstinate son-of-a-bitch!" Bill smirked to himself but remained motionless. In anger born of frustration the reporter opened the Western Union envelope and read aloud.

**"JACK REED DEAD, STOP.  APPX 07:18 LOCAL, STOP."**

Bill's eyes opened wider and he stared more intently at the stones now inches from his face.

**"FULL STATE FUNERAL ORDERED BY LENIN, STOP. REED TO BE FIRST YANK ENTOMBED IN KREMLIN! STOP"**

19

The American Way

Time suddenly distorted as Haywood realized the one overriding factor of the current American struggle. The struggle unfolding in virtually every other country on earth, yet ludicrously denied by the American leadership. The class struggle.

The one overriding factor? Death.

He pictured Jack's face the day of the support rally in Madison Square Garden for the woolen strikers up in Massachusetts. The same day he told Bill he was in love with Louise Bryant.

"His death will be banner headlines by the morning. By noon the New York book dealers will be back-ordering thousands of copies of *Ten Days*. Mr. Haywood, my editor just wanted you to . . ."

The reporter may as well have been speaking Greek. Bill was off in a trance.

*******

A cool wind meandered down the broad avenues of Manhattan on the sunny March afternoon of the twenty-fifth. One young boy, on the long road to his education concerning labor practices, entrepreneurship and the American take on economics was just starting his second shift of the day.

Butchie The Boot was glad it was Saturday. Not just because there was no school but because most of the bars opened around seven in the morning, that is the ones that closed, which meant he could get two shifts in. One around eight or nine in the morning, for the guys that didn't have to work but wanted to look spiffy that afternoon as they stumbled home half broke on the verge of vomiting in the street, and another run from four or five until late for the rest of the workers, businessmen and politicians out schmoozing with friends, clients and voters and who would later strive to follow the same well-strewn path later that night.

Jimmy Sullivan's Bar just off the South East corner of Washington Place and Greene Street was usually pretty good hunting ground. Mostly factory workers, some dock workers but on Fridays and Saturdays the place was usually loaded with at least half a dozen or so Suites. Good tippers, Suites. Especially if they were immersed in a crowd of other Suites or eligible voters.

Butchie put his back into the heavy, frosted, glass paneled door and shoved hard. As he did he steadied his home-made, pine shoe shine box slung over his shoulder by the worn leather belt nailed to the sides. He pushed and, for the umpteenth time that afternoon, had to adjust his eyes from the sun drenched Manhattan streets to the dark, shadowy interior of a sprawling, noisy bar room. A double row of dust coated, translucent glass globes, which ran down the stamped metal ceiling provided most of the meager light and the dank odor of damp oaken, floorboards and fermented hops mingled with cheap cigar smoke to fill his nostrils as he entered into his well rehearsed routine.

"Shine Mister? Shine. Shoe shine?"

Despite its expanse, the sawdust coated floor of the long, rectangular room afforded little area for maneuverability. The original wooden booths along the left wall had long ago been torn out to yield a single, narrow aisle running the length of the crowded arrangement of pedestal tables and bentwood chairs while the bar, situated along the right side running the length of the room, curved into the wall only a few feet from the front door.

With the anticipation of returning home, his pockets full of nickels, Butchie quickly appraised his potential marks. However, as the acquisition of food dominated his day-to-day existence, he was temporarily distracted when he caught sight of the long food table offset from the center of the room near the back corner. In his haste he didn't notice the big man in the dark blue, wool overcoat seated at the bar, eyeing him intently as he eyed the sandwich bar.

Sullivan's did a mediocre spread, especially compared to Morrelli's Taverne over on Mulberry. But crossing East Houston and sneaking into Little Italy to shine shoes was a risky business for an Irishman.

Sully's featured the usual collection. Bologna for the Germans, salami for the Italians and roast beef for the Irish. All sorts of cheeses, none of which Butchie could identify, were all complimented by a respectable assortment of breads. Not that the drunks gave a damn about what they were eating. What the hell, it was free, even if it was a little salty.

But it was the assortment of pickles, olives, funny little tomatoes and fishy things he'd never seen anywhere else which intrigued him. Small, incredibly tasty looking fish he'd seen Sullivan's stout Italian wife bring out every now and then and dump into the last big bowl on the right always caught his eye. Those looked really interesting.

Unfortunately there was the inevitable, strategically positioned sign. To preclude excuses Old Man Sullivan had it painted in five languages.

"SHOE SHINE BOYS, STAY AWAY FROM THE BUFFET! THIS MEANS YOU!"

Had to hand it to the miserable old bastard, he wasn't racist. He hated everybody the same. Of course, as long as their cash was green he'd take it.

"Shine? Shine, Mister?" Butchie continued the long march down the row of bar stools, all of which were occupied. "Shine?" He stood a better chance if he could catch their eye. He decided to try the little guy with the oxblood Brogans.

"Shine Mister?"

"Fuck off, ya little bastard!" Oxblood snapped back.

"What's wrong with you?" It was the big man in the dark blue, woolen overcoat on the next stool who growled to his defense.

"Who the hell are you?" Conversation in the immediate area gradually died down as heads started to turn. The small man defensively dismounted his stool. The big man couldn't be bothered to follow suit but sipped his beer then calmly answered.

"I'm the guy that's gonna kick your ass up around your shoulder blades. Shouldn't take too long seein' as how it ain't got that far to travel." There were a few laughs as some of the clientele egged them on. Butchie found the collective calmness with which the Overcoat delivered his retort unnerving.

"Kid's just trying to earn a living. What the hell ya yellin' at him for?" Then the big man did a strange thing. After a quick glance over his shoulder, he waited for old man Sullivan to get to the far end of the bar, then knocked over his own beer and started to rant at Oxblood. A bit louder and more animated than necessary, thought Butchie.

"YOU IGNORANT SON-OF-A . . ." He didn't get to finish. He didn't have to. Old man Sullivan was over the bar and between them like a champion vaulter, man-handling Oxblood by the collar and had him half way out the door before anyone knew what was going on. Butchie looked back to his left and the big man had vanished as well.

Stranger things have happened he shrugged and moved on.

"Shine? Shine Mister?"

Sullivan came back in through the front door and the bar crowd hardly rippled as the continuous clang of fire bells accompanied by horses' hooves on cobbles filled the afternoon air and flooded through the entrance.

Butchie was nearly at the back of the bar room with no takers and so figured it was a good time to go outside and see what the ruckus was. He hesitated besides the food table, quickly scanned the room and took a chance. The thick, dill pickle was in his pocket in the space of a breath and he moved to the front door with no more haste than was required. Adjusting his eyes once back out in the bright afternoon sunlight, the boy was astonished at what he saw.

Across the street a large crowd had gathered and was undulating around the largest collection of firefighting equipment and men he, or most of New York City, had ever seen.

A handful of police, with reinforcements sporadically arriving, struggled desperately to control the steadily growing throng in order to give the firefighters a reasonable working space.

"What's on that corner?" Someone just behind and to the kid's left asked. Surrounded by the crowd Butchie felt a nudge and looked up and to his right to see the big man in the dark blue overcoat who had suddenly reappeared. The man didn't look down but stood eerily still, staring out over Waverly Street. His huge hand held a sandwich the size of a small hat box dripping with two of everything from the buffet all neatly wrapped in a white, juice stained, cloth napkin.

"Some sweatshop. Triangle Shirtwaist, I think."

"Kosher pickles always go better with a sambo." The big man commented as he thrust the three course meal at the boy. With both hands Butchie snatched the prize without hesitation. As he crammed the sandwich into his shoeshine box his mind was a flurry of excuses of how to assure his mother he didn't steal the linen napkin.

Butchie's meandering concerns were suddenly forgotten as several onlookers began yelling up at the corner building across the street. He vied for a better vantage point moving through the crowd and across Greene Street, closer to Washington. Then, as something floated in the sky above, reality registered and suddenly everything jolted into slow motion.

The falling body gave the impression of being neither a body nor falling. There was no wild flailing, screaming or discernible movement. Perhaps in shock the helpless young woman resigned herself to her fate, made her peace with her god and had jumped.

Perhaps faced with little other choice she put her faith in the new contraptions they called 'life nets', or perhaps she was simply overcome with fumes and passed out.

After leaving the 9th storey ledge the dark-haired girl appeared momentarily suspended in midair, her dark, ankle-length dress spread like an angle's wing across her lower body floating in the air ever so slightly, the shock of the disbelieving crowd struggling to will her young body back up onto the safety of the window ledge.

Suddenly her blurred, flaccid form appeared in focus as it tore violently through the fireman's net and into the pavement with a sickening smack hard enough to crack the concrete, yank her would-be rescuers to the ground and crack her head open.

She lay still, eyes open, glassed over. Unrecognizable. Peaceful.

Seconds later as the fire fighters fought to recover from the shock of what happened the flailing body of a second young woman slammed into the basement entrance of the Asch

24

Building taking a section of wrought iron fencing with her.

Onlookers recoiled in horror, one woman fainted and several got sick to their stomachs and began vomiting violently. A fireman in a white helmet, Chief Worth, yelled at a cop who quickly rallied several policemen to corral the crowd closest to the building and drive them back across the street just as a fourth horse drawn fire wagon arrived followed immediately by a fifth. Canvas hoses were quickly unrolled and secured to fire hydrants along Greene Street.

William Shepherd, a reporter who had been passing by began to furiously take note of events.

Another officer, Captain Rouk over on the Greene Street side of the building ordered his men to retrieve a life net from their wagon. As he shouted the order the stunned junior fire fighters, still mesmerized by what they had seen, hesitated but quickly regained their professional bearing and where back on station in under a minute. The Greene Street crew were not yet fully set when the first body hit their net like a lead weight. One of the firemen collapsed in pain, clutching his lower back.

Chief Worth, the second in charge under Overall Site Commander Edward Croker, ran the short distance to Rouk's location and helped lift the stunned girl off the net and onto her feet. He issued instructions to move across the street and the young garment worker took only two or three steps before fainting dead away halfway to the sidewalk.

Two fireman wrestled with a ladder unstrapping it from a wagon while another team cranked  for all they were worth, swinging their turret ladder around into the building, only to have the device, the longest in the city and probably in the country, fall three stories short of the doomed victims, some thirty to forty feet up.

The sad truth of the matter was that, although New York City boasted the most modern, well equipped and trained fire brigade in the world at the time, to include a city wide grid of pressure controlled, underground water feeds, they simply weren't equipped to fight fires in the modern architectural phenomena known as Loft Buildings.

It was around four forty-five, nearly quitting time at the

Triangle, and from the eighth floor where the inferno started, the fires had climbed an air shaft and had most of the ninth floor involved. Although the N.Y.C. F. D. had arrived on scene only four minutes after receiving the alarm, the blaze now only seven minutes old, was already out of control.

The life nets quickly yielded an unexpected drawback. When the one or two partially successful catches were made, hope became tainted with belief to encourage everyone above who had seen the amazing feats to jump. For approximately the next seventeen minutes, on what was a sunny, Spring Saturday, a steady stream of doomed bodies flowed from the upper windows of the Triangle Shirtwaist Factory.

Suddenly an explosion blew out a window on the ninth floor and tongues of flame licked at the tenth floor and roof as the crowd below were showered with fragments of glass and charred debris.

Inside the man made death trap water from the fire hoses began to flood the floors and lift shafts. Down in the basement Thomas Horton, the Asch Building's chief engineer, fought furiously to maintain the circuits as one by one the water tripped the breakers killing the lights and power to the lifts. Floor indicator lights became nonfunctional and the lift operators had to guess which floor they were on. When they reached one of the upper floors and forcibly opened their doors they were greeted with dozens of terrified workers flooding out of floor to ceiling, thick, black smoke fighting desperately to cram into the small elevator car.

Finally Joseph Zito and his fellow lift operator Gaspar Mortillalo, were compelled to abandon their heroic efforts after making multiple runs back up into the burning floors.

Mortillalo was stopped as the steel guide girders running the length of the lift shaft began to warp under the intense heat, and Zito had to quit as the weight of the dead bodies tumbling down the shaft piled up on the roof of his lift preventing his car from rising anymore. Later that evening nineteen bodies would be removed from the top of his elevator and a similar number from Mortillalo's.

Between them they had saved 150 workers.

By 4:50, ten minutes after the onset of the raging inferno, six minutes after the arrival of the first of the fire brigade, dozens trapped on the ninth floor were fruitlessly screaming for help, their pathetic pleas drowned out by the roar of the flames. Dozens of mangled bodies now littered the streets, and the tenth floor was involved.

A mere twenty minutes after it started the fire yielded nearly a hundred dead between floors eight and nine, twenty-five to fifty lie sprawled and mangled on the streets below or piled up in the two elevator shafts and another near two dozen lay dead or dying in the dead-end alley where the pathetic excuse for an exterior fire escape, the only one for the entire twelve story building, had torn away from the masonry and plummeted to the ground, its cargo of fleeing humans tumbling with it.

The final body count, achieved in those few minutes would stand at 146 with scores more injured.

The primary emergency fire door exits on floors eight, nine and ten, where 60% of the deaths occurred, were locked.

Locked according to the owners, to preclude the workers from stealing scraps of cloth.

*******

Further North on the East Side, as the last of the flames were being extinguished, a group of labor activists were finishing up an afternoon of heated debate in a small, basement hall. Coincidently the debate concerned the clothing workers and centered around whether they would be better off organized by the American Federation of Labor or the I.W.W.

Three colleagues, two men and one young woman, were just exiting the building when one of the two men sighted a uniformed cop across the street, stumbling down the pavement as if drunk or wounded. The man alerted the other two.

After running to his aide the group watched in amazement as the middle-aged, seasoned officer collapsed in a heap onto the granite front steps of a cold water walk-up and wept like a middle-aged child. They listened hypnotically as he explained the horrific inferno he had just witnessed. Oblivious to the people around him, he described how young girls' bodies fell from the ninth and tenth floors, covered in flames like human torches, onto the helpless fireman below.

Every man, woman and child in that crowd would, for the remainder of their days, remember exactly where they were at half past four on the afternoon of March 25th, 1911. At least three would apply the lessons of that horrific crime to future energies, convinced now more than ever, that their cause, the cause of their union, the Industrial Workers of the World, was the only salvation of America's "poor and huddled masses".

Joe Ettor, Elizabeth Gurley Flynn and Arturo Giovannitti, as they helped comfort the police officer, had no way to know that they were now involved in the first pages of one of the most dramatic chapters in American labor history.

A chapter which would emerge nearly a century later as the class war in America that never was.

'I will have made the mistake of my life
if he isn't good timber!Clean
through the piece.'

- James Connelly
referring to I.W.W. Leader 'Big Bill' Haywood while
working with him in the New York City HQ.

## CHAPTER TWO

"Hello?" The well dressed, portly man turned his back on the rest of the office and held the phone close to mouth as he spoke in low, clear tones. "How does it look?"

"They're gonna call Chief Croker."

"Tammany Boss Croker's kid?"

"A nephew. District Attorney Whitman talked to him at the scene. Croker blames the Building Department. He'll no doubt tell them what a fire trap the building was and that they need to do something. He is held in high regard, but he's retired. Not much influence anymore."

"Hearst's Commission report?"

"We think that's pretty much run out of steam. If it comes into evidence, Whitman will likely deride Hearst and down play the report. Bad blood between 'em will probably minimize the damage there. Whitman wouldn't want it to look like Hearst was taking up his slack. It's no secret William Randolph is grooming himself for the White House. The report is just another paving stone ta D. C."

"Where's Wagner stand?"

"Senator Wagner will be feeling ill and will send his regrets he can't be there to chair the proceedings."

"So we're in a pretty good position?"

"You'll get blasted in the press. Have to wait a few months to set up shop again. But with Crain on the bench and Steuer as your defense council, it's not likely anybody's going to jail."

"Thank you Mr. Smith. Your bank draft will arrive in the morning by special courier."

"Let us know if you need anything else Mr. Blank."

"Please extend my gratitude to the Greater New York Detective agency for their services."

The two men hung up.

\* \* \* \* \* \* \*

"Michael, Michael!" The sweat soaked twelve year old ignored the rocks grinding between the soles of his small feet and his well worn, sandals improvised from rubber car tires as he negotiated the mounds, barrows and depressions of the dig site.

It had been nearly two thousand years since the great Mediterranean textile capital of Pompeii had last seen the light of day much less any significant activity. Even now only portions of the walls which formally supported her terra cotta roof tops peeked through the six meters of ash, soil and accumulated muck.

Following the 79 A.D. disaster the Emperor Augustus considered it, along with Herculaneum, a loss. Some senators argued to rebuild the city as the textile trade was vital to Rome's continued stability. Unfortunately Rome's days were already numbered as the heathen, barbarians in Hibernia and Alba had taken back most of the gains previous emperors had made and were threatening to push south into Gaul. While in the North and East, the barbarians were truly at the gate.

The huge clouds of dust raised by the army of workers as they swung their picks and shovels all but obscured the nimble boy's flight. Finally, sighting the intended recipient of his urgent message, he momentarily stopped to gasp for air and then pushed on down the hill to where three navvies were loading large baskets of excavated earth on to a flat bed lorry.

"Michael!" The tall dark one peered over his sweat soaked shoulder.

"Come stai Ragazzo?" He smiled down at the boy.

"Io non sono Ragazzo! Io sono un uomo!"

"OHH, please excuse me Pino! Yes you are a man!"

"Doctor Bennetti wants to see you!"

"Doctor Bennetti? What for?" The other two navvies stopped work and stared.

"What do I look like? Ufficio Informazioni or something?" Michael dropped his shovel, lifted the boy, turned him upside down and threw him over his shoulder.

"Okay, Tough Guy, come on, we go to see Dr. Bennetti. Only, please, don't hurt me!" Michael mockingly begged. To the amusement of the other men, the boy screamed and kicked wildly as Michael carried him off in the direction of the Site Director's tent in the center of the excavation.

At the entrance of the large, beige tent Casaburi put the boy down and tossed him a coin and the youth quickly vanished back across the massive dig site.

Ducking under the flap Casaburi entered the well equipped space as the Director was dictating to a statuesque, thirty-something secretary in field clothes sitting at a small folding table, note pad in hand.

"Address it, 'To The Attention of Dr. Joseph Jackson, Archaeological Institute of America."

"Dottor Bennetti?" The professor looked up to make eye contact with Michael.

"Si Signore Casaburi, un momento. Care of the General Secretary, 5 Washington Square North, New York 3, New York."

"Si Signor Dottore." She slung her small secretarial case over her shoulder and headed out of the large tent.

"Be sure both reports are in the evening post!"

"Si, subito."

"Michael, come in sit down." His greeting was a bit too warm to put Casaburi completely at ease. "I have some news from Naples." He poured two glasses of vodka and handed one to Michael.

"News? What news?" Bennetti handed Michael a telegram. It was in an official state envelope which had been opened.

"It's has to do with your wife . . ."

Michael dropped his glass and fell back in his chair.

*******

On the face of it Max Blanck and Isaac Harris, the co-owners and operators of the Triangle Shirtwaist Factory, were true American success stories. Immigrant laborers who rose to the ranks of management, finally earning and saving enough to open their own operation.

At first a small shop on Wooster Street in Lower

Manhattan then, after only a couple of years, in 1901, on to bigger premises. Fast forward five years and again on to an additional premises over on Mercer Street, this time with an operation christened, maybe hoping the name would bring more prosperity, the Diamond Waist Company.

It did and they were able to expand the sprawling top floors of the Asch Building with up to 450 workers crammed into each floor, working 60 to 90 hours per week. Sometimes more in the busy seasons. However, as high profiled disasters tend to do, the Triangle fire caused people to look a little harder.

Blanck actually married into his money, Harris was family, so neither really slaved his way to the top. Not exactly illegal. Things hummed along pretty good for the boys until they had their first bad break in April of 1902 when a fire destroyed the contents of the Asch Building. Fortunately it happened before work hours, so no one got hurt. Six months later, at the same location, guess what? A fire. Same approximate time, same damage, contents only.

In April 1907, there was another fire, this time in the Diamond warehouse. Also early enough in the morning so there were no casualties. April of 1910 another fire, goods burned and it just happened to be in the off-hours so no one got hurt. More importantly, no one got paid and no one manufactured any more waistcoats. That is, no one produced any more inventory.

April was the time of the Spring fashions, the time the fashion industry set the new standards and the upcoming year's fashions were dictated. Old stock was difficult if not impossible to off load once the market was set. So, what's a coupl'a of hard working business men to do when they're caught short with a load of worthless stock?

Pick up the phone and ring your local neighborhood torch.

After all, the use of gangs, violent prostitutes, known criminals and crooked cops to break strikes, discourage organizers and silence individuals who criticized the company labor policies too loudly was common practice with Harris and Blanck. Why not continue the trend of using the right man, (or the right woman), for the job?

# The American Way

These were not good men.

\* \* \* \* \* \* \*

The burning sun sat low on the horizon and a yellowish, sepia tone-like darkness bathed the small bedroom. Casaburi's deep blue eyes stared out over the swirling dust of the barren plains. He drew the window shade to obscure the view of the drought ridden, dust covered land which used to be his father's farm.

In late March Ulmi, Sicily was a tolerable place. Despite the abject poverty, the seemingly endless drought and widespread corruption, there was relative serenity. But it wasn't the same any more. It could never be the same again.

The mattress moaned as he leaned forward and his mildly trembling hand inched towards the small night table opposite the bed. He lit the well-used, thick tallow candle welded to the pewter plate and carefully replaced the box of matches. Slowly he pulled the drawer open and removed something which he sat in his lap. He unwrapped the coarse cotton cloth and stared.

The smell of gun oil permeated the air.

There it was again, glistening in the candle light, like nothing he had ever seen. Oddly enough he felt more alive than ever. He reached over and closed the drawer.

The Colt .45 was less than a year old. His brother smuggled it back from America before he returned to Cuba for the last time. He regaled Michael with stories of how the American Army designed the weapon to stop the huge Mauro native assassins of the Philippines on their suicide missions. Guaranteed death.

Suicide. What an inadequate word for the ultimate expression of grief. Or love.

Would it be enough? Enough to end the pain? A fleeting flash of excruciating agony to neutralize the insufferable pain of spending the rest of your life alone?

The Church said it would bring eternal damnation. To hell with the Church! Where was the Pope when the sea took

34

Arianna? It didn't matter, his decision was made. With stilted animation he lifted the weapon from its cloth covering.

The sun slowly receded into the shadows and a light sprinkle of sea water sprayed across his cheek. He glanced over at Arianna's soft delicate face. Then she was gone and he was encased in a cold wet cocoon of green fighting for air.

Mesmerized with disbelief and denial, he stared into the candle flame. He thought about the last time they made love. It was magic. Seventeen years, it was still beautiful. How many are that lucky? Her father continually goaded it wouldn't last. Fuck that decrepit bastard. Now the old goat's only grand-daughter was the pride of his life.

A soft whisper echoed.

In a stupor Casaburi staggered towards the shoreline and fell to his knees. He stared out at the raging sea and began to vomit violently.

They were saying good-bye at the train station. He kissed her and smiled. Then, as if someone switched off a Marconi, she was gone.

It was Signora Carlucci who led the Carbonari down the beach the next morning to where Casaburi sat, still entranced, his crystal blue eyes glazed over, staring out to the horizon. They helped coax him to his feet and get him back to the house.

"Anna?" He asked of Signora Carlucci, staring through her.

"She's okay Michael. She is in the house with Nonna."

He raised the weapon and cocked it. Begging god's forgiveness for what he was about to do, then closed his eyes and opened his mouth.

*NO!* As an afterthought he lowered the pistol and lifted a pillow from the bed. Placing it across his chest he held it in place with the muzzle of the gun. This way it would not be so traumatic when they found him.

As he arranged a second pillow behind him to lessen the spattering there was a knock at the door.

"Papa! Papa!" He pretended not to hear her calling. "Papa! Andiamo, muoviti! We'll be late! Please!" His temporary courage melted with the heat of her passionate pleas.

"Si Anna. Coming." He re-wrapped the weapon and put it back to sleep in the drawer.

Another time.

'We don't run for office. We don't hav'ta.
We own the politicians.'

**- Bugsy Moran**

## CHAPTER THREE

As the charred and mangled remains of the dead were being laid out on the Charities Pier christened 'Misery Lane', over on 26th Street, the initial political fallout from the fire began to set in as sudden and intense as the blaze itself. In all likelihood the only thing which precluded full scale riots was the overwhelming shock at the loss of so many lives in so short a time, compounded by the fact that they were such young lives, teens and twenties, approximately two thirds of which were women. There was however, one universal sentiment; "something" had to be done.

Enter a Hearst endorsed, come-from-nowhere politician.

Charles Seymour Whitman, by all accounts, was a lack-luster individual with a spectacularly mediocre career undistinguished in every respect. Until, as New York City District Attorney, he got his shot at the title. That is the potential, on that deadly March afternoon, to finally move his gold plated, matching pen and desk set into the Governor's Mansion in Albany.

Whitman was fully cognizant, as were many, if not all the New York City D. A.'s before and after him, that the key to the front door of the White House wasn't under the mat. It was between the front pages of America's newspapers. So, in time honored political tradition, even before the first chapter of the Triangle tragedy had ended, he carpe'd the diem by arriving at the scene of the fire at the Asch Building and began formulating his case before the fire was even extinguished.

The right spin on the criminal prosecution of those responsible, or at least those who could be perceived as being responsible, would snatch headlines all over the country for as long as the trial could be dragged out.

Unfortunately for the would be hot shot D. A. he was out of his league.

Whitman had never really seen much of the inside of a courtroom, so had never been pit against defense lawyers of the caliber he would face, much less genuine New York

Paddy Kelly

"mouthpieces".

Since a conviction would mean a significant and possibly permanent loss of revenue to those convicted, in this case a significant chunk of the New York garment trade, the stakes were much higher than your every day, run-of-the-mill political football type trial, even for New York.

Judging by his tactics and strategy Whitman had apparently never attempted to separate an industrialist from his money and to compound his headache, he never had tens of thousands of angry Jewish laborers, backed by irate Italians and about two dozen other ethnicities, at his back either. Throw in the fact that he publicly touted himself as an anti-Tammany man in Tammany's home ballpark and he might as well have been trying to sell bibles to Communists.

Charles didn't know it, but he was in for an education.

Ironically, both his most dangerous rivals, The Hall and William Randolph Hearst, who initially supported Whitman but also saw a golden opportunity of his own in what he labeled as 'Whitman's hesitancy to apportion blame', had as much stake in the political outcome of the fire as he did.

As a second attempt to kick-start his presidential ambition Hearst intended to run for mayor, again, and made no bones of the fact he was going to do it on the political corpse of Whitman if he could by lambasting him over his alleged 'mishandling' of the Triangle tragedy and he wasted no time oiling up his propaganda-riddled, press machines. Like so many politicians from 1798 through the generations, this is exactly the political opportunity Hearst had moved to New York City for.

No question of the three, The Hal, with their far reaching tentacles were the most well armed to lead the charge, save the day and come out smelling like roses. However, it wasn't that simple. There was a problem. Actually, there were two.

The Jews and The Italians.

Simultaneously, as Whitman, the fledgling unions, Hearst, Harris, Blank and the Boys up in Albany inventoried their war chests and stacked sand bags, Tammany was also jolted into action by the inevitable tragedy, and so were being nudged off the platform and out onto the public high wire, politically speaking.

As their former reliable constituency the Irish, English, Scots etc. had already established themselves in the Promised Land and had gradually evaporated into the suburbs and other healthier, more affluent climes, Tammany's New York votership became a shifting tide of a demographic.

With half the population of the country ineligible to vote and the latest wave of immigrants, the Italians and Jews, the inequities of the American political system were becoming more and more evident. The time was ripe for change.

To aggravate the dynamic, media circulation was growing by leaps and bounds which allowed John and Mary Q. Public to increasingly pay more attention to the news, following both foreign and domestic events which were shaping their new land. Popular opinion was shifting and suddenly Tammany politicians, as did everyone else, had to learn how to eat matzah and ciabatta instead of plain white bread.

The Jews have always been an interesting political force in America.

Centered at the time almost exclusively in and around New York City they, more so than other ethnic groups, brought with them as part of their heritage a strong legacy of radical politics originating from unprecedented persecution in every country they'd previously inhabited.

Much to their chagrin for the better part of a century, they would find America wasn't much different. From their initial shunning in New York upon their arrival to the maniacal ravings of more than one United States senator on the floor of Congress, they would be blamed for everything from outbreaks of 'feeblemindedness' due to genetic deficiencies, compliments of the Congressionally funded Dillingham Commission and William Randolph Hearst, to causing World War II.

Witness the irony of the 50 year Congressional crusade against the major, Jewish run Hollywood studios. Ironic given the fact that financing of seven of the eight majors at the time were controlled by the likes of Carnegie, Rockefeller and Morgan. The key players in financing the politicians of the American Congress.

Despite active, prolonged and organized campaigns against them as a people and much to their credit, Jewish-Americans rose to control large sectors of the economy, education and the entertainment business. However, for now the Jews would play a critical role in New York labor politics.

The Italian immigrants of the period, while also bringing their own customs, ways, language etc . . . with them, fell roughly into two categories. Those who were there to make enough money to go back to the Old Country and re-establish themselves, and those who were genuine converts and intended to stay.

Between those who chose to stay there was also an interesting delineation.

There were the Italians who took the American legal system, the Constitution etc . . . as literal and good, and these of course were the Italians who went on to contribute so many great achievements in the
spheres of Science, Education and the Arts.

Also, given that there's a pizzeria in Kathmandu, they've bequeathed America with what must be the most internationally popular cuisine on the planet.

Then there were those who saw the American social and legal systems as more of a guideline offering unlimited career opportunities in the as-of-yet not amply exploited left hand of politics, crime.

Given the way the 'law/authorities' operated in America, particularly at that time in that place, it becomes quite clear why newly arrived immigrants such as Arnold Rothstein, Alfonso Capone, Meyer Lansky and Charlie Luciano realized the only way to get ahead in the New World was to play by the same rules as the people running the show. From their first days over they were taught the reality of America. That is, that there are two sets of rules.

Witnessing people like Al Capone attack the system head on and lose, the following generation of gangsters were quick to learn the limitations of such a strategy. Better to work within the 'two sets of rules' system, that is, mimic the American politicians

Through the establishment of Tammany Hall in the late 18th Century the Irish have a legitimate claim to have established organized crime in America. However, it is an unequivocal fact that the Italians get credit for modernizing that particular career field by reconstructing it along the corporate model. But not just any corporate model.

The American corporate model.

The labor wars of the time, accompanied by the politically induced social strife, nurtured similar sympathies in the two cultures and as they did, at this significant point in history, the Jews and Italians joined forces, and not just on the labor front.

Immigrants from both nationalities saw the political corruption, industrial strangle-hold on the economy and wholesale exploitation of their countrymen as an indication of how things really were.

The Russian Jew, Meyer Lansky and his friend Bugsy Siegel, for example, came from a strong Jewish background and the Sicilians Charlie "Lucky" Luciano and Frankie Costello paired up around 1920 and later formed the first nation-wide organized crime syndicate, The Unione Siciliano, often mistakenly called the Mafia, but known by its members as The Syndicate.

As with any competently organized corporation they also had a subsidiary. Run by an Italian but staffed primarily by Jews.

Murder Inc., CEO'd by others at various times to include Umberto Anastacio a.k.a. Albert Anastasia, the man who would later engineer the burning of the T.L.S. Normandie in Manhattan harbor was, in its heyday, manned largely by Jewish hit men, Anastasia's stated preference due to their, "ruthless efficiency"

Not to be out done, the Jews had their gangster heroes Arnold Rothstein, the Jewish opposite number to Lucky Luciano, will forever be remembered as the notorious instigator of the 1919 Chicago 'Black Socks', World Series scandal and as the man who was the primary architect of the billion dollar a year bootleg industry in America.

What ever anyone's criticisms, these were unique people. People who understood the four cornerstones of American capitalism; hypocrisy, exclusion, greed and opportunity. People who would go on to establish and integrate their criminal enterprise into every aspect of American politics all the way up to the White House, just as the English and Irish did before them.

Sort of a circle-of-life kind of thing, New York style.

No small measure of the Anti-Semitism or anti-Italian sentiment which swept America in the 1910's to the 1960's arose directly from the labor struggles of this period. As a side note, it is to the eternal shame of the period press that they kowtowed so easily in the early days of government efforts against these people, efforts such as Wilson's ruthless, all out war against the Wobblies which laid the foundation for the Truman/McCarthy inquisitions.

However, one is to divvy up and draw the battle lines, ethnicity was the powder for the bullets in the class wars fought in America on the labor front.

So for William Randolph and Mr. Whitman the path was pretty clear cut as to what they would have to accomplish in order to politically ring the most out of the Triangle tragedy to help get them into office.

Over at the Irish-run Tammany Hall ambitions ran much higher. As the very bedrock of anti-reformation, they faced an uphill climb. But they also had a leg up. Since the end of the Civil War they controlled the city which they had skillfully parleyed themselves into control of along with nearly the entire state legislature, backed by the governorship.

Of course, controlling as much as they did also meant Tammany had the most to lose. So to cement their fortifications even further in late 1911 the Hall decided the next step was to get a man in the White House.

To get a Senator picked at the nomination and thus garner controlling interest in the Democratic Party was not as easy as it might have seemed, given the Hall's tenacious grip on New York Politics. The opposition had a bit of pull as well and the Boys From the Lodge were in deeper water when it came to fighting on the national level.

For a young, Democratic upstart senator who wasn't in
the New York City branch of the
Good 'Ol Boy's Club, and who once confessed if he hadn't gone
into politics he would have loved to be a screenwriter,
Tammany's desperation to control the Party was an opportunity
he saw as not to be missed.

FDR would be a true reformer through out his political
career. He would warn against ever trusting bankers, order
industrialists to negotiate with labor for the first time in U. S.
history and would forever endear himself to the film industry to
the point he was given such gifts as fighter planes, ammunition
for the Army and the privilege of "collaborating" on film
content.

But for now, he had no intention of letting this
opportunity pass.

The young senator wanted to play ball with the Hall but
wanted a 'significant' gesture from Tammany in return so he
leveraged them in their selection of a candidate. 'Significant'
being interpreted to mean helping the growing constituency
which would likely become more significant when he was ready
to make his big move to 1600 Pennsylvania Ave. The growing
constituency meaning the New York City constituency.

Essentially the Italians and Jews.

He got what he wanted and Isador Straus, owner of the
"World's Largest Department Store", Macy's, got the nod.

Almost overnight the formally marginalized masses of
the Big Apple were a serious threat to the status quo and
presented the very real potential to drag the Hall into a
Tammanyville Horror. Although these immigrants did just about
'get off the boat' however, it didn't mean they just fell off the
melon truck.

They came to New York to escape one form of political
and economic oppression or another and could damn well see
through the hocus pocus of the New York Political Machine
demanding reform, talking about reform, planning reform and
then, after getting into office, forgetting to institute reform. They
had seen it all before, back in the Old Country. A political smoke
and mirrors show wasn't going to cut it this time. Real change,

'significant' change had to be enacted especially on the issue of better work place safety.

Unfortunately for the Political Bosses that meant passing laws that their industrial partners and backers weren't going to like. Laws which would cost money by raising the fire safety regulations, the production safety rules and generally interfering with the break-neck speed production was being pushed to.

Oh yeah, and there was the issue of wages too.

*******

In the long, elaborate, marble corridor just outside court room #16 of the State Building in Lower Manhattan, Gurley Flynn and Joe Ettor waited. Joe had been sent by Big Bill to cover the State supervised hearings on the fire and do a write up for the Wobblies' weekly organ, *Solidarity*. Flynn cajoled permission to tag along. It never occurred to her Haywood agreed too easily.

Flynn sat on the heavy wooden bench directly across from the courtroom while Joe stood next to her leaning on his knee, one foot propped up on the bench. In the interim between the fire and the hastily announced hearings Ettor had done some snooping.

"Thanks to some fancy pen work and expert juggling of the books I'd say there are probably no accurate records as to how much these two 'hard working, honest businessmen' bilked from insurance companies and robbed, in wages from their employees, but from their two 1902 fires alone they collected a $32,000, lump sum. For the Triangle they carried around $200,000 in insurance. $80,000 more than the factory's total worth."

"Jesus! Did ja go to the papers with that?"

"I think you mean Jehovah, but trust me, I don't think he's in the picture. The papers weren't interested." Joe quipped.

"So, due largely to the American court system, despite the carnage and death they caused, they'll not only escape prison, but be rewarded by collecting massive amounts of insurance money!"

"And to be sure they keep the money, they further employed the law."

Flynn had seen a lot in her few years with the movement, but she was slowly coming to the realization she hadn't seen it all. "Apparently Harris has transferred all his property and money into his wife's name, going so far as to not draw a salary from his now newly rebuilt Triangle Shirtwaist Company. However his wife, even though she rarely sets foot in the place, does draw a handsome salary." Gurley Flynn was somehow shocked but not really surprised.

"Would someone actually set alight their own factory, with workers in it just to collect more money?! Money they hardly need?!"

"Probably not however, there is always the possibility that one of H & B's regular torches got a little over enthusiastic or maybe didn't wind his pocket watch the night before."

"How do you figure?"

"It's not their M. O. to start fires with workers still on the premises and it certainly isn't in their best interest to take lives."

"They didn't really have much regard for their employees and it was only a week until fashion season. And they were not above locking fire exit doors, ignoring fire safety regulations, shunning inspections and lying about their fire escapes and lift capacities to function properly to save lives. SO What then?"

"Well, there was . . . $80K in excess insurance." Joe smirked.

"Plus endangering hundreds of lives to save a few pennies was easily justified. After all the few scraps of cloth a dishonest employee might pilfer, because they weren't paid enough to buy it, might have affected the company's bottom line. Besides, with unlocked doors the even greater danger of union organizers sneaking onto the premises and handing out propaganda leaflets loomed large."

"Exactly."

"Until the fire." Flynn shot back.

"It gets better." Joe chided.

"Jesus! There's more?"

"Last week the court backed the insurance company

when it decided that each victim was worth $75 in compensation to the relatives."

"About ten weeks wages." Flynn mused.

"H&B were rewarded with $400 per casualty."

"Leaving a tidy profit of $325 per death!" Flynn quickly flipped open her note book, produced and started doing her sums.

"$47,450."

"That's allot'a sinkers!" Through the open doors they could see activity starting to stir inside the court.

"Berni, what time is it?"

"Half past ten Mr. Elkus." Abram Elkus nodded at the bench and the Vice Chairman signaled back to the Special Council.

Flynn and Ettor scurried across the hall into the court and found a place just as two pugnacious bailiffs appeared and began to close over the ten foot, oak doors in the rear of the court room. The five member panel sat at the over-sized judge's bench in front of the room and owing to the inordinate amount of spectators the witnesses were compelled to sit in the jury box while most of the gallery stood.

"The room will now come to order." The third tap of the gavel resonated through the now silent room.

The New York State Factory Investigation Commission had been convened seven months earlier, only days after the disaster as all the political parties involved instantly realized that the impact to the public was devastatingly immediate and so too should be the scramble for remedies. Whatever the outcome of the Commission, its significance was not lost on the A.F.L. or the I.W.W. Both unions had representatives in attendance.

"The Commission being present and ready to proceed, we would like to hear from c'uncil." The Vice-Chairman announced.

Whitman may have initially took a wait-and-see approach before assigning culpability, but after he was attacked by Hearst, it became a game of press wars and he virtually ordered his men to get an indictment! And in the ensuing weeks, he played the press for all it was worth.

"Mr. Elkus, you may begin."

# The American Way

"Thank you Mr. Vice-Chairman." As the men spoke spectators continued to cram into the public gallery, burrowing out nooks and niches from which to watch the biggest show to hit The City since Barnum & Bailey first rolled up Broadway.

"We all regret, of course, that Senator Wagner, by reason of his illness, is unable to be present and act as Chairman of the Commission." Elkus continued.

"What the hell is Gompers doing here?" Flynn asked leaning over to Ettor.

"Extol the virtues of the AFL?" He answered.

"Yeah, virtues." Flynn said sarcastically. "Where were they before the fire?"

"Not enough profit in the ignorant masses from the Med."

The Triangle was far from the first fire in the New York area with disastrous results. Since the turn of the century there had been no less than a dozen major factory fires resulting in over 500 deaths of workers in New York and New Jersey.

Fires had in fact become a primary point of argument for the union organizers, particularly the Socialists who early on in the American labor wars realized no one on the owner's side of the fence was going to do anything of any significance to improve working conditions, particularly if significant amounts of money were to be detoured from the profit margin.

"It is unfortunate that the occurrence of catastrophe is often necessary to awaken a people to it's true sense of responsibility." Elkus' voice now dominated the room.

"The Triangle Waist Company fire of March, 1911, with its attendant horrors and loss of life shocked both city and state. The loss of one hundred and forty-six lives in one factory fire brings to the attention of the public, with terrible force, the dangers that daily threaten the lives of employees in manufacturing establishments in the City of New York and elsewhere throughout the State."

Abram Elkus had been appointed special council to the Commission with reason over and above his political affiliations. His subtler theatrical styled blocking easily achieved the desired dramatic impact, as he carefully considered his words while he spoke.

"With your permission, Mr. Chairman, we will call Mr. Croker as the first witness."

In the gallery, as Croker was being sworn in, a folded piece of paper was passed to Joe Ettor by one of the bailiffs as he stood taking notes of the proceedings. Surprise masked his face as he read it and Elizabeth noticed his expression.

"Everything okay?" She asked.

"Hayward wants me back over at Union Square. He thinks we might have a shot at organizing Brooklyn." He handed her his note pad and pencil.

"You'll have to stay here and finish. May as well get used to it." She looked at him quizzically. At twenty-seven Joe Ettor was not only committed to the cause of labor, but was greatly admired for his organizational, oratory and writing abilities. "I think Hayward has some ideas about gettin' out a daily news letter from the New York office. He'll probably ask you to write it." Flynn glanced around the room.

"Where's that little stooge who was going to testify against Harris and Blanck?"

"Which one?" Joe quipped.

"The line supervisor who told us the reason the doors were locked was to keep the union organizers out."

"Vacation."

"In October?!"

"Company paid for him and the family to spend two weeks in the Poconos. See ya back at the ranch." Ettor made his way through the crowd towards the rear exit.

"Chief tell the Commission how long you've been with the New York City Fire Department." Elkus requested. Gurley Flynn's mind involuntarily flashed back to that cool March afternoon, and the policeman her, Ettor and some colleagues had come across on the dimly lit street.

"I was appointed Fireman June 22, 1884, went through the various grades until I arrived at the position of Chief of the Department. I served in that capacity for twelve years and retired May first of the present year."

"Chief can you tell us about the new Loft Buildings?"

Chief Croker was visibly uncomfortable on the stand but remained in control of himself.

"They vary from twelve to twenty-five stories high, have one to several occupants on each floor, and go, in some cases, round the clock."

"How many employees would each of the occupants have?"

"Anywhere from 150 to 300."

"On each floor?"

"On each floor."

"So in a ten story building you would have upwards of twenty-five hundred persons? That's almost a town in itself! Can you tell us what is generally done to protect these buildings from fire?"

"Generally there is nothing done."

"But there are laws?"

"There are laws."

"What of these so-called fireproof buildings?"

"They are not fireproof."

"But they advertise these buildings as being fireproof. That they don't burn." Croker's voice slowly assumed a tone of suppressed anger.

"They are not fireproof. They burn and they make a hot fire."

"Then why are they allowed to be advertised as such?"

"The laws allow them to be called fireproof based on the so-called improved methods of egress."

"Such as the new exterior fire escapes?"

"Yes. But very few of them have them."

"Then how do they qualify, for the law I mean?"

"They call the staircases and elevators fire escapes to qualify."

"But elevator shafts act as fire shafts, don't they?"

"Absolutely. It is routine for us to find blocked hallways, non-existent fire escapes and, as in the case of the Triangle fire, locked doors."

"What about the building inspectors, Chief?" Croker's answer was non-verbal, but spoke volumes. He looked down and shifted in his seat. To drive the point home Elkus looked at the Committee. His lawyerly instincts to win at all costs were, in this case very much intact, however there was a personal angle as well. He knew two of the girls who perished in the fire.

"I find in my experience that a great majority of the people who occupy the various establishments would rather take a chance on the loss of life than spend five or ten dollars to prevent it."

"Is that your experience?"

"Positively. They pay absolutely no attention to fire hazards or to the protection of the employees in the buildings. That is their last consideration." Elizabeth, caught up in the testimony, stopped writing.

"Tell us about these fire escapes, Chief. The stairs and the elevators."

"The stairs, mostly made of wood, fuel the fire. In the case of iron, they twist and mangle in the heat until they block the only remaining egress."

"Elevators?"

"After a fire starts, in the excitement, after they leave the floor in which the fire occurs, they generally leave the door open, and people walk into the elevator shaft."

"That is, they walk into and fall down the shaft?"

"Yes."

"Did that occur in this case, in the Asch Building fire? Did people jump down the shaft as a means to try to escape?"

"Well, we found a lot of them in the shaft. We don't know how they got there." Elkus worked his way from the Commission over to the gallery.

"Much has been made about fire nets. Have those proved useful?"

"We have never had one failure up to the Asch Building."

Flynn decided she had enough, it was time to leave. Although not an eyewitness she, as did the rest of the country and most of Europe, read the nauseating descriptions and photos of the failed fire nets in the news papers. As she made her way through the crowd her place was quickly snatched up. Despite trying to block it out, the last of the Fire Chief's testimony found its way to her ears.

"When they hit the nets, did the bodies all come together in a pile, or did the victims go right through the nets?"

"Both. When they hit the side walk the impact of their bodies was so great, due to the height, that they drove right through the iron gratings and on into the cellar." Now he moved back to the Commission.

"Chief, is it the Building Department which is responsible to ensure that the building is safe?"

"In New York City **no one** is responsible for **anything**." Croker was losing the fight to conceal his disgust. "If anything happens each blames the other. There are just as many buildings all over New York that are in the same condition as the Asch Building was, and probably is today."

"Bastards!" Flynn mumbled to herself as the bailiff opened the over-sized door and she passed back out into the elaborate marble corridor.

*******

It had been several months since the freak storm ravaged the ports of south western Italy. Although over a thousand lives were lost and the carnage was yet to be cleared, shipping was back to near normal.

The village of Ulmi, south of Palermo in Northwestern Sicily, had been a farming community.

However, following the great Risorgimento, or unification, in 1861, the Mafiosi used to enforce and collect debts and rent for the wealthy, themselves became land owners and in their ignorance, or disregard in the ways of Mother Earth coupled with the flagging economy, harvested large tracts of the forest to profit from America's insatiable appetite for timber.

It was a mere ten years until the top soil had washed away leaving the once lush tracts a denuded desert. Floods became more frequent and, unable to plant crops, the land lie fallow as it was for all of Michael's life. Some relief came from Rome in the form of municipal funds, which were skimmed into uselessness by the Mafiosi. Roads, schools hospitals, all remained in the nineteenth century until they became uninhabitable and gradually resigned to antiquity and abandoned.

In traditional rural fashion, word of the Casaburi's loss preceded them back to the village and upon his return from Palermo Michael found his house had been inundated with offers of assistance. So much so that even with Mrs. Cavallo's help Anna was occupied full time sorting out the food which was donated and she and Nonna became hard pressed to preserve and store it all.

Mysteriously, untold numbers of young men from the village and surrounding area contacted the twenty-two year old dark haired, brown-eyed beauty to offer help on the farm.

What nice boys, she thought to her self.

Her father hadn't eaten a full meal since his return and so she was compelled to give most of the perishables to the eccentric American doctor who had opened the clinic and orphanage down in the village years ago.

In exchange for her donations of food the American offered Anna treatments for her father, chief amongst which were long daily walks as a means of therapy.

Although he was notably thinner, Michael's face began to show a little color again and despite the gusty winds he had been meandering across the countryside for well over an hour. He slowly came out of his thoughts and looked up and found himself in the village's small, unevenly sloped piazza.

He had wandered aimlessly since lunch but was inexplicably always drawn down into the village. The colorful decorations ornamenting the terra cotta square in preparation for the Christmas Nativity shimmered in a light breeze. As he turned the corner and came onto a wide side street Michael perused the coffee bars and gelato stands shut up for the afternoon siesta.

Another hundred meters down the road he approached Trattoria Cavallo, now all but abandoned save for the three, dapperly dressed old men who had sought refuge from the sun behind a corner wall under a large umbrella.

Seated around a small, round table, the echo of his footsteps halted their heated exchange. Their barely perceptible movements, as they turned to identify the unexpected intruder, invoked a Hopper-esque appearance.

Not wanting to walk any more, but not wanting to stop for a drink, Michael decided to sit at the end table furthest from them and ponder his options. As abruptly as it ended the exchange resumed and gradually the conversation filtered across to him and came into focus.

The old men were engaged in a debate about the North African military campaign, which was not going so well for the Italian army when one of them recognized Casaburi.

"Michael! Como stai?"

"Cosi, cosi, Signor Cavallo." He called back.

"Come. Sit. We need a professional opinion."

"Whatever is it that my humble opinion could possibly contribute?"

"You were a government official!"

"I was a policeman." He protested.

"For five years! Come!"

"Four and a half."

"Which makes you the resident expert!" It was as much a command as a request and Michael was bored anyway. He made his way to the corner table where Cavallo poured him an Amaretto.

"What is your opinion about this movement, the Fascismo?" Michael was reluctant to respond, but given the pent up frustration of the past weeks, seized the opportunity to vent. He weighed his words before he spoke.

"The poor of this region have been little more than slaves to the land since medieval times. But have never had the right to own it. First under the oppression of self-serving kings, then came a supposed 'benevolent monarchy'. After the Greeks came the Romans and Arabs, followed by the Normans, Spanish and Austrians. Now we have anarchists. Who can say what is next? Africa may be the cradle of civilization, but we are nothing but the cradle of invasion!"

"They promise to rid us of the Mafiosi!" Challenged one of Cavallo's cohort's.

"These new, young politicians, the Socio-Fascisti,

especially this clown, 'Benito', parade under the guise of freedom for the people but in reality will impose totalitarianism. The government they propose to replace the present weak republic is a thinly disguised left wing dictatorship."

Two of them paid closer attention. The challenger remained unconvinced. Michael downed his drink and leaned forward.

"I'll tell you something else, as long as you are seeking opinions! If not for these bastardi Mafiosi, we would have our new dam with the money from Rome. The roads would be passable all year around. Maybe even a school for the children instead of that old decrepit church. But they will never be pried from their rat holes!" He sat forward and stared straight into Signor Cavallo's grey weathered eyes. "But two things are certain. Nothing will change for the impoverished people of Sicily, and no matter who lies his way into office, he will be the same as the last. He would make love to his mother and sell his sister for a vote if it would buy him the office he seeks!" Michael reached for a glass of water sitting on the table. "Of course, that is only my humble opinion." Smirking, Cavallo quickly poured him another drink. The other two stared, open-mouthed.

"Maybe you should run for office, signore Casaburi?!" Michael sat back in his chair.

"It's not possible. I don't qualify."

"No capito. Why you don't qualify?" The old man sipped his drink.

"My parents were married." Tropiano had to turn his head away to avoid spitting his drink across the table.

"But Michele . . . " The tall one asked.

"Si Signor Tropiano?"

"How do you really feel?" Cavallo broke into laughter and ordered his waiter to bring more Amaretto.

As the waiter set the drinks Michael noticed a man nailing placards to the fence line behind the fountain in the town square.

"What's with Paolo?" Michael asked nodding towards a man across the road leisurely working away, an armful of silk screened posters clutched under his elbow. Cavallo sipped his drink, smiled and turned towards Casaburi.

"Paolo has a new career, in advertising. He is going to be rich!" Michael glanced back towards the man as his full crop of jet black hair flapped in unison with his hammering.

After downing his Amaretto Michael excused himself and made his way over to the fence line to investigate.

"Paolo, what are you doing?"

"Building a bridge, what does it look like?! I'm working!"

"Working? Your hanging pictures on a fence!"

"So what? You gonna to arrest me?" Paolo missed the small nail and hit his index finger. He dropped the tool and the posters. "AGGHHH! BAFANGULO!" His hand shot under his armpit.

"Paolo! It's Sunday."

"Bafangulo for you too!" He quickly looked to heaven, made the sign the of the cross then continued to nurse his finger. "I get ten lire for everyone I hang!" As Paolo retrieved the hammer Michael picked up one of the tri-colored posters. The copy read; 'Find A New Life In America!' while a silk screened pictorial showed an Italian man in old clothes with empty pockets entering a factory. Exiting the other side he was dressed in fine apparel and holding a large white sack, a dollar sign brandished across the front in one hand and a large loaf of bread in the other while standing in front of a large, new house.

"Paolo, you thinking about to go to America?"

"You'd better believe it-a, Brother! First'a chance I get! And they gonna pay my ticket!"

"You don't worry about the big change? That everything is so . . . different?"

"Different!? You want the same?! Same like this place?! You want to be a mollusk your whole life? Keep yourself attached to some outdated traditions? Dead dreams?" For added emphasis he grabbed his genitals. "You have to take your future in your own hands! You can't expect no one to do it for you."

Along the bottom of the placard was the contact address for The American Woolen Company, Lawrence, Massachusetts, U.S.A. The bottom line read;

# Paddy Kelly

## "Fares Provided!"

\*\*\*\*\*\*\*

The case of Blanck and Harris versus The People of the State of New York went to court in December of 1911. The battle was fierce, the Press relentless and the public were permanently enamored as they hung on every word printed. However, given the surreptitious circumstances surrounding the set-up of the trial, the outcome was, as is traditional in the American court system, over before it started.

With the slick Max Steuer for the defense, Whitman's approach and background and Judge Crain's later-to-be-revealed dirty little secret, the Triangle victims never really stood a chance at justice in the court room.

In view of the fact that most of the evidence had been made public during the ensuing nine months since the crime had been committed, the judge didn't have much leeway in its manipulation. So he handed a get-out-of-jail-free card to Harris and Blanck by doing the next best thing. He manipulated the jury. Following the arguments and before turning it over to the jury Judge Crain did what judges in serious crime cases now routinely do and, thanks to the banning of jury rights in the U. S., are now permitted to do by law.

To the amazement of the legal experts who fully realized the domestic and international implications of the outcome, the press and any lay persons in the gallery who had come to watch the final phases of the trial, Crain issued instructions to the jurors, which based on the circumstances, testimony and evidence they were permitted to hear, were virtually impossible to go against.

Crain told the jury that to find that the fire exit doors were locked was not enough, even though it was agreed that being locked they caused a significant number of the fatalities.

He then instructed that they had to establish that both Harris and Blanck not only knew that those specific doors were locked, but locked on that exact day at that exact time and that

57

they had both ordered the action. An impossibility to prove in any court.

Additionally, and even more incredibly, the defense was able to get the judge to agree that this trial was only about the death of one of the 146 victims, Margaret Schwartz, essentially branding the other 145 deaths irrelevant.

It wouldn't be until decades later that Crain's prejudicial motivations would be explained.

In March of 1905 when fire broke out in an Allen Street tenement crammed with up to 200 immigrant laborers, twenty perished, including ten children, and another 20 were seriously injured.

It was the N.Y.C. Tenement House Department's responsibility to ensure the building had been up to code. Subsequent investigations established it wasn't, by a long shot. The T. H. D. Commissioner, as well as the entire department, were censured and the Commissioner, Mr. Thomas C. Crain, was forced to resign. Given this privileged background there can be little doubt he sympathized with Harris and Blanck.

Although the jury argued for a short time before announcing a verdict, their lack of awareness of their duty to the victims combined with Crain's restrictive orders forced them into a "Not guilty." decision. Far from celebrating, Blanck and Harris virtually went into hiding for fear of being lynched in the streets.

There is a strong argument for the fact that, given the point of American court rooms, to win at all costs as opposed to establishing the truth, no one could ever really have a chance at balancing the scales. However in spite of this, much good did come of the victims' deaths.

The appalling working and living conditions of hundreds of thousands of immigrant factory workers was brought into the public spotlight thus forcing action on an apathetic presidential administration. This resulted in the formation of the New York Factory Investigation Commission, which actually did have some teeth and pushed, in the years to follow, some tangible reform.

The Sullivan-Hoey Fire Prevention Law was passed in the New York Legislature and similar laws followed up and down the coast to eventually spread across the country.

That aside, by his prejudicial actions, Judge Crain was instrumental in helping launch the greatest period of labor unrest in the history of New York.

'The only men who have any place in the
labor movement of today are men with iron
in their blood. Those who think it is
something of a picnic to go up with
bare knuckles against the all
powerful trusts and corporations
of the present day had better go
home and get a rubber
teething ring.'

- *Solidarity*
**March 26, 1910**

## CHAPTER FOUR

On the labor side of things, outrage, threatened violence and drastically increased organizational activity flourished and so, in the weeks and months following the Triangle disaster the streets and avenues of New York were awash with rallies, meetings and union activity.

Neither the politicians or the labor organizers were slow on the uptake regarding opportunities to galvanize hundreds of thousands of workers normally divided along cultural, ethnic and religious lines however, probably none more so than the Socialist organizers.

So, as in the time of ancient Rome when prophets and saviors dotted nearly every street corner foretelling of the coming of the Messiah, unions and union organizers flooded New York City, mounting their soapboxes, promising delivery from the oppression of the prevalent, near slave labor conditions which existed.

From the A.F.L. to the Union of Hebrew Trades, with each successive victory for labor, even perceived victories, it seemed another union or branch with their affiliated "locals", sprang up.

Ever since the landmark, state-wide Cloakmaker's strike a year earlier, resulting in the signing of the *Protocol of Peace,* the Socialist labor movement had become more motivated by hope and belief in its cause then ever before. This was a time when the establishment of a Socialist America was a real possibility. A time when, unrealized by most of America, the country was in reality in Her last throes of a struggle to establish Herself politically before seeking safety in the refuge of the two party system.

By way of example regarding the increase in organizational activity, the union inheriting the torch from the Cloakmaker's, and who would one day come to lead the fight in the garment industry struggle, the International Ladies Garment Worker's Union, had grown from just under 30,000 to over a quarter of a million in the last three years, in New York City alone. But in terms of who would get the big prize, that is the lion's share of manufacturing labor in 1911, the field was narrow, but still wide open.

The heavy hitters were the profit oriented American Federation of Labor .

Undisputedly the most flamboyant and morally committed of the socialist unions at the time were a small group of idealists who first organized themselves in Chicago back in 1904 launching their charter a year later. They were the Industrial Workers of the World, sometimes derogatorily called The Wobblies.

The exact origins of the nickname Wobblie are uncertain. Many believe it refers to a tool known as a "wobble saw". One often repeated anecdote suggests that a Chinese restaurant owner in Vancouver would extend credit to I.W.W. members and, unable to pronounce "W", would ask if they were a member of the "I Wobble Wobble". Another has it that some politician during a strike decided to intimate they were unreliable and referred to them as being wobbly.

Regardless of these theories, the vehemence and hatred with which they were persued can be taken as a testament as to how effective their efforts were. So effective at reform was this short lived tireless, handful of organizers that by the time they were outlawed by president Wilson in 1915, nowhere in the annals of American history had so much violence, hatred and corruption been focused on one political group by so many diverse segments of the U. S., state and local governments alike.

The magnitude and level of violence perpetrated against the I.W.W. is compounded by the fact that it was propagated at every tier of the local, state and federal governments up to and including several presidents. If it can be believed, the violence mitigated by the 'authorities', for lack of a more suitable label, rivaled Hitler's efforts against the Da Da movement in Europe prior to WWII.

He ordered they all be killed.

However, in 1911 the I.W.W. were making their mark in the history books and it was the Triangle Factory Fire and the follow-on political turbulence which would give them and their cause a leg up on the industrialists. In the next two months the battle for unionization of the garment industry in America would come down to the A.F.L. and the I.W.W.

An interesting match of opponents as, aside from the fact that they both abbreviated themselves with three letters, the two organizations were polar opposites.

In the American Federation of Labor the leadership were interested solely in skilled labor, forbade racial integration in the ranks, saw themselves as a bulwark against the unwashed masses invading from Europe, distrusted and discouraged intellectualism, were as often as not industry friendly and advocated the strike as a last resort. In short Samuel Gompers saw his policies, which would reign over the union for nearly forty years, as the new Americanism.

The Wobblies were founded specifically to counter the A.F.L.'s tactics. They had a strong argument. A decade into the new century, after thirty years of organizing efforts, a mere 5% of the American working population were organized and this almost exclusively in the skilled labor sector.

Being the first organization in the United States to preach, practice and participate in complete sexual and racial integration, the I.W.W. advocated the strike as a primary weapon, were wholly committed to the redistribution of wealth in America and saw themselves as a bulwark against rampant Capitalism and were heavily rooted in intellectual principles.

The twin ironies of the situation were that Haywood, Gurley Flynn and Ettor of the I. W. W. were all native born Americans while Gompers was foreign-born. Additionally, the I. W. W.'s policies were something right out of the U.S. Constitution while the "American" Federation of Labor's policies were rooted firmly in a brand of nationalism which was already, in Italy, Germany and Japan, evolving into what would come to be known as Fascism.

So, on April the 4th, an allegorically dreary, rainy day, with nearly three quarters of a million in attendance, one hundred and forty-six young people who had come to America for a better life, slowly passed down Broadway. In their caskets.

However the name originated, the Wobblies were there.

*******

Anna and Nonna stared in disbelief as they watched Michael eat ravenously that night at the supper table.

"Nonna, pass the vegetables please." Michael requested, not bothering to look up from his plate, his mouth half full of penne. She hesitated.

"What's wrong? Never seen a man eat? Pass the vegetables!"

"Not like a starving . . ." She gesticulated with her hand. ". . . vrrrooooommm, what'a you call this thing for to clean the carpet?" Nonna replied in her newly acquired broken English.

"Vacuum carpet cleaning machine, Noona." Anna offered.

"Vaca-umm clean'a machine. You get drunk with'a Cavallo?" Nonna asked suspiciously.

"Two drinks." He held up three fingers. The women looked at each other.

"Maybe you gotta fever?" Nonna probed further.

"Of a sort." The women continued to stare while Michael continued to eat until his plate was empty. Tearing off a piece of bread he pushed back from the table and undid his belt before he spoke.

"There's no future here."

"My son the genius! No future. What was your first clue?" Noona quipped reverting to Sicilian.

"We're going to sell the farm to Carlucci. Nonna, Anna and I are going to America."

"Noona, you can now go and live with your sister."

Nonna dropped her fork and fell back into her chair. Casaburi looked up from his espresso as he continued to drink. He winked at his daughter who instinctively returned the gesture, her delicate face a glowing beacon of elation.

After a brief pause Michael and Anna were simultaneously taken by Nonna's silence.

"Nonna! For once you have nothing to say? You okay,

64

you have a fever?" There was an uncomfortable pause. Michael became concerned.

"Nonna! Say something!"

Fighting back a tear, Nonna lifted her glass.

"It's about damned time you came to your senses! Buon Natale!"

*******

Thick, grey cigar smoke shrouded the triple row of ornate chandeliers and mixed with the stench of sweat and machine oil emanating from the audience to permeate the air. Working men of various ages still pushed into the room which had been filled to capacity for the better part of an hour. The curtain was half open and the stage of the converted music hall was set with a podium and a tripod mounted megaphone off on stage left.

The Italian-American Hall just off Flatbush Avenue in Brooklyn had never seen such an assemblage. The object of the gathering was to decide what action should be taken by the men, the overwhelming majority of which were Italians, and all of whom were shoe workers from the Brooklyn factories. For the first time in their working lives these laborers harbored a faint hope of possibly influencing their own futures.

Few of the men present were in their seats as the atmosphere was far too charged with excitement. Five of their colleagues, in an adjoining factory had been fired for joining a union. Bill Hayward, the President of the Industrial Workers of the World had organized the meeting in an attempt to boost the weak membership of their Brooklyn Local, #168.

He had hoped for two or three hundred to show up. At ten minutes till show time over fifteen hundred crammed the hall and were still drifting in. A large majority of those present still held membership in the most powerful union in the world, Samuel Gomper's American Federation of Labor.

At the last minute "Smiling Joe" Ettor had requested Hayward assign young Gurley Flynn to help him in the Brooklyn dispute in order that she gain much needed experience in union organization of factory workers, a breed far different than the miners of the western plains miners and sawmill workers she had been dealing with for the last year.

As she peeked around the wing curtain from back stage, Elizabeth thought to herself how it sounded like so many thousands of separate voices. But they all echoed as one.

As over 66 million people in the Land of Plenty hovered around the poverty line, political activism was at its highest peek since the time of the War Between The States in the 1860's. It was here, in the politically charged hotbed of New York Socialist activity that Flynn learned free speech came at a price.

Six years prior, at age fifteen, she was arrested for speaking without a license, a thinly disguised charge for attempting to bring politics out of it's elite economic arena and into the common stadium, as class struggle was forced upon America. Her topic was the government's inability to institute relief for single women with children.

"Do you expect to convert people to Socialism by talking about it on Broadway?" The judge inquired as she stood before the bench for the first of countless times in her life, her father by her side. Peering back up at the artificially elevated figure the young teen gave her unwavering answer.

"Yes Sir. I do." She was let off with a warning on the provision, to which she agreed, that she cease and desist her anti-establishment rhetoric. Next day she was back on the same East Side street corner enticing the public with more self-written speeches. A year later, in 1907, secondary to her political speeches, she was expelled from high school.

It couldn't have come at a better time. She had just become involved with the I.W.W. and so immediately became a full time speaker and organizer for the growing union, being called on to travel the Eastern Seaboard to assist in garment, restaurant and miners' strikes then out to Minnesota, and a lumber strike in Montana.

By this point there was little doubt that she had inherited her mother's burning Irish Nationalism and her father's stoic Socialist's political philosophy.

Her father, educated as an engineer, was responsible for

her ideas on what at the time were termed 'Radicalism', and would later in the courts be labeled 'Socialism', 'Anarchism' and 'Anti-Federalism' and finally would be incorrectly branded by the government, through the passage of *The Smith Act*, Communism. History would show each of these terms less appropriate then the next.

Household guests included James Larkin the Irish activist and labor leader of the great 1913 Dublin Lockout. James Connolly the Irish Republican Brotherhood leader and several other prominent Irish revolutionary members who would, only a few years later, give their lives to partially free their occupied country.

Taken in all, these were not people who advocated complacency in the face of wide-spread social and political corruption but were motivated by a sincere desire to change American society and make it a better place. Even at the cost of being members of an organization that, although under every aspect of existing law was legal, were so heavily persecuted.

By 1911 Flynn was fresh from the year long Free Speech Fights which stretched from Missoula, Montana to San Diego, California to Spokane, Washington and she had more than proven her worth at helping combat a Federal government foolish enough to attempt to outlaw public speaking. However, she was yet to attain the status of a media star for her fiery speeches she would enjoy in the near future and the flammable combination of her genetics, sense of justice and altruism, would continue to yield a flame of Irish temper fueled by an overwhelming desire to help those less fortunate than herself and who had been rendered defenseless by the law. Those we today call marginalized.

"You okay?" She jumped as Joe laid his hand on her shoulder and made his inquiry. "You look a little nervous."

"No, not nervous. Scared out of my boots!"

"You'll be alright."

"How many women showed up?"

"Including you?"

"Uh huh."

"One."

"Thanks! How's their English?" She nodded towards the crowd.

"Essentially nonexistent."

"How'll we speak to them?"

"We'll figure something out."

Elizabeth's uneasiness was not propagated by the public speaking aspect of that evening's activities. Now twenty-one, she had been on and off the public lecture circuit between New York and Philadelphia ever since speaking at the Harlem Social Club at age sixteen. Those audiences however were always women or mixed gender groups interested in various social issues and were conducted exclusively in her native tongue, English.

This rowdy group of burly factory workers, most of whom came dressed in their dirty work clothes, didn't show up to discuss whether or not women should have the vote. Most of them could care less. Even the few who were allowed to vote didn't. What was the point? They fully realized they no more elected their politicians here than they did in Italy.

They had been severely abused by a group of American union organizers whom they not only put their trust in, but by contractual agreement paid to represent them. Now they were being fired for being members of that union, the American Federation of Labor's Boot and Shoe Worker's Union, and were being told the contract they signed with the factory owners, a contract the A. F. L. had endorsed, said there was nothing the A. F. L. would do to defend them.

To compound her anxiety Elizabeth had only been briefed on the whole shoe worker's situation a few days ago. But the real obstacle would be the dozen dialects divided amongst the three or four languages circulating the hall that night. Elizabeth didn't speak a foreign language.

The heavily accented voice of the moderator echoed through the hall and the men began to settle down. As quiet gradually blanketed the room a local representative took the floor to speak through the megaphone. However, no sooner had he gathered his thoughts and began to speak when a slow, rhythmic rumble originated from the back of the hall. It started with a light stamping of the feet and the low chanting of the same word repeated three times in succession.

"Sciopero! Sciopero! Sciopero!"

"What are they saying?" Elizabeth asked Joe as they waited in the wing.

"They're calling to strike." Elizabeth's eyes widened as she risked another peek around the wing curtain.

"These men are primed! Gompers really screwed up." Joe added.

At six foot two and well over 200 pounds, 'Smiling' Joseph J. Ettor had just turned 27. A Brooklyn, New York native he sported an unruly shock of jet black hair which seemed to form a lopsided triangle on the top of his head. An impeccable dresser with an infectious, perpetual smile, he had by this time worked the shipyards in Frisco, dozens of western mining communities and lumber camps, and led the Pressed Steel Car Company foreign born workers in their strike which is probably what fostered his deep affection for foreign born workers in general as well as his deep resentment of the people who sought to exploit them.

He would go on to be one of the leaders of the New York City Waiters' Strike in 1913 and the Barbers' Strike in 1914 also in N.Y.C. and would later became a member of the executive council of the I.W.W.

As the chant reached a crescendo Ettor wasted no time. He immediately made for the podium and, although he was largely unknown to the workers gathered there, when he raised his hands in the universal gesture for calm, the noise subsided enough for him to begin his oration. The moderator attempted to coax him to speak from behind the megaphone, but Ettor waved him off.

When the young organizer let out with the opening sentences of his impassioned pleas, a brief silence was followed by Pandemonium. Nearly as one the entire audience sprang to its feet and applauded wildly. Ettor was compelled to pause. He turned towards the wing, smiled at Elizabeth and took a short mock bow. Flynn's hand went to her mouth and covered the broad smile which involuntarily swept her face as she absorbed the drama of the scene. His words were not what motivated the men's enthusiasm, but how he spoke them, in fluent Italian. A true New Yorker, he spoke, Italian and Polish and could understand and communicate in Yiddish and Hungarian.

Joe continued.

"Brothers! You have seen the actions of the factory owners when you have attempted to better your lives! Thanks to your labor, profits in these factories has nearly tripled in the last ten years yet your wages have only been increased on three occasions and by a mere pittance of six percent!"

Cries were once again taken up, only this time beginning at the crescendo and continuing louder. Ettor once again gained control and skillfully worked the crowd by keeping them on track about the need for industrial action while priming them for Flynn's speech.

"At an average wage of $12 per week, that translates to seventy cents over ten years. Seventy cents! Less than what they spend on Cuban cigars in a day!" Joe slowly paced the breath of the stage for dramatic emphasis. It worked. "While your children go hungry and your wives shiver in the cold." After fifteen minutes of the ebb and flow of excitement and the cathartic effect of the energy, Ettor concluded his remarks.

"Finally there is an aspect of your, our, situation in dire need of consideration. And it is that which our next speaker wishes to address. Your families and their right to a better life! Workers, please welcome Elizabeth Flynn!'

Wild applause followed Joe Ettor off stage but the ambiance of elation quickly subsided as Elizabeth came on. Like a chilled wind, uneasy silence swept the men at the sight of a young girl taking the floor.

Dressed in a common, yet fashionably dark dress and white blouse, with pale skin and naturally rosy cheeks, Elizabeth's facial features rivaled those of a Gibson Girl. Her pale blue eyes and raven hair once earned her an offer from David Belasco, the famed theatrical producer, to be a stage actress. She turned him down on the premise that she had no inclination to read other people's lines. "I'm in the labor movement and I speak my own piece." was her final reply.

"Brothers!" Flynn was immediately relieved that her

voice seemed to carry throughout the hall. But the men were relatively quiet. The circus-like atmosphere which had prevailed up until then  had quelled. "You came to this country with promises of a better life. Promises made to you by people like the ones you work for. Your bosses. The ones whose union you joined in good faith and . . ."

"We can't hear you!"

"Speak up!" Came several shouts from across the back of the room.

Back stage Ettor slapped the moderator on the shoulder, gestured towards the stage, and threw his hands apart in the Italian for, 'What the hell's the matter with you?' The moderator understood instantly and ran onto the stage, dragging the heavy megaphone and tripod across to Elizabeth.

"The children of the owners of the factories you toil your lives away in, as well as the children of the union leaders who work hand-in-hand with the owners, are well dressed. Well fed. Most importantly, well educated.  All with money from your labor.  Do you look forward to the day your children will grow old before their times slaving away at the same job you now do on the assembly line?!" The rumbling of the audience gradually gave way to sporadic outcries. "And for little more pay than you receive now?!" Slightly shaken but undaunted she continued.
"This meeting is grim proof of what your union will do when things get rough. Gentlemen, heed the warning!"

A large man in the center aisle, clad in a jacket too small for his cumbersome frame, stood, glanced around the hall, and called up to Flynn.

"We get fired for joining AFL. Then AFL say us, 'Sorry boys, we can'a no help you'. Then they say us if we strike, we get fined ten dollars and kick'a outt'a the union. Why we gonn'a replace one American labor union with a'nutter one?" Someone in the side seats, who had been interpreting for the men around him, immediately chimed in.

"What will you do different, Signorina? Take our money for dues, say, 'sorry boys, nothing we can do.', and then fine us only five dollars?" The men erupted into laughter. Elizabeth sensed she was loosing them.

"We are not a commercial union! We do not seek to collect and stock pile large sums of money for our own benefit. For our own power! Our power originates from you, the workers!"

"So you say now! What'a happen when we strike!?" The fever pitch of earlier began to creep across the room and threatened Flynn's tenuous hold on her audience. Just as cries of 'Sciopero!' began to evolve from the back once again, Flynn put her mouth close to the megaphone and yelled.

"THE I.W.W. IS PREPARED TO WAVE THE DUES FOR ANYONE FROM THE BROOKLYN SHOE FACTORIES WHO ELECT TO LET THE INDUSTRIAL WORKERS OF THE WORLD LEAD THEM IN THEIR STRIKE EFFORTS!" She watched intently for the reaction. Silence dominated then as those who spoke some English disseminated the declaration, t
he unexpected challenge which had halted the disorganized banter, gradually gave way to tumultuous applause. Minutes later the crowd was once again transformed into an attentive audience.

Flynn glanced to her right at Ettor standing in the wing and shrugged. He returned the gesture garnished with a trademark broad smile. She was gaining momentum and tried not to think of what Haywood would say when he got word of her unauthorised offer.

"In addition to waving your dues . . ." She was cut off as a side door crashed open and several haggard looking men burst into the hall.

"BUCCAFORI, HANNO SPARATO AL CAPOSQUADRA!" One of the men yelled into the hall, and a stampede ensued as the entire hall emptied in under a minute.

Ettor jogged out from behind the curtain and stood with Elizabeth in amazement at the rush for the exits. In less than two minutes both organizers found themselves staring out across the deserted hall. Joe put his arm around her shoulder. Flynn was flabbergasted.

"When Haywood said to let you speak tonight, he told me you could get a crowd going, but
. . . I never realized . . ."

72

"Very funny!" She stared out at the empty seats. "What in the name of Sam Hill just happened?" She asked still gawking at the exits.

"Our job just got a little harder. Looks like they're going on strike."

"How do you know?"

"A worker just shot and killed a foreman."

*******

Now coated white with snow the Flat Iron Building resembled a giant slice of wedding cake. The flurries had started to dust Lower Manhattan just after lunch but pushed on into the gray afternoon as a sharp dressed man tossed a Buffalo Head nickle on the well worn mat in the center of the counter of the corner kiosk on 53rd and 3rd and snatched up a copy of the *New York Times, Late Edition.*

He opened the paper and scanned the banner as he hurried down the crowded sidewalk.

## '54 HOUR WORK WEEK NOW LAW!'

After hopping on the South bound trolley the Suit continued to peruse the front page columns.

With large swaths of Eastern Europe rapidly destabilizing, opinions of the world avoiding an impending War-to-End-All-Wars was, in 1911 pretty much split.

Juxtaposed against those who were sure it was coming, largely comprised of underpaid, underprivileged working class stiffs, were the privileged elitists otherwise known as 'The Crown Heads of Europe', a slogan frequently seen on Burlesque marquees or on the sides of circus wagons. Remnants of a soon-to-be antiquated royalty remained certain they still had total control.

Any opposing groups who might happen to show up on the scene could be dealt with by the fascists who in turn could be dealt with by the rising industrial class who in turn liked royalty and worked well with kings and queens. Most of them thought they were royalty.

This is where Billy Hearst saw his opportunity to buy political office and so launched the war against what he called the 'Hyphenates'. The Italian-Americans, Hungarian-Americans, Polish-Americans and any other of thirty or so recently arrived ethnicities who came to America to be 'American'. Probably what annoyed people like Hearst the most was the fact that the Hyphenates had no earthly idea what that meant, to be 'American', but it didn't slow them down any. Given time, they would learn.

After getting about a decade of mileage out of the 'Yellow Peril', and much to the credit of his ability to adjust fire and find new enemies as required, Hearst had recently begun to lay off the Orientals who, he contended, had come to the noble shores of the Founding Fathers with the sole intent of introducing young, white women to the seedy pleasures of opium and then selling them into slavery. He now joined the current fad of attacking Eastern Europeans. Or any body with dark hair that spoke American English with an accent.

What Billy overlooked was the fact that after going away to the Great War and being slaughtered in Great Numbers, the Hyphenates would come back harboring a sense of indebtedness bolstered by a sense of belonging and so were a little more difficult to bully around.

Thank god for Billy and his cohorts the Commies came along.

However, waiting in the wings were the ones who would inherit sole responsibility for the battle to keep the victorious Gettys, Roosevelts, and Morgans within some sort of humanitarian constraints, organized labor.

"Fifty-four hours! Won't make no difference." Declared the dungaree cover-all clad strap-hanger reading over the Suit's shoulder.

"How's that?" The man asked as he folded then tucked the paper under his arm.

"Damn foreigners too stupid to see an opportunity when it's handed to 'em! Just here to make a buck and skeedaddle back to they own country!" The business man smiled at the tradesman's eloquent analysis.

"Guess that's why they're working up to 90 hours a week for less than half the national standard with no overtime, hourly limits, medical or retirement." Replied the suit as he broke eye contact and disembarked the trolley at 41st Street.

"Fuckin' bleedin' heart!" The Jersey City factory worker mumbled.

Labor was the first price, the original purchase, money that was paid for all things. It was not by gold or by silver, but by labor, that all wealth of the world was originally purchased.

- **Adam Smith**

## CHAPTER FIVE

U nion fever was not a ploy, fad or a whim at this point in history. Something instituted and led by radical fanatics, loonies or malcontent's.

By the activists involved, unions were seen as a solution, the treatment to rectify the incredible financial inequities which had defined America until this point in her history.

As far as the Industrialists were concerned, unions were the bubonic plaque brought to America by the Norwegian rats of foreign malcontents, conspirators and Communists which, if not immediately crushed like bugs on a windscreen, would surely result in the downfall of all that was right and just which would then lead to the inevitable collapse of Western Civilization.

In reality, attempts at unionization of the labor force were a class-based, socio-political movement which, in 1911, were on the verge of erupting into full scale civil war.

The enemy were the highly organized and amalgamated employers, all of whom ultimately worked for the relatively few owners of manufacturing and production. With as little as sixty men controlling as much as 90% of America's economy, according to official estimates put forth by, amongst others, Senator Patman of Texas who made an official report to Congress, there was little doubt by anyone who controlled the lives of the 100 million men women and children living in the United States.

It took Congress more than thirty years later to seriously raise the issue of monopolization on the House floor and even then they did nothing about it. The one senator arguing for change, Senator Langer, quoting former Attorney General Wendell Berge, admitted that ". . . since 1890, when the Sherman Antitrust Act was passed, not one single person has been sent to jail or the penitentiary in the entire United States for violating the anti-trust statutes of this country." So the fact that, by Congressional decree, monopolization of any market sector was illegal, it was still okay.

The I. W. W fully realized the might of their enemy.

# The American Way

The inequity of less than .006% of the U. S. population controlling nearly 90% or more of the wealth was the first predication for the foundation of the I. W. W. in 1905.

The second was to counteract the politically conservative course chosen by the dominant, and industry friendly American Federation of Labor. A good example of the way the A.F.L. viewed its obligations to its members was the 1911 Boot and Shoe Workers strike in Brooklyn.

The B.S.W. labor force had signed with the A.F.L. and later asked the reps to negotiate for higher wages. Gomper's people at the A.F.L., after collecting significant amounts in dues all across New York, said they couldn't help the workers. Additionally, they reminded the predominantly Italian workforce that their contract prohibited strikes of any kind and anyone who chose to strike would be fined and/or sacked.

In disgust the workers struck anyway and to add insult to injury were fined $10 each and suspended from the union, mostly after they began to join the I. W. W. As if that weren't enough, the A. F. L. went on to help the company replace the striking men with much cheaper, unskilled labor workers brought in from other Eastern cities.

The third and final primary founding premise of the I.W.W. was the ineffectiveness of existing organizational efforts. No significant shift in workers' rights, safety or security of wage scale had been achieved since the onset of the labor struggle thirty years prior and the daily death toll, more than two per state per day, was climbing. Safe working conditions were an issue virtually shunned by the factory owners. The Triangle Factory fire and the overall prevailing conditions of the garment industry were harsh proof that by 1912 the 100 worker per day death rate meant nothing to the government supported industrialists.

The collapse of the Shoe Makers strike that year, due primarily to the A.F. of L. working hand-in-glove with the company, certainly hurt the workers but it was a major blow to the I.W.W.

In spite of the fact that they had remained faithful to their membership throughout the costly and bloody Free Speech Fights of 1909-1911, single-handedly organized tens of thousands in the construction industry and lumber mills of the South and West, established unionization in the steel mills for migratory farmers, the I.W.W. had not been doing so well in the unionization of Eastern workers, the country's sector with the highest concentration of industry on the continent, and one of the highest in the world at the time.

To compound matters the Wobblies couldn't seem to maintain the union shops after they were set up but just as important, they couldn't get that 'Big Win', the one against the important industrialists which would bring them large measures of positive national attention and net a significant increase in membership, thereby arming them further against the likes of the Rockefeller's and Morgans. Competition with the larger unions, especially the A. F. of L. greatly exacerbated their situation.

Samuel Gompers and his union leaders, founding their union on financial rather than humanistic principles, fully realized the potential economic impact of the unskilled, foreign labor force they refused to represent. The union actively fought to assist the government to regulate against the Eastern Europeans flocking to 'their' country. Flocking to the country not in the hopes of gaining a foot hold through labor in the manufacturing sector and causing a major shift in the American economy as argued by Gompers, but simply to put food on the table.

The leaders of the I.W.W. and other organizations like them, variously labeled as Communists, Socialists, subversives and Anarchists and who were beaten, arrested and imprisoned, were in fact the people who did 'hold the truth to be self evident'. 'That all men are created equal'. As evidence of the A.F.L. versus the I. W. W. philosophies witness their membership policies.

Foreign or native born, skilled or unskilled, male, female, black, white, red or yellow, all were welcomed for membership and representation in the I.W.W. but more revealingly, all paid the same dues and had an innate right to be guaranteed the same wages for the same jobs.

Idealistic, across the board dues scales for blacks, women, unskilled labor or other 'minorities' weren't an issue for the AFL. None of these people were even allowed to join.

Perhaps this idealistic, egalitarianism on the part of the Wobblies was a little impractical, as Haywood, Flynn, Ettor and the rest never really understood that they were fighting a financial war of survival of the fittest versus a financial war of the ideals of wealth distribution. Ironically, their struggle was not without influence on the wealthy.

It was, for example Eleanor Roosevelt who introduced FDR to what is euphemistically termed 'Left Wing' politics, as anyone in America who is a little too pro-constitutional rights has always and still is branded. This in turn was an influence on his drafting and implementation of the National Recovery Act in 1932 which officially compelled manufacturing to get along with the unions for the benefit of the overall economy.

Additionally, J. P. Morgan's own daughter actively supported the reformation of worker's rights as did Taft's wife, Helen Herron.

In the interim however, the A. F. L. would enjoy the overwhelming support of the local, state and national governments and continue to exploit the I.W.W.'s primary weakness, their policy of not building cash reserves to fight what was developing as one of their costliest battles to date.

To this end there are two guiding principles which transcend, yet define the boundaries of American jurisprudence and in turn can be extended to all spheres of that government.

One, who ever has the deepest pockets is the one you go after and two, how much will it cost to out spend the other guy in the costly court battle it will take to get whatever it is he has thta you want? This gives way to the founding principle of the American Holy Trinity; politics, law and business, and why it's about amassing the biggest war chest.

Essentially, 'He who dies with the most toys wins!'

Activists like Flynn, Ettor and Haywood saw this and were out to alter the status quo. Men like Carnegie, Rockefeller and Morgan knew it and were out to stop them. At all costs. Of course little people like the Wobblies were not really taken seriously by the Big Boys.

That was about to change.

# Paddy Kelly

Elizabeth shifted the small heft of trade dailies she held tucked under her arm and lifted her ankle-length black skirt with the other hand to ascend the stoop of the Victorian, brown stone at 60 Cooper Union Square. Halfway up the granite steps she caught site of the wooden sign board hung on the wall to the left.

"Very original." She mumbled under her breath. The newly hung sign which read, 'I.W.W. Headquarters' had been defaced, again, the prominent letters, I.W.W. had been repainted in broad, red brush strokes to read, "I Won't Work Headquarters".

"Delinquents!" She commented and made a mental note to get the sign cleaned.

Most of the second floor of the five storey walk-up served as the New York Headquarters of the now six and half year old labor union. The Lower East Side office wasn't elaborate by any standard, but was extremely functional. Flynn came through the front door and, after cursory greetings to the two or three staff members scurrying around the front office moved straight to the back of the converted tenement.

She entered the improvised conference room in the middle of a conversation between Bill Haywood and Joe Ettor who had his feet propped up on the table editing an article for *The Call* as he spoke to Haywood.

"Apparently he was told he had to work a double shift a couple of minutes before the whistle blew and he refused. An argument ensued and the foreman came at him with a shoe last intent on hitting him. There are a dozen witnesses. He was attacked and shot in self-defence."

"They'll hang him." Offered Haywood.

"Without a trial if they think they can get away with it." Ettor added.

A miner from Utah, at six foot three inches tall, 250 pounds and missing one eye due to a childhood accident, 'Big' Bill Haywood wasn't a man who escaped notice.

One of the twelve founding members of the I.W.W. by late 1911 he was perceived to be forcibly taking on the mantle of sole leader. In an organization founded on strict Socialist principles, this was beginning to cause increased discontent in the hard core membership and no doubt scared the hell out of some as well.

Bill shifted his chair at the table and rummaged through the variety of trade and union papers Flynn had brought in. The I.W.W. were in the process of establishing their daily, literary organ but understood the criticality of reading everyone else's to gauge the political weather and plan their tactics state and nationwide.

"Why didn't he just work the shift?!" Flynn asked as she plopped a second, smaller stack of newspapers onto a table and removed her heavy wool coat.

"It was his little girl's birthday." Joe answered as he wrote. "The foreman hates Italians and gave him a hard time about it."

"New York Central Labor Union has ordered all other unions to stop sending us defense fund money for the Brooklyn campaign." Bill announced without looking up from the paper.

"They think we're stealing it?!" Flynn asked.

"Better than that." Bill added as he threw the folded newspaper across the table. "Read the quote, column two."

"In a widely distributed letter, the A.F. of L. have warned that . . ." Flynn read aloud. "I
didn't see any letter! Did you see a letter?"

"Must've got lost in the post." Joe chided.

". . . if the I.W.W. succeed in their war against the Boot and Shoe Workers Union . . ."

". . . the next trade they attack may be your own! Take action now!" Bill mockingly finished.

"Oh good! Now we're fighting a war on two fronts!" She realized aloud.

"Three. Billy Hearst had another editorial yesterday on the 'anarchistic' activities of the I.W.W. and it's 'well known' Communist members."

"The Brooklyn local is fast dissolving and the strike is falling apart." Joe added with a wry smile.

"Can't blame them. They came to the land of milk and

honey to drink contaminated water and eat stale bread while trying to learn the language. Worst yet, they try to preserve their cultures in a land where your culture is the single biggest weapon used against you." The door creaked open and one of the young office volunteers peered her head in through the door.

"Would any one like tea or coffee?"

"No thank you, Louise. And you don't have to serve us. We can make our own tea." Elizabeth instructed.

"Hold on there Flynn! Don't go gettin' too Socialist on us!" Joe corrected. "I would like some coffee, Louise!"

"Ignore him. His mother dropped him."

"Whatever you say Miss Flynn."

"And don't call me Miss Flynn! Call me Elizabeth. Or Gurley Flynn."

"How would you like your coffee, Mr. Ettor?" Flynn gave him a look.

"Thank Louise. Apparently I don't want coffee." Joe made a funny face at Louise behind Flynn's back.

"They're dealing in two or three different languages, there's wide spread suspicion of the provincials by the rurals, plus the six or seven trades refuse to work together."

"AFL tactics work every time! Wait, don't tell me. The neighborhood police are also picking one or two at random to beat and arrest as intimidation to the others. The judges are increasing bail each time a worker is dragged in and . . ."

"And, we've got a strategy meeting to conduct here. Media sympathy is something we're likely never gonna get, so let's stop worring about it and get down to business!" Bill interjected. "There are eighteen other actions across the country we're fighting and the Brooklyn action isn't over yet!" He pushed the dailies aside.

"I guess it's safe to conclude things are not going well in New York?" Flynn inquired.

"Things are not going well on the east coast!" Joe answered.

"Maybe here's our chance to turn things around. Got a telegram from the local in Lawrence." Bill announced as he passed the message across the table.

"Didn't know we had still had an active local in Lawrence." Joe commented.

"Didn't know we had a Lawrence. Where the heck is it?" Gurley Flynn asked.

"Massachusetts. Twenty-five thirty miles north of Boston. Sure Joe, knows that." Bill quipped.

"I do?"

"You were up there little more than a year ago."

"I know that."

"Then why didn't you say something?" Flynn inquired.

"Just wanted to see if Bill remembered." He Joked. "So, what's the story?" Although conditioned to Ettor's antics, Haywood was not amused.

"The State congress passed the 54 hour work week, food prices are up, and being just after Christmas, the mills have increased quotas for the fourth time this year, and the workers think there'll be a wage cut."

"Sounds like the workers have lost their sense of humor. How many members in I.W.W. Local number . . .?"

"Twenty. Around a thousand."

"That's not bad. How many dues paying members in good standing?" Bill consulted his notes and while still staring down at them he addressed Elizabeth.

"That reminds me, Gurley." Bill slowly turned to her with narrowed eyes. "We must have a chat about dues when we're done here." Flynn looked at Joe who threw his hands up, palms out in a don't-look-at-me attitude.

"Local #20 has about two hundred members in good standing."

"That's not good."

"Will they strike?" Flynn asked.

"We have no way to know for sure, but if they do it's a cinch the AFL won't want any part of it." Bill added.

"And if they back down, we'll have wasted how much precious time and limited resources in preparation?" Ettor suddenly became eerily serious.

"Why would the AFL not help them?" Flynn interrupted. "The New England mills are some of the most productive in the world, and they're the third largest trade in the country! Why wouldn't Gompers jump at that?!" Flynn asked.

"Two reasons. They've got the United Textile Workers up there already, and these are laborers asking for help. Not tradesmen"

"Here Joe, they addressed it to you. Hold onto it and give it a think." Joe reached across the table and took the telegram from Haywood.

The meeting was, by Monday standards, short and after about twenty-five minutes began to wind down. There was a knock at the door then it opened about halfway. It was Louise holding a steaming cup of coffee.

"Shall I set it on the table, Mr. Ettor?" Joe beamed with mock satisfaction. Flynn was not amused.

"No Louise. I have to get Downtown with this copy for *The Call*. And I'd better have this outside." Exiting he took the coffee and headed out into the hall. Flynn, still sitting at the table, took up a pad and pencil and began to sift through the trade dailies for relevant information being reported on the Wobblies as Joe took his coffee and left.

"I've seen Joe do remarkable things with people, but is he going to be okay alone if he takes on Lawrence?" She asked, head down, as Bill making ready to leave.

"No."

"NO!?" She looked up in astonishment. "Then why did you give him . . .?"

"I mean 'no' as in no you're not going to Lawrence."

"I didn't ask . . ."

"There are in the neighborhood of forty-five thousand workers up there all together. Local 20 has only two hundred members. That's smaller then the Brooklyn Local who's workforce is less than a quarter the size. We're not in a position to squander resources. Besides . . ."

"Besides what?"

"You're not going to Lawrence." Haywood reiterated.

"I still don't see your point!"

"This time next week there won't be a Brooklyn local and every cent we've invested in time and energy might as well have been flushed down the toilet! Worse yet, we'll be one more step closer to having a reputation for not being able to win strikes!" Flynn found Bill's uncharacteristic pessimism disheartening but was at loss for a retort." And don't think I don't know why you want to go up to Massachusetts!"

"Yeah? Why?"

"Free membership maybe?" He half-heartedly mocked. He moved closer and made eye contact. "What the hell were you thinking?!" Flynn sat silently as Haywood crossed the room and took a seat at Joe's empty chair just opposite her.

"They were wavering! Besides, most of them will pay it anyway! It was to prove a point!" She was defending herself for the free dues offer she made to the Brooklyn local. "You're the one always sayin' we have to emphasize we're not like Gompers' crowd!"

"Not stockpiling thousands in funds is one thing! How do you propose we pay the rent this month, let alone the three trials we got going on? Ask for credit?! Even the damn landlord is Republican!"

Flynn, although one of only a couple of women actively involved with the New York headquarters full time, was no less caught up in the all but out-of-control political events of the times.

"We'll raise enough funds from the donations for the trials!"

"I know we will. But don't do it again!" Flynn realized Bill was just blowing steam.

Although a strong, independent leader, some in the organization suspected that there was resentment by Haywood of Gurley Flynn's growing popularity in the press. As the very authorities who sought to put him away for the rest of his life or better yet execute him, controlled the American 'free' press, he had precious little good press while Gurley Flynn was, for the most part, widely touted for her unwavering humanity and enthusiasm in terms of embracing causes concerning equality.

To aggravate the situation the I. W. W.'s idealistic belief of not stockpiling large sums of dues money combined with a lack of follow-ups in areas where strike victories had occurred, all exasperated by Gompers' new tactic of trying to cut off what little funding they did get, was beginning to take its toll.

"Gurley, it's not about the money."

"What then?"

"Picking your fights." Flynn sat back in her chair not sure if she was being chastised or not, or even if they were still arguing. Mostly she hoped this wouldn't turn into another of Father Bill's sermons to his surrogate daughter.

"Gurley, forget about the Asch fire." '*Too late for that!*', she thought.

"Pray for the dead and . . ."

"Fight like hell for the living."

"If the I.W.W. are going to stay a viable organization then we have to pick our fights."

"Then organize me, damn it! Give me something else! Something big enough to make me forget the Asch building! Let me go up to Lawrence."

"No, I need you elsewhere. Besides, we don't even know if they'll go through with a strike. Joe has strict orders to get a firm nod or walk away. As it stands it's only a few of the two dozen mills and one group or another of them has threatened strikes eight or ten times in the last year alone. The one they did try was so pock-marked with in-fighting they lost in a few weeks and had to go back at a **lower** wage." Not previously privy to the research Bill had done, the picture slowly came into focus for the young Gurley Flynn who remained at the table as Bill headed for the door.

"You want to go to Lawrence to help lead them in a crushing victory against the industrialists in revenge for the Triangle fire." She looked over at him with creeping suspicion. "We all want that." He added. Unimpressed Flynn returned to her note taking. With the door half, open Bill hesitated. "How are things at home?"

"What home? We've been living apart for nearly five months now." She didn't bother looking up as she answered.

"Who knows about it?"

"Mom, dad and the two of us. I'd appreciate it if . . ."

"Don't even say it. It's nobody's business. I saw it coming

anyway, it was inevitable. You two are opposite ends of the spectrum. Him with his political agnosticism and you and your 'god-damned illogical anarchistic activities'." He said, imitating her husband's mannerism.

"You're a hoot Haywood! I hear the Orpheum's looking for a comic."

"How's Freddie?"

"He's teething. A few late nights, other wise he's good. We're living at my parents for now. Until I get settled."

"When's the last time you saw Carlo?" Bill asked as he let the door close behind him and headed down the hall.

"Tresca!?" Flynn jumped from her seat and opened the door. "Is he alright!? Did they arrest him again?" Bill continued down the hall. "Damn it, Haywood! Talk to me! Is Tresca okay?"

"You tell me, Flynn." He said over his shoulder as he vanished through the front entrance. "You're on the 2:15 to Pittsburgh."

Flynn dropped back into her seat and smiled. Carlo Tresca, Flynn's clandestine lover since her marriage had run aground, was based in Pittsburgh.

"Bastard!"

\*\*\*\*\*\*

The Sunday before the Triangle factory fire the Brooklyn Shoe Workers strike, led by the I. W. W., had run out of steam. In only a matter of a few weeks the workers had been starved into submission. With the arrest and conviction of Frank Buccafori the ensuing bad press gave Gompers and his A. F. L. the excuse they were looking for to put their anti I. W. W. campaign into high gear and petition other unions to stop sending relief money to the Industrial Workers of the World.

Despite the fact there was clear evidence corroborated by testimony that Buccafori was attacked with a tool by the foreman following an argument and Buccafori fought back in self defense, he was found guilty. The defendant and his fellow workers were not even on strike, however, the fact that the I. W. W.'s name was even invoked during the trial did not fare well for the defendant.

The plethora of witnesses in favor of Buccafori were easily dealt with through death threats and intimidation and, as was the custom of the time, the jury were stacked against the defense by the existing selection laws. Buccafori got ten years in Sing Sing.

Since then jury selection laws have been strictly monitored. So other methods have evolved to assist the outcome of trials in the U. S. The judiciary employ what are known as the 'rules of evidence' to say what the defense can and cannot introduce on its behalf in order to assist the prosecution.

*******

Whether or not Haywood harbored an ulterior motive concerning sole leadership of the union is largely academic. The reality was that Haywood understood the need for decisive action in the face of an increasingly totalitarian government where the rule of law simply no longer applied. Where, largely due to the I.W.W.'s greatly increased public persona and hence an ever increasing effectiveness in unskilled labor organization against unsubstantiated arrests, denial of council and fabricated charges accompanied by extraordinarily long sentences which had become routine, an ever increasing portion of the populace were falling in behind the Socialist Wobblies. And, for the leadership of the country and the men who commanded them, a Socialist America was never going to be tolerated under any circumstances. Even to the extent of voter rigging, violation and atonement of "Democratic" principles to the point of virtually ignoring the so called rules of law.

There can be no argument these acts of unmitigated violence against the workers and organisers were the desperate actions of a few unscrupulous men in high places however, the serious knock-on effect was that the entire American system was clearly seen to be coming apart at the seams. Additionally, Haywood was one for the liberal application of King Hammurabi's code.

If they, 'the authorities', had no compunction regarding the use of unnecessary force, circumventing the law and bending the rules to their breaking point, Big Bill reasoned all bets were off. Ironically and much to his defense, there are no substantiated recorded incidents where he or the Wobblies ever propagated violence against anyone who did not attack him or his members first.

Haywood came by his opinions on how to get things done honestly. He had been arrested, beaten and tortured by various state and federal authorities routinely for the last seven years.

One of the first leaders in American history to forbid racial or sexual segregation in any form in an organization, by 1914 he would find himself on the 'unofficial' most wanted hit lists of every major U.S. Government, state and municipal agency in America. Not forgetting every one of the major industrialists as well.

Oddly enough, despite their current personal conflict, Gurley Flynn's first gig with the Wobblies was speaking at a protest meeting in Schenectady, New York defending Haywood and his colleagues who had been illegally arrested and framed for murder in the famous Haywood, Pettibone and Moyer Trials, a true landmark case in the history of the American class struggle which manifested itself as the labor wars. It was in December, 1905 when he was the President of the Western Federation of Miners, during a strike that Haywood's reputation and henceforth his career, was launched.

The governor of Idaho, Frank Steunenberg, had used labor to get elected and once in office refused to support the workers then called in the U.S. Army against them when they struck. One night returning home, hen opened his front gate which detonated a bomb. Steunenberg died on the spot.

On the 8th of January, 1906 the Pinkertons were called in to find the murderer or murderers. A Detective McParland was the man assigned the case and it was little trouble to arrest a plausible suspect, in this case a dodgy itinerant miner named Orchard.

McParland, who had previously engineered the frame-up of several of the executed Molly Maguires in Pennsylvania, made it crystal clear to his rube they had damning evidence on him, which of course they did not, and as soon as court reconvened he was going to the gallows. However, if he decided to name names in court The State might consider leniency. However, not just any names would do.

McParland instructed Orchard to specifically name Haywood, Moyer and Pettibone, the leadership of the Western Federation of Miners, sworn enemies of the Mine Owner's Association who were the primary backers of The Governor. This instruction was given despite the fact that all three were 100 miles away in another state at the time of the killing and had nothing to gain by the victim's death. Incidentally, as was usually the case, there wasn't a shred of evidence of any involvement on the part of Haywood, or his colleague's.

With a practiced hand, McParland embellished Orchard's 'confession' over the days ahead and when he was finished, much as senators Dies and Thomas would later present 'evidence' that there were hoards of thousands of Communists massed on the Mexican boarder poised to invade America, McParland presented 'evidence' that there was a national conspiracy, led by the I.W.W. to assassinate employers all over the country, to possibly include the president of the United States, and to bring about the downfall of Democracy as they knew it.

No doubt McParland had political ambitions of his own for he seized this opportunity with vim and vigor to toot his own horn at every turn describing his "clever" apprehension of the defendants to the Governor as ". . . having unearthed the bloodiest crowd of anarchists in the civilized world . . ." From this and other writings concerning the case, there is no doubt this virtual unknown was grooming himself as some kind of superhero, much as J. Edgar Hoover would do a few years later.

Of course no evidence was forth coming or ever presented, in court or otherwise. All that remained for the Pinkerton to assure himself everlasting glory in the annals of criminology was to arrest Haywood and company. But there was a legal snag. The men not only weren't anywhere near the crime scene, they weren't even in the same state. So before they could be hanged following their fair trial in Idaho they would have to be extradited from Colorado.

McParland hit on a solution.

# The American Way

He contacted the Head of the Colorado State Supreme Court, enlisted the assistance of the Governor, and with their collusion and tacit approval, plans were made to kidnap the three victims and transport them across the state lines to Idaho where they could be legally arrested.

On this illegal legal authority the three were kidnapped and whisked away to Idaho on a heavily armed secret train specially commissioned and well stocked with dozens of heavily armed vigilantes, chains, arms, ammo, and of course, multiple cases of beer and liquor.

After the legal mob beat them their rights and 'arrested' the three men, a lengthy appeals process followed whereby the local and state courts essentially said that, even had they not the commited the murder, they needed to be in custody anyway so, even though there were no other warrants out on them anywhere, all was okay. The fact that they were abducted in another state and transported across state lines, outside Idaho's jurisdictional territory with no corroborating evidence, all on the word of the unemployed transient who later openly admitted to committing the murder himself , (as well as several others), although illegal, was okay.

When the case was finally brought before the U.S. Supreme Court several months later the actions of the private detective agency were deemed illegal but, as the men were already in Idaho, the nation's highest court cowered from a decision stating there was nothing they could do about it.

Additionally, about three weeks before the trial a grand jury investigating land fraud indicted one of the prosecutors, William Borah, making him a felon under Federal law. His new found status as a felon of course did not preclude him from assisting in the ever increasing show trial. Haywood was the first to be tried, as a victory against him was seen to make it easier to hang the other two.

By this point, in May of 1907, international indignation in the labor community was at a peak. Public pressure was building thanks to the few sympathetic press organs which were not owned or controlled by the Mining bosses or William Randolph Hearst. Additionally President Teddy Roosevelt was besieged by union leaders realizing they too were potential targets of the no-holes-barred legal system. Despite his many public claims to be 'a friend of the working man', still he refused to intervene in the case. International Heads of State, legal and journalistic experts all over the country criticized his procrastination of public comment until the eve of the trial.

Condoning the kidnapping conspiracy, Roosevelt stated that the three were deemed, ". . . undesirable citizens" and therefore anything McParland and company did was irrelevant. A rather strong statement from a politician who proclaimed himself to be a citizen's rights activist as well as a friend to the working man. No one involved in the men's defense, headed by the unpopular Clarence Darrow, could have known that Governor Gooding and Roosevelt were working hand-in-glove with the Pinkertons through daily communications.

To further tip the scales of justice, Pinkerton Operative #21 had been cleverly manipulated onto the defense council's team and dispatched daily reports which were forwarded from the Governor's office and then onto the White House. This while Roosevelt repeatedly publicly assured the nation the three would receive a 'fair trial'.

The entire mid-western miner's community went into shock, particularly the Owner's Association when, after a dramatically heated trial and 20 hours of deliberation, in spite of the fact that McParland and the mine owners had a plant on the defense team and believed they had sufficiently 'packed' the jury, the twelve men returned a "Not Guilty" verdict.

As if the plot wasn't convoluted enough, there was one last interesting twist.

About three months after the trial it emerged Orchard, who really did commit the murder, had been hired by the Pinkerton's to actually commit the crime presumably to frame the I.W.W. leadership. Pinkerton's who were themselves in the employ of the Miner's Association, a group who were no friend to the Governor!

Thus was Bill Haywood's background and baptism of fire in the American labor struggle.

These sorts of events ensnared by this style of dynamic

were to set the tone for the I.W.W.'s fight against the so-called authorities all over the country. The fact that this case got as far as it did, handing three men's lives over to a jury on fabricated evidence and perjured testimony, would pave the way and dictate tactics for the remainder of the labor struggle.

The fact that the three were exonerated was not seen as a triumph of the American judicial system, but as a sick perversion of it. A decision, which took nearly an entire day to deliberate, if going against Haywood, would have certainly resulted in the execution of two other innocent men, Moyer and Pettibone as well.

These considerations are not exclusive of the fact that the three had spent a half year in prison subjected to the daily abuse and sometimes outright torture acceptable for the times, and lost hundreds of thousands of dollars in precious union funds.

But then again, that was the general idea, wasn't it?

This behavior would set the tempo and pattern for all of the major labor actions to come. The police or militia would murder a civilian, (unarmed in nearly every instance), the strike leader or leaders would be charged and tried and, as the authorities learned to modify their techniques, nearly always found guilty.

A tactic which infuriated the authorities however, was that the I.W.W. would increasingly play the smart hand and become more firm in their advocacy of non-violent resistance, much to their credit, in the face of ever increasing, State-sponsored violence.

'Sixteen and time to pay off. I get this
job in a piss factory inspectin' pipe.  40
hours a week at thirty-six bucks. It's real
bullshit but ya know, it's a pay check Jack.
It's real hot in here too, hot like Sahara
but all these bitches are too lame to
understand, too grateful to get this job to
realize they're gettin' screwed up the ass.
Meanwhile . . . I wasn't sayin' too much
neither.'

- **Patty Smith**
*Piss Factory*

## CHAPTER SIX

Straddling the banks of the Merrimack River, just north of Boston, the city of Lawrence was billed as the "Worsted Center of the World". It hadn't always been so.

A long time ago, not long after the natives were chased from the territory for the last time, some well dressed men rode into the small village in a fine, private coach. They stayed for a couple of days, walked around a lot and, were careful not to muddy their boots too much and, except for an occasional question, kept mostly to themselves. After a day or so in that place they climbed back into their fine coach and went away. "

A few days later, back in Boston, deals were struck, hands were shook, and the Essex Company was chartered.

A short time later, teams of surveyors came back to the village followed by gangs of men with little red flags who were in turn followed by an army of laborers. After the town folk were offered good money for their plots, homes, shops and possessions, swaths of land along both banks of the river were cleared.

Speaking their strange, incomprehensible language, Irishmen came by the hundreds and uprooted trees and shrubs then planted steel rails in their place while several large brick buildings began to rise out of the ground at the same time wide, deep trenches were rutted out along the banks of the mighty Merrimack. The dam and buildings were finished, the trenches were flooded and the trains started coming. Sporadically at first then on a regular basis.

The directors of the Essex Company sold land on either side of the river which was earmarked for planned housing for workers and managers, planned stores, planned churches and planned schools as well. Everything was planned, by the directors. Speculators need not apply.

The directors were the interlocked families of the Lawrences, Lowells, Appletons and Jacksons, families already steeped in the traditions of industry control in the New England textile sector. Lawrence was the final and most ambitious of the New England planned textile-manufacturing cities developed by the Boston entrepreneurs competing with New York for bragging rights to the Eastern Seaboard and credited with launching the Industrial Revolution on the West side of the Atlantic. That was well over a century ago.

Unfortunately the social and technical advances of the Boston associates gave way to the "Robber Barons" who, after gaining prominence in the later part of the19th century, further exploited foreign labor, reaped profits at the expense of modernization and had a complete disregard for the values of humanism and nature conservation first envisioned by the founders of this potential, but now mythical Shangri-La of industry.

Now in 1911, The American Woolen Company, by far the most powerful woolen mills in the country, had three of their largest factories in Lawrence, the Wood, the Ayer and the Washington. These three facilities alone employed nearly fourteen thousand.

Additionally there were four cotton mills in the city, The Arlington, the Everett the Atlantic and the Pacific whose total rosters tallied fifteen thousand workers. The Pacific mill was the largest producer of printed cotton goods in the world and was responsible for over a third of all these employees.

There was one independent woolen mill, The Kunhardt, two small cotton mills and one dyeing plant, the U.S. Worsted Company. These factories employed about 2,650 people. There were also several smaller mill operations.

So in the bustling metropolis of Lawrence, Massachusetts there were 12 major mills, employing about 32,000 men, women and children, the overwhelming majority, foreign born, half of which were under twenty-one. More significantly, less than 10% of all of them spoke English.

Soon after the Wood Mill opened, William Wood built the Ayer Mill directly across the street. The Ayer Mill was labeled unique because it housed the largest clock tower in the country, the E. Howard Clock, built specifically for Wood. At a height of 276 feet, the tower's four dials were lit by over 400 bulbs. The town father's praised it as a monument to architecture. Wood praised it as a monument to maintain the punctuality of his ignorant workforce. The workforce praised it as a monument to Wood's greed and tyranny.

The new mills were a subsidiary of John Pierpont Morgan, who in 1911/1912 was estimated to be worth two times the Gross National Product of America and who controlled shipping, steel, rail road and textiles and an appreciable sector of American banking. Despite the fact he controlled their lives, he had no idea the people of Lawrence existed.

In less than two weeks they would make their presence known.

*******

It was six twenty-seven a. m., Tuesday morning when Michael took his place among the gathering crowd in the pitch dark cold of mid-Winter, outside the towering, steel factory gates. Well-worn eyes of all ages glared into the distance as condensation rose from their faces and gently floated above their heads. They took in the frigid morning air and waited outside the barriers to breathe life into the dormant behemoth of the massive structure before them.

Contemporary writers and journalists described the mills flanking the river as looking like prisons, but for Casaburi, with memories of the decrepit, dirty factories of Sicily, located almost exclusively in the derelict or barren parts of the ancient towns, these mills were well maintained, brick and steel modern marvels.

The giant factory's location, near the city center was another feature which flushed Michael with an unexpected rush of pride as he peered through the wrought iron fence. Elated with his good fortune and new place of employment he patiently waited.

Not only had he been introduced to Alfonso Affanoso, a man from Palermo who knew several families familiar to the Casaburis, the day he arrived at the boarding house, but he was also given a job. It was instantly apparent to him that he had made the right choice to come to America and pursue a new way of life. His new life.

"In Winter they wait to let us in." Affanoso announced over his shoulder to his new charge.

"Why?"

"Colder we are, faster we work." Michael made no comment but put Affanoso's remark down to acquired complacency.

"Sometimes they leave some of the windows open all night."

"You sound like an American." Casaburi quipped. The frigid December cold found its way through everyone's clothing and by now not a man, woman or child was able to stand still in the dark.

"What time does the sun rise?" Michael asked.

"Not for three hours." The woman next to him answered in a heavy Slavic accent.

"Sie kommt jetzt! Die Flutliche!" A young boy, his pale white face peeking from between the tall iron railing, called out from the front of the crowd as he pointed to the roof of the mill. The veteran workers covered their eyes and turned their heads away from the direction of the factory.

Michael, with a handful of other new comers was temporarily blinded when an intense, wave of light washed over them as powerful flood lights blasted to life.

Almost immediately two Stentorian steam whistles shattered the quiet of the morning, signaling the armed guards inside the factory compound. The over-sized, barbed wire capped gates slowly swung open and throngs of men, women and children poured through into the rear yard. After a full minute the offensively loud whistles ceased and rows of pathetically inadequate, overhead lights inside the factory began to flicker on bathing the machines and spaces in a haunting iridescence.

As the crowd pushed through the single pair of large double doors, all anxious to reach the relative warmth of the open floored mill, Casaburi felt like he was entering an auditorium to hear the Prime Minister speak. Upon entering the expansive main production area he was momentarily stunned and stood still.

Hard pressed to see the far wall of the tremendous work space he scurried around some machinery and gawked down a gangway.

"What are you looking for?"

"The other end!" He exclaimed with a healthy measure of curiosity. He stared up at the heavily sky-lighted ceiling. "So much glass. So much weight! How does it stay up?" He asked in amazement.

"On our shoulders."

"I mean, it's so big! Where does it end?"

"It never ends. Come on." Affanoso shot back.

Within minutes several thousands were at their respective work stations. Overhead belt drives groaned into motion and well oiled feeders, thrashers and looms awoke and settled into a rhythmic hum until the factory rose from its sleep and gradually but firmly manifested a life of its own.

Having only worked with or ever seen mid-nineteenth century farm machinery before, the gradual unfurling of the voluminous amounts of modern technology and shear expanse of the operation at the Washington Mill combined to mesmerize and intoxicate Michael as he walked with Alphanso across the factory floor. To effectively communicate, the two men were compelled to yell over the now deafening, mechanical din.

"The oil . . . smells sweet!" The metallic melody of the machines reminded him of an overgrown version of the typing machine he had once seen in the Palermo post office.

"Signor Affanoso, I can never repay you for your help."

"You are right, you can't. So don't worry about it. Besides, all I did was take you to the office."

"And get me hired!" Michael protested.

"I didn't get you hired. You met the primary condition for working in Wood's mills. You are breathing. If fifty women and children walked in off the street this morning they would be working before lunch. Bastardi would have them do the work applications on their break. Which reminds me. Be sure to report in after shift so you can fill in your work form."

"What about my entrance visa and birth certificate? Who do I show them to?"

"Nobody. Don't worry about it, you won't need them."

They walked a bit more.

"I want to thank you anyway." Michael reiterated.

"They'll start you at thirteen cents an hour. Work is six-thirty to six. We're only paid for ten hours. Saturday only seven." Affanoso explained as he escorted Michael to his position at the end of a production line.

They passed a large side room filled with children scurrying in and out hauling buckets of something Michael could not see. The young boys hauled the nearly filled buckets up the long narrow room and little girls returned, running with the empty pails.

A little further on a boy, no more than nine or ten, stood at a machine bare foot, his clothes
pathetically inadequate for the frigid air of the mill. Oblivious to his own shivering, he operated the
complicated device with admirable dexterity, an unlit cigarette dangling from his mouth. Michael gave a stare of curiosity as they passed. The boy noticed him.

"Buon giorno." Michael smiled.

"Ciao Mack!" The boy waved, nimbly throwing levers and simultaneously operating a set of six foot pedals.

"Yes. This is a family business. The whole family must work to survive." Affanoso added. Michael narrowed his eyes at the comment. "You have family?" Affanoso inquired.

"A daughter. Anna."

"Women get seven to ten cents per hour, children four cents." He nodded towards a pair of empty buckets being returned to the water room. "You have to pay for your drinking water. Ten cents every two weeks. Only go to the toilets on your time. If not, you're docked. You don't keep up with the Overseer's quotas, you're docked." They were over taken by a young man hauling an over-sized tool box. "You're docked three times in one week, you're fired."

"Why is he running?"

"He's a Fixer. He has to tend five looms at once. If one goes down the Overseer won't get his quota and they are both docked. If it happens twice he'll be transferred from the looms to a lower paying job. Overseers, Slashers and Menders get bonuses if they exceed production quotas."

"What is quotas?" Micheal switched to English.

"How much linen we must to produce each day."

"How much must we to produce each day?"

"Completely arbitrary. Wood sets them whenever his cow of a wife needs a new set of panties."

"What does it mean, Pann-tees?"

"Mutandine." He gestured grandly with both hands around his hips.

"Ahhh! She's so fat?"

"Why do you think we work Saturdays?"

They turned a corner, weaved between rows of machines and continued on, stopping at some sort of storage bay. Large bolts of cloth half filled the chamber.

"What about us?"

"Peons, rabble. Unskilled. But if you come to work every day for four weeks you get a five cent premium. Problem is bastardi keep moving the four week period. You miss one day you have to wait until they set the next period."

The large, poorly lit room was at the end of production line #7. A long concrete loading dock sat in front of six pairs of double wooden doors, all closed in an attempt to keep out the Winter cold.

"This is you." Affanoso pointed to several green-enamelled hand trucks lined against the far wall then at the large rolls of cloth which had come off the line.

"You put the bolts on your hand truck, then roll them over there into the corral. Pack them tight, make sure they are all the same weave." Michael's face displayed a puzzled look. "Here, on the top, this number shows you the lot and weave. Last three numbers and two letters must be the same. If not, put it aside and ask the foreman what to do when he comes around."

"Capish?"

"Si."

"I'll be back before lunch, make sure you're alright."

"What is it exactly you do?"

"Same as him." Alfonso gestured towards the production line where there was a man with a pencil and clipboard with a stop-watch stuck to it. He was arguing with one of the middle-aged women about something which was indiscernible over the offensively loud noise of the machines. Affo switched from Italian and answered in his heavily accented English. "But I'm not an ass hole about it."

Five and a half hours later Michael strained under the weight of another of the six foot long bolts of wool as he lifted it off the production line and wrestled it onto his hand truck. By now he had become adapt at balancing the two hundred and forty-seven pound rolls on his hand truck and found the 100 yard trip to the storage corral had gotten easier.

Unloading his cargo he saw a dark haired man, another Italian, or maybe Sicilian, standing in the doorway, pad in hand, counting the bolts of fabric stacked in the corral and noting the time. When Michael looked up again the man was gone. On his return trip to the production line he noticed, squeezed into the tiny shipping office at the end of the loading dock, Affanoso talking to the shipping dock supervisor. They nodded and shook hands.

Affanoso made straight for Michael and, yelling over the machinery, motioned for Casaburi to come with him.

"Come'a outside, we gonna have a smoke."

"The cloth?"

"Fuck the cloth! Andiamo." Michael became concerned. "It's okay! If'a the checker come the supervisor tell him the line brake down."

Affanoso led Michael through a steel fire door and outside onto some granite steps where he produced his tobacco pouch and rolled two cigarettes. Michael took the cigarette offered and tucked it behind his ear for later as he continued to blink his eyes in an effort to adjust to the bright, late morning sun reflecting off the crests of new fallen snow. Taking in the crisp, clean air he awaited a cue from Affanoso he looked away and gazed out over the river towrads the low hills.

"Eets beautiful, eh?"

"Yeah." Casaburi glanced down.

"You still'a think about you wife?" Affo asked with genuine affection.

"Not like before, all the time. Now only sometimes." Affanoso lit his cigarette, then peered at his new charge.

"So?"

"So what?" Michael asked.

"So how you do?" Casaburi smiled before responding.

"It's not what I thought." Michael switched to Italian.

"It's not what any of us thought."

"I don't know, but . . ."

"But when you see the placards back home and the incredible rate of pay, your imagination runs away with you, no?" Alfonso sensed Michael's mood was worsening.

"A loaf of bread, fifty cents! That's four hours wage!" Michael shifted his position.

"Don't be embarrassed. None of us could know it would take four hour to earn one loaf of bread. Much less two and half days to earn one pound of meat!"

"What were you talking about with the supervisor?"

"New work week."

"What new work week?"

"American Department of Labor, decide the bosses have to make a, a . . . how do you say in English, *ammettere*?"

"Concession. They have to concede something." As he promised to help Affo with his language skills, Michael went back to English.

"Yes, they have to concede something. So they say we only have to work 54 hours per week instead of 56."

"Some concession. Two hours!"

"Yes, and it only take'a them two years. The American hierarchy, impossible to navigate. Vespuchi would flip over in his grave!"

"ROLL over in his grave, Alfonso. No flip."

"Why you talk such good English?"

"I was a police man. Rich English and American tourists often came to our district. Also my father believed as in the old days of Rome when everyone spoke Latin, in the future New York will be the new Rome. So I should learn English."

"Smart man, you father. Where I was?"

"Where was I?!"

"Fongulo!"

"Americo Vespuchi."

"Okay roll, flip, dance who cares? In the end it comes back to the factories. They control the government."

"It's democratic country. The people do what they like."

"It's 'democratic' country on'a the outside. In reality it's industrial country. Less than half the tax paying population is allowed to vote. Industrialists control who run for office and so, who get elected."

"There's more to it than that!"

"Oh, the hole is very deep my friend! And don't worry, they cover all'a the possibilities along the way."

"Like what?"

"Big contributions for both political parties so who ever get into office will help them. Crushing of opposition no matter what. But most important, control of'a the labor unions. Especially A.F.of L."

"Di che cosa parli, A.F.of L.?"

"American-Federation-of-Labor. They control almost entire voting population of the labor force."

"Un'unione?"

"Si. One union."

"They don't control us?" Casaburi protested.

"They don't have to. We can'a no vote."

"I still no understand the problem with 54 hour work week. How can it be bad?"

"They reduce our wage!"

"So? We work less hours!"

"Yes, and we get less money! True the law apply to women and children only, not men. But, in ten years we get no one but two reduction in pay! No raise! Reduction! New machines, faster production, same hours, less men, same wage! Increased production and so more profits, same wage! When is enough?! You tell me!" Michael suddenly had the sensation he had fallen in love with a beautiful woman only to find out she was a prostitute.

"Also, some'a of the Germans and Poles have'a good reason to believe they reduce our wages without reduce the hours! But, even if'a they reduce the hours, for some it mean one, two, maybe three loaf of bread less each week. For some, who have meat one or two time each month, it mean no meat."

"You think they gonna reduce wages this close to Christmas?!"

"No, they evil, not stupid. They know what they do to us. The bosses always discuss strategy with one another, so they can work together. Not like'a the workers. The workers always bitter with each other!"

"Bicker with each other!"

"Yeah! That's what I say. Fight!" Affonoso flicked his spent cigarette into the snow. "They would wait until after Christmas when they know we are without much money and would not dare to strike for fear of starvation and must still face the worst'a of the Winter."

"STRIKE?! WHAT STRIKE?! I can't believe they talk of a strike?! I just arrived!" Michael was astounded.

"NO! Relax! I only explain to you how they think." Casaburi turned away and grabbed hold of the tubular banister with both hands.

"Michael I sorry! Truly, but you have to realize we no longer human here. We are like, like
. . . cattle. Numbers at the end of'a ledger sheet . . ."

". . . expendable commodity." Casaburi finished the thought as he hung his head. His friend turned to go back inside. Michael stared intently into the distance. Alfonso put his hand on Michael's shoulder.

"You okay?"

"Anna sailed for America two days ago. She will be here for Christmas."

The lunch whistle blew and the two men made their way back into the mill as most of the machines were shutting down for the thirty minute midday break.

"I think you should'a come with me later. There is'a something I want to show you about." Alfonso suggested. A young man near the far wall pulled back on a series of large wooden levers rising out of the floor disengaging the machines from the overhead gang drive shaft. One by one the rows of looms shut down and the workers drifted away from their machines. Michael followed his friend, considering the open-ended proposition.

The two men continued to weave their way through the sun lit, slowing machinery and headed for the side exit where the Italians took their lunch each day.

As the last of the giant overhead drive shafts slowed and came to a halt they were passing through a double archway in the far wall.

"Come with you where?"

"Saturday night we meet . . ."

"AAAGGGHHHH!" Chills ran up Michael's spine as Affo was cut off in mid-sentence by the agonized scream of a woman. Casaburi was in the lead as they raced back past the phalanx of machinery towards the ever loudening screams emanating from the other side of the factory.

Affanoso glanced up at the sign over the doorway as he entered and commented half out loud half to himself. "'DYEING ROOM'. Appropriato." Neither of the two men were prepared for what they found. Pushing his way through the small crowd which had already gathered just inside the entrance to the Dyeing Room they both stopped dead at the sight which greeted them.

Turning the corner Michael was the first to catch sight of what appeared to be a copious amount of diluted blood running down a dye drain. A dozen women huddled around a young girl, lying on the concrete floor desperately gripping the edge of a steel dye trough, her long, dark skirt up around her chest, legs wide as she gasped rapidly for breath in the advanced stages of labor.

More women filtered through the crowd and, realizing what was happening, began to chase the men away and form a rudimentary cordon around the patient. An older woman, kneeling between the young girl's splayed legs, calmly shouted orders and gave directions in some Slavic language Michael didn't recognize as she rolled up her sleeves. Another, younger woman comforted the soon-to-be mother removing then, folding her wool coat and sliding it under the young girl's head.

"AAAGGGHHH!" Michael, no stranger to emergencies,

felt a discomforting sense of helplessness as he noticed the girl's lower lip ooze blood as she slowly bit into it. He pulled a bobbin from the machine next to him, removed the wooden pin and gave it to the old woman who had taken charge. She understood instantly and gave it to the woman on her knees at the patient's head who forced the twelve inch dowel rod between the young mother's teeth.

"ERE NOW! What's all 'iss then!?" It was Higgins the section foreman. The short, middle-aged man had been with Wood's mills for twelve years, back when his hairline was three inches further down his forehead. A young boy and two little girls scurried away, the rest virtually ignored his presence.

There was nothing even the mighty Mr. Wood could do to stop a child coming into the world when nature said it was time. Although, some of them pondered, if he could he no doubt would, annotating the lost time due to the birth as a business expense. But he couldn't. It was their lunch hour.

Forcing his way between the spectators to the center of the action, Higgins' face became a little paler than usual as the baby's head presented and the mother gave way with another agonized scream.

The squeamish foreman involuntarily drew in a deep breath, retched and quickly turned away upchucking into the floor drain.

After making his way back outside the crowd he regained himself just as the old woman again spoke in her native tongue. Quickly tossing a nod back to the old woman one of the younger girls near Affanoso reached into his knife pouch and removed his folding knife. She pushed back through the bevy of spectators and headed for the front of the dye line. Wiping his mouth Higgins gawked in amazement as she nimbly mounted the feeder platform with the open knife clenched in her teeth, sliced off a sizeable swath of cloth and returned to the scene in seconds flat.

"WHAT IN THE KING'S NAME . . .?" Higgins took the wanton destruction of The Mill's property as a personal affront. "RIGHT! 'At's IT!" He raised his all powerful clipboard and never-dull pencil to the ready. "Youse are all going down on my list, youse are!"

"On jest bardzo maly zeby byc duzym mezczyzna!" Added fifteen year old Agnieszka, the one who had fetched the cloth.

"Yes, he is awfully short to be such a big man." Commented the woman at the patient's head.

"You want the baby to lie on the cold stone floor you heathen?!" One of the by-standers snipped in a heavy Russian accent.

"That's it! You're first! Tragit . . . Traajig . . ."

"TRAGENSKI, TRAGENSKI! Get it right for once, you STUPID ENGLISH BASTARD! T-R-A-G-E-N-S-K-I!"

At's it! You're on my list you are!"

"Sie sind auf das Liste! Ihre Frau besuche wollen haben, acshloch!" Another woman snapped at him before walking away.

"What'd she say!?" The incensed manager demanded.

"She say, if Frau Tragenski's name go in to office, your wife have a visitor. Sir." Even Higgins recognised a cue and stomped off to pout in the small office at the front of the mill.

"Eto vsjo ravno sluchitsa." Volunteered the old woman as her nimble fingers ligated the umbilical cord and cut it with Affo's knife. Using her pinky finger she began to clear the newborn's throat.

"What . . . did she. . . say?!" The new mother panted as her wailing, healthy infant was placed on her belly.

"It would be a great thing if he wife find out about how he blackmail some of the new girl for sex!" The Old women responded, in her passable English.

"Don't worry, she will find out." Another of the women chimed in.

Affanoso backhanded Casaburi on the chest.

"Told you. A family business." Casaburi mustered a half-hearted smile. Alfonso, realizing there was nothing he could contribute, turned and began to push his way through the crowd. Michael, without response, remained leaning against the dye machine, taking in the last of the scene. "Welcome to America." Affonoso added as they made eye contact. "Saturday night. Italian-American Club, on Madison. Be there."

The mother's previously pain contorted face slowly melted to joy as she cuddled the crying new born now lying on her sweat-soaked chest. Casaburi found her broad smile infectious as she briefly glanced up at him, tears streaming down her cheeks. Michael was compelled to smile back.

"Benvenuto all'America." He mumbled.

'Poorly paid labor is inefficient
labor, the world over.'

**- Henry George**

## CHAPTER SEVEN

From 14th Street south to John Roebling's Brooklyn Bridge to Centre Street and halfway across Manhattan lay the boarders of the Lower East Side. To say life was raw was to say J. P. Morgan did okay for himself. As in the heyday of Rome, without exception, anything could be bought. How illegal whatever it was you wanted to buy had no significance save the price. Wine, women and whiskey were just the hors d'oeuvres. Chinese would sell the best drugs, thieves would sell you back your own property, and politicians would sell their mothers for a vote. The American credo was, they had a right to do to you anything you let them do.

And they did. Many would argue little has changed.

The Lower East Side was the sixteen year old Anna Casaburi's intended port-of-call, but for the next 24 to 48 hours the humid, smelly steerage hold of the *Laura Keane* would remain her home. The slow moving, double funneled steamer had taken the better part of two weeks to cross the turbulent, wintry Atlantic and was now temporarily anchored a half mile outside New York Harbor. Third in a queue half mile from Ellis Island.

"Yew got sumbody waitin' on you, Dearie?" The former Mancunian prostitute inquired as she filed her nails and lounged on the narrow, bottom bunk.

"Yes." Anna covered her mouth as she spoke, embarrassed at answering while chewing her last few pieces of salami. "A friend from my father's will meet me in'a the town square."

"Town square!? Where do you think you 're, Love? Back 'ome in the vill?"

Of the four other women sharing the cramped birth, Anna had befriended Mabel NLN, (no last name), during the voyage. It wasn't a 'woman thing' or some magical moment. No emotional connection. It was a matter of practicality. Anna's Italo-English and the linguistic ability of the English street walker were roughly on the same par.

112

"Yew any eyedear 'ow big New Yawk iz?"

"No. But I was'a told you can have almost three Romes inside'a New York! I can no wait to see this place!" Mabel put her nails on hold.

"You 'ear me well, Dearie! Remember you 'free fings! First, don't EVER lose sight of your baggage. DON'T ever talk to strangers. And DON'T EVER agree to 'ave a drink wiff a man! Lessen 'e gives you the money up front. You get me, Sweet'art?"

"Si Mabel. Io capito. I understand." The ship gently but continuously rolled in the 25 knot winds and 7 to 10 foot swells.

"'Ew's meetin' you then?"

"Signor Affanoso. He knows'a my family in Ulmi."

"Yew stick buy me, Dearie. I'll sees you get to your Meester Affanosio awright."

"Graci, Mabel."

Mabel helped herself to a chunk of salami.

*******

As if the heavily ornate and gilded Herter Brothers bookcases and desk were not enough to impress, in opposite corners like two prized statues at the ready, stood a pair of servants decked out in tie and tails. To eradicate all doubt as to Mr. Wood's economic status, there were two well decorated maids of non-descript European origin occupying the other two corners. These servants, part of a small army of domestics, were permanently housed in this one of Wood's two palatial homes. Once asked in court how many automobiles he owned, Wood replied he wasn't sure. He'd never had time to count them.

Although there were only a half dozen men gathered in the room, to include their host, Cubanas smoldering, brandy glasses swilling, the egotistical display of affluence was typical Wood.

"If they strike, you, we could get hurt pretty bad."

"What's this 'we' shit, Fletcher? You got worms?" Compulsory laughs rippled. "Don't be stupid! First off they haven't got the balls. Second, if they do decide to go out, there's no chance the skilled labor's gonna join them, so there really is no 'they'. Third, it wouldn't last two weeks!" He held his glass up as he spoke and in seconds, as if by magic, more Glen Maurangy appeared in the glass.

"How can you be sure?"

"In the middle of Winter, on what's left of their wages after Christmas? They'll be starving in less than a week!" The tall guest seated on the far side of the room suggested.

"Plus 80% of them have kids. Not eating won't fly too good with the wives." Added one of the senior mill agents in gratitude for the size of his Christmas bonus check.

"Besides, there's two chances enough of 'em will be organized to institute any effective action. Slim and none. And Slim just left town!" The comment was tagged with the cursory repressed laughs. Not too much, just enough. "Come to think of it, a walk-out might be a good thing." Wood speculated further.

"How in the hell could a strike be a good thing?"

"Because after their defeat, which, I reiterate, will take less than two weeks, they will return weakened, starving and broken." Nods of approval were offered. "I believe there's a better than even chance we may even be able to gain back what we lost last year to the skilled laborers!" Half lit from his third snifter Wood extended his predictions. "Jenkins, get a memo out to all the agents on Monday. I want . . ."

"Mr. Wood, Monday's New Year's Day."

"What's your point?!" The sarcastic inquiry was met with silence. "Get a memo out. Make sure everyone gets it. No agent, manager or office personnel to respond to inquiries by the press, general public or workers."

"But Sir, what if they . . . ?"

"I think I hear the dinner bell boys. Let's go have us a feed!"

*******

Anna chose her latest friend well. It was a good thing Mabel was along for the ride too, otherwise the driver's decision to take the ladies up into Union Square via the East Side by Brooklyn Bridge would have gone unnoticed. However, after being introduced to Mabel's trusty sidekick, Shiny Jack, a ground down kitchen knife, he politely corrected his miscalculation of the fare and settled for the standard ten cents per passenger and five cent surcharge for baggage.

Mabel said she understood when he didn't dismount the driver's bench to help unload the bags. "After all, one 'as to be careful in 'eese parts. Ain' they, Dearie?" She sarcastically queried.

The driver readily agreed.

Standing centered on the perfectly screed concrete sidewalk of the wide avenue, Anna missed the gist of the banter of the special relationship between Mabel and her American cousin as her young mind was mesmerized by the magic of the Christmas season Manhattan cityscape, now being softly blanketed in Winter's first snowfall.

Poised under an ornate, gaily decorated, electric street lamp she involuntarily held out her bare hand, palm to the heavens to catch some of the white stuff.

"I have only seen eet in pictures! It's so beautiful!"

"Not 'eff ya 'ave ta sleep it in it, Dearie!"

"But where does'a it come from?" She stuck out her tongue and delighted in the cold, wet sensation of the melting flakes.

"Someplace I'm never likely to see Love. Now grab ya bag. Let's go find 'es uncle'a yours before it's dark. Won't be so beautiful den I promise." They crossed Cooper Union Square amidst an ever increasing crowd of men and women, apparently gathering for some event.

Anna paused, removed her small diary from her handbag and consulted the last page. She gazed around the large triangular square.

"There!" She pointed several doors up at an overhead swing sign. *Frankie Donavan's Hardware & Iron Mongers,* the gold leaf and black beaded schmaltz sign announced. "The restaurant next to that place!"

The small rally in the square was quickly growing larger by the minute as the two settled on the north west side of the landmark intersect and huddled in the door way of Piccorino's Restaurant.

Although no one seemed to come in or out of the large eatery, several people inside the hardware store leaned over the large barrels of nails and stacks of ax and pick handles to peer out the expansive window to peer into the square.

By the time the girls noticed men setting up a short row of folding chairs on the wooden dais at the base of the bronze statue on the north end of the square, Anna was growing excited and worried at the same time. Several dozen policemen in heavy blue overcoats passed in front of her and casually cordoned off the area immediately in front of the platform. The whole time Mable assessed her prospects.

Finally a large oil cloth sign with black and red lettering was unfurled and roped off across the front rail of the platform.

"What means I.W.W.?" Anna asked. Mable didn't answer. She was halfway across the street, under the arm of a pugnacious looking dockworker ostensibly bumming a cigarette.

"Be back in a bit, Love. Not to worry! Your uncle should be 'ear any time now." She called back as the two melted into the crowd.

Now the teen genuinely began to be more concerned. The crowd had swelled to the point of overflowing the sidewalks and she was not the only occupant of the cramped doorway. Twenty minutes later a very frightened Anna made the decision to find a policeman and ask for help. Suddenly a burly man grabbed her by the arm.

"Anna?" The terror gradually melted to reason.

"Si! Yes! Who are you?"

"Alfonso Affanoso. I am the friend from you father's."

"Thank'a you so much for . . ."

"Speak Italian! Are you okay? Did you eat? Do you want some food?"

"No, thank you. Can we go to my father?" She spewed out in relief, quickly switching to Sicilian.

"Yes of course! He had to work a double shift for the money! But he is very excited to see you."

"Me also."

"Come on. We have to take a train, but we've plenty of time. It leaves in about one hour."

Affanoso took Anna's bag as they made their way north through the crowd to Grand Central Station. "What news from Palermo?" Once they cleared Cooper Union things quieted down and it was easier to talk.

"They are talking about withdrawing from Ethiopia. Mussolini says it would be a mistake and that the President is weak. It will show weakness. But the Prime Minister is weak and stupid. He says it was a mistake to commit to help them in the first place."

"And if he is elected he will bring peace and prosperity to Italy." Affo sarcastically added.

"Most young people don't think Mussolini wants to be Prime Minister, just to help the country. Maybe someone so non-political will be good for us?"

"And the rest of the people?"

"I don't think they care. They just want work. But all anyone talks about is America. America, America! The only chance for a better future. To have something."

"A-mer-i-ca!" He echoed. "If only they knew!"

The trek north to Lexington and 42nd, through the ever increasing snow flurries, took about half an hour and once inside Grand Central Affanoso slowly and deliberately perused the immediate area around the two. Anna was enamored with the enormity of the station.

"Every thing's'a bigger and better in America! Eh uncle Alfonso?"

"Definitely bigger, Bella. Definitely bigger." He again suspiciously perused the massive lobby.

"Anna, open your coat."

"What?"

"Open your coat, hold out the flaps like this and stand close to me." Anna did as directed and was puzzled as Affanoso took a small handful of bills from a hidden pocket sewn onto the inside of his shirt and moved in close to Anna. He held the notes close to her, well hidden between the wide flaps of her long, woolen coat and counted out just enough for the tickets before quickly stuffing the remainder back into the secret pocket and doing up his shirt. Again he looked around before moving off to

117

the ticket counter.

"Mind your bag. I'll get the tickets."

People act so strange in this country, Anna thought to herself. As if everyone is out to take something from them!

Paddy Kelly

'If  we do not revolt, we are
either morally insensitive
or criminally selfish.'

**- Herbert Read**

# CHAPTER EIGHT

**A**s in any criminal case it's not only what the criminal did do which helps give the police a complete picture, but what he didn't do. So in the weeks leading up to the Christmas holidays when no mention of a shift in hours or a reduction in wages was mentioned by any of the mill bosses or their respective managers most of the senior workforce had become suspicious.

As predicted by William Wood and the Bosses by the first week after Christmas things looked bleak for the 40,000 plus work force. Money was low, food was beginning to be less available and the bitter weather showed no signs of letting up. By New Years Day, the day the new hourly work week was to take effect throughout the country, it was assumed that the bosses were planning something. Something the workers of the Lawrence mills would not like.

While there was no general consensus on organization amongst the mill workers of the various mills or even the ethnicities themselves, it was the largest group, the Italians, who banded together to take the lead.

On Wednesday January, 3$^{rd}$ the current President of the I. W. W. in Lawrence, Angelo Rocco, quietly passed the word to assemble at the hall for a general meeting of Local #20.

The same age as Joe Ettor, Angelo at 27 had already spent nearly a decade in and around the labor struggle. A dark haired, dark eyed Italian immigrant he carried his short frame with pride, Rocco was well respected by the local Italian population and now was head of the tiny contingent of members in good standing of the Lawrence Local of the I.W.W. Stemming largely from distrust of non-Italians in America, of the thousands of Italians working for American Woolen only around 200 were partially involved in the union however, being no stranger to strikes and strike strategy, Rocco had already given much thought to organization of the workers.

After the improvised committees to function as intermediaries and organizers of the 15,000 plus Italian contingent were formed and Rocco was formally elected overall Chairman for the Italians, they decided to elect committees to visit each of the A. W. C. mills to gauge the temperament of the other ethnic groups. Rocco's next action as head of the committee was to direct that a query letter be drafted to each of the mill agents asking them to clarify the company's position on the new 54 hour work week.

Rocco was a natural for the position. Not only had he been through several smaller actions at these mills before, but he was known to be a level headed individual who not only had worked his way up through the ranks but was someone who was familiar with the Bosses' behavior patterns. Perhaps more importantly than anything else, he believed heart and soul in the I.W.W.

Following the meeting Rocco called Affanoso off to the side.

"Affo, we have to start to organize on a wider scale."

"We still don't know what Wood will do. We have the main committee selected. It's early yet." He shrugged. "What about the letter to the company?"

"The letter is only a means to an end. The next step in the game. A reply will come or not. We can't afford to sit and wait."

"What do you want to do?" Affo was more confident now in Rocco than ever.

"I want to draft a letter to Wood. Send it to him at his home."

"His home? Nice touch."

"If we hear nothing from him, we can assume the worst. Also, pick twelve men, tell each to pick someone to help and we'll have them approach each of the twelve mill agents. I'll have the secretary draw up a brief letter."

"Okay. I'll have a list of the twelve apostles in the morning." Rocco snickered at the remark.

"I'm going into Boston in the morning. Bring it by the house tonight for dinner. We'll have a last supper."

"Things go as we suspect, we could be living on bread and wine for a while." Quipped Affo.

121

# The American Way

It was a typical New England Winter's day, cold and clear, when Wood's butler trudged up the double wide staircase to the master bedroom with a small silver tray in hand.

Wood rolled over in his double king sized bed in the center of his palatial bedroom. He groaned with irritation as there was yet another knock on the polished oak door.

"Mr. Wood, Sir?" There was no answer. "Mr. Wood, Sir?" Finally a slightly hung over Wood sat up, alone in his bed.

"WHAT?!"

"Sir, letter for you."

"Leave it on the dining table! I'll read it at breakfast!"

"Sir, it's half past noon, and the letter requires your signature."

"MY WHAT . . . what for ?"

"It's a special delivery, registered letter, Sir."

"Slip it under the door!" He ordered. "Great way to start the fucking week!" Wood mused.

Over the next three days a few agents met with some of the I.W.W. sub-committees, most declined to even speak to them but all refused to give any answers as to whether there would be any alteration in men's wages. To the man, all queries met with the same rehearsed answer.

"All inquiries must be directed to the office of Mr. Wood in Boston."

A little less than a week later a small committee of Loom-fixers garnered a successful meeting with a couple of the mill agents which the Fixers had been planning just before the Italians launched their effort, but they were told in no uncertain terms there would be no adjustment in wages to offset the two hour shortage of the new work week. As the Loom-fixers were skilled labor there was no association with the unskilled, general laborers so no communication between the two groups took place.

Upon meeting procrastination, vagaries and outright refusal by mill managers to speak with the sub-committee members and no answer from Wood or any of the Trust was forthcoming, it became apparent that the owners fully intended to lower the wages.

All too mindful of their past failures when taking on the American Woolen Trust, it was throughout Monday the 8th and Tuesday the 9th that there were meetings between the improvised mill committees feeling each other out and trying to assess the general situation. On Wednesday the tenth a mass meeting was held in the Franco-Belgian Hall. So crowded was the meeting that a running commentary was required to keep those outside the hall, standing in the freezing snow and ice informed of the proceedings. The uncontested upshot of the two hour assembly was one of the few things the small hodge podge of ethnicities had agreed on in the last ten years; to launch a strike if pay was reduced.

Later that day the committees met at Ford Hall to clarify details of what had been decided by the local leaders. When their decision to strike if the pay was short was announced Rocco, sitting in the back room of the hall, dropped his head and sighed when he heard the wild cheers of elation.

"You seemed relieved?" Affo, sitting across the small table from him, half asked half stated.

"If they were going to blow it, it would have been here, over this vote."

"Maybe they're seeing past their petty ethnic squabbles." Rocco stared out into the mobbed dance hall.

"Or maybe their anger has become their temporary mistress. Of the nearly 40 ethnic groups in this place we have less than a dozen out there. And there is no one from any of the larger groups." The two traded glances. "We take up this strike we'll sure as hell find out if it's just temporary anger."

On his earlier visit Ettor had taught the workers well. Organization and solidarity were the keys to success. Organization came easy.

Solidarity would be another matter.

123

*******

"I spoke with my wife. We will go home!" The despondent worker spoke with folded arms looking down at the floor. The dozen others were scattered about the parlor of Gino's apartment.

"GO HOME? To what?! You sold everything you had to get here! What do you have here to sell to go back? And back to what? To trade one kind of fascismo for another?! My family and I intend to stay here and fight!" Declared Affanoso.

"How? With what? At least in Sicily we know what they're saying when they curse us! Besides, you think the others are going to risk what little they have to fight? The Slavs, the Greeks and Lithuanians? The Syrians!? If we lose no, **when** we lose like all the times before, we will be forced to go someplace else and start all over, again! Or worse, stay here and work for less!"

"Gino, what do you think?" The short brooding Sicilian considered his answer by looking at both men before he spoke.

"Better to make a stand here than to run and have to start again." He quietly replied to no one in general.

"If we fight we can't go to war alone. Who we gonna ask to help? Golden?!" Gino's sister had just entered the room and began to set coffee cups out. The remark about Golden struck a chord and several of the men mockingly spat on the floor in contempt of the head of the United Textile Workers.

**"Che è la questione con lei?!"** The teen yelled at the men as she threw her dish towel at Gino's face and ordered he teach his heathen friends manners or take the meeting outside.

John Golden was not the only one of the majority of A. F. L. officials who had continually demeaned the Italian and Eastern European workers branding them "unskilled, foreign rabble" and barred them from the union under orders from Samuel L. Gompers himself.

"We need help!"

"Than we get help!" Gino proudly declared in English.

"Who?"

"We get Ettor!" When Gino switched to English the ones who could followed suit.

"Who?"

"Joe Ettor! That guy from I.W.W. The one never stop smiling."

"He speak to us last year. He speak Italian."

"Thank god!"

"Why you say thank god?"

"Because his Italian can't be no worse than you English!"

"What's'a matter for my English?!"

"I.W.W.?! They don't come here!"

"Why not!?" He challenged indignantly.

"We don't got big enough members!"

"We don't got **enough** members!"

"You don't speak no good English."

"And you do?!"

"Got, go, don't got! Still 200 members . . ."

"208!"

"OKAY, 208! Big'a fucking deal!"

"Watch your language! Heathen bastards!" Came blasting out from behind the kitchen door.

"Okay, 208 members no gonna bring somebody all'a the way from New York City to help us!" A momentary malaise blanketed the bevy.

"We gotta to try." Gino pleaded.

"Okay, we try." two of the others conceded.

"Hey, Luciana, where's the coffee?!" Gino called into the kitchen.

"GET IT YOURSELF!"

*******

Involuntarily foregoing the coffee Gino had suggested they go over to the Franco-Belgium Hall on Mason Street because it was equipped with a small telegraph station and it was only fifteen minutes before the self appointed contingent were piling through the doors of the gaily painted hall.

They were met by a smaller, but defensive group of

Belgians and Dutch who were scattered around several tables sipping strong coffee and lagers engaged in a near replay of the Italian's earlier discussion, that is whether or not to return to Europe or stay and fight.

Startled by the dramatic entrance, the Northern Europeans sprang to their feet, several of them grabbing chairs in preparation for the impending Donnybrook. The Italians, already in an advanced stage of agitation, halted and spread out assuming a defensive formation.

Gino then pushed his way through to the front and spewed a prolonged, impassioned flow of Italian at an unintelligible rate. The Italians stood down, the Belgians lowered their chairs and a young, attractive Dutch woman from the other side of the room called over to them.

"Do one man here English speak?" The ensuing stampede of Italian men scared hell out of the blond haired beauty as they threatened to trample each other to death.

They immediately coagulated into pockets of arguments and Gino again came forward and introduced himself. The girl returned the gesture, politely not correcting his mispronunciation of Gerta.

"Wat willen zij?" A man behind her asked.

"Why here you come, Sir?"

"We wish to use'a the telegraph."

"Voor welk doel?" The man growled.

"What for?" The words sounded sweeter when she said them, thought Gino as he leered up at the thick-necked, blond, Aryan type towering over her.

"We talk'a with New York." By now most of the Dutch and Belgians had migrated to the point of parlay. Gerta turned to the crowd and explained in Dutch which was in turn quickly disseminated in Belgian and half a dozen dialects.

"Waarom?" One of the men inquired. Assuming the role of intermediary, the girl translated.

"They wish to know why you want to talk with New York."

"We wish to bring here a Meester Ettor. He ees from the unione of the I.W.W. And we believe he can help us to make'a this fight."

"They are going to fight." She announced in Dutch over her shoulder. While not overly enthusiastic, the middle Europeans were mildly impressed. Thick neck mumbled a snide remark and they all drifted back to their Weiss beers. The Italians looked to the girl.

"They say, eets about time."

"Whatt'a do you mean?"

"They decide to fight last week." A few minutes later a telegraph message was being painstakingly drafted.

As it was recalled that Joe Ettor was half Italian the task fell to the Italians to draft the Western Union and as Gino was the one who could read the best it followed he should compose the critical document. It would be sent in the name of the Local's President, Angelo Rocco.

To speak English well enough to make yourself understood was one thing. To be able to write the words in their backwards order with all their unnecessary letters and mis-use of vowel structure which, for no apparent reason, you didn't pronounce half the time anyway, was quite another.

"Dear Meester Ettor . . ." He recited as he wrote to facilitate the translations simultaneously occurring behind him.

"Stop." A Neapolitan leaning over his shoulder volunteered.

"What Stop? I just start!"

"NO! Stop! S-T-O-P. It mean dees little dot." Taking the pencil from his colleague's hand he demonstrated by placing a period after the salutation.

"You make-a thees mark when you finish what you say."

"Si! Io sapere fare uno punto! Who write, me or you?"

"They call this one 'Stop'!"

"I know theese one!" Gino unconvincingly reassured his co-workers.

"Very good Gino, but maybe the strike be over before you finish to make thees little dot!" Another helpful colleague offered.

"Bafangulo!" Gino thanked him.

"What means, Bafangulo?" Asked Gerta.

"Eets Sicialian. Eet mean . . . 'thank you very much'." Gino explained.

"Dear Meester Ettor, **STOP!**" He garnished his terminal comment with a brief glance at the Neapolitan then carried on. "We wish'a you to come to Lawrence, STOP! We the members of the Industrial Workers of the World . . . che?"

"'Weesh-for-you-to-help-us.'"

". . .weesh for you to help us. We will make a strike." He handed the paper to his less literate workmates for approval. Following a cursory inspection by an impromptu committee in the immediate vicinity approval was unanimous and the message was passed to the young Dutch girl who glanced over the page and passed it to a young Dutchman who was careful not to let on he didn't speak a word of English much less read, but nodded his approval in an impressive authoritarian manner.

Gino stood and offered Gerta his chair.

"Bafangulo, Gino!" She politely thanked him.

*******

At the time the Lawrence local of the Industrial Workers of the World with its 208 members, out of a 32,000 plus workforce, supported by ten to fifteen thousand ancillary support workers, security, management, office staffs etc., and casual workers, seemed all but non-existent. But this core membership provided several vital features to the dynamic.

First it demonstrated there was a chance, however slim, that there was a potential for the twenty-five plus nationalities to unite and therefore possibly do some damage to the mill owners.

Second, it allowed the I.W.W. to demonstrate that they gave a damn about otherwise neglected foreign-born labor, and gave the workers and therefore the union, a nucleus to build on. However, and perhaps most importantly, they had been introduced to Joe Ettor.

Less than a minute after it was sent, the wire arrived at the Penn Station telegraph center in Mid-town Manhattan where an elderly Western Union agent typed it up, slipped it into an official dark amber, windowed company envelope and shuffled to the back door. The old man made an entry in a log book near the rear exit then punched a time clock on the wall which spat out a small paper ticket.

Peaking his head through the rear door he yelled out into the narrow alley.

"COURIER NUMBER SEVENTEEN!"

A young teen on a black Swinn Flyer bicycle snuffed out his half smoked cigarette, put the butt in the head band of black cap and scurried to the door.

"Get this down to Union Square, the I.W.W.'s Headquarters."

"Yes sir Mr. Grieg." He put the envelope in his cap, popped it back on his head and manned his bike.

"And don't expect no tip!" The boy took off as Grieg shuffled back to his desk.

"Anarchist bastards wouldn't tip their hats!"

*******

Ettor sat with an upturned collar, hands in pockets on the wooden bench towards the rear of the platform. He glanced out over the sea of bowlers, fedoras and Windsor caps crowded into the square and was encouraged to note the bitter cold of the encroaching evening hadn't dampened the spirits of the five or six thousand crowding Cooper Union in Lower Manhattan late that Wednesday afternoon.

The short, squat speaker now at the rail spoke with a conviction which exuded an over animated sense of conviction. He spoke through a tripod mounted megaphone.

"Industrial unionism . . . is little more than a pipe dream! A fanciful notion which will in the course of time, a very short time I remind you, prove to be an impossibility."

By all accounts Morris Hilquit, the prominent Socialist lawyer, who now had the attention of the slowly swelling crowd, out gunned Haywood in all aspects of the public debate. A firm advocate of the school of belief that unskilled labor, especially foreign-born unskilled labor, was a lost cause as a demographic for unionism. Hilquit didn't speak, he preached. Not necessarily motivated by a sense of racial prejudice he, as thousands of other union organizers did, simply believed that the quilt work of European ethnic diversity and organization were mutually exclusive concepts. Presently he railed on against industrial organizational efforts.

"Industrial labor has little to contribute. They can't plan. They can't design and they can't create! You pay peanuts, you get monkeys!" The shadows across the square grew longer. Hilquit replaced his hat and took his seat to appreciable applause.

Ettor glanced over at Big Bill and nodded towards the front of the stand, indicating the he would go next. Haywood shook his head in the negative, rose and walked to the rail.

His over-sized fedora gently flapped in the brisk breeze and as usually was the case, and despite it being January, he wore no over coat. Scanning the crowd with his one good eye, he launched into his defense.

"The working class and the employing class have **nothing** in common!" Haywood always brought the advantage of starting out at a run, being already emotionally charged when he took the platform.

As he sat there listening to the debate, Joe removed a cable from his breast pocket, opened it and reread it for the third time that day. The grammatically incorrect communiqué, scratched together by a few insignificant employees of the American Woolen Company, hot on the heels of the Brooklyn failure, perplexed him as to whether or not he should commit valuable time, money and energy to another potentially lost cause. Particularly at a time when the Wobblies were so desperate to make a national breakthrough and breech the East coast industrial union barrier now all but sewn up by the politically and profit oriented A.F. of L.

All this was compounded by the fact that if he did accept this request on behalf of the Wobblies, he was picking up the steel gauntlet of the man who could, save J. D. Rockefeller, buy and sell any of America's millionaires twice over. The man who helped maintain Carnegie, Mellon and, in its infancy, the Kennedy's American dynasty. The man whose net worth at that particular time in history was an estimated 150% the Gross

National Product of the entire United States of America.

*"HUH!"* Joe laughed to himself. *"More than the GNP! And just yesterday morning Bill was yelling at Gurley Flynn for wasting paper!"*

However, this cable was different from the dozens of others the I. W. W. HQ received each month. This one had . . . passion. Not desperation borne of frustration compelling its composers to turn to any sympathetic ear.

"We weesh for you to help us make thees fight!" These workers were going up against the Bosses with or without the Wobblies. At least they sounded committed.

By the time he was finished reading it he had come to a decision. This time tomorrow he would be in Lawrence.

"There can be no peace so long as hunger and want are found among millions of the working people and the few, who make up the employing class, have all the good things of life!" Bill turned slightly to address the crowds on the side of the platform and caught sight of Joe re-reading the message.

"Between these two classes a struggle must go on until the workers of the world organize as a class, take possession of the means of production and **abolish** the **wage system**!"

This began the ten minute ebb and flow of tumultuous applause, shouting and calls of support from the now 5,000 strong former crowd, now welded into an audience. Haywood stepped back to the rear of the platform to allow the crowd to build catharsis.

"WHO DO YOU WANT TO TAKE WITH YOU?" He was compelled to shout back at Joe as the din of the crowd echoed off the brick and granite buildings filling the triangular square. Joe was taken off guard that Bill sensed his intentions.

"THERE'S A GOOD NUMBER OF ITALIANS. ARTURO I THINK. MAYBE GURLEY FLYNN?"

"NO, I NEED HER HERE. BESIDES -"

"HERE, OR IN PENNSYLVANIA?" Bill gave him a look. "CARLO OUT THERE?"

"BESIDES . . ." Bill ignored the query and stepped back towards the workers slowly approaching the rail with both arms raised, hands out. A near dead silence befell the throng as he once again addressed the motivated laborers.

"I am going to put the workers of this country into such a tremendous organization, a union with such enormous strength and power, that we shall be able to **abolish** the wage system and **starve** out those hell hounds of capitalists!" Haywood had them. "Instead of the conservative motto, 'A fair day's wage for a fair day's work', we must inscribe on our banner the revolutionary watchwords, '**Abolition** of the wage system.' It is the historic mission of the working class to do away with **capitalism**!"

He paused and stepped back to Ettor as the square resonated with wild cheers and applause.

". . . BESIDES, THIS THING GAINS MOMENTUM THEY'RE GOING TO BE GUNNING FOR YOU, JOE." Ettor smiled. "I MEAN IT! THEY'LL KILL YOU IF THEY THINK THEY CAN GET AWAY WITH IT! WATCH YOURSELF!"

Joe's smile slowly evaporated.

"TRESCA'S OUT IN PITTSBURGH. GOT ANOTHER PAPER SET UP. ORGANIZING THE MINERS" Bill added.

"I HEARD. HOW'S HE DOIN'?"

"MUST BE DOING SOMETHIN' RIGHT. FEDS ARE FOLLOING HIM NEARLY DAY AND NIGHT. THEY KEEP CONFISCATING HIS PAPERS. WRECKED THE PRINTING OFFICE LAST WEEK."

"HE'LL KEEP PRINTING THEM. YOU KNOW THOSE GOD-DAMNED ITALIANS!" Joe commented.

"YEAH, THICK BASTARDS, AREN'T THEY?" Haywood smirked as he returned to the rail. Joe followed him up and, before he could again address the gathering, yelled over his shoulder.

"I'LL GO UP ALONE, LET YOU KNOW THE SITUATION ON SATURDAY."

Haywood watched Ettor descend the steps at the rear of the platform and disappear into the evening shadows around the corner.

'The world's civilization started
from the day on which everyone
received reward for labor.'

**-Andrew Carnegie**

## CHAPTER NINE

As the train pulled into the Lawrence station early that Thursday morning Ettor, who caught the midnight run from Grand Central in Manhattan, was met by a small committee the head of which spoke passable English. They offered to take him for some food and drink but Joe had eaten prior to the two and a half hour journey north and so declined and insisted on being taken directly to the Italian American Club. As the rail line ran close to the Merrimack River it was only a short walk through town and over to the hall on Mason Street.

Originally called Ford Hall, it was one of the largest of the dozen ethnic community clubs in Lawrence and recently converted for use by the Italian-Americans, it was built to accommodate about twelve hundred. However, in spite of the late hour and the freezing cold Ettor was forced to follow behind a makeshift, multi-manned bodyguard/escort to gain entrance through the crowd surrounding the hall's entrance.

The temperature was somewhere below zero and in little more than four hours the work day was scheduled to begin but word had spread and, in addition to the two thousand plus crammed into the hall, the throng outside numbered well over three thousand. The fact that this represented less than a third of the Italians, which in turn were less than half of the town's mill population impacted heavily on the organizer's initial perceptions of the current situation in Lawrence.

The noise inside was deafening, the mood angry yet restrained and consequently you could cut the tension with a knife. Every man in the hall was cocked, primed and ready. With one word these three thousand plus Italians were themselves ready to shut down New England's largest mill town. Ettor was in his element.

He was led to a small multi-purpose room in the back of the utilitarian hall where several women worked preparing food for the visitor. As was the Italian custom, enough food to feed an army of visitors.

The I. W. W. representative and the Strike Committee

leaders gathered around a small, rectangular table and pulled up seats. As Ettor took a seat on one side of the table three of the improvised committee sat opposite. The proceedings were quickly set into, in the native tongue. Angelo Rocco, sat between two younger men. In as much as they had cabled New York for help, it fell to the Committee to initiate the parley.

"What's the situation?" Joe inquired.

"After they posted the 54 hour notices in the mills, some of us became suspicious." Offered one of the younger workers.

"We were suspicious long before that!" Someone interjected.

"Be quiet!" Rocco ordered. "After the notices we wondered if they would cut our hours also."

"What did you do?"

"We went to speak to the mill Supervisor."

"What did he say?"

"After a very short discussion with him . . ."

"Who with a detached attitude explained he cannot give the committee the information they seek . . ."

An intense look of disdain flashed the desired message again and the younger, more emotionally charged worker held his tongue. Rocco continued.

"It was decided to contact the owner of the Wood Mill, as we believe this to be the key to all the other mills. It is widely known that as goes American Woolen so the others follow."

"And . . . ?" Ettor prompted.

"We had to go through the mill agents, first here then in Boston, and that was another three days."

"Did they give you an answer?"

"What do you think? They told us to contact Wood's Boston office."

"Did you?"

"Last week. Still no answer." Ettor sat back and smiled before replying.

"There's not going to be an answer." The few workers standing around the table looked insulted. "They're trying to stall you until pay day."

"For what purpose?"

"To start the game ahead of you." Ettor explained. "They are already making plans for you to strike."

Silence blanketed the dozen or so in the small room. Rocco gestured for a man to pass the word to the thousands waiting out in the hall.

"NO! Not yet." Ettor ordered. The messenger hesitated at the door, then returned to his place.

"If word gets out, it will be misinterpreted as a strike is imminent."

"A strike IS imminent!" Declared Gino.

"Probably, but it will be much more difficult  . . ."

". . . and expensive." Added Rocco as he lit his small Italian cigar.

"And expensive, to control a wildcat strike!"

"And, we don't want to tip our hand yet." Gino deduced.

"You are right, Mr. Ettor." Rocco conceded. "What do we do?"

"When is your next pay day?"

"The day after tomorrow."

"Friday. Makes sense. They'll have the advantage of the weekend as well."

"Yes."

"We will have definite proof then. Have you made any definitive plans?"

"Simple. If they cut the pay we strike."

"I understand." Joe sat back in his chair. "First, it is absolutely imperative that you are all in agreement. We have just lost a very important action in Brooklyn. There was no agreement between the factions, the Bosses were united and a worker killed his boss."

"Sounds like a good start!" Someone a safe distance from Rocco contributed. Joe fought back a smile.

"We want to help but we have to be careful how we use what little resources we have." He continued. "We have to know your people are really committed."

Rocco reached into his waistcoat pocket and produced a letter. He removed it from the envelope and gave it to the only man in the room who didn't realize its significance. Joe continued his commentary as he reached across the table to take the letter.

"You may think this place, these mills, your situation is unique. But this is the same exact story all over Massachusetts, New England and the rest of the U.S." Ettor advised.

"America, Home of the Slave!" Came another offer from the peanut gallery. Joe didn't try to fight it this time.

"I should take some of you guys on the road with me." He unfolded the letter.

"*Dear Angelo*; . . .this letter yours?"

"No no, another. A young Wool comber in the Ayer mill. One of his friends, Pino, 'borrowed'
it to show me." Rocco explained. Joe continued to read to himself.

*"We understand about not sending the same amount last month. As for not sending any money this month, don't worry. We took in a boarder and he seems to be a very nice man. An American writer, from New York. His mother is Sicilian. But I am sure she is a very nice woman anyway. After all, not everyone can be Tuscan, but everyone must have something to aspire to. Otherwise there would be no hope."*

"I like this lady." Interjected Joe.

*"We are all very happy about Maria. It sounds like the baby will come in August. Perhaps on the 15th? That would be very lucky to be born on the feast day!*

*As for the strike. If you think you should leave, leave. But in your heart of hearts if you think you should stay and fight, then stay and fight. For if you don't you will regret it the rest of your days. The workers will win or lose. No matter the outcome you will be remorseful of not being there with them in their hour of triumph or defeat.*

*You are right to be concerned for Maria and the baby. But if she says you should stay, then listen to her. It is her child too and she understands the situation as well as you do. Just because a woman is pregnant doesn't make her stupid. Women can do stupid things without being pregnant. She wasn't pregnant*

137

*when she married you, eh?*

*You write that the women must also work to pay the bills. Then things are too expensive in that country. But more importantly without the women there can be no homes and so I say that that society is doomed.*

*But when you say the children must work . . . that they are taken from the schools and playgrounds to be strapped to machines so that their laughter, their joy their very childhoods are taken from them and woven into cloth to be coined into dollars, then those mill owners are pitiless bastards who deserve to rot in hell! This man Wood must have been so named because that is what his heart is made from.*

*We love you and remember, whatever you do we will love you no less. We pray for you.*

*Please write soon.*

*Love,*
*Mamma*

*p.s.- If there are any Tuscans making this strike with you, stay. You have already won."*

Recognizing Rocco's tactic Ettor carefully refolded the letter and held it between his middle and forefingers as he offered it back across the table.

"Does Angelo know Pino took this letter?" He asked.

"Doesn't matter. Angelo is dead." Ettor heard the roar of the boiling pasta water in the kitchen over the silence. The man standing to Rocco's left spoke.

"He and Maria left nearly two weeks ago. They went to Pittsburgh. He was offered a job in the mines. Better money."

"Last week he was clocking off shift. The brake on a hand car failed. He and three others fell almost a thousand feet." Gino finished. After fourteen years Ettor never adjusted to these stories.

"Maria?" He quietly asked.

"The Bosses gave her a . . . " Rocco started.

"Twenty-five dollars!"

"And made her sign a paper that she wouldn't go in the

courts!" Contributed Angelo.

"That's all a man's life is worth!"

"Not even that if you interrupt me again!"

"Scuzi Signor Rocco!" The young man backed away.

"If you think something like this is going to sway me . . ." Joe nodded at the letter. ". . . it's not." Braced for a possible refusal of help the others exchanged glances in disbelief. Was this the famed Joe Ettor from the great I.W.W. looking to fight against the industrial Bosses anytime, anywhere? "But, just in case, I'll wire New York tonight to prepare for a possible strike."

You'd think Roma FC just beat Chelsea for the world cup. The applause and yelling was so loud it warranted an investigative committee from the kitchen where one of the younger girls was cursing the oil she splashed on her only white waist coat in reaction to the eruption. The older woman of the staff, obviously in charge, out yelled the entire room.

"BE QUITE! QUITE, you idiots!" The cheering swiftly died down. "You want to announce your plans to all of New England?!" There were no arguments, the reverie subsided.

"Angelo, you **must** understand that it will take 100% commitment from all the workers! Not 25%, not 50, not 75%. One-hundred-per-cent!" Slowly and with ceremonial deliberation, Rocco sat forward, folding his huge hands on the table.

"Mr. Ettor. When we struck last year we lost, but we won. We lost the fight but not the war. We won, because we learned about commitment. Commitment, fortitude and strategy. Commitment and fortitude we can offer you. Strategy is what you must offer us in return." Rocco perused his colleagues. "Tell us what to do."

This is exactly what the I.W.W. rep had come to Lawrence to hear. He wasted no time in seizing the initiative.

"The first order of business is to form a proper strike committee. How many skilled laborers in the twelve mills and are any of them going to support the strike?"

"Two, maybe three thousand altogether. How many will strike, I'm not sure. Why?"

"We should have their support as well. We might avert

trouble by asking some of the skilled workers to sit with us on the committee."

"For what? Golden will tell them they can't. Besides, they have no concern about us, why should we care about them?" Rocco countered.

"They don't even talk to us!" To emphasize his point the young man behind switched to English. "We are rabbis under the feet to them."

"Rabbis?" Italian or English, Joe was lost.

"You know, the dirt and'a rocks under you shoes!"

"It's rabble." Joe corrected. "They may think you're rabble, but trust me when I tell you, they will follow a strike very closely because they realize how it will affect them and their situation and, if it's successful . . . in one day your ranks will swell by their numbers." There was some sporadic discussion, comments & translation. "But there is a more important reason to have the support of the skilled workers." Ettor continued.

"And that is . . .?"

"And that is because they are Wood's ace-in-the-hole. You can be replaced. There are thousands of you walking the streets in Boston, New York, Chicago. But the skilled workers, they are not so easy to replace and, just like the Bosses, they stick together. One goes out they all go out."

At hearing the argument and strategy he never considered Rocco sat back, self vindicated at having asked for Ettor's assistance.

"We are not sure if they will go out or not. Hard to say. Some of them sympathize but they all belong to the A. F of .L."

"If they refuse there will be problems." Joe admitted.

"Don't worry. They won't." One of the men standing behind Rocco reassured Ettor.

"Thank you Godfather Carlucci! Now shut up!"

"Si Rocco."

"We'll have to avoid trouble for as long as possible. But all of you must understand these mill owners have a lot to lose. J. P. Morgan owns or controls the majority of them. If we strike and win he won't take it lying down. He'll fear the same thing could happen with the steel workers, the shipping or his rail workers!" Ettor was making one last probe of their fortitude. "They will do everything to stop us! He owns half the politicians in this country. You understand what I'm saying?" Angelo met the challenge head on.

"For decades conditions here have grown worse and worse. First, they bring in a few machines, then more. More people lose their jobs. Then they get rid of more and more skilled workers to save money. Two years ago the two-loom system and then we have to work twice as fast, for the same money." Joe realized that subconsciously he had been egging Rocco on. "Last year they try to **lower** our wages. Those who kept their jobs earned less than $8.50 a week for nearly sixty hours of work. We don't give a shit about Morgan, Rockefeller, Carnegie or any of those bastards! They eat steak, drink scotch and sleep on silk sheets off the back of our labor! Time we made something too, not just scraps! Our women and children deserve bread and roses too, Signor Ettor! You help us, yes or no?"

Ettor was as convinced as he could be concerning the Italians' commitment to take action.

"We might possibly avert trouble by asking someone from the United Textile Workers to sit on the committee with us."

"Angelo, we could ask Franco to talk to the Belgian, the weaver with the U.T.W., what's his name?" Gino suggested.

"LaFette." Rocco recalled.

"Maybe he will talk to someone for us."

"Good Idea." Rocco commended. "See that Franco gets the word." Joe pushed on.

"Next, select a committee of two to represent all of you."

"Only two?"

"If we are successful and the others join us we will need to work with up to twenty five or more nationalities. That's fifty workers plus our selves. Not counting translators." Rocco nodded, the man on his right took notes.

"How many Italians are there?"

"We don't know for sure, but maybe fifteen and a half, sixteen thousand."

"Good, that puts us in the majority. If we act as one there

is a better chance of the others to follow. But we must present a united front! Subdivide yourselves by mill, then by groups and committee. NOT by trade! Or job." He emphasized.

"Or national region! We are not in Italy anymore." Angelo reminded the room.

"Could have fooled me!" A young man offered.

"Where do the Eastern Europeans stand?" Joe asked. Rocco sat back in his chair as a half smile crept across his weathered face.

"Get Pino." He quietly commanded. Several men scurried to the door and the call, "PINO!" was passed down through the ranks and out into the hall. "He's born in Spain, but he's really Italian. He speaks Spanish, Italian, Polish and a little Russian. His English is so-so" Both men, speaking several languages themselves, were impressed.

"He's not a bad chef either." Someone volunteered.

Minutes later a short, wiry young man with unruly, curly black locks sparking from his head squeezed his way into the room. To indicate he should do the same, Rocco spoke to him in English.

"Pino, this is Mr. Ettor from'a the I.W.W. He come to help us to make this fight. It is'a very important he knows what is happening with our Eastern European friends at the moment. Capito?"

"Si Signore Angelo, capito! Buon giorno Signore Ettor. We have heard much about you. Thank you for coming to help us." In concert with his respectful salutation Pino removed his cap prior to commencing his delivery.

"As concerns the Eastern Europeans . . ." A shrug of the shoulders as he stuffed his hat into his back pocket emphasized his sentiment. ". . . pretty much'a the same as back in their respective homelands. As you know, the Balkans' peoples are at'a war with us. The Germans are at'a war with the French in Africa. Hungarians, Poles, Russians and Lithuanians are seen by the Americans to be 'all'a the same thing'. They call them Dirty Honkies, Dumb Pollocks, Filthy Ruskies or Lazy Lithos. When they are being polite, of course."

"Of course." Echoed Ettor.

"The Turks and the Greeks, traditional enemies, are on the brink of war in the Adriatic, and now petition the Germans, Dutch and French for war materials, so hostility with one another mounts here also. However, none of those people are doing well either because of the some 1,500 plus deaths from tuberculosis here last year. Also here in Lawrence, the infant mortality rate is nearly seven times the normal." Ettor fell back in his seat. *This guy speaks better English than I do!"* He mused.

"Wonderful. Is there any good news?" He asked half sarcastically.

"Actually, there is. Here the Turks and the Greeks they don't fight each other."

"That's a start!" Ettor was encouraged by the sliver of light. "Why?"

"They refuse to work in the same room together." Ettor hung his head, simultaneously relishing and regretting the irony of his position.

"Is there anything else?" His face in his hands he inquired.

"Yes. The Middle Easterners are despised throughout the community for their 'strange cultural habits'. And they smell."

"You mean, the others think they smell?"

"No they actually smell. It's fucking awful! Like, like something crawled up inside them and died -"

"Graci, Pino!" Rocco interrupted as he nodded towards the door. Cut short in his graphic description the resident social historian took his leave and the impromptu committee sat in silence.

"One last thing." Joe prompted. "We must shut down **all** the mills! A primary reason for failure of the other strikes was chaos and disorder and this will come if only some of the mills are not kept from production. If production is allowed to continue the Bosses will have hope and the workers will eventually become discouraged."

"We understand."

"Once the police or the militiamen move in they will have control of the mills and they will try to bring in scabs. If they do this . . ."

"Don't worry about scabs, Mr. Ettor. At least not in the Washington mill." Rocco assured.

"Angelo, if we do this thing don't start it off by attacking others." Joe cautioned. To emphasize his point Rocco switched back to English.

"We no gonna hurt nobody. Trust me, Joe." Ettor wasn't sure how to take the comment, so he let it drop.

"Organize your staff, make your notes and get me two people who know the town backwards and forwards." Joe stood and put his coat on as some of the women started to place plates of antipasto on the table.

"You want to eat?"

"Later. Right now I need to walk around and get to know the layout. Send anybody you don't need home. Tell them to rest. I'll be back in few hours."

"I'll come with." Volunteered Rocco.

Unrealized by anybody in the I. W. W. things were far worse in Lawrence than they initially appeared during their assessment back in New York City.

Of the now potential 32,000 workers threatening to strike, less than a tenth spoke English. There were over twenty-five different nationalities speaking forty-five different languages and close to a hundred dialects. The diversity of nearly two dozen religions, one of the biggest obstacles to be surmounted, rounded out the Tower of Babel that the Lawrence mills had become.

Rocco conducted the two man tour and after about an hour of wandering the lamp lit streets they found themselves on the North bank of the Merrimac near Bayside Road West of Broadway.

Joe picked up a rock and glanced across the quarter mile of raging river. The giant buildings of Wood's mills were silhouetted by the compound's powerful security lights and spanned nearly a mile of the high ground along the South bank.

"500 years and little has changed." Joe observed.

"How's that?" Rocco asked.

"The castle, the moat, the fortifications. The opposing army planning the siege."

"One thing has changed." Rocco smirked.

"What's that?" Joe asked.

"Now it's the peasants who'll storm the castle." Joe smirked.

"So, what do you think? About our chances I mean." Rocco asked as he passed Joe a copy of the official 54 hour work notice taken from the Washington mill. Joe smiled down at the notice.

"A few thousand uneducated, non-English speaking, unskilled immigrant laborers in a country which hates them worst than the plague, picking a fight with the richest man on the planet backed by the most powerful government in the world?" Joe scratched his head and did up his great coat, shrugged and turned to head back up the riverbank. "No problem!" Rocco followed.

"I've been waiting my whole life for this." Joe uttered.

'To live outside the law, you must be
honest.'

**- Bob Dylan**

## CHAPTER TEN

**M**ayor John Scanlon stared at the pulp leaflet given him by the Deputy Mayor that morning when he showed up at his City Hall office.

**STRIKE! STRIKE! STRIKE!**

### BETTER TO STARVE FIGHTING THAN STARVE WORKING! WORKERS UNITE AGAINST THE MILL BOSSES!

### VOTE TO STRIKE!

He was conflicted whether or not to convene the Town Council and discuss the situation or to follow his gut instinct. After weathering several of these strike threats in the last four years he decided to go with his  instinct.  He flicked the toggle switch, picked up the hose to the Edison Megaphone on his desk and spoke into the horn.

"Linda, send Mr. Howe in please."

"He's not in the office, Mayor."

*Great.*

"Find him, please!"

"Yes sir."

"Thank you."

Scanlon reasoned Lawrence was a mill town and that was that. Whether they made cloth in New England, steel or coal in Pennsylvania or canned fish in California this sort of thing was the price of doing business in a modern machine age and had to be taken with the overwhelming prosperity of the region the factories brought with them. He rang again.

"Linda, put a call into the Editor of the *Sun*. See if they have anybody talking to the workers.  If so get him to get a hold of me, please."

"Yes Mayor. Mr. Howe just walked in sir."

147

"Send him in." The Mayor replaced the horn on the hook on the side of his desk and began to arrange some papers as Howe entered.

"Sit down Frank, we have some work to do. I'm drawing up contingency plans for this strike thing, if it happens." Not quite as relaxed as he would have liked to have been, Howe took a seat adjacent to the big desk just as Scanlon come around from behind it.

"I need you to contact all the members of the Town Council, tell them I'd be immensely grateful if none of them made any plans to leave Lawrence for the next week. We'll have a short meeting Monday at ten. Strictly to put our heads together and make sure we cover all the bases. I'd like Police Chief Sullivan and the new Fire Chief there as well." Scanlon adjusted his stance. "Get a hold of Mr. Wood's office in Boston. Tell him he can count on this administration's support if the workers do go out." Howe looked up from where he scribbled notes on the back of a sheaf of papers.

"Anything else?"

"Yes. Get a hold of the officer in charge of the Militia. Don't rely on the phones. Tell Sullivan to send a mounted patrolman."

"Are we expecting trouble sir?"

"No, not really. Tell the officer I would like a company of his men to spend the night in the armory. Just as a precaution. Maybe do some periodic patrols around the mills, just the American Woolen ones. No need to worry about the North side. I don't think they'll cross the river."

"Sir the Governor will need to be notified."

"Let me worry about Foss."

"We'll need to get a hold of the armory today, before lunch. They're locked up on Fridays, except for drill weekends on the first of the month." Howe informed.

"Okay. Do that first." Scanlon agreed as he made his way back to his chair. "Soon as we're done here."

"Who's in charge over there this weekend?" Linda buzzed through.

"There's no answer at the *Sun*, sir."

"Thank you." Howe consulted a hand held note book.
"A Lieutenant . . . Giancottii, sir." Howe replied.
*'Fucking great!'*, thought Scanlon.
"I think he's Italian. Would you like me to check?"
Scanlon hung his head.
"No."

*******

The ten story Georgian-styled office building just off Massachusetts Avenue in Cambridge was fully rented a year before construction was finished. The avenue side of floor ten was where Wood had his office with the rear half of that level dedicated to a small hall able to seat fifty or so of the top share holders.

The Annual January shareholders' report and meeting was scheduled to start ten minutes ago but people still hob-knobbed, made deals, set meetings and mingled. But mostly they just drank the free booze at the thirty foot bar manned by four bartenders, two backs and one very annoyed manager. Very annoyed at being called in to work by the agency at ten o'clock on a Thursday morning.

The formally residential Boston suburb had recently been acquired by the City Council and re-zoned 'Commercial'. The property's tripled value was pure speculation and in reality not worth a third of the price paid by the American Woolen Company, formally the American Woolen Trust. However, with capital stock valued in excess of $60,000,000 plus, dividends increasing 10% per year for the last decade and $2,800,000 in dividends paid out in 1911 alone, that didn't really much matter.

Backed by his father-in-law Fredrick Ayer, William M. Wood established the American Woolen Company in 1899 and began to build his empire. The A.W.C. was originally the product of the era of trusts, however, overproduction, competition and poor management brought the American textile industry to its knees by the 1890s.

The largely family owned trusts, the main shareholders of most of the mills, raked in high dividends in lieu of making the necessary capital improvements required to keep up. It wasn't long before they were in deep kim chi and Ayer and Wood were able to move in, buy out and consolidate eight of the financially troubled mills. Frederick, a successful Lowell merchant, purchased the Washington Mills in Lawrence and hired his son-in-law, Wood to run them.

Wood had already successfully turned around a small, bankrupt mill in Fall River and with Ayer's financial backing, he brought together various under-performing mills with the aim of reducing competition and increasing prices.

He convinced investors to reinvest profits into new plants and machinery and continued the highly profitable trend of hiring only immigrant labor at a fraction of the industry standard wage level to save costs. He'd learned early how to manipulate their wages and, in the absence of any regulations or unionization ability, simply got rid of anyone who complained too much. Governmental regulations of course weren't a consideration as the incumbent administrations were put into office almost exclusively by the 'Captains of American Industry'.

A modern promo for the company boasted; 'Because Wood utilized the most modern machinery and techniques, the A.W.C. was by far the most productive and largest single manufacturer of woolen and worsted fabrics in the nation.'

Certainly not an exaggeration. They **were** the most productive and Wood did use the most modern machinery and techniques. Techniques such as premiums, fining and grading.

Premiums, about 5 cents a day, were paid to the weavers. To maximize profits by minimizing payouts the line was sped up, the Weaver had to go faster and so the Loom fixer, and all the looms he tended, had to keep up.

The wages of the Overseer of the section depended on the slowest Weaver as well and if he didn't keep up, no one got their premium and the Weaver was moved or sacked.

For unskilled labor a premium, also 5 cents, was paid on a four week basis providing the worker showed up every day, on time and met the arbitrary quotas Wood set. If he, for example, went three weeks and became sick, or his machine broke down, as they often did, he got no premium money. When Wood decided to pull back on premiums he simply manipulated the four week periods changing the dates and thus avoided paying out.

After fining, (deducting wages for imperfect material regardless of cause), was deemed illegal by the Massachusetts State Legislature, Wood and the owners instituted a system of 'grading' under which they paid various, arbitrary wages for material tagged 'inferior'. With the ever increasing speeding up of the machines it was impossible to produce perfect cloth thereby guaranteeing most of the cloth being graded as 'inferior'.

Water from the factories' plumbing was undrinkable and so 10 cent a head per week was charged for cold drinking water.

Five or ten minutes of lateness was a one hour fine and three offenses got you fired. Additionally, the first week's wages were held back to give the company the chance to cheat the worker out of their last week's wage for a variety of reasons.

Thus, the most modern techniques.

While Blanck and Harris were entering their third week in hiding in fear of their lives as the Triangle Factory fire paid rich dividends, William Wood sat at the center of an eighteen foot long, veneered conference table in the front of the heavily paneled meeting room, scanning the small crowd which had helped make him rich beyond his wildest dreams.

The meeting had been called to order, the role taken and old business reviewed. The moderator reminded the investors of how much they got in dividends last year and finally, Wood was introduced.

With a mildly restrained flamboyance he strode to the podium, leaned forward and placed both hands on the heavily varnished, ornate podium. He then scanned the room and, with a melodramatic air, addressed the assembled stockholders and guests from the Manufacturer's Association.

"Stockholders, fellow manufacturers, ladies and gentleman. I trust everyone had a bonus of a Christmas?" There was sporadic laughter and a few cheers. "When the three wise men visited the baby Jesus they came bearing gifts. Immigrants to His country bearing gifts. In these modern times immigrants of different nationalities have successively come to this country and been given, by folks like us, you and me, the greatest gift of all. They have been given the opportunity to attain new and higher standards of living. They have in turn been assailed and displaced by a new alien race, which has brought with it its own, lower standards.   And so the battle of the standards has continued.   And it is **our** mills which constantly reach down to the lower strata of society and lift them higher!"

The drama wasn't completely necessary but, in light of the strike rumors Wood wanted to be sure any wavering souls were soothed. He knew that, although it was only January, most of them already had their 1912 end of the year dividends spent. The young recording secretary at the far end of the table slid her glasses to the top of her head, rubbed her eyes and began to doodle at the top of her legal pad.

"It is a fact, as has been said by one long familiar with the textile centers of this country, that the entire textile life of the United States has always depended upon the low paid help, made up largely of immigrants who have begun their lives in the mills of this country.  Partly because they are acquainted with that sort of employment and partly because they are incompetent to take up any other line of work."

Some of the gathering offered their support with a ripple of applause. Some except the proper ladies and gentlemen. They nodded.

"But low as the earnings of the unskilled operatives may be, as touted by some, these people have been able to get ahead in life's battle. Thanks again, to our mills." Two or three in the back straggled to the bar. "This fact is shown by the $21,000,000 in deposits in the savings banks of Lawrence! And the money sent each year to foreign countries.  The postal money orders issued yearly from 1907 to 1911, inclusive, average $125,406!" The young secretary suddenly became less bored as she scribbled the numbers quoted by Wood.

'$21 million?' She thought to herself. 'He's probably talking about the merchant's money in those banks. But even if he's not . . .' She scratched out some quick sums. 'That's $131.25 saved per year per immigrant over five years? That's four and half to six month's pay! And that's just in his mills alone.' She sat up straight. *'That's impossible!'* She paused to digest her thoughts. *'Plus they've been here over a decade, and there are thousands of other immigrants besides the ones in his mills!'*

With a mother from Italy, a father from Ireland and an aunt working in the Duck mill, she became even more attentive. As Wood bragged on she continued her self analysis. *'Postal money orders to foreign countries? $125,406 divided by five by 32,000. Wow! A whole 78 cents each, per year! Geesh! At that rate they'll be able to retire and go home any time now. Say around . . . 1980!'*

"Other statistics show . . ."

"Mr. Wood! Question from the floor, please!" It was a sharp dressed, conservative looking man, fifty-ish, off to the side. Wood cleared his throat to buy time to clear his head then acknowledged the man with a nod.

"Thank you, Sir. Mr. Wood, I am J. G. Lansing. I hold controlling interest in the Pacific mill . . ." He was cut off by a man at the bar.

"NOT FOR LONG J.G.! I GOT THAT OTHER 8OO GRAND AND I'M COMIN' AFTER YA'LL!" There was sporadic laughter in the immediate vicinity of the heckler but the speaker maintained his composure and didn't bother to turn around as he spoke.

"People of your caliber will **always** come **behind** me, Mr. Jones!" The comment garnered more laughs. The benefits of the open bar were kicking in. Wood wasn't amused.

"Mr. Wood, we are all more than grateful for the way you have parlayed our money into the fortunes you have however, would you not agree that if we are to stay the course we must stay one step ahead of, for lack of a better word, the Jones'?" Widespread laughter erupted as the meeting just became more interesting to the handful of bar flies at the back of the room.

"What's your point, sir?"

"My point is, should we be concerned about the possible scaling back of the Schedule K Tariff Act?"

In the time it took for the question to set in, the ambiance of the meeting transitioned from joviality to near morbidity. Was there something somebody had the inside dope on that wasn't being circulated? Some scrap of information or a rumor that could change the tide of battle in favor of the enemy? The quiet murmurs were deafening. Wood was losing control.

"Mr. Lansing, if you have some information or ideas that may help us all I wish you'd speak plainly, sir!"

"Mr. Wood, is it not true that the mills are facing a general strike within the first quarter of this new year?"

"NO! It is not true! And it is very irresponsible of you to attempt to start such a rumor!"

"Your answer is a relief, sir. Thank you for your candor." The stockholder took his seat.

"Ladies and gentlemen, I . . . " Wood began damage control, but didn't get far.

"Mr. Wood! Apologies, but just one more thing." Wood was now visibly distressed. "If there were to be a strike, and there were . . . shall we say problems, is there a possibility the government might take an interest?"

Wood was stumped. He, as well as of the rest of the industry, had for nearly a decade floated along downstream on the back of industry friendly presidential administrations, to include the self declared 'anti-fat cat' Teddy Roosevelt during his first stay on Pennsylvania Avenue. The tariff literally guaranteed them run of the market against cheaper sometimes higher quality imported goods at a fraction of the tax they would otherwise pay. That is Schedule K afforded protection of up to 80% of their manufactured goods, thereby virtually guaranteeing inflated and progressively increasing dividends.

Additionally, in virtually every dispute against the A.W.C. and the mills the Tariff Board clearly sided with the Mills and the owners. This was particularly true in the cases of the living conditions of the workers throughout New England when investigated by the despised 'do-gooder', bleeding heart, so-called 'Sociologists' now coming out of the Ivy League schools in the East.

"Believe me Mr. Lansing, the last thing any of us want is Uncle Sam snooping around or muscling in on our operations because some Italians are getting snippety about how much spaghetti they can afford to eat every day!" The audience was now fully attentive. "There are currently no plans to halt production for a strike, and no known plans for the workers to strike! A small contingent of the Washington mill are negotiating wage rates relevant to the 54 hour work week rule however . . . " He paused and perused the room. Most of the crowd seemed to be buying it. ". . . I and my agents are in constant communications with their various committees and have the situation well in hand!"

Wood never did finish his well rehearsed opening spiel, but relinquished the podium to the moderator who stumbled through a few more questions then called the meeting to a close.

Ten minutes later Wood entered his office, pulled the blind and locked the door behind him. Without hesitation he crossed the room to the liquor cabinet, poured half a glass of scotch and plopped down behind his oversized desk.

"Well god-damn! That was pleasant!", he informed the chandelier as he gulped his drink.

*******

The bolts of cloth seemed lighter, the Overseer's barbs didn't sting as much and the work day moved at a quicker pace. Michael was at the happiest he'd been since the death of his wife.

Saturday's were the best. Not for the afternoons he took off, as much as it jeopardized his job, but for the anticipation of spending time with Anna. Taking her out and showing her the town. The incredible selection of restaurants, shops and parks. None of which closed for three hours in the afternoon for siesta, or because of torrential rain and mud slides.

The first Saturday she was over he took her to the city for a rushed tour and by six o'clock had made their way to a new restaurant just off Campagnone Common. Michael sensed Anna's preoccupation with her new environment and ordered the food to go.

"Why don't we eat on the Common?" He proposed.

"What is 'common'?"

"This park over there." He pointed through the window

155

of the restaurant. "In New England it is called a Common."

"Okay." With the large white bag of food they crossed the street to the well groomed park.

"Are you cold?"

"It's cold. But I love how everything is so clear!" She marveled. They took a seat in the large Victorian gazebo.

"In Manhattan, when I was waiting for uncle Affo, I saw snow! It was beautiful! Will it snow here?"

"Yes I'm told quite a bit." Michael handed her a wax paper wrapped hamburger.

"Have you been taking care of yourself?" She asked.

"Yes."

"No bullsheet!"

"Where did you learn to speak like that?!" Michael demanded.

"On the boat. From a friend."

"What else did you learn from this friend?"

"How to act in polite company!"

"And how do you act around boys?"

"Papa, I'm here not even three days! You think all I think about is boys?"

"Yes. At least I hope a little. This old man should be thinking about grandchildren."

"I have many more important things to think about! My English for example. Do I want to go back to school? Do I want to stay in the mills?" Anna bit into the small, square burger.

"But . . . " He prodded.

"But . . . mostly I think about meeting a boy." Michael was on his second burger and chased it with some thin stringy fries.

"What do you think of the food? Great isn't it?! They call it, 'White Castle'! You see . . ." He pointed back towards the corner eatery. "Because it's shaped like a castle!" Anna wasn't impressed as she stopped chewing, peeled open the burger bun and stared down at the burger she held.

"Doesn't make them taste any better!" She slowly peeled back the burger patty and inspected the brown meat.

"They have one in Boston and two in New York! Soon

they will be all over the country!" He triumphantly declared in between chews. She spat her bite out onto the paper and waded up the mess.

"Bravo! Maybe if they keep opening them they will learn to cook!" Michael stared at her puzzled.

"What's wrong?"

"This food is revolting! I want penne!"

*******

That afternoon as he sat at his desk Wood decided to devote a little more time to the strike threat scenario. Annoyed that there was at least one individual who wasn't following on blind faith, he sensed the potential for a ripple effect of descent in the ranks. That's what he considered the people who financed his mills. Not stockholders or financiers who made his phenomenal wealth possible, but soldiers in the ranks, not much different from the tens of thousands of cogs in the wheel who worked the factories. Except of course two or three times a year he had to sit down to dinner with these cogs.

The reality was that if one of the stockholders decided to pull out, based on the A.W.C.'s past stock market record, there were dozens more waiting to get in the door, so there was no real threat, at least none of any financial danger. It was the bruised ego Wood was grappling with.

"Mr. Wood, it was one stockholder." The Chief Mill Agent offered as he pulled up a chair in front of Wood's desk.

"One bad apple!" Wood replied.

"These workers are virtually incapable of cohesive action. They're mules."

"I know that answer! Now tell me what YOU think, damn it!" He poured his right hand man a drink.

The mill agent's comments regarding the foreign born work force's inability to unite were common knowledge amongst the management and ownership of the mills in New England and much of the United States. The idea was that if they did strike, which due to their poor judgment they probably would, how best could the company maintain production and minimize financial

157

dips in the cash flow situation during the strike.

Based on twenty-five years of past mill history, it would only be a couple of weeks or less, before they could be starved out, so the goal was how to shift the production work load around the various mills to support the numerous present orders for cloth. Orders which were coming in not only from large clothing corporations which would help broach the national market, but some of the first orders from the U. S. government, to include Roosevelt's legacy to Taft, the ever growing military.

The Mill Agent reached over to the desk for his drink which he held neatly in his lap while answering the sixty-four dollar question.

"I agree with Gompers' man, Golden. They have a complete inability to unite, they're not smart enough. They're too busy fighting each other. This ruckus over in the Balkans has half of them wondering should they go home and fight? Should they stay and work? Even if half of them went home tomorrow they'd be going against the traffic. We'd have them replaced in less than a day." He shrugged and twirled the Wexford crystal glass.

"The only ones really making any noise are the Italians and hell they're a nickle a dozen. None of them speak any English, all any of them want to do is to save enough money to go home and raise grapes. They never get anything done because they're too busy making pasta and bambinos." He downed his drink. "Ever see Italians try and organize anything? It's a Chinese fire drill." He replaced his glass on Wood's desk.

"They've got a union in Lawrence."

"The Industrial Workers of the World! Bunch of New York Commie Jews! I've seen better organized riots. Besides, the local in Lawrence isn't really theirs."

"How the hell do you know?"

"I've got a Pinkerton on it." Certainly that deserved another drink. He eyed his glass. Apparently Wood didn't think so.

"Less than two hundred members, nobody pays dues. The October quarterly meeting nearly had to be canceled because they couldn't raise a quorum." He shifted in his seat. Was he saying something Wood already knew? "The United textile

Workers issued a report back in . . . I think ought five. Said it was a waste of time and money trying to organize them. It'd be like trying to form some international political organization of nations, uniting them all under one roof to try and stop wars. Might as well try and sell Marx's Manifesto to the Vatican."

"That your honest opinion?"

"I'm around them every day! You'd have more luck trying to get Taft to lose weight." Again the agent glanced at the empty glass without results.

Satisfied with his man's response Wood directed him to set up a strategy and production meeting with all the agents first thing Monday morning in the Wood mill offices. Understanding his orders, the Chief Agent made for the door.

"Meanwhile, no contact with workers, committees or do-gooder groups. Got it?"

"Will do, Boss."

"Or fucking press!"

\*\*\*\*\*\*\*

Unknown to Wood and his agents was that less than three weeks earlier a strike organized by Gurley Flynn and Arturo Giovannitti and the radical Carlo Tresca, had just ended.

The four month battle in Minersville, Pennsylvania had a significant outcome.

Although the workers lost the fight outright and were forced back under worse conditions, due largely to Taft and the government's intervention on behalf of the Mine Owners' Association, the I.W.W. came away with English, Pole and Italian branches who joined with the French and Belgians to sign up with the racially neutral I. W. W. This was an unprecedented unity of formerly clashing cultures.

This in effect put the Wobblies on the tote board as the most racially integrated organization not only in the labor and trade unions race, but in the entire United States of America.

\*\*\*\*\*\*\*

159

It was nearly five a.m. and despite the fact he hadn't been to bed in over 48 hours, and had his first hot meal in two days only three hours ago, Ettor had no intention of letting up just yet. He figured the amount of lasagna & bread they fed him for breakfast would hold him over for about week. Add to that the three cups of industrial strength, prescription espresso, which kicked in about two minutes after the first one went down, and Joe reckoned he could do that week straight through without any food or sleep.

It was the critical day. Today would tell the tale and determine the immediate future of nearly 100,000 workers and residents in the greater Lawrence area to include the suburbs, possibly most of New England.

*"No pressure!"*, thought Joe to himself as he stepped out from the back room of the hall, rubbed his eyes and perused the rhythmic activity of the union hall. *'Everybody busy as little bees!'*

Partially due to its location and partially to try and convince the skilled labor they were part of the fight as well, the Franco-Belgian Hall on Mason Street was set up as the permanent strike headquarters. Orderly lines of 'committee' tables neatly lined three of the walls, a handful of the 200 union members scurried about from table to table and the kitchen was in full swing. Save those at the impromptu strike headquarters, every mill worker in the city showed up for work that day.

"Ciao Joe."

"Ciao, Angelo. Any word?"

"What is the time?" Joe reached into his waistcoat pocket and glanced at his watch.

"Quarter past seven."

"Another forty-five minutes or so. We've got people watching each of the mills. They'll bring word here."

"Anybody else doing anything?"

"More or less. The Lithuanians have put together a small committee with the Russians, Poles and Czechs. The Hungarians refused to cooperate because of the Russians and have formed their own committee. The Greeks say they will wait and see what happens. The Arabs, Syrians and Turks say they aren't going to form any committees or participate if there's a strike. They say most of their people are considering leaving this place anyway. 'Too damn cold!' they say. Not worth fighting for." Joe folded his arms and looked down at the floor.

"What about the Belgians?" Queried. Rocco knew full well their disposition as well as that of the Dutch, but he wanted to end the topic on an up note.

"They're still committed. But they're less than 3% of the work force and the fight hasn't started yet."

"You think they'll waiver?" Joe felt the first pangs of apprehension as he shifted his weight from one foot to the other.

"I don't think so. The core that are committed are very committed and will hold the others together. A lot depends on how the first few hours go. We'll know then who's with us and who's not."

"The critical thing is control of the workers in the first few days. If they lose their heads and go crazy the police will shoot first and not ask questions later. Then the militia will come in, followed by the Army. Then we'll face an uphill battle, something we don't want in the middle of Winter. In the middle of Winter." Joe informed.

Rocco gave Joe a slap of reassurance on the arm as he walked into the room behind them.

"Cops and militia get cold too." He said. Joe smiled back, not sure if he was being pessimistic or weakly pragmatic. "Let's get started." Prompted Rocco. Ettor followed him in with Gino and three of the men chosen to act as translators who had just arrived.

The primary order of business, until they got word of a development, was to form a tentative General Strike Committee. This, along with three or four other preemptive tactics were critical measures gleaned from lessons hard learned by no small amount of blood, life-long prison sentences, police firing squads and government sponsored lynchings.

There was no completely accurate count of how many Wobblies had been murdered since their inception, but taking into account the Wheatland Affair, the Spokane, Washington atrocities and the Southern Lumber Drive, the body count was well into the hundreds. Those imprisoned for significant parts of their life, ten and twenty years, was easily triple that.

"Gino, your English is pretty good. With Angelo's permission I think you should form the core of the Secundos." Ettor proposed.

"Okay. Secundo to what?"

"The Primos."

"Okay. What's a Pr . . ."

"The Primos are what we'll call the primary translators. There'll be two for each committee. Along with one Secundo."

"What do the Secundos do?"

"Keep an eye on the Primos! The Pinkertons have Italians, Poles and Jews also and they will try and infiltrate. Even more dangerous, a small handful of dollar bills to a hungry worker with a family for a few hours of handing out misinformation is tempting." Explained Rocco.

"Each of the 60 committee members to include me, you and Rocco, must have replacements trained to do our job and ready to step in at a moment's notice. One of their first tactics will be to try and take out the leadership." Gino felt proud at being included with men such as Joe and Rocco. But at realizing he too could be 'taken out', pride froze into a block of reality in the form of fear.

Having been hardened to the ruthless tactics of the Pinkerton's, Ettor took another precaution. Each committee member had to be personally vouched for by several others, his supposed place of residence had to be checked out and work records had to be produced and verified. And there was one last measure borne out of bitter experience. He called them over to a secluded corner.

"I brought this dossier down from New York." He handed the folder to Angelo. "Make copies and get them circulated. These are photos and descriptions of all known Pinkerton's operating in the Northeast. They will be here. Trust me. We are their meat and potatoes! They will pose as sympathizers or show up with phony work papers supplied by the mills. Appoint teams to memorize them, and once they are found I want them kept under constant surveillance. Record all their movements and report them to the sub-Committee for Tactics and Strategy!"

"What happens if they see us?"

"I want them to see you. Let them know we know who they are. Let them know they have a shadow!"

"How do you want the information listed?"

"You'll find blank copies of Pinkerton's standard surveillance reports in the back of the folder. Use those."

Rocco smiled.

'From The Monongahela Valley, to the Mesabi
Iron range.
To the coal mines of Appalachia the story's
always the same.
700 tons of metal a day, so ya tell me the
world's changed,
once I've made you rich enough, rich enough
to forget my name.'

**-Bruce Springsteen**
*Youngstown*

## CHAPTER ELEVEN

In 1879, long before there was an American Woolen Trust, little Jimmy Lynch started in the mills. However, he was now known as James T. Lynch, or Mr. Lynch to every one of the office staff at the Wood mill. The unwavering respect shown him did not emanate from his years in service. It came from the fact that he was the Pay Master.

"Mr. Lynch. Excuse me Mr. Lynch. I think there's a mistake." Every penny filtered through the mills to the various echelons of employees passed through his hands first.

Lynch turned back to face the first of the seven Assistant Pay Masters, with three others standing around him, all about to make rounds in the mills and hand out the pay packets. Naturally they were handed out while the workers were still at their machines.

"You have the Everett mill listed to be paid first."

"Oh good. You can read. I was concerned there for a moment." The bewildered assistant stood like a dog just been shown a card trick, then blinked at Lynch.

"Question Mr. Arrows?"

"No sir. Everett mill to be paid first."

"Good. Bye! Next!"

That Friday morning, the first pay day of the New Year, on orders from Wood himself, Lynch varied the pay routine. The Everett, one of the four cotton mills and manned primarily by Polish women, would receive their pay packets first.

As the Paymaster's Assistant left the expansive office on the top floor of the mill, one of the small army of women behind the six rows of the massive typing machines casually stood to stretch her back. Her desk was near a window and, satisfied that no one was paying any attention, she looked out and down, across the street and pretended to adjust her clothing then nodded twice out the window. The boy across the street on the corner of Carver opposite the Ayer mill tipped his hat and shot his eyes to the front door of the Wood mill.

Between sales staff, maintenance personnel and visitors

there was considerable traffic in and out of the front entrance of the mill late that morning, but the A. P. was easily sighted by his brown leather, shoulder pouch. The boys' mind briefly fantasized about the $14,000 plus cash in the pouch. Then he instinctively looked about ten paces behind the clerk.

The two Pinkertons made no effort to hide who they were. They carried their 12 gauge Remingtons at high port, cocked and ready and were careful to allow their brown, ankle length MacKinaws to flap open revealing their shoulder holsters and automatic pistols.

No doubt they were busy fantasizing about their $100 bonus if they shot a would be thief.

The trio turned left and headed north. The boy followed. Through the mill streets, past secondary workshops and around corners. Down laneways and across expansive lots of the town within a city which the American Woolen Trust's mill complex had become, finally ending up at the front entrance to the Everett mill.

About ten minutes after receiving the covert signal, his mission accomplished, the boy broke off from tailing the Assistant Pay Master. He ran for all he was worth back through the streets and lots and across the canal bridge into the city. Once off Water Street he cut across an abandoned building site, on to Mason Street and burst through the union hall doors.

"IT'S THE EVERETT!" He yelled across the expansive floor to Rocco and the small committee sitting at tables in the back.

"YOU SURE?!" One of them called back.

"SI!"

"VIENI QUI!" Rocco called out and the boy scurried to the back of the hall.

"Why the Poles first?" Gino asked Rocco.

"To see what they will do! They are probing our strengths. If the Poles do nothing, it's likely so will the rest of the Easterners. That leaves us, the Belgians and the Dutch on our own!" Rocco said.

"Almost cuts our numbers by half!"

"Don't be a doom sayer!" Rocco admonished. He handed

the boy a nickle. "Pisano, go and get Mr. Ettor. He's at the boarding house. Wake him. Tell him it's started."

"Si Rocco!" As the boy dashed out one of the others speculated.

"They will likely leave the Wood until last."

"Maybe, maybe not. We wait."

Back at the Everette at the front entrance of the noisy, massive work room, stood the Pinkerton's who adjusted their positions accordingly to allow them to cover the entire expansive space as the A. P. worked his way down the ranks of spinning machines towards the rear door checking the numbers on the pay packets. Numbers were used to identify the workers in lieu of names for several reasons.

The management had no need, desire or ability to learn all those foreign names, even if they had had an interest. Management's apathy towards them was just fine by the foreigners given the pent up animosity generated by their continual mistreatment. In turn the new comers figured the language barrier was a good thing. The less they had to talk to the bosses or their lackeys the better.

The A. P. turned the corner and continued up the next rank having the workers sign for their wages then moved on. As it was forbidden to stop working to open your pay packet the women merely exchanged glances, and stuffed the small brown envelopes into their work aprons or pockets to wait until the pay party had left the room. All except Mrs. Poluski, third machine from the end in the first rank.

At the ripe old age of 37 going on fifty, able to down a quart of vodka at a baptism, wedding, or funeral, nine kids, three husbands, (two of them dead), and a three cigar-a-day habit, there wasn't much left to intimidate her.

The A. P. was nearly half way up the second line when he looked over and saw her disengage the swing arm of her machine from the overhead gang drive and stop to open her packet. He waved over the din to the Line Supervisor who had just wandered into the room and pointed to Poluski's station as he didn't want to make a scene himself.

He wouldn't have to.

As Lawrence merchants tendered their deliveries, part time militiamen lined up in the chow hall over in Cambridge and Mayor Scanlon was just leaving home, late for work after arguing with his wife, the Great Melting Pot boiled over.

At approximately 12 noon, Friday, the 12th of January, 1912 one of the largest industrial actions in the world to date was initiated.

The heavy set Polish woman stood, stepped over to the clutch bar of her machine and wrestled it from the floor slot permanently disengaging it from the gang drive. She had been shorted 32 cents for the week.

With some effort, as the machine gradually slowed to a halt, she climbed up onto the cast iron mount of the comber and held her packet in the air. The A. P. and the Line Super hurried back towards her work station.

"Lady, what are doing? You know you can't . . ."

"Come on down Mrs. Poluski. You know you're not allowed . . ."

"Short pay! Short pay!" She cried alternately in English and Polish.

"You want us to take care of her?" Asked one of the Pinkertons who had dashed over to the scene of the crime. The rest of the women began to react.

First the machine operators to her left and in front quickly checked their wage packets then, as they disengaged their machines the illegal checking of packets spread across the floor until all 750  machines were unmanned. Several other women climbed up on their machines and took up the battle cry of 'Short pay!' The Line Supervisor, Paymaster's Assistant and both Pinkertons unconsciously moved a step closer to one another.

The Line Supervisor stood in awe just as the last rank of workers joined in the protest and had taken up the chorus which now reverberated across the expansive bay louder than the mechanical whine of the few dozen machines still running. As one by one the last of the machines died to a halt, the P. A. got the message.

"I handle wages boys, not riots! Let's get the hell out of

here!" The Line Supervisor glanced over his shoulder just in time to see the pay party vanish through the rear door and out onto the street. By the time he grabbed his hat and coat nearly the entire room had one machine left running and nearly 1500 women yelling "Short pay! Short pay!" as they gaggled into orderly ranks and poured out of the mill.

Ten minutes later out on the icy street their passion and anger grew in intensity the closer they came to the gates of the mill compound where they were met by small groups of other agitated workers which had also begun to congregate there.

"Rocco! The Easterners at the Everett just walked out!" A worker from the mill informed Rocco back in the hall.

"We know. All of them?!"

"The whole mill! Even the Checkers!"

"Where did they go?"

"Nowhere they're just milling around!"

"Milling around! That's pretty good!" Quipped Gino, which earned him a slap on the head from Rocco.

Uptown at the boarding house the boy was told Mr. Ettor had gone to lunch at a local deli a few blocks away on Appleton Street, just south of the Common. He found Joe seated halfway down at the lunch counter.

"Signore Ettor! I cominiare!"

"Proprio ora?!"

"Si!" Joe dropped his corned beef sandwich and dashed past a dozen stunned lunchers, out of the deli, the boy close behind. They headed straight south down Appleton and turned east on Canal four blocks from Broadway and the widest point over the Merrimac.

"Anybody hurt?"

"No Signor. They just yell and scream but no police come yet!"

"They come now!" Joe nodded down the street.

They were halfway down Canal coming up on Broadway when, a hundred yards ahead were two squads of police in a straggled formation running straight at them. Joe grabbed the boy by the collar and dragged him into a tenement doorway then slammed the door behind them and leaned on it, panting, listening and waiting. The cops' footsteps grew louder, peaked then faded to nothing. Joe sneaked his head out the door and saw the cops turn right and scramble across the foot bridge over the river.

"Let's go kid!" Holding the kid's hand they dashed out of the door and ran back in the direction the police squads had come from.

"They run from the fight?"

"No. To the back of the fight! Come on!"

"Where they are going?"

"They're heading to the Washington and the Ayer. To protect Wood's mills."

"They waste they time! They never make eet." What the boy knew and Ettor didn't was long before the Wobblies were invited to the dance, the festivities had been planned.

Rocco and his countrymen made the decision that if it was a fight Wood and the Bosses wanted they would have to strike the first blow. However, once they did, they would be made to understand why the Marquis of Queensbury didn't come from Italy.

The Washington was primarily manned by the Italians and was located south of the Merrimac in the same area as the Wood and the Ayer, both of which also had large numbers of Italians in the workforce. Taken together they employed over 16,500, half the entire workforce of the Lawrence mills. All three were large six story structures which spanned half a mile long. The three behemoth factories were only accessible by the Union Street bridge over the power canal.

After trudging through their gates day in day out for years Rocco, and his men, aided by their primary school educations of medieval castles, moats and sieges, were quick to grasp how their size, proximity and isolated location could be used against them. Especially if the invading force were already inside. But there was one other critical factor even Ettor didn't see until Rocco explained it to him.

All three mills supplied the raw material to the other mills of the company, located inside and outside of Lawrence. Neutralize these three and none of the others, even with the protection of the authorities, the militia and all the scabs in the world, could operate.

Runners were standing by and less than ten minutes after the Everett action was confirmed, men at the Washington, were passing the word.

Like a well drilled army of saboteurs the Italians at the end of the production line, nearest the back of the mill and the loading docks initiated their assault. Their signal to begin was a poetic act of pure inspiration.

A worker swept through the long floors, wildly excited, waving an American flag shouting, "Sciopero! Strike! Sciopero! Strike!"

Arming themselves with the picker sticks used to move the cloth, they went from machine to machine, dropping off in teams of five, six or seven and began to shut them down then smashed the wheel cogs or cut the drive belts with stilettos or straight razors . After the machines ground to a halt, the workers destroyed as many of them as possible to preclude the standard tactic of bringing in scabs.

The few faint hearts which were reluctant to join the fight or leave their machines were persuaded, sometimes by knife brandishing Sicilians, that it would be healthier if they vacated the premises.

The crowd now coming from the Everett and the north side of the Merrimac coalesced into one big mass, and moved over the Union Street bridge.

Across the compound, nearer the main entrance,  a small group were attempting to reach the hated clock tower, the clock which reminded them daily of their indenturement, and destroy it. Wood's clock.

Thousands poured out into the streets and choked the roads. Within twenty minutes Broadway ground to a halt and still they pushed on blocking cars and suspending traffic while at the same time hooting and howling, some groups hoisting speakers and leaders up onto their shoulders. In little over an hour all the mills targeted had come to a halt and were abandoned. In just over two hours, as if someone had disengaged a giant floor lever from that great drive belt in the sky, the whole of Lawrence had ground to a halt.

Wood, Turner and company may have fired the first shot, but the workers drew first blood.

*******

It's not as if problems weren't expected. Certainly the police, as did nearly every one else in the city, suspected there was a pretty good chance of something happening with the mill situation. But an all out, spontaneous riot by tens of thousands of workers bent on destruction was unthinkable. Kind of like that famous unsinkable ship which in a few months, alsmost to the day, was going to sink.

The assumptions were predicated on two common American falsehoods. It's never happened here before and those foreigners aren't bold enough or smart enough to pull it off.

This reasoning was also predicated on a master stroke of industrial/political propaganda. Propaganda heralded by the industrialists up through Morgan to President Taft himself. They're getting paid better here than they did over there so they really have no bitch. And, worse yet, they don't even speak English, so how smart can they really be?

True the workers were getting paid more then in their homelands. But not better. What use is even fifty cents per hour if a loaf of bread is 25, 50 or even 75 cents a loaf?

As for never happening before, two words. Haymarket Massacre.

The American's lack of knowledge of their own recent history combined with the Hearst controlled, government generated tripe, concerning situations in other countries had taken its effect. Culture, as Ray Chandler pointed out, is dominated by politics. America is a political machine, one of the largest in the world. In American terms these workers had too much culture. In European terms the Americans didn't have enough. The end result was that at some point, like any system that far out of kilter, it had to collapse. And without exception, violence was an integral part of the dynamic.

For the first time since the Civil War church bells across

the city sounded in alarm. Most of the citizenry wondered at the racket but attributed it to some special noon day ceremony.

About twenty minutes after the Everett was shut down the police were notified and the alarm went out. Acting Police Chief Sullivan saw his chance. He hated the Eastern European scum worst than the murderers, thieves and rapists in his jails. At least they were red blooded Americans. By two o'clock that afternoon the call had gone out for every regular, special and reserved police officer and detective in the city limits to include night watchmen.

By the time Ettor made it the half mile south from the Common to the intersection of the Union Street bridge and North Canal the rampage had gained such momentum that it developed its own dynamic. The Washington, Wood and Ayer mills were in a shambles and the mob, now nearly 10,000 strong, were pouring over the bridge heading north up Broadway.

"STAY WITH ME!" Joe shouted to the boy as they fought their way through the throng and across the bridge.

Because the front of the mob had collided with the Broadway traffic and slowed both to a halt the workers were kept from coalecing into an ucontrollable surge and swinging wildly around and into the city. This also allowed Joe and the boy to make to the south side of the river and into the yards. By this point the reality of the anger and frustration of the out-of-control workers hit home with Joe and he became even more desperate to find the main body and try and prevent a full scale riot.

They reached the main rail head just as the bulk of the them were congregating on the main factory road.

"Stay here! In an hour, maybe less, they will all be over the river and the trouble here will die down. Make your way back to the hall and stay there! You understand?"

"No problem, Mack!" As he spoke the mob surged around them like a swollen river. By shear luck he sighted Angelo leading a large group of combers and spinners and sent the boy off to a safe doorway. Ettor's six foot two, 200 pound plus body served him well as he barged his way across the street and through the tide of thousands of angry workers.

Seconds after he headed Rocco off and pulled him aside

there was a pick handle across his neck  and he was fighting for air. The attacker was instantly on the ground but several others swarmed over Joe before Rocco fought them off and identified Ettor who was compelled to shout above the clamor.

"LISTEN TO ME! ROUND UP . . ."

"YOU OKAY?" Ettor guided him by the arm away from the surge of the crowd and into a doorway.

"Never mind that! Round up as many of the committee men as possible and get the hell back to the hall!" He directed as he composed himself.

"Now?! This is the fight we have been waiting years for!"

"Rocco! I'm telling you not to go. The cops are waiting for you! They were tipped off it would start today!"

"Good! Then we can have this finished once and for all!"

"Don't give them the excuse they're waiting for! This is supposed to be a strike not a mob riot!"

"We must show them who is in control!" Joe switched to Italian.

"When it comes to violence THEY are in control! The police will shoot first and no one will ask questions later! DO YOU UNDERSTAND WHAT I AM TELLING YOU!? There is them and there is us and only one is subject to the law!" In English he added, "And it ain't them!" Rocco glanced at the determined, disorganized mob as it surged by.

The catharsis of the mob screaming for blood had an irresistible allure. However, the level of  Ettor's collectivity in the midst of the chaos was frightening but logical.

"What about them?" With the axe handle he was now holding he gestured towards the mob.

"The police know if they get to the other mills the workers there will join the strike. They'll head them off and fight them back at some point. The workers will retreat, try to regroup and then wonder around like lost sheep for awhile. That's when we'll have our chance to take control. But we must have an agenda! We have to organize a permanent general committee followed by a mass meeting as soon as possible! Only then we will be in a position of strength to negotiate!"

174

"I can organize it tonight and we can hold the meeting tomorrow afternoon."

"NO! That's too late. With this mess going on we are even with the Bosses for control. It could go either way. If the violence escalates we may never gain control! Start right now! Get up to Colombo's and get leaflets printed off immediately, at least ten thousand to start. Schedule the meeting at seven in the morning on the Common!"

"Tu?"

"I'll go to the telegraph office and signal New York. If this thing gets as big as I think it will we'll need reinforcements."

Ettor knew the dynamic well. The Pacific and the Prospect mills were exactly where the crowd were headed and that's where the first of the trouble started.

*******

Sullivan and his men were waiting and as soon as the workers turned the corner and marched  down the side road towards the gates the police formed a double cordon, locked arms and drew there batons.

At first the lead workers were puzzled at the tactic. Four or five dozen police against four or five thousand workers? It made no sense. At a slower but steady march the workers advanced.

Sullivan, standing unseen behind the last cordon put a whistle in his mouth. The center officer in the front cordon raised his baton.

"Do they mean to charge?" A Pole near the front asked his colleague.

"Hard to tell what they are thinking!"

"They haven't a chance!" He added.

Now, with the crowd at about 100 feet from the police, the baton fell, the whistle sounded two short bursts and the police ranks split in half and scurried off to the sides of the frozen road. Once the police were clear of the road Sullivan sounded three more short bursts and the workers began their education in American strike tactics.

The American Way

The freezing water fell from several locations catching them off guard and saturating half their ranks in less than a minute. Strikebreakers and Pinkertons on the roof tops of sheds, adjoining buildings and the Pacific mill itself, were manning four inch hoses. Fire hoses originally intended to protect workers' lives.

The freezing temperature of the ambient air quickly became another of Sullivan's allies. The worker's ranks scattered and many fell back. But not all.

Angered by the unprovoked attack, many surged forward including the Norwegians, Fins and other Northern Europeans inconvenienced but not intimidated by the cold.

As the police attempted to retake the road, behind the deluge of fire hoses, the workers rushed the bridge, forced the gates and broke into the mill yards. Cheers went up as some of Sullivan's men were forced into the high pressure water stream as well then blown off the bridge.

As the workers slowly but surely streamed into the yard groups of strikers in twos and threes climbed on to the roof of the railroad structure that pierced the mill's perimeter and dropped down into the mill yard. From there they ran through the mills, urging all hands out.

Those who didn't storm the bridges ran to the freight cars in the railroad yard, and collected large rocks of rail bed gravel and fist-sized lumps of coal. With these they demolished the windows in the weave-shed of the Pacific, gained access and then joined the infiltration of the mill.

As the roof top heroes saw the squads of workers streaming into the Pacific they dropped their hoses and abandoned their battle stations and the water streams died down and stopped.

The temperature by now was near zero and the road instantly formed a new sheet of ice.

The police outside had regrouped and been reinforced by about three dozen strikebreakers, and cut the flow of workers in half.

The new front line of rioters now advancing, the police attempted to slow and stop them but the momentum of the mob

176

pushed forward. Within the space of half a minute the unfortunate front runners had two choices. Fall to the ground and get trampled or crash into the police lines and get beaten to death. Choices had been predetermined.

The ones closest to the sides had time to readjust positions, the ones toward the middle of the twenty man wide column then involuntary formed a wedge. At the last minute a maniacal cry erupted from somewhere.

"IF"A WE GONNA GO, GO ALL'A THE WAY, GOD DAMN IT!!" To the surprise of both sides, the lead pack put their heads down and ran at full force. The wedge easily broke through one cordon after the other scattering police, strikebreakers and workers to the frozen ground however, it was a pointless victory. Under Sullivan's direction the more disciplined police slowly regrouped into teams of four or five then into squads of fifteen or twenty.

The road leading up to the mills was just narrow enough that neither side could outflank the other and this combined with the fact that the ethnicities were spending so much time and energy attempting to locate and regroup with their own, Sullivan had the breather he was looking for. The police cordons reformed then, stepping over the two dozen or so broken and bleeding workers slowly and systematically began to beat back, what was now, a disorganized mob.

Then the police fall back tactic was initiated.

From somewhere in the direction of the two main mill buildings shots were fired.

The two Poles who were in the first assault party over the rail shed roof and were now at the south end of the mill building, and took cover as soon as the shooting started.

"Pistol shots!" One offered.

"How do you know?"

"Count the shots. They are coming in sixes."

"Those bastards are **actually** trying to **kill** us!"

"Maybe, maybe not." He calmly reassured. Several more short vollies rang out across the yard.

"WHAT THE HELL YOU MEAN, MAYBE, MAYBE NOT?!"

"With shooting like that they either have very old pistols or put their worst shooters in the front line to be safe. Over two dozen shots and they've hit nothing!"

While the workers ducked for cover the police fell back behind the gates, closed them over and quickly erected makeshift barricades of pallets and scrap steel rods successfully stopping the bulk of the crowd from gaining access, the few dozen who were inside the yard slowly realized they were trapped.

The end of the battle was signaled with the growing wail of sirens closing in on the location.

Sullivan ordered the strike breakers to stay and man the gates while he and his men rounded up, beat and arrested the infiltrators.

*******

By the time Rocco was at Colombo's print shop near the Common and Joe made his way through the ever increasing traffic jams and chaos of the city streets along the river it was coming up on half past four in the afternoon a little over 10,000 mill workers were out and the thirty-five to forty thousand shop keepers, shoppers and residents were preparing to transition into commuters.

At least that would have been the Friday evening routine. Dark was swiftly approaching and Broadway north to Melvin just above Essex and Canal to Amesbury was already at a complete standstill. Over a half mile radius north from the Wood, the Ayer and the Washington was one big gridlock. Sirens of emergency vehicles sounded all up and down the roads and the church bells of all the major churches continued to contribute to the cacophony.

Joe burst into the telegraph office and startled the three or four patrons scattered around the room attending to their business as he ran to the counter.

"I need an operator right away!"

"See what I can do, Mista." The old man shot back in slow motion. He shuffled over to the oak box on the wall and turned the generator crank several quick turns. "Whear ya callin' too?" He called over the counter as if his valium just kicked in.

"New York."

"New Yawk it is!" The old fella lifted the receiver from the hook and shouted into the mouth piece. "MAYBELL?! JED OVER TO THE WESTERN UNION."There was a short pause. "OH SHE'S DOING FINE, THANKS. I'LL TELL HER YOU WUZ ASKIN' AFTER HER." Ettor rolled his eyes in frustration. "GOT A YOUNG FELLA HERE NEEDS TO SPEAK WITH NEW YAWK. UH HUH. UH HUH. THAT'S RIGHT. NEW YAWK CITY. YA, MUST BE IMPORTANT AWRIGHT. UH HUH. JUST A MINUTE, I'LL ASK HIM." He turned to Ettor. "Is it important?"

"No. I'm frantic and out of breath because the news stand was out of Hershey bars! YES! It's an emergency! Please hurry!"

"SAYS IT'S AN EMERGENCY AWRIGHT. UH HUH. UH HUH. JUST A MINUTE." Again he addressed Joe. "She wants ta know, is somebody hurt?"

"MACK! Can you please just get me a line to New York!?"

"HE'S IN AN ALL-FIRED HURRY MAYBELL. BETTER SEE WHAT YA CAN DO." Another agonizing pause. "I'LL CERTAINLY TELL HER YOU SEND YOUR LOVE. OH, I'D SAY SHE'LL BE AWRIGHT. THE VET'S HAD A LOOK AT HER SAID THERE'S NUTHIN' TA WORRY ABOUT. JUST A LITTLE CONSTAPATION, THAT'S AWL. BYE BYE MAYBELL. GAWD BLESS." He shuffled back over to the counter. "Mabel says she'll rush things right threw for ya. Be 'bout half an hour." Ettor stared in disbelief.

"I need to send a cable." He uttered through clenched teeth.

"Where to?"

"New York." Joe answered, trying not to rip off the edge of the pine counter he now gripped.

"That'll be five cent for the first ten words, penny a piece after that." Joe slapped a silver dollar on the counter. The old man reached under the window and produced a blank cable form, took a stub of a pencil from behind his ear, licked the tip and said, "Shoot!"

179

*"If only!"* Joe involuntarily thought. Instead he started to dictate in as a controlled voice as he could muster. "Pandemonium here, STOP. Upwards of 10,000 out, STOP. Rioting started around noon, arrests have already started, STOP. Workers temporarily under control, STOP. GET A.G., REPEAT GET A.G., STOP. Tell him to get next train out, STOP. Real opportunity here, STOP. No telling what the bosses will try next, STOP." The old man passed the form under the window to Joe who signed it and passed it back through the window.

"That'll be 48 cent."

"Can you send that immediately?!"

"No problems missta . . . Eetta. Be in New Yawk in a few minutes. You want to wait on a reply?"

"No. When it comes send it over to the Oak Street boarding . . . no wait, to the Franco-Belgian Hall. Can you do that?"

"Oovaa on May-sun Street. No difficulties, saa. That'll be five cent cash money for the delivery." The man passed Joe his change who took it and turned to leave.

"You still wanna tawk with New Yawk, young fella?" Joe left without answering. The old timer shuffled to the cash register to deposit the takings.

"Young ones. Always in a hurry!"

*******

Situated on pub strewn Massachusetts Avenue in the Boston suburb of Cambridge, not far from the scenic Charles River is Harvard University.

Her hallowed grounds have helped produce presidents, generals and captains of industry. Her general reference stacks date back to the 10th century A. D. Her rosters boast the top lecturers who are world class in their respective fields and her kitchens employ internationally rated chefs.

However, if any of those teachers, captains or world renowned chefs wants to use the toilet, they need to rely on the hired help. Unskilled labor.

To access those thousand year old books one must

negotiate acres of well groomed pine, elm and oak lined paths trimmed with meticulously cultivated foliage and shrubbery. As if the bushes were not testament enough to her surgical attention to detail, just to be hired on as an assistant grounds keeper one was required a four page application, three references and a personal interview. Or as Danny Boyle, Boston Southie and recently hired Assistant Grounds Keeper might observe, a trial by fire of the anal retentives.

Danny looked up from his raking duties just in time to see a student fly by and dash up the granite stairs of the male dorm.

The blond haired, blue eyed student raced through the dormitory hall with a determined sense of purpose. Ignoring the two students he had barged through, he then crashed through the door of a room unannounced even before the books and notes hit the ground behind him.

"JOHNNY BOY! Get your gun! We're goin' ta war!" The young, slightly underweight Johnathan Gugino, sitting at the desk turned and slowly removed his glasses.

"David, I realize you're from Texas so I'll speak slowly and avoid as many polysyllabic words as possible. Aside from getting in the habit of wearing shoes, not spitting your tobacco on the parlor floor and learning to use indoor toilets, part of the reason you come to an Ivy League school is to learn manners. To include how to knock before entering another's room."

A third student who had overheard the other students down the hall cursing as they cleaned up their mess, meandered in through the open door.

"Taft's got us involved in North Africa?!" He asked.

"Hell no! We goin' ta' Lawrence!" David shot back.

"The North Africans have landed in Lawrence?" The new arrival asked. The young man at the desk snickered. Blondie was indignant.

"We's going ta put them damn anarchist strikers in they place!"

Heidelberg, Cambridge and Trinity may have set the standard in science, business and literature, but the last word in American jurisprudence remains Harvard.

"What's all the hub-bub, Bub?" A fourth student asked as he pushed pass David and into Johnathan's room.

"We gonna get ta crack some heads out in Lawrence!" Tex bragged. Johnathan felt the pit of his stomach fall out.

"We been called up?!" Asked future war hero #3.

"Not yet, but a runner just came through the R.O.T.C. dorm five minutes ago! Assembly in the drill hall 13:00! In full kit!"

"'Bout time somebody went in to stop them bastards!" New Boy exclaimed.

"Sweep-em Away Sweeter!" #4 chimed in.

American military officers were generally required to hold college or university degrees prior to commissioning. As degreed individuals upon graduation, especially from the likes of Haavaad, slid into the private sector on greased grooves as highly paid professionals, motivation across college campuses to join up wasn't very high and dropped even further following the U. S. expansionist policies in the Caribbean and South Pacific, where you had a pretty good chance of going off to some god-forsaken, foreign land and getting your ass shot off for less pay then a janitor. A public school janitor no less.

So, in order to boost the ever sagging body count of commissioned officers in the military, the Washington brain trust hit on the idea of paying tuition for selected students in return for a hitch in the Army. 'Selected' taken to mean, upon qualification', taken to mean breathing and had a pulse.

As the others piled out of his room Jonathan didn't bother to get up and close his door, he just turned back to his desk and stared out the window across the campus. He watched as David, flanked by the two newest Volunteers of America, stumbled down the granite stairs and splattered his books and notes across the path.

Across the path the old man helping Danny Boyle load dead branches and foliage into a wheelbarrow shook his head.

"Take a good look, son. There goes your future leaders." Danny kept working and didn't look up.

"Assholes couldn't lead a piss up in a brewery!"

# Paddy Kelly

By six o'clock that evening a blanket of cold and dark had engulfed Lawrence, and approximately 15,000 workers had wrecked their machines and abandoned their work stations. Police reserves from all over the county were on alert and all but essential emergency services were available.

To the uncomprehending general populace, the twin evils of a transitioning Europe, Anarchy and Bolshevism, had somehow crept onto America's shores and launched an unprovoked attack on peaceful, god-fearing city of Lawrence, Massachusetts.

'Who will not suffer labor in this world,
let him not be born!'

- **John Florio**

## CHAPTER TWELVE

A cold but mild breeze snaked its way up Broadway and fanned out into the side streets of the city. Two dogs over on Tremont just off Haverhill had knocked over a full garbage can and were rummaging through the remnants. With no luck they moved on to the next can, also full to overflowing. The Sanitation Department had been forced to cancel their Friday rounds due to the rioting, so the two mongrels would have a full day but retire with empty stomachs that night. Even stale bread was being saved at this early stage of the strike.

The city's population was nearly 86,000, 60,000 of whom depended directly upon the payrolls of the textile mills. The carnage in the mills north of the canal was minimal. But the Wood and the Ayer would be hard pressed to re-open without a week's maybe two, worth of repair and clean-up. Scabs would be of no immediate use as nearly one hundred per cent of the machinery had been destroyed or damaged and most of the windows broken out. The thin sheet of snow over the machines closest to the exterior walls would soon melt and swell the few leather drive belts which hadn't been cut and, start to rust gears and destroy what there was of the cloth and raw materials lying dormant in various stages of production strewn around the expansive floor. As a guard against future action company engineers had moved in overnight and welded heavy, iron re-enforcement rods across the main gates and the rail entrance near Salem Street.

However, the near complete desolation of the city streets that morning was deceptive. In a local shop basement on Chestnut Street, not far from Campagnone Common, a furious planning and strategy meeting was underway. Not wanting to chance being arrested at the Hall, Ettor had Rocco moved the first big organizational meeting to one of the few trade shops sympathetic to the workers.

The space was needed as, much to the pleasant surprise of the Wobblies, far more workers joined in the Friday action than initially expected. Unfortunately, with over half the workforce out, a whole new set of problems cropped up.

"Rocco?" Joe handed the reins over to the I. W. W. Local's President. As the entire gathering of two dozen plus, to include the two or three women present, were Italian, Angelo spoke in the native tongue.

"Okay, here's where we stand. Due to so many brothers joining in the fight, the . . ." There was a loud but short cheer from his fellow conspirators. Rocco fought back a smile fully realizing it was early days. ". . . communication requirements have tripled, relief efforts and supplies, originally planned for 7 to 10,000 for one month, would at present levels last less than two weeks and that's not taking into account those who are still wavering or haven't joined in.

Three of the toughest yet most important groups are the Germans who, don't forget, harbor the majority of the skilled workers, the Middle-Easterners who are split into a half dozen different nationalities and who never see themselves as any sort of an entity anyway, and last but not least, the Jews."

"Those firery, fiercely independent Jews!"

"Don't mock! We can certainly use some of that fire!" Joe immediately realized that the present situation far transcended the county, state or even regional levels. Unlike any other action he or most of the Wobblies had previously been through, in less than 48 hours this industrial action had been catapulted on the road to national level. A master of organizational skills, he focused on the immediate.

"Joe?" Rocco nodded across the plank supported by two kegs of nails. Ettor took the helm.

"First order of business on the agenda, is the formal election and formation of a General Strike Committee of 60 members, with the 14 largest nationalities given four reps each, but every one of the nationalities must be represented."

"What about Ed Reilly? " Someone called out. The following uproarious outburst puzzled Joe who looked over at Angelo.

"He is our Irish committee member."

"So get him another one or two, whatever he needs." Joe instructed. Gino shot back.

186

"Okay, if you pay for the ticket from Ireland." His quip was again followed by an outburst of laughter.

"You mean he's the **only** Irishman we have?"

"Oh no. There are plenty of others. But they're all cops or Pinkertons!" Rocco quietly explained. "He's the only Irishman working in the factories whose is in the union." Joe smiled and shook his head.

"Won't take long for his committee to vote then, I guess!"

Later when asked by a pressman if he thought the Irish would stop fighting amongst themselves long enough to join the cause Reilly replied, "The only reason we fight each other is because there are no other worthy opponents. That's why they sent me out here."

"Why's that?"

"To see is there anything worth getting excited about."

At the meeting it was determined that the General Strike Committee would be authorized to act as an executive board directly responsible to the workers and would be imbued with complete authority to conduct the strike and act on everyone's behalf. Any decisions they made could only be changed by a popular mandate from the workers. Through this system all mills and all component parts to include tradesmen, laborers and any sympathetic administration workers would be represented. No one was excluded.

One member of each ethnicity was then assigned to each of the five sub-committees; Relief, Finance, Publicity, Investigations & Organization. They were then left to elect their own committee heads and assistant heads.

Each of the sixty committee members, as did Ettor, Rocco, and Giovannitti, had picked their replacements and begun to train them in all aspects of their respective jobs. There was less than a weekend for them to be ready to step in at a moment's notice. There would be arrests, probably mass arrests which is why committee heads and critical leaders were to be kept apart as much as possible. At all times Ettor was careful not to dwell on the worse specialties of the Pinkertons and other 'detective' agencies like them. Blackmail, kidnapping and murder.

# The American Way

The next major task was to arrange for daily mass meetings. These, the Wobblies had painfully learned through the western strikes, not only kept the lines of communication flowing but forged solidarity in their sense of purpose amongst the workers.

Later after the meeting broke up Rocco briefly lamented about the Germans and Jews but Joe reminded him the priority now was to force a response from the owners to enable the committees to plan their next phase of strategy.

The last order of business before dispatching the General Committee reps to the afternoon mass meeting was to draw up their list of demands, which were surprisingly simple.

At the number one spot was a 15% increase in wages followed by time and a half for overtime, abolition of the premium system, and the reinstatement of all strikers on settlement of strike.

Each classification of workers were advised what to ask for, but in keeping with the Wobblies' true Democratic guidelines, each was also given complete autonomy on their final list of demands. Joe additionally suggested they add that all strike meetings be public meetings, with the exception of the executive meetings with the mill-owners and public authorities or those which they did not desire to be made public.

At the end of the meeting the vote was unanimous on all counts and an official General Committee was in place.

Just twenty-four hours after its initiation what started as a spontaneous, hate fueled orgy of violence, had by one man and the principles of one small union, been transformed into a well organized revolt.

There can be no small wonder at the intensity of fear and hatred the U. S. government, later to include those normally viewed by historians as supporters of the people's rights such as the Wilson administration, would later harbor for the I. W. W.

*******

The two elderly Sicilian gentlemen, draped in conservative, blue flannel suites with shiny elbows and dark ties

188

shifted nervously from one foot to the other. The long handled, wicker baskets they steadied themselves with had developed a slight bow.

For the better part of half an hour they had stood in the rear of the church flanking the vestibule doors, staring up the wide aisle at Father Mariano Milanese, who currently played to a packed house. The Italian priest, whose passion had been propagandized as 'radicalism' by Father O'Reilly over at St. Mary's, was just finishing a verse from Colossians, 4:1; *Employer-Employee Relationships* while O'Reilly, at nearly the same time, was preaching to the more well-to-do residents of the city by reading *James 4:1; The Causes of War.*

As was the case with all of the masses being said in Lawrence's ethnic churches, the sermons were in the native tongues of the congregations.

"The Monsignor has sent word from Boston that the Bishop has denied The Holy Rosary Church permission to donate **any** funds from the Sunday mass collection to the strike relief effort." Padre Milanese explained to his flock. A ripple of mumbling broke over the crowd. "The Bishop stated that the funds collected by Mother Church are specifically to feed the poor!" With both hands firmly gripping the pulpit, he leaned forward and looked out over the sea of parishioners. "Sorry you are all so rich!" Sporadic laughter echoed through the cathedral-sized church. "So I regret to inform you that ALL of the collection money will have to be given to the Italian Socialist Federation's soup kitchens located through out Lawrence, to be used in relief of the hunger now sweeping our fair city as a result of these terrible times!"

You'd have thought Verdi himself had just finished conducting the last act of *La Triviata.*

The applause caused an elderly couple outside to stop and glare up at the church doors.

"What do you suppose they're celebrating in there?" The woman asked, staring up at the granite edifice.

"Must think mass is a party or something. Damned Eye-talians!" The husband commented. She smacked him on the arm.

"Rufus! Mind your language, it's Sunday!"

"Hope it's Sunday!" He answered as they shuffled away. "Hate ta think we went to church for nuthin'!"

The two basket bearing gentlemen, who had now moved from the vestibule, stood a little more upright as involuntary smiles simultaneously swept their weathered faces. "Now we will pass the baskets for the weekly offerings. As we do I ask you to remember; God helps those who help themselves." He leaned forward both hands resting on the edge of the podium and peered down at his flock. "But God help those who get caught helping themselves!" Laughter from the congregation again punctuated the Father's remarks. "Go in peace, and may the Lord be with you!"

Out, on the portico of the entrance, morale in the congregation was never higher as the church slowly emptied and the people clustered around Milanese to shake his hand and thank him.

Michael and Anna Casaburi were amongst the last to exit and, at Michael's suggestion they headed across town to a neighborhood drug store to enjoy one of the latest crazes, a frap. An old fashioned milkshake with fizzy water. What some people were starting to call a 'Sunday'.

Not suspecting that Michael had an ulterior motive for the walk, Anna broached the subject that had been eating at her since last week.

"Papa, what will happen eef'a the mills don't'a reopen?"

"Why do you always speak English to me?"

"What? You got'a so good at English because you never spoke eet?"

"Touche." He shrugged. "They will, they have to. They are too important."

"Important to who?"

"To whom! Important to whom."

"TO WHOM! TO WHOM, Signor Profssori!"

"They are the life's blood of all of New England and New England is too important."

"To WHOM is New England so important?" Michael playfully grabbed her around the neck and pulled her close.

"Did uncle Affo teach you to scutch me like that?"

190

"I don't need no help from uncle Affo to scutch you! I know you every flaw, Old Man!" He smiled as they walked for a bit in silence.

"This part of the country has traditionally tipped the balance of the election of the president. And soon there will be a big election here."

"Ah hah! That explain the book!"

"Which book?"

"*A Hees-story of the American People.* You are studying to became historian now?"

"No. I have thees book for different reason. Besides, it won't matter if the mills reopen or not."

"And why is that Mr. Hees-story Professor?"

"Because, we won't be here." Anna froze in her tracks as fear crept up her spine.

"What . . . why?"

"Because fortunately for us America has gang violence."

"So does Italy, so don't tell me we are returning to Italy!"

"So does Italy, and we are not returning home. We are going to Chicago."

"Chicago?!" She asked with restrained excitement.

"Because most of the gang violence is from the Italians and that is where the Italian gangs are becoming a problem and so they are looking for policemen who can speak Italian."

"You'll take the police test?! But how will I find work?!"

"You won't need to work. You will finish your schooling, then do as you wish. Maybe even go to that big design school in New York." To dumbfounded to react, Anna just stared straight ahead.

"Are you okay?" She gave no response.

"You . . . you have to be a citizen first, no?"

"If I pass the police exam, they will help me to get my citizenship. I spoke to Affo last week. He made some inquiries. The exam is in March." He carefully watched her face for a reaction. It was exactly what he hoped for. "Or, if you like, we can go back to Sicily." He teased.

"Ha ha!" Her beautiful, broad smile lifted him to where, only three months before, he believed he could never again be.

"Ora si che ci siamo, Baby!" She grappled his arm and led the way. He pulled back from her.

"Che?!"

"Now-you-are-talking, Baby!" Michael shrugged. "Eet's American! It mean, now you are talking, Baby!" Michael stared. "Eet's mean bene, molto bene!" He still didn't get it. "Never mind."

She pulled him towards the door and into the crowded drug store.

"I spend five years at night to learn this language, and now they change it!" He mumbled.

'. . . an evil power which roams the earth,
crippling the bodies of men and women,
and luring the nations to
destructions by visions
of unearned wealth,
and the opportunity to
exploit and enslave
labor.'

**- From the novel** *Oil*
**Upton Sinclair, 1926**

## CHAPTER THIRTEEN

Despite the freezing weather that Monday morning the first mass meeting went ahead. The I. W. W. had set the meeting and when Scanlon got wind of it, for obvious reasons, he suggested they hold it outside the City Hall. The entire General Committee was there as were some of the merchants and most of the state-wide press. An estimated 10,000 members of the striking workforce surrounded the City Hall area. Scanlon ensured he was first up at the podium.

"The fifty-four hour work week is at the root of our problems here today. The fifty-four hour work law is unfair, unjust and unnecessary! The existing wage law hours are more than fair and allow a hard working man to support his family." For the first time Scanlon clearly revealed that he stood squarely on the oopposite side of the fence from the workers. "Above all we must keep the peace! It is in no one's interest to propagate violence! I am compelled to say that I am shocked at the level of violence of your actions!" The workers patiently let his remarks go by. Most of them had no real first hand knowledge of where the Mayor stood and so no strong opinions about his place in the fight. That is until now.

"There should be no opposition to those workers who desire to return to the factories. Those who wish to keep their families fed and clothed in these desperate times! They have the right to work if they so desire. It is to this end that I suggest we form an alternate committee. Not to conduct this non-productive action, but to negotiate, in good faith, with the mill owners. So that we may all return to work as soon as possible and return our town to its former, productive state!"

There was no telling what kind of response Scanlon expected, but the reality was signaled by the faint, sporadic applause of some of his most staunch supporters and some of the merchants. He proposed nothing original, or practical as far as the workers were concerned, but he certainly nailed his colors to the mast. Or rather, in between the masts.

Joe spoke next but made no pretense at neutrality. Scanlon offered a weak hand to Ettor as he ascended the steps to the timber framed platform. It was a wasted gesture not lost on the workers who were in a position to witness the act.

After stepping over to the podium he paused to survey the crowd, workers, merchants and a collection of interested citizens, huddled in the crisp, mid morning air.

"This struggle is not an accident. It is an incident in the world-wide conflict between capital and labor. The mill-owners have conspired to defeat the fifty-four hour law, though signed by the Governor, challenged and upheld by the Supreme Court.

The winning of this strike means more bread for the workers and less dividends for the Capitalists. In order for you to have any show at all you must have organization. You have that. You must have a committee, as advocated by the Mayor. You have that." Capitalizing on the dead silence, he paused and perused the mass of ill clothed garment workers specifically.

"But by **all** means make this strike as peaceful as possible. In the last analysis, all the blood spilled will be your blood. And if any blood is spilled, it will be on the heads of the mill-owners, for they will be responsible for it." Now the crowd, overwhelming comprised of the workers, began to react. "Given the severity of the wages and non-existant benefit systems in these mills, especially compared to the national averages, and how many years this situation has been allowed to go on, the reality of the present circumstamce is that it is surprising that there hasn't been more violence!" The workers rose to their feet but with his outraised hands Ettor stayed them to calm.

"For a strike to be peaceful, to be successful, there must be solidarity in the ranks of the strikers. Division is the surest means to violence. Violence means the loss of a strike. You can hope for no success on any policy of violence. Therefore, instead of taking the Mayor's advice and staying away from the mills, you should go to the mill and urge all the workers to shut down completely all the mills. Then there will be solidarity and no occasion for disturbance among you." It was the first time since their inception as a workforce that the workers began to feel and understand themselves an entity.

"Remember, the property of the bosses is protected first by the police, then the militia. If these are not sufficient, by the entire United States Army. Remember also that you too, are armed. Armed with your labor, a power which **you** can withhold. Provoking violence will serve as a pretext to start a blood bath in which the workers' blood will be spilled. You have formed a strike committee. This committee should try to settle the strike and provide finances and relief as long as it shall last."

Joe made eye contact with Scanlon who shied away. "Victory lies in a complete tie-up of all the mills!"

By the end of the day the ranks of the Italians swelled with the addition of many of the Americans, Poles, Lithuanians and Franco-Belgians.

Scanlon, as did the Bosses, fully realized that solidarity meant victory for the workers. So the next day, not having achieved his initial goal to weaken the strike, Scanlon upped the stakes by issuing a threat to call out the militia. Down to the last man and woman, every striker knew this meant Scanlon advocated violence to back his flaccid rhetoric. Furthermore, Ettor let it be known that Scanlon didn't have the authority to call out The Militia. This would have to be done by the Governor, which in turn indicated Scanlon's fear of the workers.

Round two to the strikers. But it was still early days.

*******

Father James T. O'Reilly anti-Socialist, anti-reformationist and stalwart, unwavering self-appointed, life time President of the imaginary International Anti-I.W.W. Federation had 'informally' set a meeting with one or two of his parishioners that Sunday after mass. It was no coincidence that both invitees were Lawrence town council members.

Bill Jenkins' gout was acting up so he had to beg off which left Father O'Reilly and Frank Oz to have their flapjacks, bacon and black coffee alone.

"I say we start our own campaign! I already spoke to most of the clergy. Ninety per cent of 'em condemn the strike. But that don't mean we don't think some of those people don't need no help. We can do both, with some kind of action committee." Frank wasn't completely clear on what O'Reilly was sniffing around for, but he wasn't completely hazy about it either.

"A Citizens' Association or something."

"What makes you think that, Father?" Frank asked without looking up from his last morsel of grease-soaked, crispy bacon.

"Well, out at the Ecumenical meeting in Boston last week some of the other clergy mentioned they'd feel pretty good about a priest leading the struggle . . ." O'Reilly continued to twirl his juice glass. Frank wiped the corners of his mouth with his napkin as he sat back in the booth. ". . . but we can talk about that. Main thing is we gotta have some kinda show of support from the public sector. Let 'em know the citizens of Lawrence are Americans first, last and always!"

"I thought we were god-fearing Americans first, Jim?"

"That goes without saying!" O'Reilly sat forward and plunked his elbows on the table. "Understand something Frank, this is not a damn strike! All that sh. . . stuff about higher wages, better conditions and family support is a bunch of whoey! This is a war-against-society! A WAR against the American way'a life! These people's goal is the destruction of the present social order!"

"I hear Father Milano supports the strike?"

"He's the only one of the priests who does. And he's Eye-talian! Long as he has enough wine he don't care! Waitress can we get a scotch? You want a drink?"

"Yes sir." She answered.

"No thanks." Frank declined.

"Get those damn Socialist agitators outta here! Outta our town, outta our state and outta our country! Got no damn business here anyway!"

"What about Scanlon?"

"Scanlon! Hang Scanlon! Who runs this town?! Him or us? You want your kids learnin' Eye-talian in school?! Besides, this time next year he's out and some other idiot wanna-be-governor is in!"

The waitress dropped off O'Reilly's drink in route to

somewhere else. "Look what happened with that supposed 'massive' letter campaign to the mill owners to let the workers march! Scanlon agreed straight away to reverse his stance against 'em and let 'em march!"

"He met with the council and we agreed to 'peaceful' marches. Not unreasonable. Then Sullivan decided to get heavy-handed and went after them. Chased them away by force." Frank countered.

"EXACTLY!" O'Reilly slammed the table, spilt the milk and caught the attention of everyone seated at the lunch counter. "Exactly what he should'a done! Peaceful picketing! What the hell is that?! A pickett line's somethin' invented fifty years ago in the War Between the States! A tactic you use in war! Not in industrial relations fer cryin' out loud!" The newly invented 'pickett lines' had continued unabated, 24 hours a day, seven days a week for the now nearly two weeks of the strike with no sign of abating.

"They were told they could march." The councilman countered.

"That's my point! We need a show of strength and unity here. To stand as one. They think they're splittin' our ranks and it'll give them more impetus to push harder! Only a matter of time before we see unrestrained lawlessness, chaos and riotin' in the streets." The good Father leaned further forward and narrowed his eyes. "I'm tellin' ya Frank, they're out to break our rice bowls!"

"Jim I'm not sure they're out to take our rice bowls . . ."

"Break em, damn it!  Break 'em so's we can't never use 'em again!"

Two more scotchs and fifteen minutes later the vote was unanimous. A citizen's association would be formed.

*******

"Man must earn his bread by the sweat of his brow! You ever heard that before?" The judge's downward glare was met with a steel hard stare of indifference by the defendant. "Well you ought to have. It's in the Bible! "

Paddy Kelly

"That's fine Your Honor. But I'm a woman, or hadn't you noticed?!" A ripple of laughter erupted through the courtroom as she hefted her over-sized breasts attempting to escape from behind her waistcoat.

"Councilor! Your client looking for a contempt charge on top of her sentence?"

Judge Mahoney was notorious for his anti-labor bias. He was well reputed for submitting unsigned, condemnatory, double-column editorials to the local press berating the Wobblies and anybody remotely related to the Labor Movement. Now, as is common in the American judicial process, he sat "impartially" in judgment of their membership.

"Judge, before my client is sentenced we are opting for trial by jury as proscribed in article 17 . . ."

"JURY!? You must be stupid son! I got over 100 of your criminals to see ta'day. What makes you think I intend to waist taxpayers' dollars on 100 trials?!"

"Long before the rioting started your Honor the police were given orders to beat the women on the ribs and breasts so as to disallow the bruises to show."

"OHHH! They were, were they?! Looks like we got us a psychic!" Mahoney performed to the room. There was the occasional giggle. "How do you know what the police were told, son?! Were you privy to their morning meeting?" The union lawyer found it increasingly difficult to contain his anger.

"No Your Honor, but . . ."

"MAYBE YOU'LL NOTICE THIS!" The woman began to undue her waist coat.

". . . the orders were issued at the scene **after** the rioting broke out!"

"That's what we call in legal vernacular, 'hear-say!' son!"

"HEAR SAY THIS!" The woman shouted as she pulled her shirtwaist from her waist band and exposed her breasts. "YOU FASCIST BASTARD!"

Hoots, hollars and cheers mixed with gasps of horror peppered with applause as she exposed herself to the gallery and control of the court was temporarily wrested from Mahoney.

199

It was a wonder the mother of four was in court at all. One breast was so swollen that it looked deformed and both breasts and her entire right side were a mass of ugly black and purple welts. All bruises were clearly in the shape of policeman's batons. The lawyer hung his head.

Several bailiffs immediately made for the front of the court, tackled her and dragged the exposed woman from the court.

"One year for rioting and one day for contempt! Next case!"

Although they would take up to six months to be overturned by the State, at a cost of tens of thousands to the state and union, every one of the I.W.W. arrested that day were pronounced guilty by Mahoney and sentenced to prison terms, most for one year. All without hearings, much less trials.

Out in the hall there was a dull thud followed by the shriek of pain of an injured bailiff.

*******

"Damn greasy Italians are like a bag of snakes! And these two Vaudevillians, Ettor and Geo-spaghetti are the heads!" Wood sat on the 18th century King Louis settee as he grumbled to Turner, President of the Duck mills. Turner was at his bar trying to pour another glass of Bombay in peace but not having much success. He was surrounded by a dozen of his young wife's legendary dog collection.

"God-damned dogs!" He glanced down the long corridor of the mansion and yelled again. "DO SOMETHING WITH THESE GOD-DAMNED DOGS!" One of the miniature schnauzers was humping his leg and he spilled some of his drink. "BEFORE I DO!" The small dog yelped as it bounced off the adjoining wall.

The meeting at his country home was one in a series Wood had arranged with several owners to coordinate and plan strategy. A bit ironic for them to apply the word 'strategy' to what they were doing as it implied intricacy, planning and forethought. To this point, a little over two weeks into the fight, their entire strategy was based on previous blueprints. Starve the workers back into the factories, strip them of their dignity then lower their wages.

"500 fuckin' dollars in Chicago for steak to feed these little bastards! You believe that shit?!"

"You took her dogs on your honeymoon?"

"If I didn't I never would've heard the end of it! At least they had their own god-damned Pullman."

"I been thinking, you know how Jason killed the Medusa don't ya?" Wood asked returning to the subject of the meeting.

"Cut off her head." Turner replied as he pulled up one of the dozen Chippendale chairs and took a seat.

"That's right! Cut off her head." Wood downed his drink and made his way to the bar. As he did, the small herd of dogs trailed behind.

"You're not thinking of killing them are you?" Turner asked with more anticipation then surprise. The dogs began to cluster around Wood's feet, sniffed his trouser legs and quickly scattered across the large dining room yelping as they ran. Turner froze in mid sip from his glass and stared.

"How the hell'd you do that?"

"Chili pepper in the leg cuffs. I got an idea I want to run by you. I know this funeral director in town . . ."

"Ethel! ETHEL!" An instant later an immaculately dressed, young black maid appeared in the doorway.

"Yes'sa Missta Tooiner?"

"Tell the cook from now on I want a pound of red chili peppers in the kitchen! You got that?"

"Yes'sa Missta Tooiner." The maid turned to leave.

"A pound! IN ALL THE HOUSES!"

"Yes'sa Missta Tooiner." She replied over her shoulder.

Back in the kitchen Jonesy the cook had just come in.

"What he want now?"

"What he always want?"

"Yell at somebody."

"Dats it!"

"What he want wiff red chili peppers anyway?" The cook asked.

201

"I dunno. But you bess get him some red chilli peppers! A pound in every house!" She laughingly mocked.

"Girl! You bess keep yo voice down for we boff be living on red chili peppers!" Ethel's heart-warming smile melted from her face as she stared at Jonesy while he hung his coat and removed his over shoes. He glanced over his shoulder.

"What's you shakin' yo head at, Sista'?"

"Damn shame."

"What's that?"

"Youse some good lookin' man!"

"And youse some good lookin' woman! So tell me sumthin' I don't know!" Ethel fought to muster enough determination to fight back a tear.

"So enlighten me, Sista'! What's you cryin' for?" She drew a breath before she spoke.

"We wash and dress they kids. We put ow hands all in they food. We even use they toilets! But we still gotta come in thu the back doo." Jonsey's face broke into a broad grin as he approached Ethel and took both her shoulders from behind.

"I prefers to calls it . . . my 'Private Entrance!" He proudly exclaimed, his retort laced with stoicism.

Ethel shook her head and smiled through her tears.

\*\*\*\*\*\*\*

"JOHN! JOHN, where the hell are you?!" Detective Inspector Rooney was not a happy Boy Scout as he slowly weaved through the gravestones and monuments in the frigid dark. He got John Breen's surreptitious message about an hour before going off shift which was bad enough, but with things relatively quiet in town, now that the Staties had been asked to help out, Friday was supposed to be his drinking night.

"Over here!" Came the subdued whisper. Not subdued enough to keep Rooney from stumbling over a broken headstone.

"God damn . . ."

"Hey! You're in a cemetery!"

"You think I don't know I'm supposed to be in a tavern instead of a bone yard!? I hate this cloak and dagger shit! You got something for me or not?" Rooney leaned on the monument in front of him. Breen, a local undertaker and former school board member moved closer and spoke in a hushed tone, presumably so 'Mary Markowitz, Beloved Mother of Three, Deceased' couldn't pick up on the conversation.

"I got a tip two Italians came in from New York this morning, in a hired truck." Rooney stared at the shadowy face across the marble slab.

"Well, well, well! I guess that solves the Haymarket Massacre mystery." Rooney mocked.

"They brought explosives." Rooney, about to light a cigar, froze and made eye contact.

"This on the level?"

"There's at least three cases. Maybe more." Rooney didn't light up but instead threw his match to the ground and stowed his cigar.

"Wood and the mill bosses have over a hundred and fifty detectives working for them around the clock. How is it a humble stiff handler came by this information?"

"They were seen unloading it by one of my guys. He came back after collecting a payment for a casket we sold last week and he went by a tailor's shop, some Arab fella . . ."

"Mared's?"

"That's it! He saw them unloading a case of something covered in cloth. Only the cloth is too small to cover the whole box, ya know. He got scared 'cause of the violence and all. So he came to me. Now I'm coming to the coppers, which is you."

"That all you got to go on?"

"No. I asked around and some friends said they thought they saw somebody out here."

"There's lots'a bodies out here."

"It's disrespectful to joke in a cemetery!"

"Sorry, Mary." Rooney tipped his fedora to the head stone. "I'm still listening."

"I didn't want to send you on a snipe hunt so I came out to have a look around. That white oak over there? All I saw was one case, partially opened. A couple of sticks were missing. But you'd better have a good look around yourself. I'm not a policeman."

"If what you're telling me is true, sounds like you oughtta be." Rooney's attitude shifted into professional mode as he gave a precautionary glance around. "You'd better get out of here. Any of those strikers find out you were talking to me they'll put two and two together."

"Okay. Good luck!" Breen was glad to be leaving. "One more thing. There's a print shop owned and run by a guy named Colombo, just off Maple I think. He belongs to the Italian Socialist's Federation."

"So?"

"He's the guy printing all the strike leaflets."

"Man's got a right to earn a living. Doesn't mean he's in cahoots with anybody."

"He does them for free! So I heard. You might have a look. Better to ere on the side of justice."

Rooney made his way across the single lane, dirt road to the tree indicated and there, hastily covered in mulch and dead foliage was a 100 stick case of industrial grade dynamite.

"Son-of-bitch!" Rooney tipped his hat back towards the grave stone. "Humblest apologies, Mrs. Markowitz."

Paddy Kelly

'A mule will labor ten years willingly and patiently for you, for the privilege of kicking you once.'

- **William Faulkner**

## CHAPTER FOURTEEN

"**M**oham, put on your shoes." The dark, cherub-like two year old looked up and pointed to his shoes next to the prayer mat. His mother smiled down at him and pointed to the tiny shoes as well which caused a broad smile to break across his tiny face. He got the idea, fell back on his bum and began to fumble with the black leather pull-ons.

His father finished the last of his morning prayers, rose from the floor and took Moham's infant sister from his wife as she moved to the prayer mat.

Ferris had taken it as a good sign that Oak Street faced due East when he rented the shop and converted it into a tailor's shop a few years ago.

The baby had fallen asleep so he set her in the crib, parted the curtains separating the back room from the front of the shop just enough to see out to the service counter and took a seat at his treadle sewing machine which doubled as a desk just near the back door. He began to sort his day's work.

The rear door burst open so hard it knocked the tailor off his seat. The six burly state troopers piled in so fast his wife was still on her knees. It took young Moham until he saw the four cops breaking through the front door and piling into the back room to start screaming in terror. A half dozen shotguns and assorted pistols were aimed at point blank range towards the terrified family.

"GET YOUR HANDS IN THE AIR! DON'T MOVE!" Mrs. Mared instinctively moved for her son and one of the deputies cocked his 12 gauge and aimed at her head.

"NO!" Fortunately the Lieutenant next to him slapped the muzzle up and pointed it away from the mother and child. The deputy looked at him like a chimpanzee seeing his reflection in a mirror for the first time. "Go watch outside!" He ordered the young deputy who refused to move. "Go watch outside! NOW!" The young zealot reluctantly moved to the front entrance and took up a station near the front door. "Mared Ferris you are under arrest for the illegal transportation of explosives with intent to do bodily harm and destroy private property."

A few minutes earlier similar scenes had been played out at a shoe repair shop one block South on Lawrence Street and over at Colombo's print shop in the same neighborhood. The deputies spread out and began to search Mared's shop. A few minutes later the trigger happy deputy returned to the Lieutenant.

"We just got word. They found another case last night. Over near one of the mills. It was broken open."

"So, maybe this isn't a bum stear." The scene commander mused.

"A local detective found it behind the fence line. Not very bright, leaving it in the open. But, whatt'a expect?" Trigger Boy commented.

"Probably got spotted. Had to dump it in a hurry. Alright let's get this over with. Give the place a good search. Try not to shoot if you . . ."

"HEY LIEUTENANT! DOWN HERE!" The Lieutenant made his way over to the narrow wooden stair case and down to the basement while two deputies cuffed and restrained Mared. He was back in less than a minute led by two local police carrying a case of dynamite.

"MARED!" She yelled at him. Knowing it was a plant but not wanting to tip his hand to the cops he silently glanced at her but his look screamed "Be quiet!"

"You want her too?" A uniform asked.

"No. Warrant's for him only. If we need we can come back." The Lieutenant replied. As they led Ferris out the front door he looked back pass the curtain, through the door and at his wife holding the crying children.

"She's not going anywhere." Commented a deputy.

"Good thing you were saying your prayers lady. He's going away for a long time." Trigger Boy reassured her.

*******

It was only a matter of a couple of hours the morning the dynamite story broke before the entire merchant class of Lawrence had firmly decided to throw its support behind the mill

207

owners.

Some, like Jake Garfield even made the decision to look into O'Reilly's Citizen's Association.

Garfield's wife stood at the stove fixing his usual six eggs, six strips of bacon and three pancakes. He sat at the table reading the *Lawrence Sun Times*.

"Listen to this! Arrested were a one Ferris Mar-eed, tailor with a shop on Oak Street, **a known** Syrian and **known** friend of the strikers, who has led parades of his countrymen!" He read with the enthusiasm of a child reading his first bed time story unsupervised.

"Urbana DePrato, with a shoe repair shop located at 78 Lawrence Street, next to the printing shop owned by a one Antonio Colombo, known Italian and Italian Socialist Federation member. His printing shop is known to have printed thousands of leaflets for the strikers and serves as the location where Joseph Ettor, I. W. W. member and covert strike leader receives his mail. Sounds like a who's who of terrorists!"

His wife was preoccupied with the breakfast and wondering if there was any credence in the *Ladies Home Journal* article she read yesterday. It told of a study at John's Hopkins where doctors believed an excess of salt could lead to early coronaries.

She glanced over at the Morton's salt container then threw in a couple more generous dashes just in case.

"Three cases a dynamite they found! And they suspect there's probably more!"

"Why don't you wait till we get the whole story?"

"Because my Dear Nai-eve-ness, this is a Hearst publication! The whole story's right here!"

She placed his plate in front of him then shovelled the food onto it. The Morton's salt container followed.

"Here. In case there's not enough." He continued to parrot the commentary.

"They have sources which **prove** that the explosives were imported from outside for the **sole** purpose of sabotaging the mills and **creating** anarchy. The I.W.W. leaders could **not** be reached for comment."

He triumphantly folded the paper and set it aside before diving head-first into his cholesterol infested breakfast.

"So much for no violence perpetrated by the strikers, Miss Flynn!" He emphasised his political commentary with a sprinkling of salt.

*******

Ettor was on his way to the train station to meet the latest of his re-enforcements coming from the New York headquarters. The "A. G." of the telegram Ettor sent the first day of the strike referred to Joe's long time compatriot Arturo Giovannitti activist, orator, poet and I. W. W. organizer.

Easy going and soft spoken Arturo maintained a gentlemanly demeanor even in the worst of times. His tall frame contrasted considerably against the largeness of Ettor and Haywood in that he was graceful without being gangly. Accompanied by "smiling" Joe Ettor they sometimes had the unsettling effect of causing their enemies to wonder if there wasn't something the two knew that they didn't. When taken together they were considered the Ying and Yang of the labor struggle.

The 28 year old Arturo arrived that afternoon representing the news paper *Il Proletario* on behalf of the Italian Socialist Federation Relief Committee. As of yet the Federation wasn't embroiled in the nuts and bolts issues of the strike, but from its outset when the Italian flag went up in Lawrence that was enough and a trickling of help was sent. Arturo was there to change that.

Arturo had met Gurley Flynn in New York so they could travel North to the mill town together. Joe met them both in Lawrence and the three drove up to the union hall from the train station. As they rounded the corner and turned off Broadway Flynn noticed a speaking platform just off to the side, protruding out into the street. It had been strategically erected in front of the state public clinics.

"What's that for?"

"Well Elizabeth, that's what we call in the trade a

209

'speaking platform'. It's used for making . . ."

"Ya know Joe, I almost missed you." Arturo and the taxi driver chuckled in unison.

"So many workers came out so fast, to keep up we had to set them up all over, wherever we could. Only way to get all the rallies and speeches in."

"Could you please pull over?" She addressed the driver who turned back and shrugged to Arturo. Giovannitti said something in Italian and the car pulled up to the curb and the driver shut off the meter.

"What are you gonna do?" Joe asked.

"We came here to work didn't we? Unless you just want to sit on your backside all day and drink tea?" Arturo turned to Joe and shrugged.

"Looks like she's going to make a speech."

"Good idea." Concurred Giovannitti. As Flynn mounted the platform Joe, fighting back a bigger smile than usual, stepped into the middle of the deserted street in front of the platform and began to applaud.

"I haven't said anything yet!"

"Just warming up for when you do!" As he applauded a few curious clinic workers outside on a smoke break drifted over into the vicinity of the platform. Flynn introduced herself as being from the I.W.W., explained their goals and then said she would like to say a few words about health care in the United States. Soon, a small crowd had gathered.

She reached into her skirt pocket and produced a sheet of notes. As was her forte, Flynn had done her research and plotted her attack strategy long prior to arrival at the front.

"I have here some interesting comments. Comments written by one of your most diligent clinicians. Dr. Elizabeth Shapleigh, a health official with the State government and practitioner right here in Lawrence. This is from a report she compiled, wrote and submitted late last year. Dr. Shapleigh has discovered that, in regards to the Lawrence population, and I quote, 'A considerable number of the boys and girls die within the first two or three years after beginning work. Thirty-six out of every 100 of all the men and women who work in the mill die before or by the time they are twenty-five years of age. Average life expectancy is 22 years less than the rest of the country. The mortality rate for children is fifty percent by age six!'"

The small crowd of medical practitioners knew their city was behind, but not that much behind. Flynn noticed a few doctors had gathered on one of the hospital balconies over looking the street. One, a female doctor, watched with what appeared to be particular interest.

"Victory in this strike will not only mean more reasonable wages for the workers but a realistic hope of higher quality health care. Health care which means an improved standard of living for the entire city of Lawrence." Flynn turned her attention the ten or fifteen health workers who had gathered.

"You who have spent years of your life studying and working to save lives and improve life will no longer have cause to be ashamed or embarrassed that this city, this modern metropolis is one of the nation's leaders in infant mortality, decreased life expectancy and neglected public health." Joe and Arturo had separated and now, from opposing locations, egged the gathering on.

"We need your help. Your expertise. Right now, over on Mason Street, we have six brave doctors and ten courageous nurses working night and day to care for 15 to 18 thousand workers and their families! We need your help. Real help, not mere support. Please help the workers with your time and expertise. Please volunteer! Two, three even one hour a day will make a difference! These people came to this country, our country for a better life. Help them find it. Thank you." Flynn paused for a ripple of mild applause and glancing around caught sight of a woman in a long white lab coat up on the balcony.

Dr. Shapleigh quietly smiled, nodded and stepped back into her office.

*******

The Reserve Officer's Training Candidate Hall was in reality the main gymnasium of the athletic complex in the Northeast corner of the Harvard campus. Sunlight streamed in on the hanging racks of duck pins and rows of dumb bells above the medicine balls as uniformed student-candidates gradually filed in. The Battalion First Sergeant had arrived a half hour earlier and it was Colonel Sweeter, the Battalion C. O. who approached the grizzled enlisted man as he finished directing the set up of the podium.

"First Sergeant."

"Colonel."

"You look stressed, First Sergeant."

"Worried about these kids, sir. They're greener than green."

"They'll be alright. As long as they remember their training."

"Training Colonel? They're law students at an Ivy League school who meet once a month to learn some drills. These are not professional soldiers. I hate to think we'd lose any of 'em to some disgruntled immigrant workers." The student soldiers continued to stream into the gym.

"'All enemies, foreign and domestic'. You took the oath same as myself."

"Yes sir." The First Sergeant turned away to take his leave. "I remember."

"Best if you keep your eye fixed on that First Sergeant!" The First Sergeant's look of disdain was tangible. "You may assemble the men."

"Old Blood 'n Guts! His guts, our blood!" The Sergeant mumbled as the officer strode to the front of the gym. It was an angry First Sergeant took his place in front of the podium. "FALL IN!"

The command initiated a mad scramble and in less than a minute, squads, platoons and finally the companies had taken head count and reported to the First Sergeant now standing at the head of the battalion formation. He executed a sharp about face.

"Third Massachusetts Battalion, R.O.T.C. all present and accounted for, sir!" He reported. Although perfectly capable of issuing the order himself, Sweeter again directed the senior enlisted man.

"You may stand the battalion at parade rest, First

Sergeant." The order was issued and the Colonel dramatically took the podium then slowly perused all he surveyed.

"Gentlemen! We have received a preparatory order from the Governor of the Commonwealth of Massachusetts! As you are all educated men and good patriots you have no doubt been following events in the mill town of Lawrence. It would seem the Bolsheviks have been considerate enough to provide us with some training to fight them over here before we have to fight them over there!" The Colonel's opening comments sparked laughter by some in the formation.

Standing in one of the back squads Jonathan Gugino, first generation American, only responded by grinding his teeth.

"We are the United States military. We are the defense of this country regardless of the political orientation of its leaders and as such are expected to behave in a politically neutral manner. Therefore I will assume this posture in what I say here today."

Just in front of the podium the First Sergeant smiled as the pretty Filipino waitress brought him another banana rum daiquiri in his private quarters over looking Alangapo Bay on the main island.

"These foreigners come to our shores in a desperate act to better their miserable lives. We provide them with jobs with which they may in turn provide their families with food and shelter. And how do they demonstrate their gratitude? They destroy our factories! The very factories which provide their daily bread!"

Save for the uniforms, someone entering the hall late would have guessed it a high school pep rally. Out in the hallway several passing students took time to peep through the main entrance doorway and investigate the commotion.

"In the event we are activated, it will be our duty to show them the error of their ways!" This time cheers were accompanied by applause. "I have personally guaranteed Governor Foss that I, we, will do just that! And know you now, one and all, that as a Harvard man it will be my honor and privilege to lead you Harvard men into battle, anytime, anywhere!"

# The American Way

Several large bodies of students had by now congregated outside the four exits of the gym to investigate the commotion. As the cheers died down Sweeter started up again.

"And what ever our future holds, always remember! Trust in God! Trust in your family. And, as Americans . . ."

*"Cue dramatic pause."* Mused Gugino.

". . . always put your trust in your government!"

"Thank you ladies and gentlemen! It's great to be back here at the Palace!" Gugino's comments were drowned out by the wild uproar.

\*\*\*\*\*\*\*

Coney Island, New York boasted two things. The largest amusement park at the time and a rapidly expanding Russian-Jewish community. The park was simply known as Coney Island and featured two 250 foot parachute towers, one of the first roller coasters in The States, and 'The Cyclone', a large wooden slide where for two cents you could climb a thirty foot ladder, slide down a long wooden slide, slam onto a large rotating disc and be flung, skinned knees, elbows and torn trousers, back out into the waiting crowd. Occasionally someone fractured a limb.

It was a hoot.

The young couple walked arm in arm along the expansive beach side boardwalk with the park as a backdrop. Passing a news stand, the young man pointed to a front page photo on the *New York Times* of strikers demonstrating in Lawrence. Several of them carried signs in a foreign language.

"What's that say?" He asked his Russian-Jewish girlfriend pointing to what was written on the signs.

"Ja rabochi. I am a worker. Something like that." Masha replied.

"Workers huh? Not any more!"

"Why's that?" He then pointed out the banner headline which by now had swept America.

## 'ANARCHISTS PLOT TO BLOW UP LAWRENCE MILLS!

---

214

## 8 ARRESTED!
## CONSPIRICY SUSPECTED!'

"Now they're criminals."

*******

The Governor swung his chair around to face the picture window behind his over sized desk. The serenity of the snow flurries outside seemed to lighten the tense atmosphere in the office.

"What was the exact wording on the message from Bill Wood?" The man sitting across the room shuffled through some papers and produced a scribbled note.

"'Tell Foss to get the god-damned militia in here to protect my god-damned mills!'"

"Eloquent and articulate as always." The Governor commented. "What was their response when you and Howland offered the workers state arbitration?"

"They refused outright." Responded the Governor's Secretary, Dudley Holman.

"Arrogant little bastards, those Commies!"

"Actually they're Socialists."

"What's the difference?" Foss had entered the meeting that morning with Holman aware there was a strike in Lawrence and that the mills of his 'very good' friend, William Wood, were involved, however, not much beyond that. Suddenly he began to polish up his 'political opportunity' spectacles so he could read the situation a bit more clearly.

"Said they'll only talk to the owners directly. All the owners or none of the owners."

"Is there an official request from Mayor Scanlon?"

"No, but he intimated that if he didn't have a response by the morning, he would make it one." Foss swung his chair back around and perused the memo again.

"Did you run this by the Attorney General?"

"Yes sir. " Holman looked grim. "It's called *Posse*

215

*Comitatus.*"

"What's that in English?" Holman thumbed through his notes.

"It was a rider to an appropriations bill back in 1878. Chapter 263, Section 15. It's a statute specifically forbidding the use of United States armed forces against its own citizens unless expressly authorized by Congress."

"You mean I'd have to go through Congress to send in the troops?"

"That or a Presidential edict."

"To stop a bunch of uneducated immigrant mill workers?!"

"Only if you want to use the Militia or the Army. The Coast Guard's exempt."

"So we send gunboats up the Merrimac?" Foss was off
balance. He needed a loophole. "Way
I understand it, most of those people aren't citizens." Holman took a seat in front of the Governer's desk.

"We don't have a count on how many are and how many aren't Americans, but there are a goodly number of bona fide citizen's in the mill's workforces."

"If I give the okay could it become a state budget issue?" Holman consulted his memos from the meeting with the State's Attorney General.

". . . no money appropriated by this act shall be used to pay any of the expenses incurred in the employment of any troops in violation of this section. Any person willfully violating the provisions of this section shall be deemed guilty of a misdemeanor and on conviction thereof shall be punished by a fine not exceeding ten thousand dollars or imprisonment not exceeding two years or by both fine and imprisonment." Foss adjusted in his seat. "I don't have the figures on cost per day sir, but the A. G. rang the State Militia's Headquarters, they've been following developments out there, and their best guess estimate is a strike under the present conditions wouldn't run much past a week. Ten days at the most. Budgetary considerations for keeping the military in Lawrence for seven days should be minimal. In terms of political strategy, the small amount spent on troops for a week balanced against the expected campaign contributions towards your presidential election campaign from the American Mill group . . ."

"I get the picture." Foss swung his chair around to face Holman. "This comitatus thing ever been tested before?"

"Not in Massachusetts. Militiamen have never been considered to be used against civilians. There's a lotta people in the Senate thinks it'd make us look like a bunch of Bolsheviks."

"Didn't Idaho send in the troops back in ought . . . something? Against the miners?"

"Yes, sir they did. Ought five I think."

"And . . . ?"

"Things were done. Lives were lost."

"Ours or theirs?"

"Both." Foss turned back to face the window. But only halfway.

"Put the call into Fort Devens. Let the Army decide how many they want to send out there."

"Yes sir." Holman rose to leave.

"And Dudley, tell them to put somebody in charge with a level head. Last thing we need this close to election is a blood bath of the 'poor, honest workers!' You get me?"

"Yes sir." Holman headed for the door.

"Holman . . . " Dudley paused in the doorway. "They crush that strike in Idaho?"

"Completely, Sir."

"The Governor get re-elected?"

"No Sir. What they could find of him was determined to be ineligible for office."

"What?"

"They blew him up. At his home after the strike was crushed." Holman left.

Foss stared at the closed door.

'Due to their constant abuse, words such as Liberty, Justice and Freedom have come to be meaningless.'

**- George Orwell**
*Politics and the English Language*

## CHAPTER FIFTEEN

**G**eneral George Armstrong Custer was a warrior. The protection of his people had always been his paramount consideration. Good guys and bad guys were clearly defined. He was a good guy. They were different. They were the bad guys. But today, he was tired of winning the west.

In the back yard of the Kennely household just off Ames Street the next generation of young Americans were about to find Cowboys and Indians a trite game.

"How come you always get to be the cowboy?! Why can't you be the Indian for once?!" Young Jimmy demanded, oblivious to the fact that his mother was going to have no sense of humor about him sitting in the wet dirt wearing his freshly cleaned pants.

"I'm tired of Cowboys and Indians! Let's play somethin' else."

"Like what?"

"I dunno. Maybe . . ." Suddenly a faint rumble slowly grew louder and the ground under the two young boys shook. The sound of powerful motors suddenly filled the air and the two warriors ran to the front yard fence to investigate. Mounting the bottom rail of the white picket fence the two boys stared in awe.

With Colonel Sweeter prominently displayed standing in the lead vehicle, swagger stick appropriately tucked under his right arm, a seemingly endless convoy slowly snaked it's way south on Ames heading towards the river. The small warriors stayed on tip toes, glued to the fence for the entire forty minutes it took the convoy to vanish up Water Street. They even held on a few minutes longer, just in case.

"So whatta ya wanna play?!" With the effort of Archimedes attempting to discover a new algorithm his young mind receded deep into contemplation until it reached the obvious conclusion.

"I KNOW! LET'S PLAY ARMY!"

"YEAH! ARMY, WOW!" Delighted with his playmate's

reception he once again prepared himself to escape mundane reality. Until the argument resumed.

"You be the strikers!"

"Why should I?! My father ain't no arachinist!"

There was no joy in Mudville that day.

Sullivan, along with the Mayor and a small crowd of town officials who wanted to get a good look at the big boy toys now rolling through the streets of Lawrence, met Sweeter at the armory.

Sweeter wasted no time demonstrating his command abilities and even before being properly introduced made a point of issuing a series of orders to his Captain and Lieutenants in front of the town's reception committee.

Scanlon couldn't help but notice that although the junior officers hopped to on Sweeter's command, the crusty old First Sargeant stayed buried in his clip board full of paper work. There was a good reason. He, as did the junior officers, had already heard all the orders on the way into town. Essentially the same orders which were agreed upon when issued back at the drill hall prior to marshaling and move out.

After preliminary introductions Sullivan made it known he was anxious to be part of the game. "Colonel, I have my men posted all along the gates of the major mills." He assumed the appropriate pseudo-military posture. "I thought we could have a strategy meeting -"

"Chief Sullivan, Gentlemen, make no mistake about it. This is not a strike by some disgruntled workers. This is not an industrial action prompted by an argument over a few pennies more or less per hour. This is nothing less than an anarchistic revolution to wage a war of class struggle throughout the United States which threatens our way of life, and must be stopped at all costs!"

Although he was yet to realize it, John Scanlon, Lawrence's elected leader, was no longer in charge of his own city.

* * * * * * *

# Paddy Kelly

An Eighteenth Century French philosopher once wrote that you can judge a society by how it treats the most helpless of its population, its prisoners and elderly.

The Commonwealth of Massachusetts has remained one of only four commonwealths in The United States because she prides herself on her legal system. A system which is significantly different than that of the federal states. More even handed. More equitable. More representative of what the Founding Fathers had in mind. So goes the theory.

These thoughts of equitability were the last thing which ran through Judge Mahoney's mind as he raced down the spacious, marble-lined corridors of justice and commerce in the Boston state House on Court Square that chilly, early February morning.

As the location of the public arraignment was kept confidential, (which is why most of the press were there), court room 606B was nearly devoid of members of the public.

After considerable trouble Joe, Rocco and Gino found the room and took a seat in the back of the nearly full public gallery.

All stood and waited as Mahoney, well known for his anonymous contributions of weekly, two column articles on anti-labor to the local press, floated into the court room on a wave of black robe. The side door slammed behind him and he quickly took the bench.

Surrounded by pistol wheeling, burley bailiffs Antonio Colombo, Urbana DePrato, Ferris Mared as well as several others branded as 'accessories', were in chains off to one side of the court.

Mahoney was known as an efficient man and so didn't bother with the formality of calling the hearing to session, acknowledging who was present and who wasn't or asking the charges. He already knew them, as well as the outcome. He just picked up the single sheet of paper in front of him and read aloud.

"You are charged with illegally transporting dangerous explosives across state lines. Illegal possession of dangerous explosives. Planting dangerous explosives with intent to do bodily harm. Attempt to do bodily harm. Planting dangerous explosives with intent to commit murder. Intent to commit murder. Intent to destroy private property. Each charge carrying a maximum sentence of five to twenty years. How do you plead?"

"Defense wishes to enter not guilty pleas on behalf of all the defendants, your honor." The young lawyer stood alone behind the defense table to the right of the bench. "Additionally for the record your Honor, may I state with the exception of Mr. Carlucci, all the defendants are bone fide citizens of the United States and established businessmen of the Commonwealth."

There were so many lawyers at the prosecutor's table two of them were required to stand as all the chairs were occupied by District Attorney Pelletier and half his staff.

"Making their crime all the more heinous, councillor, as it marks them as traitors as well! Bailiff, alter the docket! Trial will commence this day next month! Jury selection will be set for the day prior. Dismissed!" The defendants, having expected there to be more than the heated exchange, stared in bewilderment.

"Well lads, at least we'll get a speedy trial!" The young lawyer remarked still standing in front of the juror's docket where the eight prisoners were now additionally guarded by no less than six shotgun bearing sheriff's deputies to reinforce the ten bailiffs.

As the police started to guide the shackled prisoners out of the room one of the younger Italians had just enough time to say something to Colombo who passed the question off to the I.W.W. lawyer.

"He ask, 'what just happened?'" Colombo relayed.

"Justice." Quipped the lawyer. Sensing the fear they felt he put his hand on the young Italian's shoulder as the gang of bailiffs began to lead them away. "Tell him not to worry. It'll be okay." Colombo held eye contact with the lawyer then relayed the message, minus the lack of conviction.

Rocco and Ettor who had, along with about half dozen supporters, all the judge would allow in the courtroom, had witnessed the farce from the gallery. Rocco looked at Ettor who spoke first.

"Now it's getting serious. If anything happens to me first

222

thing you do is get Haywood down here! You got that?" Rocco just nodded. "There's something else." He glanced around the courtroom at the reporters still milling around. "Let's go outside."

Overwhelmed by what he had just witnessed Angelo glanced to his left. Gino was smiling at an attractive, twenty-something reporter in the press gallery. She did her womanly duty and ignored him. Rocco elbowed his mate hard in the ribs.

"Hey! We have work to do!"

"I am working!" He smiled at her again. "Meet you back in Lawrence." He whispered to Rocco who shook his head as Gino made his way over to the reporter.

"Buono fortuno! She's out of your league!"

"I don't need no luck!"

"Idiota!" Rocco mumbled. Gino moved in for the kill and Rocco left to meet Joe out in the hall.

"Let's duck in here." Once inside the toilets Joe washed his hands until the lone occupant left then took Angelo over to the rear window.

"I'm going to ask you this and I want a straight answer. I already know the answer . . ."

"Save your breath! It's none of my people!"

"You're sure?!"

"As a precaution I will check it out, but with us all working 16 to 18 hour shifts when the hell would they have the time? Where would they get the money to buy that much dynamite? And you think any of my people would be stupid enough to leave a whole case out in the open? Besides, and more importantly, what would we have to gain by it!?"

"Exactly what I said when they came for me."

"Came for you?! When?"

"At Morretti's on Lawrence."

"How did they know you were in his drug store?"

"I've been followed night and day since I stepped off the train. Now you will be too." Angelo looked down and shook his head.

"I told you it would dangerous."

"What happened at Morretti's?"

"They seized my satchel. Broke it open then tried to take

it."

"You stop them?"

"No. Dr. Morretti, bless his little old heart! He knew they'd plant evidence. Said he'd testify in court that there was nothing in it when they took it. They gave it back and disappeared."

"Now what?"

"Follow up, make sure none of you're people are connected to any of this. I'll let New York know what's happening."

\* \* \* \* \* \* \*

It was only a matter of days before the strike leaders realized that Sullivan's police had decided they were no longer subject to the jurisdiction of the City Council and its elected members after they forcibly halted mass picketing despite Scanlon and the City Council's promise to allow it. To counteract this the strike leaders quickly adopted a new tactic. Passing slowly enmassé through the stores and shops of the merchants, the majority of which now avidly supported the mill owners. This tactic so intimidated the local shop's' clientèle that for the better part of a week the downtown shops remained all but deserted.

By Thursday, to the detriment of the I.W.W., the alienation of the merchants was complete. Sweeter now had the excuse he needed to outlaw groups of people larger than three. This encouraged some stupid police to harass and in several cases arrest, anyone they desired including lifelong citizens of Lawrence, some of them even members of the City Council.

Meanwhile, back at the ranch, O'Reilly's Citizen Association was transitioning into a state of crisis. Actually, transitioning is not totally accurate, as they had been conceived and formed in a state of crisis. Beyond riding out of the fog like a herd of American Valkyries and saving the chastity of Lady Liberty, they had no idea what the hell to do much less how to accomplish it. Then again, these things happen when you're disorganized and leaderless. So they held a meeting.

# Paddy Kelly

"I say we march, damn it! Just like the strikers! Right down the middle of Broadway! Let 'em know we're here!" Herb Stimple suggested as he broke the five minute silence with the first of the suggestions called for by the Chair. Half the table and a quarter of the people standing around the room in the cheap seats groaned and covered their eyes.

"Is that the best you can come with, Herb?"

"Hold on! He might be onto something!" Interjected O'Reilly. "If we can show them anarchists what it is to be true Americans, they'll get the idea this country ain't up for grabs!"

"And what better way to do it then to take over the streets with a good old fashion American parade?!" Herb defended.

"That's right! Take back the streets! Let them know our town ain't just free to anybody, damn it!"

"Frank! Language!"

"Sorry, Mrs. Abecromni."

"We'll get the band from the fire house to play the national anthem!"

"Good idea! They use bands all the time! Works for them should work for us!"

"We gotta have flags, damn it! Lotts'a flags!"

"LANGUAGE! Gentlemen."

"Sorry, Mrs. Abecromni." They answered in unison.

"Where we gonna get so many flags on such short notice?!"

"The dry good store's got 'em on sale!"

"Yeah, but they ain't got nearly enough!"

"We could get somebody to make them up!" Someone suggested.

"Yeah but who we gonna get to make up so many flags on such short notice?" O'Reilly countered.

"Hold on." Herb scurried to the back storage closet and was back in a flash and half with a small wooden crate.

"Herb? What in Tarnation you doin'?" Herb answered as he rummaged through the crate of various sized American flags.

"One of the old Council memebers had a pot full of flags made for the Fourth of July a few years back! A coupl'a dozen

225

cases. This is the last of 'em." He found one he was happy with and started searching along the seams. "Ought to be a manufacturer's tag here some where."

As a solution to the last hurdle in the cunning, foolproof plan fell into place, Herb Stimple had the full attention of the room. A short man stepped forward from the standing room only back wall just as Herb found the tag.

"Well, where was they made?!" Short man asked. Herb's smile melted from his face and dripped to the floor.

"Wood's Mill's Lawrence, Massachusettes."

\* \* \* \* \* \* \*

Harriet Beacher Stowe, following her success with *Uncle Tom's Cabin*, enjoyed a royal invite to England by invitation of Victoria. On a tour of the Scottish Highlands during the infamous brutal 'Clearances' she was in full agreement with the Queen as to the justification for the inhumane proceedings and commented that the peasant rabble had indeed to be removed to, ". . . make way for progress." One can only speculate how strongly Stowe would have condemned the Eastern and Middle European mill workers and their dwellings in the Lawrence of 1912.

So bad were the domicile conditions of the workers that a Presidentially appointed senate committee found that so far below the national standard were the housing conditions of the immigrant workforce that they defied measure under the present ratings.

"Gurley Flynn!" The tall, balding, bespectacled man called out.

"I'm here!" Elizabeth sprang from her chair and moved to the tall counter. After an hour and a half wait she was happy to move anywhere. Even if it was just across the sprawling municipal office.

"What is it I can do for you, Miss Flynn?"

"I'm in Lawrence with the I.W.W."

"The I Won't Works." Someone mumbled in the background. The Assistant Chief Building Inspector betrayed no reaction.

"I'm interested in what you can tell me about the mill worker's housing situation?"

"You must have a pretty good idea by now. You were out there yesterday. And the day before. Wednesday as well I'm told." He let it sink in.

"Yes, I do. The entire mill workers' neighborhood is made of single tenement lots holding two tenements each. The rear tenements are only accessible through dank narrow allies, one person at a time. The buildings are all timber with no fire escapes." His only discernible movement was a single blink. "I visited over a dozen of the four story tenements. Each with **one** common toilet for the entire tenement. With four to six people per room that's up to sixty people per toilet. You ever heard of dysentery?"

"Miss Flynn . . ."

"Cholera? Of the fifty or so families I spoke to, all of them have had to take in boarders to make ends meet . . ."

"Miss Flynn. Each year . . ."

"You do understand there are federal regulations regarding basic living needs and that . . ."

"MISS FLYNN!" Hallway traffic halted, paper stopped shuffling and cumbersome typing machines fell silent. He adjusted his glasses then, as if made of granite, he stood motionless. "EACH . . . year . . . Each year without fail, I have recommended to the City Council to take up the matter of revising the building ordinances. And each year the proposal is buried by said Council."

"A council no doubt dominated by members who are property owners and don't want taxes increased?"

"Very good! And, who believe that these conditions are good enough for the likes of the 'Honkies, Wops and Poles' you so self-righteously defend. These mill owners live in Boston, New York and elsewhere. They could care less about the housing situation in Lil 'ol Lawrence, Massachusetts. They pay no taxes here and thanks to the Federal tariff laws, and other factors . . ."

"Laundered books, bribes, pay-offs . . ."

"Other factors! The mills pay only a nominal tax. Which

leaves the homeowners and shopkeepers to bear the tax burden. Do you think for a New York City second these people want to pay more money so foreign born laborers can improve their standard of living while taking jobs away from legitimate Americans?"

As she exited the office, Flynn was angry but gratified that the hour and a half wait and the one minute visit rose to her expectations.

"NEXT!" The clerk yelled out once again.

Although she knew the tariffs existed, the full impact of their shield had just begun to sink in. As she descended the narrow staircase she made a mental note to dig deeper into the Schedule K rulings.

Exiting onto Lawrence Street she looked up from buckling the waist strap on her heavy wool over coat in time to see two soldiers quick-stepping behind a young officer, moving in her direction. Flynn stepped aside to allow them access to the doorway. But they weren't there for City business.

"Miss Elizabeth Flynn?"

"Yes?" By this early point in her career Flynn had been arrested too many times to get flustered in front of the enemy. She knew the routine better than most lawyers.

"You're required to come with us."

"Oh? Am I under arrest?" The Lieutenant's military bearing showed only the slightest sign of cracking, but it was enough.

"No Ma'am."

"Then under what authority are you detaining me?"

"Orders from Colonel Sweeter, Ma'am." He stepped closer to her, out of earshot of his smirking riflemen. "I'm not arresting you Miss Flynn. They want to ask you a few questions, that's all. You'll be home by dinner time."

"Said Mrs. Lincoln as they left for the theatre." The older of the two guards laughed.      "Let's go Pershing!" She took the lead.

Flynn fought back the sensation of mild alarm as they passed a long column of troop transport trucks parked all along the avenue. Disembarking troops were merging into company formations and even to Flynn's untrained eye it was apparent that this sector of the city had been turned into a marshalling point.

"More troops?!"

"There are anarchists in league with the workers. The Colonel thought it prudent to call up another twenty-two companies."

"TWENTY-TWO companies?! Think that'll be enough?" Then her professional bearing broke as she stopped walking and stared in disbelief.

An M. P. was directing two of the trucks to pull up and clear the intersection of Lawrence and Canal. Several horse drawn caissons appeared hauling small artillery pieces.

"My god! You people never learn, do you?"

"Learn what Ma'am?"

"The question was rhetorical, Lieutenant."

\* \* \* \* \* \* \*

Foss was in the en suite bath adjoining his office tying his tie when Holman entered the room.

"Give it to me short and sweet. I want to get this press conference over with as soon as possible. I've got to get out to Springfield to the fund raisers' dinner."

"Your car and driver are standing by. There are as many as eight in custody with more arrests expected." Holman read from a single sheet, typed report as he addressed the Governor from across the expansive office.

"The State Police report half a dozen cases were found, possibly more. Enough to blow up the largest of the mills and then some."

"I want maximum penalties handed out to these bastards, you understand?!"

"I'll see the right people get the word, sir."

"And I want the state's Attorney General to handle this himself." He ordered as he crossed the room to exit.

"He intends to sir. Also, I've already drawn up press releases for the campaign tying this in with your 'Tough On Crime' platform."

"That's good! I'll use that at the fundraiser dinner tonight."

"Good luck Governor!"

"Thanks Holman. " Foss crossed the room and poured himself a drink. "New Times, Harsher Crimes, more Time! Somethin' like that. How's that sound?"

"Catchy, sir." Right before Foss opened the large wooden double doors to exit he turned back to his Secretary.

"Looks like the Commonwealth of Massachusetts has successfully tested that statute."

"Looks like it, Governor."

Foss stepped through the doors and out onto the capital's balcony overlooking the massive lobby. Holman remained in the office and quietly closed the doors behind the Governor as a plethora of magnesium sulphate flashes flared in rapid succession.

*******

Although Sam Gompers wasn't short on self righteous arrogance and liked to preach that the Industrial Workers of the World weren't recognized in the adult world of labor unions, he wasn't stupid.

As events in Lawrence escalated and began to leak into the mainstream press, Sam, in an effort to attempt to undercut the Wobblies and get a foot hold in Lawrence, made the decision to make a brief trip up there to consult with his top man, Golden. Neither had expected the press to pay any attention to their get together, but were not taken off guard by the dozen or so reporters which now cordoned themselves across the steps of the U. T. W hall as they tried to enter. Quickly realizing they had a real P. R. opportunity, they paused on the top step to allow questions.

"Yes, we believe the workers are justified in striking. But the outrageous manner in which the leadership is conducting the strike is totally unacceptable." Gompers retorted in answer to the first question thrown at him.

"Mr. Golden, why are you here? Are you here in the

capacity of United Textile Worker & the American Federation of Labor's representative? "

"Actually, yes I am. I was asked by the City Council to come in and quell the strike."

Golden threw him a sideways glance.

"When did you meet with the City Council, sir?"

"Earlier. Next question!"

"Are you here to cooperate with the I. W. W.?"

"There's nothing to cooperate with. The A. F. of L. does not recognize the I. W. W. as an organization."

"Mr. Gompers, is it not a fact that over 32,000 men and women are out on strike and are organized? By the I. W. W.?"

"I suppose they are. But what of it? This is nothing more than a class conscious revolution. A passing event that is not intended to be an organization for the protection of the immediate rights or promotion of the near future interests of the workers."

"Mr. Gompers, would you not agree that in a 'Free Society', these workers have every right to choose whom they wish to lead them?" Gompers hesitated before responding.

"They have the right to express themselves as their conscience dictates." A tall, gangly reporter elbowed his way to the front and took advantage of Gompers' pause to shoe horn his question in.

"Do you believe that it is the spirit of the workers that is most dangerous to mill owners, sir?" Gompers frowned and looked away. Mary Heaton Vorse, veteran labor reporter pushed the issue. "It's as if the tired gray crowds constantly ebbing in and out of the mill had suddenly awakened and opened their mouths to sing! Wouldn't you agree, Sam?" She purposely quoted one of her own recent editorials. He paused with the massive entrance door half open.

"While I don't share your enthusiasm Miss Vorse, in light of the current I. W. W. induced violence, I'm not sure singing is going to contribute to the labor struggle! Thank you. That's all."

"There are reports that your A. F. of L. are putting forth a feverish effort to keep the skilled workers from joining the strike."

"Thank you. That'll be all for now. Thank you for your cooperation, Ladies. Gentlemen."

Scurrying towards a back office Gompers pushed Golden for details on the skilled workers.

"Any of them talking about going out?" Being exposed to the atmosphere of the situation first hand, Gompers was dealing with the reality of his skilled laborers aiding the strike efforts, voluntarily or other wise.

"Going out's not the problem. It's getting them back in! Only certain departments of three of the mills are running due to most of the laborers being out and not generating any raw material for the tradesmen and so, even though technically they're open, they aren't producing anything!"

"Then why in the hell is Wood keeping them open?"

"He says they'd rather run them at a loss then give in to those 'anarchist bastards!'" Gompers picked up the pace as they neared the office. "Besides, not too many of the tradesmen are willing to go up against three or four thousand picketers at one time."

"Our best bet is to keep the skilled workers and tradesmen from joining the strike." Gompers offered.

"Shouldn't be too difficult. The Germans have already separated themselves and refused to join in."

"Good! Then we issue an ultimatum to the owners. Separate negotiations with the U.T.W. and the skilled workers by . . .by . . ."

"Two weeks?" Golden consulted his pocket notes. "By the . . . twentieth?"

"By the twentieth. Either they start talking to us or we walk. We want 15%, double time for overtime and elimination of the premium system. They'll be a few other things to throw in there later. I'll get a list to you by day after tomorrow. Get it to Wood right away. Put the onus on them to light a fire under Sweeter's ass and get those troops to do their job and open those damn mills!"

They entered the U.T.W. Office and took their seats, Gompers behind the massive desk.

"Let's wrap this up. I've got the Shop Stewards coming in five minutes."

Now in the middle of the fifth week several of the many infiltrators sent by Sam Gompers reported that as the owners predicted, the combination of the harsh Winter, the worst in 50 years recorded history, and lack of money was already taking it's toll on the mill workers. Some households were compelled to scavange for fire wood, burning articles of furniture to supplement what they could beg, borrow or steal for fuel to keep the young children from being claimed by the elements.

Fully realizing the implications of the outcome of the 'Battle of Lawrence', Gompers had ordered daily updates on the situation.

"Now an immediate, strategy, What do they need most?" Gompers asked.

"Food." Golden shot back. "Some of our agents report that some of the Syrians are on one meal a day."

"Good! Set up a relief station. Soup and bread, that sort of thing, nothing fancy. Give them all they need." Astonishment laced Golden's face. "With a condition." Golden smirked.

And with that, the A.F.L. leadership hatched the Great Lawrence Soup Plot.

*******

Gompers may have, as did Scanlon, Sweeter and even Foss at various times, seen himself as the great savior come to Lawrence to " . . . quell the strike.", but Wood and the owners didn't see it that way. Gompers' and Golden's 'offer' to them was virtually ignored. Not only did the Bosses let the deadline come and go, they didn't even acknowledge the telegram.

A few weeks later, in a terse reply, they offered a 5% across the board, no extras, take it or leave it. Gompers, having backed himself into a corner, took it knowing full well he couldn't push them any further. However, his ham-fisted approach combined with the unwavering attitude of the strike leaders, put the U. T. W. in a worse position than before. By this point so many laborers were out, none of the mills could operate anyway.

To compound Gompers' headaches many U. T. W. members had been gradually deciding to join or support the strike and by now a noticeable number of them had seen the logic in the Wobblie's arguments. Combined with the slap in the face of an inferior counter offer by the mill Bosses, most of them made up their minds, were pushed over the edge and took to the Pickett lines.

Ironically at this time in the struggle, how the U. T. W. would come out of the fight now depended solely on how the I. W. W. conducted the rest of the battle.

However, with this welcome development came bad news. Gompers' efforts to dry up the Wobblies' national contribution fund, although having been only partially successful, were strongly bolstered by the negative press brought on by the dynamite plot.

Overnight, donations slowed to a sporadic trickle.

Paddy Kelly

Lawrence bore no resemblance to a typical
American city. The entire inner-city
district had now become a series of armed,
military camps replete with machine gun
nests, roving patrols, and, just in case
the Bolsheviks had booked passage on H.M.S.
Lusitania,         artillery.

**- Anonymous**

## CHAPTER SIXTEEN

L ate that afternoon, as he was not called for picket duty, Alfonso was at home. Returning from the community toilet at the end of the hall he entered the two room, dilapidated, timber-framed apartment where he and his family resided. He was shocked to see his wife entering the front door just ahead of him, tears streaming silently from her tired eyes as she listlessly shuffled into the main room. It was obvious she had been crying for some time.

The four children looked up from their various positions on the floor where they were occupied with their wooden toys. Alfonso quickly moved to her.

"Como stai?!"

"Bene, bene!" She said weakly.

"NO BENE! What's wrong?!" He took her firmly by the shoulders with both hands.

"We went down to . . ."

"Speak English!" He nodded to the children scattered around the floor of the cramped room. Her speech became stilted and deliberate.

"We go down to . . . the new relief center. Some men are going through dee street and they say, 'free soup and bread, free soup and bread', and hold'a up signs."

"Okay." Due to her emotionally drained state she relapsed into Italian. Alfonso, more enraged by the tears welling in her eyes, didn't notice.

"They said the food was compliments of the A. F. L."

"Who you go with?"

" Signora Poropolus."

"Okay Bella, tell me."

"After two hours of standing in line, in the freezing cold the man asked me, 'How many people are in your family?' I said to him, six. He said, 'Good, then you can have double ration.' My heart soared! I gave him my pail, but he pushed it back to me. I was confused. Then he said, 'First, you must sign this paper.' I said, 'What is this paper?' He said, 'This paper says you and your husband, and your children will be members in the A.F.L. and no longer members in the Industrial Workers of the World."'

.  "Did you sign this paper?!" Her look of indignation was more than answer. His reaction was immediate. He did up his braces as he charged into the bedroom emerging seconds later checking the action on a Barretta 9mm.

"What kind of people do this thing?" She pleaded.

"Where is this relief station?" He demanded.

"Cherry Street, near the butcher's. What are going to do?!"

"Get some soup. Stay here with the children . . ."

"Alfonso, if . . ."

"DO YOU UNDERSTAND ME?! NO MATTER WHAT HAPPENS!"

"Yes." Having heard the row Mr. and Mrs. Poropolus were standing across the dimly lit hall in their doorway as Alfonso stormed through the narrow hallway and started down the staircase. Mrs. Poropolus immediately moved to comfort Signora Affanoso. Hugging her friend tightly she realized her husband was still standing behind her leaning on the doorjamb. Reaching over she slapped him on the side of the head.

"What are you gawking at! Go and help him!"

"ALRIGHT! I GO! Only don't hit!"

"You need hit sometimes, you big mule!"

"ALRIGHT! Only don't hit!" Scurrying down the narrow hall after Affanoso, Poropolus took time to turn back to his wife who was now watching over the shoulder of Alfonsos's wife as they embraced. "You hit me, maybe I get hurt, then you don't get none of this!" He gyrated his hips with his hands behind his head.

"I don't need none of this! I need younger man!"

"OHHH! Good luck to you, old woman!"

"GO! Just GO! It will be finished before you start! As usual."

Grateful for the opportunity to regain her composure, Affanoso's wife was hard pressed to curtail a giggle at the middle-aged, Greek couple's banter.

237

"Thank'a you, Angelica."

"Agghh! Some day we all have nice place to live. We have big dinner with all the families, and we tell stories." Angelica comforted.

"Yes . . ." Affo's wife added as the Greek woman wiped a tear from her neighbor's cheek.

". . . but what kind of stories we tell?"

Down at street level a half dozen other mill hands from the tenement were outside in the cold Winter's air shifting a donation of coal from the back of a small, open bed lorry to buckets and various containers. Observing Affanoso storming down the street still clad only in his shoes, trousers, braces and undershirt, they instantly sensed something was up. From his agitated state they instinctively knew what ever it was it had to do with the Bosses and so couldn't be good. They straggled after him bringing broom handles, shovels and various improvised weapons with them.

Although it was a weekday, the military patrols ordered by Sweeter had not only cleared the mill districts but secondarily discouraged most other traffic in the city giving the city streets a temporary early Sunday morning feel. Overnight a thin layer of snow had coated the city and so the only sound discernible that mid-day was the crunching of the snowy crust as the men strode west on Maple Street.

Five minutes later the small group turned onto Cherry Street and a policeman on the corner saw them. Given the heightened, panic-stricken atmosphere of the last few weeks he wasted no time and ran towards the nearest military post, three blocks west.

By the time they reached the kosher butcher's shop Affanoso saw a group of about twenty women engaged in a heated argument in the doorway of the relief station across the street. He pushed his way through the gaggle where there were two men behind the long soup counter engaged in busy work and a third standing by a mill hand bent over a table apparently signing his name to something.

Affanoso may have been hot tempered but he wasn't stupid. He kept the Baretta tucked neatly in his trouser pocket as he entered the store-front shop. The two soup workers didn't immediately tick on to the developing situation but the one with the mill worker looked up at the overtly aggressive man.

"Which one of you is Golden?" Asked Affo.

"I am!" He answered, bolstered by a false sense of confidence.

Affanoso wasted no time but vaulted the counter and with his left hand clasped Golden by the throat and slammed the terrified agent backwards against the wall behind the counter and thrust the pistol under his chin. One of the younger women screamed.

Two of the men with Affo moved to stand on either side of the mill worker who had only began to sign the A. F. L. application form. A quiet, "Get out!" was all that was required for him to understand his position. The women parted like the Red Sea as he scurried through the front door and vanished down the quiet street.

One of the Armenian women gathered in the entrance quickly dispatched her two children to the opposite ends of the street to act as lookouts.

"How much is the soup now, fangulo?!" Alfonso asked, the bile of contempt welling in his throat.

"I . . . I was just . . ."

"SHUT UP'A YOU FACE!" The other two men stood stark still. There was no question, Affanoso was in charge. "YOU, give them soup!" The women in the doorway stared in disbelief. Affo leered back at the women. "You want soup?! GO!"

The women scurried to the counter, pails in hand. The two men were already there, ladles dripping with vegetable broth, to greet them. "Bread too, assholes!" The men immediately complied.

"What are you doing?! You just can't . . ." Golden weakly protested.

Suddenly from the corner of Maple and Cherry one of the Armenian youngsters sounded the alarm. The women looked to Alfonso who instantly began to give orders.

"You two in the back! Now! You, give me your coat."

He ordered one of Golden's men. "You stay here!" He ordered Golden. "Take off your coats!" His fellow mill workers complied while he donned the white clerk's jacket.

"You two, get busy doing something! One of you collect all the shovels, put them in the back. You with the broom, the floor is dirty."

"Si Alfonso!" He began leisurely sweeping up. By this time the women had formed an orderly line along the counter.

"If there is shooting , you will be the first!" Affo kept the gun at his side hidden from plain sight by the tall counter but still in sight of Golden. "You came here to help us, so help! Fill the pails!" Golden was relegated to dispensing generous portions of the steaming soup to the women.

A squad of soldiers holding their weapons at high port with the policeman in tow, double timed up to the shop and while six of them formed a cordon arching into the street the rest shoved their way in and cleared a path through the women. Through the front door strode a well polished young Lieutenant who may have seen one too many picture shows. Anxious to assert his command, pistol drawn and held at waist level, he quickly surveyed the premises.

"Don't forget your bread Mrs. Zaydoon." Affanso happily offered. With tears in her eyes the thirty-something woman going on fifty took the bread without answering and scurried around the officer and out the door. In the back Golden's men froze but the mill workers carried on as if the soldiers weren't there.

"We got a report of a disturbance. Everything alright here Mr. Golden?" Golden felt the pistol muzzle pressed into his lower ribs.

"No problem fellas. Everything is in hand."

"You've got extra help today?" The officer noted.

"Yeah, big day today. Volunteers from the U. T. W. Hall."

Hesitantly, but satisfied, the L.T. holstered his revolver and retired to the street where he sharply issued a series of orders and assembled his troops into squad formation and marched them back from whence they came.

More women, some with children in tow, began appearing at the soup kitchen.

Just as the situation seemed to resolve itself a boy in his late teens, merrily bounced through the front door and approached Affanoso and Golden.

"Who?" Affo quietly demanded of Golden.

"Our daily courier. From headquarters."

"So Gompers **is** behind your little scheme!"

"He's nothing to do with it."

"Don't tell me. He doesn't even know?!" He mocked.

The women continued to eagerly collect their double rations of soup and bread.

"Morning Mr. Golden."

"Morning . . . Stewart." Golden choked out his reply.

"Here for your afternoon order sir."

"Oh, we'll go for the same . . ." The pistol pressed harder into his flank. " . . . ahh better double, ahh, triple the order Stewart. It's going pretty good down here."

"Wow! Mr. Gompers' office will be thrilled when he finds out! See ya at two Mr. Golden." As the courier exited more women lined up and the queue now snaked out the front door and halfway down the block.

"How much your normal order?"

"Two hundred loaves of bread and a fifty gallons of soup."

"Very nice. You and you stay with me." He was careful not to use his colleagues names.

"We wait until two. You others get out and tell rest of women to be here at two when trucks come."

As the ones with food left the station Poropolus made a comment in Greek. Golden, who was still dolling out generous portions of soup was puzzled. Affo translated.

"He say, don't you feel better now you do the right thing?" The union official, unamused continued to stare at Affanoso.

"Don't forget your bread ladies." Alfonso pleasantly reminded.

# The American Way

*******

Gino's air of self presence was as strong as it had ever been in his twelve years in America as he entered the spacious lobby of the Hearst Press Building just off Broadway. As if his ego needed support he felt an inflated sense of importance when the elevator operator grandly announced, "Fourth floor, sir!" He turned right and headed for the Editor's office.

"Good morning."

"Good morning." Gino responded to the clerk at the counter of the City Desk. There was an awkward pause as he suddenly attempted to plan his strategy.

"Can I help you?" The elderly gentleman asked.

"Yes. I would'a like'a to see you copies from'a the . . ." He rummaged around in his trouser pocket for a non-existent note paper.

Nina Vorst's desk was in the back of the office but close enough to recognize the heavy accent as the funny little Italian who approached her in the court room. Was he back here for her or did she smell a story? Only one way to find out.

Tea cup in hand she took the long route around the room and passed within inches of the desk clerk. Gino's smirk told her she was on the right track.

"Miss Vorst, this gentleman would like to access the files."

"Thank you Henry. I think I can handle him." Henry retired to more pressing business at the coffee station in the back, Gino turned on the charm and Vorst turned on the cooling fans. Let the games begin.

"I noticed'a you in'a da court the other day."

"I noticed you noticing me in the court the other day. In English we call it gawking."

"Gawking. That's'a nice. Eet means something good, no?"

"It means something good, no. You always go to court rooms to gawk at reporters?"

"No, no, no! I'm'a actually here doing'a report on'a Italian-American relations."

"What sort of relations Mr. . . "

"Perrelli. Gino Perrelli. My friends they call me Gino."

"What can I do for you, Mr. Perrelli?" Gino knew the jig was up.

"I need'a somebody to help me."

"Take a number."

"To help me with'a information." She casually sipped her tea.

"What kind of information?"

"What'a time do your press setters come to work?"

"You're with the Wobblies!"

"What'a time do your press setters come to work?" Gino noticed a well dressed man in the back office, sitting at a large desk gawking at him through the partition window. The Assistant Editor had always noticed Vorst in and around the office. Now he noticed her at the counter with the dark-haired stranger.

"I need'a to know when the paper of'a the twenty-fifth was'a sent to press."

"You're investigating the dynamite plot! What do have!?" She set her cup on the counter and moved closer. "Have you been to the *Boston-American?*" She made no attempt to hide her suspicion.

"The what? No! I come into you first!" She breifly gagged as she went to sip her tea.

"You wanna reword that, cowboy? "

"What'a you say?" She was suddenly convinced of his innocence. Nobody that naive could be a spy.

"They come in at around half six and start work at seven. By midnight the type is set and printing starts. Why? What are you onto?"

"The papers? What'a time the papers go out?" Her curiosity was too aroused to let this one get away. Just as the Assistant Editor approached the pair Vorst caught sight of him.

"Follow me Mr. Perelli."

"Can I help you, Miss Vorst?"

"Thanks Bill. We got it." She let Gino through the small swing gate and guided him back to the shelves of files.

"*The Boston-American?*" Gino queried.

243

"It's a Hearst sheet, like us and *The American.*" She pulled a bound, broadsheet sized volume from the morgue shelf. "Here. This is the volume with the reproduction sheets up till yesterday. You'll find your paper in there. Stay here! Don't wander off. I'll be right back."

A moment later she returned with her note book as Gino sat at a small table perusing a paper he had pulled from the shelves.

"Early edition seven o'clock. So eet was off'a the presses and on the stands maybe about'a six in the morning, si?"

"Yeah, six, half six, depends where in the city. Joe Donohue wrote the article. He said he had a line on a hot story the day before. Gave it to the Editor around half eleven, twelve that morning."

The penny dropped.

"Gino!"

"Miss Vorst!" He teased.

"Stop that!"

"What?"

"Listen to me!"

"You have all my ears. And'a my eyes and'a my heart, bella! Teamo! Marry me!" Her answer came by way of her note book. She flipped it open to a certain page and held it in front of his eyes.

"The Prosecutor submitted the evidence. On the avadavat the official time of discovery by the detective was five p.m. of the twenty-fifth." Gino sat bolt upright.

"He had'a the story before they find'a the dynamite!"

"Five hours or more before they find'a the dynamite!" She teased back.

"We have to get'a this to the Persecutor!"

"It's prosecutor and don't waste your time. They've probably already seen it!"

"Then we must to get'a this to the other papers!"

"Forget it. They won't print it."

"Why?! Thees exonerate us and'a the I.W.W.!"

"Which is exactly why they won't print it."

"Well, we no just gonna sit here and do'a nothing! What

do we do, miss fancy reporter?"

"The cops must've had an informer. . . ."

"How you know?"

"Because if they did it on their own there'd be a long windy story of how they cracked the case, then there'd be handshakes and drinks all around followed by a medal or two with Scanlon making a speech."

"Oh. Just like in'a Italy."

"We need to find the informer, and then get the story out to the New York papers."

"Shouldn't be hard. It got to be someone in Wood's . . ."

"Excuse me." Bill The Editor suddenly appeared and confronted Gino. "Can I help you?"

"No thank'a you. I . . ." Bill narrowed his eyes at Gino.

"You with the I.W.W.?"

"The what? "

"He's doing a story . . ." Vorst intercepted.

"No, I with the I.W.H.A. "

"The what? "

"The Italian World History Association. We are doing a study on'a the great Italian explorers of'a the fifteenth Century." The Editor glared at him then at Vorst who was barley able to suppress a smirk. Gino read him like a telegraph. He swung around in his chair and threw a casual arm over the back cross piece. . "Did'a you know eet was an Italian who first discover America?"

"Oh yeah? I happen to know Columbus wasn't the first to discover America! We ran a story on it last year. Happens we know there were others here long before Columbus!"

"Actually hees name was'a Colombo, but you are right! He wasn't'a the first." Gino gave him a friendly tap on the arm. "Was another man."

"So I'm right, Mr. Eye-talian Historian!"

"Yes, you are right! It wasn't'a Columbus." Bill's smirk would have lit an auditorium. But only temporarily.

"It was Americo Vespucci.

'There is something tragically wrong with
a system of justice which can and does
make criminals of honest men and can
only convict gangsters when they
don't pay their taxes.'

**- Raymond Chandler**
**In a letter to James Sandoe,**

## CHAPTER SEVENTEEN

**D**ue to their loyalty to the mill owners and lack of sympathy for the foreign workers, later reinforced by the mass picketing maneuvers used by the strikers, the shop keepers had initially been a major influence in the over all anti-strike activity. While not wanting to appear to take sides, they consistently supported Scanlon, Sullivan and Sweeter with any ordnance or regulation they wanted to implement as long it was in line with their self interest and the leaders promised to keep the strikers away from the shopping district.

It took Gurley Flynn less than a day to run her idea by the committees who endorsed it wholeheartedly, then get word to the prominent shop keepers about the open meeting. To her surprise most of the merchants she invited showed up that afternoon for her meeting at the Syrian Hall.

She started off by talking to the group who were scattered around the room, about the unity of the major capitalists and the elimination of their differences. How they split the forces of labor with their unity, employers' associations and their control of the police and military. They pit labor groups one against the other, skilled against unskilled and worse, children against parents as in the Wood and Washington mills. This is why, she argued, the A. F. L. belongs to the employers. They protect only skilled, domestic labor, and do that only in conjunction with the employer's ambitions. She paused and perused the room. She turned to the burley man leaning against the far wall I the back.

"Mr. Garfield, thank you for coming."

"Don't thank me yet, lady. It's early!"

"I was in your shop yesterday."

"Oh yeah? Buy anything?!" A few jeers were thrown out as Garfield drew first blood.

"You have some very fine items of jewelry."

"Yeah, too bad I can't display them all!"

"Why is that?"

"One of those Wobbly friends of yours is likely to walk

off with them!" Laughter followed.

"Has anyone here been burgled by any of the mill workers?" She posed the question to the room in general. Other than the sounds of merchants shifting in seats there was complete silence. Finally one of the less overweight ones mustered some courage.

"This strike looks like it has a long way to go. We're in early days yet, Miss Flynn."

"Has anyone **ever** been burgled by **any** of the mill workers. Ever?" Same reaction.

"Vandalized? Cheated?" Still no response. Flynn pulled it back on track. "Mr. Garfield . . ."

"Why you picking on me?!"

"My apologies Mr. Garfield. I'll direct my question to the other gentlemen as well. Gentlemen, with the exception of Mr. Garfield, although I've never met Mrs. Wood . . ."

"She's a fine lady!" Someone called out from the back.

"Doesn't go around the country stirring up trouble for honest, decent merchants!" Another added. Flynn's strategy of isolating and treating the merchant sector of the city as a separate entity was about to be vindicated.

"What exactly does she look like?" She asked.

"Tallish, for a woman . . . Dark hair." Someone shot back.

"Not so tall I think. And her hair is brownish, not so dark." Another added.

"So you've seen her? Up close I mean." Flynn prodded as she moved closer to the group.

"Well . . . once at a parade. Fourth of July."

"I saw her up close! She was in my shop." Came a terse challenge from the rear of the room.

"What did she buy, sir?" Silence again ensued. The formally defiant air of the challenger evaporated into borderline meekness.

"Nothing. She was just shopping. Nothing wrong with that."

"Not at all! Woman's god-given right to shop, isn't? Where'd we be otherwise?" Flynn's comment elicited a mild ripple of laughter. "The point is gentlemen, the lack of patronage by the mill workers is not an indication of their like or dislike for the merchants of Lawrence. It is a direct result of the starvation wages they are expected to live on! Despite the fact mill profits have soared **forty per cent** in the last seven years, the workers' wages have not only not risen, but been reduced by three per cent!" Flynn briskly crossed the room.

"How would you greet me Mr. Jensen, if I strolled into your bakery and said, 'Why that's a fine loaf of bread, sir. But I think I would prefer to pay you three per cent less than that price you ask.' What would I get?"

"A boot up the . . . I would ask you to leave, Miss Flynn." Another ripple of laughter followed.

"Starvation wages! Starvation wages which fluctuate up and down at the whims of the mill owners every time one of their wives or children wants a new suit of clothes."

"Which they will promptly run out and buy!" Garfield fired back.

"On Mass Avenue in Boston. Or on the North Common. Or during a weekend trip to New York. Anywhere but in Lawrence, Massachusetts!" Flynn countered. There was dead silence.

With the subtlety of optic surgery and the impact of a train wreck her point was driven home. She pressed the attack.

It is the police and the Militia - "

"They're here to protect the citizens of Lawrence from the hooliganism of you Wobblies!" A man in the back challenged. Flynn directed her rebuttal straight at the merchant.

"We've said it to The Press, we've said it to the public and I'll say it to you here, again. The goal of this strike is not to instigate a revolution. Not to riot, loot or steal."

"What about the violence?!"

"If you would be so kind. Please site to me, Sir, in the last four and a half weeks of this strike, what violent incident has been perpetrated by myself or any member or supporter of the I.W.W?" There were no takers. "Without exception any violence thus far has been perpetrated, and will continue to be perpetrated, solely by the mill owners, the police and the military authority."

249

"What about the dynamite?!"

"Did anyone actually see any union members plant that dynamite?"

"Who else'd be that stupid? Leave all them explosives layin' around in the open?"

"That remains to be seen." She had been told of Gino and Vorst's discovery but was under strict orders not to reveal what the Wobblies knew. "The purpose of this strike is to gain a decent wage for the men, women and children of the mills. A decent wage which will offer them a decent standard of living." Having done her homework, Gurley Flynn knew the key members of her audience. She made eye contact with the butcher. "One where they can eat meat more than once a month." Then dry goods dealer. "Buy new clothes for the children when the old ones are in rags. Or maybe some nice fresh tomatoes once a week for Sunday supper." The greens grocer feigned nonchalance, but just barely.

"Doesn't matter how much them Pollacks get! You won't see them buying meat in my place!"

"Why's that Mr. Petersen?"

"They all get their sausages posted to them from New York that's why! Meat through the mail! Never heard of such a thing!"

"You're shop has a postal box, does it not?" He grunted yes. "Why don't you research the shipping costs, bring it in at wholesale and offer it at the going price minus what they pay for postage? They get their sausage, save money and, you get to corner the market on pig's knuckles and kielbasa!"

"How about that? Petersen's Polish Pigs Knuckles and Perougies!" One of the other merchants chided. There was outright laughter now.

"Think of it, lads! Upwards of 45 to 50 thousand customers for your relatively few handful of shops!" Two or three sat upright. "And Wood building yet another factory!"

"What do you want from us, Miss Flynn?" It was Garfield who made the next move.

"Support the strike! If you can't find it in you to support the workers, then stay neutral. Don't antagonize them. Don't root for the militia when they attack the strikers."

"What about this mass picketing through our shops?! My legitimate customers are terrified to come in any more!"

"You give me your word as gentlemen not to support Wood and the owners, or at least to remain neutral, and I will give you my word the strikers will no longer picket through your shops. In fact they won't even picket outside your shops so as not to intimidate your regulars."

Sporadic grumblings floated through the room.

"Why should we?!"

"Why? Because, believe me gentlemen, we will win this battle! But if we do not, the result for you will be the same. Haywood will be gone. Ettor, Giovannitti will be gone. I will be gone."

"Thank heaven for small favors!" Someone murmured.

"The door swings both ways. But yourselves and those tens of thousands of workers will remain. They will remember who stood on which side of the fence. And they will spend accordingly."

There was little discussion before Garfield headed for the door.

"Leaving so soon Mr. Garfield?"

"Understand Miss Flynn I'm not swayed by your arguments. But you keep them out of our shops and I'll try and remain neutral."

He didn't bother to shake her hand as she offered, but at least he seemed conciliatory.

\* \* \* \* \* \*

Rabbi Shankum had twice before refused to allow anyone to speak for political purposes in his synagogue. Historically the Jews were no strangers to political strife and have always made it their business to fight for what they believed was right. But in Lawrence, the Rabbi had seen how the Christian community was being manipulated and torn apart by the pulpit politics now taking center stage in the largest of the Catholic churches.

"The first prayer one utters upon entering the Temple. .

251

." He patiently explained to Joe who sat on the other side of his desk, ". . . whether it is a weekday, the Sabbath or a holiday, is the *Ma Tovu*. It is a series of five verses taken from the *Torah* and the prayer is named for the first verse. Ohalekna Ya'akov . . ." He spoke with the hallmark deliberation of a scholar.

". . . mish-kena-tekho, Yisreal. How lovely are your tents, O Jacob, your dwelling places o Isreal!" Ettor finished the prayer. The Rabbi gave a shrewd stare and sat back in his Queen Anne chair.

"Mish-keno-tekha, Yisreal!" The Rabbi corrected right before he removed his glasses. "I am not easily impressed young man. I have known people before to learn just enough to pass themselves off to get what they want. I appreciate your reading about our culture before you came, but . . ." Joe leaned forward and smiled.

"Rabbi, do you mind if we speak Yiddish?"

Twenty minutes later Ettor emerged from the office with a concerned look on his face. The Jews, as were many of the ethnic faction, critical to the cause if the I .W. W.

Gurley Flynn, waiting in the vestibule sensed the bad news, stood and came towards him.

"It's alright we'll try again in a week or so, Joe."

"It's no use. Besides, we won't need to."

"But these people are . . . why won't we need to?" She stopped while Joe continued ahead.

"Because. I've been invited to speak to them this Saturday."

"Does being a bastard take practice or does it just come naturally?"

"Language Gurley Flynn! Language. We're in a house of God!"

\* \* \* \* \* \* \*

"We got a problem." The Chief informed his Lieutenant as the former sashayed into his boss's office.

The Lowell State Police Barracks, situated on the outskirts of the town of Lowell, Massachusetts, was one of the dozen state wide barracks of the oldest state-wide police force in the United States. A fact which garnered no small amount of pride from the State Troopers who were posted there.

"What kind of problem?" The battle worn Lieutenant didn't bother looking up from his pile of paper work.

"A rather interesting one."

"Make it short. We got another damn motor car accident. Some one was run down."

"Dead?"

"Yeah. Old fella named Henry somethin'. Getting' off streetcar. Hit by a taxi."

"Taxi driver?"

"Not hurt but they got him over at the jail. Chargin' him with manslaughter."

"God-damned machines are wicked bad! They need to start getting' more regulations on those damn things before they get out of hand and more people die."

"Either that or out law the damn contraptions altogether! Okay, whatta you got?"

"We traced the origin of the dynamite in the Lawrence case. There's four authorized dealers in the greater Boston area, another three between here and mid-state. On the off chance they came through one of the Boston dealers we checked all the sales records in the last 90 days."

"Why only 90 days?"

"I had a chat with Harry Franklin . . ."

"Seven Fingers Harry, the janitor?"

"Yeah. He's retired army. Demolitions Engineer, was at San Juan Hill. Says the stuff gets unstable in warm weather. October was un-seasonally warm, and the strike only started last month."

"You should be a cop."

"Thought about it. Heard the pay was shit."

"Not after you make Lieutenant."

"Yeah, I know. More access to graft money."

"You got something or not?!"

"We determined by the serial numbers that the stuff came off a building site in Boston, the Southside. When we sent a couple guys around to ask about it, foreman said he reported three cases to the owner as stolen about a week ago."

"And?"

"No one in Boston P. D. has a record of the theft." The Lieutenant raised a brow.

"Talk to the building company owner yet?"

"No. I wanted to run this by you first." He slid a report across the Lieutenant's desk.

Underlined, in the middle of the page, were three serial numbers.

"The serial numbers on the crates are from manifests traced to stock in the Washington Mill.
In Lawrence."

"The dynamite came from the Washington Mill building site?"

"Yep."

"So when does it get interesting?" The Lieutenant sat back in his chair.

"The Washington has been surrounded and fortified by the Militia since ten days prior to the discovery. So . . ."

"So the explosives couldn't have originated with the Wobblies?"

"That's why you're the Lieutenant."

"Sometimes I amaze myself!"

"When does it get interesting?"

"Very funny. Get me detective what's his face?"

"Rooney."

"Detective Rooney's original report then invite the good officer down here for a chat."

"Anything else, Your Amazement?"

"Yeah. Find out who hired the building company." The Chief was already halfway out the door and into the hallway.

"We already know." He called back. "It was the mill owner. William Wood."

The Lieutenant looked up from his desk and stared out into the hall, amused at the irony of possibly having helped clear the I. W.W.

The Mass State Police were founded specifically to help quash union activity.

# Paddy Kelly

It took a half hour of convincing, and several Amerattos, but Arturo finally agreed to wear a yarmulke. He took a seat in the men's section and waited for the worship ceremony to start. The Cantor sang the opening prayer, the Rabbi performed his part of the ceremony and next up on the bill was Joe.

With a joy fed of an inner confidence which intimidates most people, Ettor took the alter, greeted the congregation in Hebrew and launched into one of the pivotal speeches of the Lawrence Strike.

"Greetings on God's Sabbath and thanks to your Rabbi for allowing me to address you." He looked up at the women. "My message is simple." They were unusually attentive. "There are but two nations in the world. The nation of workers and the nation of shirkers. There are but two races, the race of useful members of society and the race of useless ones. The man or woman, whether Jew or non-Jew, that works for a living, has interests and hopes that can only be advanced and realized by the solidarity and common understanding of all the workers. Among the workers there is only one nationality, one race, one creed.

No doubt, many of you left your home countries because of persecution or the fear of persecution, and to better your conditions. But you did not leave the labor problem behind you in Russia, Poland, or the Saarland." He stepped out to mid alter. "The moment you arrived here you found yourselves confronted with that problem, probably in a different way. But you found here too, the struggle between those who work and those who do not work.

Forget that you are Hebrews. Forget that you are Poles, Germans or Russians. Remember always you are workers with interests against those of the mill owners. The master class has but one flag. The rag of profit. They have but one nation. The field of exploitation wherever found. They have but one god. The dollar. The workers too should put one flag, one nation, one god, in their class unity."

He steppped to the front off the alter.

"They murdered, assassinated and massacred the Jewish workers in Russia, in the hope of destroying them. But the scaffold has **never yet** and **never will** destroy an idea or a movement!"

More than anyone involved Ettor realized the path to victory was not one man, one woman or one skilled or unskilled worker at a time. But one ethnic group at a time.

To complete silence Joe once again thanked the Rabbii, the congregation and took his seat on the left of the alter, next to a grinning Arturo.

After the final ceremony, frought with humility, Ettor questioned his effectiveness. A little over 48 hours later his doubts were put to rest. Monday morning not one Jewish worker showed up for work. But a small committee, representing all the Jews, was sent to the hall on Mason Street to ask what was needed of them.

\* \* \* \* \* \* \*

The meeting room at the American Woollen Company Head Offices in Boston was uncharacteristically crammed full. Supervisors and senior personnel of the six most prominent detective agencies in the United States drank, mingled and rough housed like kids at a playground.

The New York Detective Agency, the Federal Investigation Agency and the ever present, notorious Pinkertons were all there as were several minor agencies such as the Central and Sammon & Son.

Between professional detectives, strikebreakers and thugs, the owners, led by Turner and Wood, had amassed just over five hundred men.

The time to force the strike to a head was at hand.

A former Army NCO who had served in the Philippines with Roosevelt stepped up to the podium and adjusted the large Lawrence city map mounted behind him and began to speak. His commanding tone compelled the adult adolescents to settle down and pay attention.

"The workers have demanded a meet with the owners. The

owners have no intention what so ever of meeting and negotiating with this rabble." He was offered a drink but declined. "Our strategy is based on their stupidity. They believe they will meet the owners through Scanlon in the morning. They've got another think coming."

The men started to applaud but he continued over them. "O'Hara, you and your squad will be stationed here, just off Broadway. Harrison and Ford, their so-called 'General Strike Committee' will be lured over to the police station. After they realize they're not going to get their meet they'll give up and come out. When they drift back towards Broadway, where they think they're gonna have a parade, that's when you go into action. The Pinkertons know what they have to do."

A half dozen men in the back started passing out boxes of black arm bands. "I'll be floating around tracking events. These are so we can identify each other. Make sure each of your men get one. Ford make sure your guys keep your bands off until the last minute, but have them on by the time Sullivan and his cops arrive!"

"Will do, Boss!"

"When I cross Broadway here, that's your signal to start. Any questions?" The mood had turned serious. Even the most inebriated were drilled through with hate for the foriegn usurpers. Turner took to the podium to address the troops one last time.

"Gentlemen! Thanks to Taft's wife buttin' her big nose into places where it don't belong, there's talk of a Congressional Committee being sent up here to 'assess' the situation! I don't know 'bout you fellas, but I don't remember votin' for Helen Herron!"

Shouts of "HERE, HERE!" Filled the room.

"Make no fucking mistake! I want this strike over by the time they finish fucking with all their red tape down there and drag their fat asses up here!" The seasoned coach pumped up the team before the big game. "We need to shut this thing down! Right here! Right now!"

The booze fueled banter and bravado went on into the night.

# The American Way

## * * * * * * *

It was just before 6 a. m. and still dark when the workers began to congregate on the north side of the city. Joe, Arturo and Rocco had been at Campagnone Common since four that morning. By half six there were dozens of groups of men and women huddled around flaming steel barrels scattered along the park's Northeast perimeter. Aggression tempered by hope pervaded and there was no shortage of argumentative speculation as each worker in turn contributed to the forecast of the upcoming events.

The three leaders and their immediate staff were gathered in a small red brick pavilion just inside the main gate of the park.

"This meeting will tell how they intend to conduct the fight." Joe informed Rocco and the small group.

"What's our strategy?"

"Stay firm. Don't be intimidated, don't trust Scanlon! And above all, no violence!"

After he learned of the workers intended outdoor meeting, Scanlon again offered they hold the gathering outside City Hall. The idea of an open air, public meeting appealed to Joe. "If you have any hot heads in your respective groups, leave them behind!" Joe cautioned. Rocco smiled.

"I understand. Scanlon's arranged this get together to look like the great healer. It's a primitive tactic but will serve us well for now. As you say, when we show up we'll at least find out the rules they intend to play by." As he spoke Rocco noticed a mild change in Joe's demeanor.

"Si" Joe produced a Western Union from his breast pocket and offered it to Rocco.

"There's a change in plans." He said.

"What?"

"We got this last night inviting us to send a speaker to the rally in Germantown." Rocco perused the telegram.

"That's great news! What do you suggest?"

"I discussed it with Arturo. If you don't object, we'll go out there today. But, that'll leave you alone against Scanlon."

"And the Bosses!"

"There aren't going to be any Bosses." Arturo quickly added.

"Scanlon's aide said . . ."

"Scanlon and Scanlon's aide are full of shit. Wood's still in Boston, at their headquarters."

"Turner?"

"Turner's probably at home with his wife and dogs." Suddenly the light came on.

"You sneaky bastard!" Rocco complimented.

"Not me. Tresca. He's been in touch with New York through Bill from Pittsburgh. He suggested we send people to tail Wood and Turner around the clock."

"I'm glad he's on our side."

"He's made his life's work learning how to use their tactics against them." Joe asked if there were any other questions or anything more to discuss. There wasn't and the meeting broke up, the others disbursed and Joe nodded Angelo off to one side.

"You're doing a helluva job, Rocco. The workers trust you."

"They trust me but they believe in you. We all do."

"Arturo and I should be back with news from the Germans one way or the other by nightfall." Ettor turned to leave.

"Joe . . . thank you."

"In bocca al lupo!" Joe challenged.

"Crepi il lupo!" Rocco added.

"Crepi Wood!"

Rocco laughed. They shook hands and Ettor left to meet Arturo who was waitng over on the corner.

*******

The loading dock behind the Duck mill was a convenient rally point for Turner and the detectives. At about five past seven that morning a cargo truck backed into loading bay No.7 and the driver was caught off guard as he dismounted the cab and was confronted by over a hundred men. He presented a docket to

259

Turner.

"I got a special rush order. Says here I don't need no signature?"

"That's right. What's your name?" Turner asked.

"Harold. Why?" The mill boss produced a fifty dollar note and stuffed it into the delivery man's waistcoat pocket.

"Harold, this is for you." He smirked at the dumbfounded driver. "Why don't you go get yourself a cup of coffee. We'll have your freight off loaded in about twenty minutes." Even as he spoke the truck's tarpaulin had been unhitched, rolled back and the men had formed a daisy chain and were off loading the wooden crates. The driver shrugged and meandered away.

After the crates were unloaded and pried open the knives, clubs, guns and ammo were distributed amongst the assembled 'authorities' as everyone did up their black arm bands.

Similar scenes were being played out in half a dozen locations across the city as a senior mill agent from the mob approached Turner.

"I don't get it. Scanlon's given them permission to march, you know that?"

"Which is exactly why we decided a week ago that he ain't running the show anymore."

\*\*\*\*\*\*\*

A team of Clydesdales rested behind the seemingly endless beer tent where over a dozen bar men rhythmically drew stein after stein of lager and passed them across the make shift bar of oak planks spanning empty beer kegs, to husky waitresses, some of which wrestled six steins into each hand before dissapearing into the crowd.

Just outside hundreds of bratwurst sizzled on three giant grills, a sea of thick pea soup simmered in a giant caldron and Ump-pa-pa music clanged away as old men argued, women gossiped and children romped through the beer garden.

It was Joe and Arturo's first exposure to how the Germans spent their liesure time and both were enamored with the overt lust for life which pervaded the atmosphere. They took their warm welcome that afternoon as a good sign and realized Italians weren't the only people who took their food and drink seriously.

Without warning silence enveloped the crowd as the brass band on the patform at the far end of the tent struck up the German national anthem. Men, women and children of all ages stopped what they were doing and gradually rose from their seats around the large round tables scattered across the expansive beer garden. German patriotism suddenly dominated. Following the last chorus, the crowd remained standing for the playing of the American national anthem.

At its conclusion a moment of silence was observed for some reason neither union organizer quite understood but then an explosive round of applause erupted. The band settled their instruments into their racks and dutifially sat back down as a distinquished elder, impeccably dressed in a dark suit stepped up to the megaphone. Arturo and Joe recognized him as the man who greeted them with the buckboard at the train station that morning.

There were no empty spots within a hundred feet of the stage and as he began to speak, the crowd drifted forward. Neither man spoke German but the central message was pretty clear.

About twenty minutes into the Elder's rousing remarks a young man came up from behind and put his hand on Joe's shoulder.

"Entshuldig, Herr Ettor, you vill speak next please?"

"Yes, of course. Thank you." The young man left and Joe smiled at Arturo. "It's show time!"

"Break the leg!" Arturo, who remained outside, took a quick whiff of his rindwurst he had been handed followed by a polite nibble. He then looked around to no one was watching and discreetly deposited it into a nearby garbage can.

In the giant tent the Master of Ceremonies made a short announcement and Joe took the stage. He set the megaphone aside and tried not to be intimidated by the dead pan audience or to remind himself how much depended on the Germans.

"Thank you for having us. I will speak plainly and to the

point. The days that have just passed have demonstrated the power of the workers. The power of the workers consists of something greater than the power of the capitalists. The power of the capitalists is based on property. Property makes them all powerful, socially and politically. Because of it they control the institutions of attack and defense, they have the laws, the army, everything!" He noticed the crowd appeared only politely attentive.

"They can employ agents to go around to plant dynamite and to provoke disorder among the workers, in order to defeat them. In spite of all that, the workers have something still more powerful. The workers' power, the one thing more powerful than all the property, all the machine guns, all the gallows and everything on the other side. The common bond of solidarity. Of purpose. Of ideals.

Our love of solidarity, our purpose and our affection for one another as workers, bind us more solidly and tighter than do all the bombs and dynamite that the capitalists have at their disposal. If the workers of the world want to win, all that they have to do is to recognize their own solidarity. They have to do nothing, but fold their arms, and the world will stop."

There was a ripple of applause. Joe wished he spoke German.

"The workers are more powerful with their hands in their pockets than all the property of the capitalists. As long as the workers keep their hands in their pockets the capitalists cannot put theirs in there as well. With passive resistance, with the workers absolutely refusing to move, laying absolutely silent, they are more powerful than all the weapons and instruments that the other side have for protection and attack." Save for the scattered Germans whispering translations to various pockets of other Germans, there was dead silence.

"The policeman's club and the militiaman's bayonet cannot weave cloth! It requires textile workers to do that." The silence, originating from German politness, didn't last long.

\* \* \* \* \* \* \*

262

"Gino!"

"Si Rocco!" Gino appeared as if dropped from tree.

"Pass the word for the workers to remain here. After we meet with Scanlon we'll send a runner up to tell them where to meet for the parade."

"SI ROOCO!" He snapped his heels. Gino's antics elicited exasperation.

"Assemble the committees and get all the assistant committee heads to stay here. Tell all the heads to be sure all the assistants are fully briefed on what has to be done."

"Okay Rocco."

"How much time do you need?"

"Twenty minutes?"

"It's nearly half seven. Meet me with the committees over on Haverhill at eight. Okay?"

"No problem, Cappo!"

"Never mind that! Today is an important day, focus!"

By the time Gino, with the committee heads and translators met Rocco four or five thousand workers had congregated around the Common.

Fifteen minutes later the small group of fifty or so were approaching City Hall when the man to the left of Rocco stopped and pointed down the street.

"Are those militia tents?" Rocco didn't have to answer. A militia encampment, obviously thrown up overnight, surrounded the City Hall grounds.

Suddenly a whistle sounded and several squads of soldiers from around the camp double timed to the ready and formed a cordon around the City Hall. None of the workers spoke. Rocco glanced over his shoulder at his colleagues, paused then moved on. The formation followed him as one.

An NCO took up a position out in front of the imaginary skirmish line.

"STAND AT THE READY!" He shouted to his troops.

"What the hell are they thinking?" Gino asked to no one in particular.

"God only knows what a boy thinks when you give him a gun and tell him he's a man." Rocco answered.

# The American Way

In response to their campaign of thousands of letters requesting permission to be allowed to peacefully protest, Scanlon, through the City Council, gave the General Strike Committee the okay to march. Unbeknownst to Rocco, after Sweeter was given word of Scanlon's okay to march, along with a request for the Wobblies to hold their meeting at City Hall, Sweeter without consultation, reiterated his orders to his troops to 'shoot to kill anyone resisting a lawful order or perceived to be a danger' to include attempts at protests.

As soon as the worker's contingent reached the road in front of the hall a second order was issued by the outwardly nervous NCO.

"FIX BAYONETS!" The clatter of chrome slapping gun barrels echoed across the grounds. When they were about fifty yards away, across the road from the militiamen Rocco halted the committee.

"Wait here." He instructed the others.

"YOU ARE ORDERED TO STAND FAST AND NOT ATTEMPT TO ENTER THE BUILDING!" The NCO yelled across the road. Rocco fought back his anger but kept slowly walking towards the soldier who had now positioned himself between Rocco's path and the City Hall building.

"YOU ARE ORDERED TO REMAIN . . ." Rocco continued to approach holding Scanlon's written invitation aloft.

"We are here by invitation of the Mayor!" Rocco attempted to approach the NCO and show him the message from Scanlon. The soldier-turned-cop responded by ordering his men to stand by to advance. The ranks lowered their rifles to the ready and took up a defensive stance.

Several yards behind Rocco, Gino and the committee heads closed ranks and started to cross the road.

Rocco made eye contact with a blond haired soldier in the front rank. The soldier grinned widely from underneath the brim of his Rough Rider campaign hat.

"Fellas, fellas, fellas, please!" Suddenly the Deputy Mayor appeared scrambling through the front portico and down the wide granite stairs. Scanlon's assistant pushed through the soldier's skirmish line to take up a stance between the warring factions. He approached Rocco. "You must be Mr. Angelo?!" He held out his hand. "Ahhh . . . Mr. Rocco, President of I.W.W. Local #20?" Rocco's hands remained at his side.

"Mr. Rocco, we felt . . ." The D. M. waved hid hand in a downward motion towards the NCO who his men to stand down.

"We?" Rocco queried.

"The Police Chief and . . ."

"And his new boss, Colonol Sweeter?" The politician fought back his embarrassment. "It's okay, we understand. Mayor Scanlon is no longer in charge."

"I didn't say . . ."

"You don't have to say it. Is there an alternative plan?"

"We thought it might be better if we held this meeting over at the police station."

Up on the top floor of the Hall, in the corner of the building, the edge of a window curtain was pulled back just enough to peer through.

"The Mayor believes this situation is just a miscommunication. A mistake. Police Chief Sullivan & Colonel Sweeter have agreed to allow the meeting at the police station."

"Will the gentlemen of the mills also be attending?" Rocco snidely queried.

"I'm not sure if they will or not Mr. . . Mr. . . ."

"Rocco." *Idiots can't even keep track of who they are fighting!*

Rocco ordered Gino to send out a runner who returned fifteen minutes later and confirmed with a message from the station that they were expected and would be allowed to meet unmolested.

As planned the Committee were manipulated over to the drill hall of the police station, through the back door and into the large, non-descript room where another two and half hour wait ensued.

Again as planned, they waited in vain for the mill owners to arrive and just as their patience was wearing thin Scanlon himself showed up. He reassured the workers 'something' was being done to contact the owners but was short on specifics.

After another ten minutes Rocco figured to try and make

the best of a bad situation and attempted to begin a dialog with an increasingly nervous Scanlon.

"As long as we are waiting . . ."

"Must be some weather out n Boston. Maybe the roads are bad?" Scanlon stalled.

"Yes, bad roads. As long as we are waiting perhaps you and I, as representatives of our respective sides, could have a dialog?" Scanlon looked puzzled but soon refocused and nodded in agreement. They stepped off into a corner and Rocco sat on a bench bolted to the wall expecting Scanlon to take a seat next to him. He didn't.

"Mr. Mayor, on behalf of the Committee I would like to ask you to shut down all the mills as has been done with the Everette. At least until the strike is settled. There has been no violence there since it has been shut and I think it is in both our interests to avoid any more violence. Rocco didn't expect honesty but at least politeness. He got curtness.

"Mr. Rocco, it is no function of the local government to interfere in such matters."

"Then why are the strikebreakers always so heavily armed?"

"Such as when?"

"Such as the ones at the gate incident on the twelfth."

"There's no proof of that."

*So much for dialog.* Mused Rocco. Rocco shook his head and walked away.

The atmosphere grew more tense until nearly two hours later it was apparent that there would be no negotiations as there wasn't going to be any bosses. Gino drifted over to where Rocco was standing and leaned in to him.

"What do we do?"

"We march." In anger Rocco decided to send runners back to the Common. "Tell them to meet us at the intersection of Lawrence and Canal." Twenty minutes later the police and militia had taken up their stations and the workers were congregated at the intersection.

*******

In the hallway just outside a glass paned door marked, 'C. O.'s Office' Sweeter's adjutant appeared and apologised to Gurley Flynn for the delay. For the third time in the last two hours. As he left to disappear into the bowels of the armory Flynn rose, gathered her things and prepared to leave. The soldier happened to glance over his shoulder and saw her walking towards the opposite end of the hall.

"Miss Flynn! MISS FLYNN!" Flynn didn't halt but addressed him over her shoulder and kept moving.

"What?"

"The Colonel would like to speak with you."

"Then tell him to send one of your errand boys over when he's ready to speak to me. You know where to find me." By now he had caught up with her.

"You can't just leave."

"Oh?! Why is that?"

"Because Colonel Sweeter wishes to speak with you!"

"Am I under arrest?"

"Well, no. But . . ."

"Bye!"

As Flynn made her way down the hall the Military Police corporal guarding the office entrance turned to the officer.

"Sir?"

"What?"

"Shall I bring her back sir?"

"No. We know where to find her." The uncomprehending NCO looked at the officer.

"I SAID NO! QUESTIONS CORPORAL?!"

"Negative Sir!"

*******

The parade route had been previously agreed by the Committee and Scanlon and so they started off South along Canal. It was only a matter of three blocks before they ran into the first road block. The Militia had dispatched reinforced squads to act as flying columns and it was from one such column that the soldiers cut them off just a few blocks after they started. Remembering something Joe had done in a new York strike in a similar situation, Rocco merly deviated the marchers up a side street and continued the parade/demonstration south towards the yards of the Atlantic and Pacific mills. When they arrived about fifteen minutes later they were faced with a scene from a war film.

Machine gun nests and light artillary manned by fully battle ready militia surrounded the gates and were strung along the entire perimeter fencing. A defensive cordon of troops was stationed along the canal and barbed wire obstacles had been erected across the front of the bridge.

Further uptown Sully's people, as per orders, were stationed behind Sweeter's soldiers all along Broadway. Assessing the developing situation and fearful he might miss some of the action, Sullivan decided to pass the word to his men to drop back and move East towards Franklin.

Predictably, given the tactical situation, it was Compton & Franklin was where the first clash occured.

Un-noticed, a small group of Pinkies had earlier spread out and drifted up Franklin in teams of twos and threes until they were just South of Compton. The afternoon traffic was light but steady as they spread out and occupied all four corners of the intersection. Sullivan had briefed his men how to I. D. the Pinkies, so the stage was et.

It started with a face-off composed primarily of police and a handful of workers. For a few minutes it looked like trouble might be avoided as neither side appeared ready to initiate, but with sharp eyes watching from a safe distance, the signal was given and nearby, just over on Broadway the Pinkertons, dressed as workers, went into action.

At first they just lightly attacked the sparse traffic. With animated and boarder line ridiculous gesticulations they banged on car roofs, kicked at lorries and randomly jumped on running boards to give the illusion workers were attacking residents.

As the police knew who they were and the workers didn't recognize them, neither group reacted.

Then, realizing they weren't getting the desired results,

the hired thugs became more aggressive. As the traffic began to back up on Broadway, they began to develop a target-rich environment. Soon, any pedestrians unfortunate enough to be in the area began to be pushed and shoved, then punched. Blackjacks and clubs were produced.

The police and workers at the stand off didn't react immediatly, but when a group of Pinkies overturned a trolly car, all hell broke lose.

The police rushed the crowd of workers which parted but didn't scatter. Although a portion of the workers tried to flee back along the streets there was just enough pent up hatred that a majority waded into the fight. Taken by surprise that the foriegn rabble didn't immediatly fold, the police, some running in panic, began to wildly open fire.

A volley of three shots rang out and a house window shattered. An Italian worker who ducked behind a parked Model T withdrew a long barreled pistol from his great coat pocket and fired in the direction of the shots. Another volley ripped through the black cloth roof of the Tin Lizzy and the front wind screen shattered.

Rocco was across the street and yelled several times at the mill worker turned street fighter, but to no avail. Two more shots rang out and the right front tire exploded and deflated but the worker, craning his neck, couldn't see where the bullets came from. Rocco suddenly appeared and wrestled the crouched worker to the ground.

Recognizing Rocco from the Committee meetings the man ceased his struggle as Rocco grabbed the pistol from him.

"What are you doin?!" The worker demanded.

"What the hell's the matter with you? You stupid or something?"

"The police are shooting at us!"

"It's a trick you stupid'a! You play right into their hands!" Rocco emptied the revolver, closed the cylinder and returned the empty weapon to the man. "It's not the cops, it's the detectives! It's the oldest trick in the book! They shoot high to try and get us to shoot back. Then, once they know where you are they open up with everything they've got!"

# The American Way

By this time a squad of cavalry had arrived and were hacking a wedge through the widest concentration of workers. A half dozen seeking refuge under the granite portico of the library were spotted and immediately charged by a zealous young officer recognizing the soft targets. As the soldier's steed took the steps two at a time two or three of the younger workers vaulted over the edge of the porch and escaped through the hedges. An older Greek worker ducked behind a pillar just as the officer raised his saber to strike. The horse bucked, reared up on its hind legs and threw the officer who slammed into the stairs and tumbled back down to the sidewalk.

More than pleased with this turn of events the Greek shouted out across the melee to no one in particular.

"You see!? Horse I.W.W. too!" Seconds later he was butt stroked across the face by a private who had crept around the other side of the column before being dragged off, unconscious, by two others.

Suddenly soldiers arrived in force and it was only a matter of minutes before marchers were scattered all over the streets. The detectives, who were supposed to preserve their identity by melting back into the crowd, saw that between the police and the combat armed militia the marchers were being pummelled into submission, and so happily joined in.

It was at around this point that more infantry doubled timed around the corner of Compton
and the workers were attacked with a vengeance from a new angle.

Shots were now fired directly into the unarmed crowd. Several fell, some scattered, some of the men even charged. Thoroughly enraged by the apparent, unrestrained wholesale slaughter some even tried to outflank the charging militia in a vain effort to silence their indiscriminate guns.

John Ramos an 18 year old member of the Syrian marching band, who had been at the center of the former orderly parade, stopped and stared, along with other band members, at the spectacle in disbelief. Then, confronted with two soldiers coming straight at him with bayonets fixed he, as did most of the rest of the band members, dropped his instrument and began to run. Dozens of civilians were now being chased up allies, through gardens and into and through houses.

At this point, locked in a life and death struggle with two policemen, Rocco could see it was obvious the police were running amuck and the soldiers had lost all discipline and were under no one's control.

Ramos was corralled towards a house and in desperation scurried up the front porch. Seeing one of the two soldiers chasing him closing in on him with his bayonet gleaming Ramos panicked and began banging on the front door.

The residents, a mother, father and three children, had been watching the mayhem through their front window but quickly moved away and huddled in the corner as John burst through the front door and froze in the middle of the parlor.

The sight of the combat ready soldier bursting through the front door after him caused one of the young family to scream but the militiaman made straight for the teen now paralysed with fear.

John never knew what hit him.

He turned to run towards the kitchen but looked down in time only to see the bloody tip of the bayonet protruding from his lower chest. He instinctively reached to push it back in but the soldier had already braced his foot against the teen's lower back and pushed as he pulled back on his rifle. Exactly as he had been taught.

John crumpled to the floor and began to convulse.

Huddled in the corner the husband covered his young daughter's eyes as the soldier took point blank aim and fired one shot into the boy's convulsing body, turned to glance at the terrified family and withdrew from the house, being careful to close the door behind him.

Outside several bystanders, townspeople actually, were surrounded and beaten into unconsciousness before being collected by the police and thrown into wagons.

A block up Broadway the soldiers again brandished their weapons and bayonets at the unarmed strikers only now the aggressive momentum had shifted.

Two reinforced squads of militia, led by a young First Lieutenant had formed a skirmish line forty or fifty yards in front of a large group of women demonstrators who had been working their way over to Broadway, and stood, following the shooting just a block away, in two ranks with fixed bayonets facing the women.

A twenty-two year old Syrian girl moved to the front of the crowd and out into the narrow No-Mans-Land created by the standoff. From under her great coat she unfurled a large American flag and wrapped herself in it. The crowd quieted as she slowly walked closer to the soldiers. At less than twenty yards away, she stopped.

"Shoot now! You yellow bellies!" Struggling to suppress her trembling born of a mixture of fear and anger, she found renewed courage as she peered directly at the young Lieutenant standing behind the double rank of soldiers.

"I SAID SHOOT! SHOOT THROUGH THE FLAG, YOU COWARDS! OR DO YOU ONLY SHOOT US IN THE BACK?!" She made direct eye contact with the officer, turned her back to the ranks then closed her eyes and remained motionless. Hour-long minutes passed. Having been propagandized into believing they were shipped out to face hardened Commi and Socialist anarchists, more than a few of the soldiers were at loss as to how react.

Some of the soldiers allowed their trigger fingers to slide back off the triggers and onto the trigger guards. More time passed. The officer began to perspire as his glassy eyed stare scanned the faces of the angry women.

"ORDER . . . ARMS!" The squads retracted their weapons. "FALL IN!" The soldiers quickly formed four orderly ranks and all the women breathed a sigh of relief. Finally as the order to withdraw was given the crowd erupted into *Le Marseillaise* and rushed to surround the young girl as she was enveloped by their ranks.

Along with the untold numbers injured or wounded that day, news of two fatalities reached Rocco's committee at the Hall that evening. One was John Ramos, the young Syrian boy. The other was a young Italian girl.

Michael wouldn't find out until late that evening that he was now alone in The New World.

'The authorities arrested them and more
came. They crammed the jails to bursting.
In one town there were so many in jail that
they let them out during the day. We
outside had to feed them. Every night they
went back to jail. At last the Wobblies
decided that when the jail opened they
would not come out. People came from far
and near to see the Wobblies who
wouldn't leave jail.'

- **Gurley Flynn**
**Fordham University**
**New York City 1961**

## CHAPTER EIGHTEEN

Although Germantown was only a few miles outside Lawrence, Joe and Arturo didn't return until late. Before leaving Lawrence Rocco had briefed Joe of the German's past strike history. As skilled labor they were treated better than the general labor workers but not by much, just enough to keep them from joining most of the past strikes and, in the few instances when they did, they always negotiated and settled separately.

True to form, the Germans that day hadn't given Joe and Arturo any indication that they would or would not join in, on the return trip neither man was overly optimistic, but neither ruled out future participation.

It was well after dark when the *Boston Flyer* steamed in and screeched to a halt at the Essex Street station about a mile North of the river. Arturo rose to get off and Joe slid over from the window seat to follow suit. Just as he did he glanced through the frosted over glass just as the steam enveloping the platform was clearing. There in a doorway were two men in black MacKinaws.

"Arturo, attenzione!"

"Che?"

"Something is wrong. Sit back down!" Joe nodded out the window and Arturo spotted them as the conductor passed through the carriage.

"Essex Street station! Essex Street!" Arturo replaced his satchel in the overhead rack and took a seat opposite Joe.

"You awright, Saa?" The conductor drawled at Giovannetti.

"Sorry wrong station."

"Where'd you want to go to, Saa?" More Pinkertons accompanied by a squad of police began to scour the station and peruse the dozen or so passangers disembarking.

"Lawrence but . . . "

"This is Lawrence!"

"We'll get off at the next station, Conductor." Joe

intervened.

"Next station's South Canal. Other side the river."

"That's okay."

"Suit yer'self, young fella." He punched their tickets and moved on.

"What do you think?" The whistle sounded two short bursts.

"Not sure. But I've got a bad feeling." Joe avoided looking dirctly out the window as he spoke.

"What do they want?"

"Us!"

"They'll be at the next station."

"Which means we have about five minutes to make a decision."

"ALL ABOARD!" Out on the platform the conductor retrieved the footstools.

"We stay!" Arturo was adimate.

"I didn't mean us. I meant you."

"What . . .?"

"These people are running amuck! You are technically here as a Pressman. However we do it, we need more international press. One of us has to get word to New York about what's happening up here! They're here to arrest us, after they do, there's no telling how far they'll go. Tell Bill to get the story to Jack Reed!" Unphased by the impending danger, Arturo folded his arms and smiled at Joe who pushed further. "I've seen this in Spokane, San Diego, the lumber camps through out the South! Depending on what charges they fabricate, this could drag on for months. More than enough time for the Bosses to crush this strike!" To add weight to his words Arturo leaned in to Joe.

"Listen to me. Unless these sad little men intend to arrest 30,000 workers or more, this fight will go on. You trained them well. And Rocco is a good man."

"And if he . . ."

"Everyday the Bosses back themselves into a smaller corner. The more tyrannical they become, the tighter they close their fists, the more of us slip through their fingers. Even if they hold us incommunicado, think of the press we'll get!" Joe sat back as the train slowed into the next station.

"SOUTH CANAL STREET STATION! SOUTH CANAL!" Arturo leaned over to Joe.

"The *Il Proletario* editor has instructions. If I fail to contact him twice a day for two days, he is to assume something is wrong. He knows Jack Reed's editor at the magazine. He will contact Reed and they will go to the New York Editor! No matter what they do, someone will know!" Joe smiled at Arturo's forethought and offered his hand.

"Graci fratella!"

"Crepi lupo!"

"Crepi Wood!

They were surrounded by a dozen rifle wielding soldiers the minute they stepped off the train. Sullivan and his half dozen cops stood obediently by while an Army Lieutenant-turned-cop read the charges.

"Joseph Ettor and Arturo Giovannetti, you are under arrest for inciting and provoking violence, suspicion of the transportation of illegally obtained explosives and on the charges of accessories to murder on two counts." The last charge caught the two completely off guard.

They were handcuffed and manhandled into a nearby military truck and minutes later, the armored convoy sped North, back across the river.

\* \* \* \* \* \* \*

With both hands Mayor Scanlon leaned on the window of the small office and perused the barbed wire and machine gun nests surrounding the armory. The Chief of Police and Colonel Sweeter sat just behind him at the desk. The Deputy Mayor sculked in the far corner.

"You gonna shoot, shoot! We gonna have a funeral procession!" Sullivan read the note aloud. "Sounds like an ultimatum to me, John!"

"It's **Mayor** Scanlon to you, **Acting** Chief Sullivan!" For the first time since it had all begun Sweeter was impressed. He didn't think Scanlon had it in him.

"Acting Chief . . ." Sullivan gave a slight grimace at Sweeter's emphasis. ". . . I am, as are most of us here, all for the closed shop policies of the mills. It's what keeps the mills and factories of New England, hell the whole United States, going and so is everyone's bread and butter, but . . . " Sweeter was cut off by the Deputy Mayor who saw his chance.

"We have arrests for people speaking in public! Ever heard of free speech, Acting Chief Sullivan?!"

"Those people were arrested for preaching anarchy and disrupting the peace!" Scanlon struggled to surpress his anger as he slowly turned from the window.

"I have a copy of the arrest report right here along with notes on the 'anarchistic evidence' they were supposed to be preaching." He shuffled through a sheaf of papers and held one aloft. "They were reading the BILL OF RIGHTS, FER CRYIN' OUT LOUD! You can't do that! Where the hell do you think ya are? Russia?!"

"Mr. Mayor, we can't be seen to be giving into threats!" Despite the way things were shaping up Sullivan continued to see himself as the answer to all their prayers. The hero who'd ride in on the white horse and save the day.

"Threats?! THREATS?! I got a dead sixteen year old girl and an eighteen year old kid who played in a band stabbed in the back with a bayonet and then shot! What was he threatening you with? His fucking tuba?!"

Sweeter was disgusted. It hadn't quite turned out to be the noble cause he had envisioned weeks ago in the cozy command environment of the Militia drill hall.

"Mr. Mayor that striker was forcibly dispersed by my troops, not the police, only after he refused to follow a lawful order." Sweeter offered.

"Oh, failure to disobey an order? Well that's a relief! As long as it wasn't something serious like . . ."

"Spitting on the sidewalk." The D. M. was Johnny-on-the-spot again. Scanlon picked it back up.

"I can see the fucking headlines now! 'The Boston Massacre, The Haymarket Massacre and now the Lawrence Massacre!'" Scanlon fought to collect himself. "Colonel, you were sent in here to keep the peace, not to kill my citizens and take over my city!"

"I believe it was you who requested us, Mr. Mayor." Even 'Sweep 'em away Sweeter' realized that unless he was willing to open fire on an unarmed crowd during a funeral procession, there was little he could do to stop the workers on this one.

The meeting of the minds was decided upon the morning after the murders, but had been long overdue. Entering the fray with the sole strategy that 'might makes right', the three heads of the imposing force had finally come to the realization that a bit of forethought was now called for.

Scanlon fully realized that the opportunity to bring peace and appear as a savior was probably lost, and this could be his last opportunity to consolidate and gain back political ground he had lost in the last weeks. The Town Council had been purposely excluded from this phase of the decision making process and wouldn't take it well when they eventually found out. Additionally, he had made the decision to sideline O'Reilly's Citizen's Association once and for all.

"I want viable suggestions!"

"Don't let them do it! It's not a funeral procession they want. It's just another anarchist protest march!" Sullivan implored.

"Colonel, you got anything a little more level headed to add?" Sweeter glanced at Sullivan before answering.

"Stay away, let them march. Get it out of their systems. I'm not saying we vanish, just keep a low profile." Sullivan sat back in disgust. "I'll station squads along the route and if they act up, we'll move in."

Sullivan, I want your men behind the Colonel's at all times."

"Mayor . . ." Scanlon stared straight into Sullivan's eyes as he reiterated his order.

"At ALL times! Do I make myself clear, Acting Chief?!"

"Yes. Mayor."

*******

Affonoso hadn't seen Michael for the entire day and began to get worried. He knew that Michael brought a gun with him from Italy, wouldn't handle the news about Anna very well and might go off looking for revenge. He decided to return to the tenement and see if Michael was home and if not, to wait until he showed up.

"Michael! You in there?" He knocked again and the door swung open. Affonoso quietly closed the door and returned to the hallway and into his own aparetment, walking past his past wife.

"Did you see Michael?!" She asked.

"Yes."

"Did you tell him about Anna?"

"He already knows." He drifted over to the front window and stared out the back of the  tenement.

Elenora crossed the narrow hall to Casaburi's room, pushed back
the door and peered in.

Affo closed his eyes and hung his head as her partially stifled scream echoed through the tenement.

Michael's face was unrecognizable. The blood splattered window shade next to the bed was all the way down. The .45 was still in his hand and the flies had already begun to swarm around his distorted head.

\* \* \* \* \* \* \*

A sea of oversized black umbrellas, derbys, black kerchiefs, and great coats clogged Broadway as a dozen ethnic marching bands spread over the length of the quarter mile long procession took it in turn to play slow marches and funeral dirges.

An estimated twelve to fifteen thousand were in attendance and even the Pinkertons just loitered about and took notes. Despite warnings from the authorities, as if to taunt the strikers, there was sporadic traffic but the marchers showed great restrain when taunted by the some of the drivers. The Pinkerton tactics of dressing their men like mill workers who then harassed and attacked the citizens had left an indelible impression.

Although it was primarily the Socialist press which covered the funerals of the slain workers there was a smattering of mainstream coverage in New York.

At the head of the procession the I.W.W. leaders were the first to reach the improvised memorials of the two slain teens and after a few solemn words laid a wreath and then stepped aside for all to pay their respects.

Following the three hour ceremony an emotionally drained Rocco returned to the hall on Mason Street. The sight which greeted him did not lift his spirits.

Although not jam packed the hall was full. To aggravate the general atmosphere of frustration and sorrow, anger had begun to take hold and scattered around the hall, multiple arguments were underway. A wake of silence followed Rocco as he made his way through the emotionally charged crowd and he realized he wasn't emotionally prepared for this. But he was expected to say something to the troops.

He mounted the small presidium stage in the back of the hall and removed his great coat and handed it to an assistant. A pool of faces glared back at him and courtesy borne of respect yielded silence. He spoke quietly and without a megaphone.

"I know you are frustrated. I am too. I know you are angry and want revenge. So do I. But understand . . ."

"We have to do something!" A voice yelled out.

"They're killing children!"

"Which means they are willing to kill anyone! So we do exactly as Joe taught us!" Rocco countered.

"Then what DO we DO?"

"We keep our heads, NO violence! We keep calm and give them **no** excuses!" An older worker pushed his way to the front to break the uncomfortable stand off.

"What is our strategy . . . Mr. President?" He calmly asked. Rocco nodded to him.

"I've wired New York. Haywood will be up in a day or so. I want daily visits to the jail. Make sure Mr. Ettor and Mr. Giovannetti have everything they need. Also, be sure their names have been added to the food and medicine lists."

# The American Way

"Already done! A man's on the way over there now."
Someone called out.

Part of the city's tactic to help Wood break the strike was
the use of the jail system to reinforce the corrupt judiciary. This
took the form of cramming 100 men into 20 man cells, spraying
them with cold water in the unheated spaces and either not
feeding them or feeding them one cold bowl of porridge a day.

The Wobblies countered this at first by smuggling food
into the prisoners then later as the body count went into the
hundreds, they advertised the torture tactics to the community,
state and national press. That is the few even-handed press
organs which existed at the time.

Eventually, Gurley Flynn organized feedings en massé
twice a day.

"And then?" One of the union members pushed.

"And then we march! We march and we pickett! I want
pickett lines twenty-four hours a day, seven days a week until
this is over! Rain, sleet or snow! Mr. Haywood's promised to
bring in more strikers. As many as we need. Enough to fill all
their jails!"

"Scuzi, Rocco."

"One minute Gino! Just because they are in jail, nothing
changes! Assistants take over from the committee heads where
necessary."

"Rocco!"

"Che?!"

"One thing will change." Rocco was exasperated as Gino
handed him a telegram. "This came during the funeral." Rocco
was shocked that it was from the United Textile Workers. He
slowly lowered his head along with the Western Union. Then
raised his smiling face to the workers and held the telegram aloft.

"The Germans are in." He quietly informed the hall.

They heard the cheers across town in the City Hall.

*******

The crackly voice coming in over the wireless sparked a
sudden interest from the busy hotel desk clerk. He stopped filling

282

out the guest's registration card and without so much as an 'excuse me', meandered over to the back counter where he stood by the radio next to the expansive key rack.

"This is an I.W.W. strike! It's a Western strike in the East! A strike in New England conducted by Western miners who have brought here the methods and the spirit employed by them in Idaho, Colorado and Nevada, improved, if you please, by their experience there and by radical philosophies from abroad!" He turned up the volume and put his ear to the walnut encased Marconi.

"Only time will tell if the legions of the working class have chosen the right time and place to rise against the likes of the one of the world's richest man, J. P. Morgan! This is Lincoln Steffens reporting!"

"Radical philosophies from abroad my ass! Nuthin' but damned Bolsheviks at it again." The world-wise, fifty-one year old assistant desk clerk returned to his duties.

"Ought to give that Sweeter fella orders to shoot-to- kill! That's how Napoleon did it!" The well-dressed guest added from the other side of the counter. This of course gave impetus to his fur draped, poodle-cuddling, overweight wife to chime in.

"Why all these foreigners feel they have to come over here and stir up trouble when they should be grateful we've given them jobs just makes me feel . . . feel like. . . " Both men unwittingly leaned slightly forward. " . . . well, I don't know what! But it makes me feel something!" She emphatically alluded. Both men finally exhaled.

The Biltmore Hotel in downtown Boston was a classic of its time. Save their size and notoriety, The Klondike in Frisco, The Chicago Hilton or The Astor in New York had nothing on her luxury accommodations and furnishings.

The lobby, covered in three inch, wall-to-wall, plush Asian carpet, was tastefully accentuated with hand-carved Corinthian columns, elaborate balustrades and smartly uniformed bell hops. Just to make sure all the boxes had been checked, there were the mandatory Coco-Baroque chandeliers which never seemed to give off enough light, but looked expensive.

Just off to the right of the brass plated revolving door

serving as an entrance was the bar where guests could be reassured that they were in the right place by virtue of the fact that beers were twenty cents instead of the usual nickle and were served in fluted glasses rather than crude mugs which held too much for a proper gentleman to drink in one go.

It was just after lunch, so despite the lobby being busy there were only a handful of people in the bar area and only one of those, a man, off to the left, was at the bar.

He wore two marks of distinction which labeled him as being out of place with the local hoi paloi. An ill fitting suit and a very nervous look on his face.

Ernest W. Pitman was a successful building contractor. He often met clients at the hotel to negotiate or close deals. Today he would make a different type of deal. One he had never made before. A deal for his freedom.

He was waiting for a very important man, Boston District Attorney Pelletier.

Pelletier arrived a few minutes late and they moved to the end of the bar for more privacy. Ernest ordered another scotch before they began. Pelletier initiated the festivities.

"How ya holdin' up Ernie?"

"Fine."

"Ya okay to do this here or ya wanna get a table?"

"No. No I'm fine. Let's get it over with. Whatta ya need?"

"The Suffolk County Grand Jury convenes again next week, Tuesday or Wednesday. All I need you to do is take the stand and, in your own words, relate what happened."

"That's all?" Pitman timidly inquired.

"Just relate exactly what happened. There might be a few questions, but don't worry, I'll be there to coach you along."

"And I won't do time?" For the first time he looked the D. A. square in the eye.

"Not at all. A fine and suspended sentence. That's about it." Only slightly, Pelletier dropped his gaze.

"And all this is strictly off the record?!"

"One hundred and ten per cent off the record!" Pitman still wasn't convinced. "Ernest, believe me, you made the right decision. It was only a matter of time. If you didn't do it this way, and we found out on our own, god knows how long you would have gotten. I understand how you feel. Really I do!" Anyone within a mile of the conversation could see Pelletier was a seasoned pro. He had his fish, trick now was not to let it wriggle off the hook. Pitman needed time to let his situation sink in.

"We may not be on the inside track, but we like to think we're not stupid. Anybody knows that dynamite costs money. That much dynamite a good deal of money. So where would these working class anarchists get enough money to finance their attempted sabotage? Worse yet, what would they gain by blowing up the only place they can work?"

"Exactly!"

"Taken in conjunction with the fact that there is enough food and clothing to continue this  strike for so long in the dead of such a brutal Winter, there has to be outside financing. Which could only mean one thing . . .

"Exactly!" In coordination with his affirmation Pitman threw back his drink.

"A national conspiracy!" Ernie suddenly looked puzzled. "Sure they're revolutionary anarchists hiding behind the flag but . . . " The D.A. continued.

"I never thought of Wood as hiding behind the flag!"

"I'm talking about the anarchists! We need names, times and places!"

Pitman's leg began to vibrate on the rung of the stool.

"Bartender can I have another one please?"

"Right away, Sir."

"Make it a double." Pelletier added just before he cast his best sympathetic look at the builder. "Now, just take your time. Start at the beginning." Ernest took a deep breath and jumped.

"I know Mr. Wood because I built the Wood and the Ayer. He's got me working on a third mill just outside Lawrence at the moment. . . "

"Yeah, yeah, we know Mr. Wood. We need the intermediaries, the guys the anarchists hired to plant the

285

dynamite." Pitman's drink came and he took his time responding, as if he were wrestling with a decision. He chose his words carefully.

"Mr. Pelletier, I don't know nuthin' about no anarchists. All I know is what Wood wanted us to do with the dynamite." Long minutes passed while the wall behind Pitman seemed to trombone forward and the D. A. stared through his star witness digesting what he had just heard.

"Wood, what he wanted you to do . . . with the dynamite?" The flabbergasted lawman queried.

"That's right. It was me, Breen, Dennis Collins and a fella named Fred Atteaux."

"Who's . . . who's this Collins fella?" Pelletier reached across the bar and finished the last of Pitman's drink then flagged the bartender for two more.

"A friend of Breen's. I got the stuff off the building site, gave it to Breen and he passed it off to Collins who took it into Lawrence. They met later and planted it around the place. They picked spots they thought the workers would have used had **they** actually planted the explosives."

"Were you paid?"

"Of course! We all were."

"Tell me about it."

"Wood paid us fifty bucks each. We picked it up the night before, off the building site."

"And that's where the dynamite originated from? Wood's new mill site?"

"Yeah. There and the Washington."

"And the site foreman?"

"What about him?"

"Was he in on it?"

"No. He didn't know nuthin' about it."

"Go on."

Forty-five minutes later, as Pitman's speech became increasingly slurred and the D. A. figured he had enough information, they called it quits.

Pitman never caught sight of the young stenographer sitting at the table behind him off to his right.

Paddy Kelly

'And they were working people, poor people,
whose money was their strength, the very
substance of them body and soul, the thing
for which they lived, and for the lack of
which they died.'

- *The Jungle* ,
**Upton Sinclair, 1906**

## CHAPTER NINETEEN

**A**staticy, nasal voice filled the all but empty, dark bar room just off the South East corner of Washington and Greene in Lower Manhattan as the radio commentator spoke rapidly and with child-like enthusiasm. The Saturday, NBC afternoon news traditionally wrapped with a political commentary.

"The political, social and public stages have been set and, perhaps unbeknownst to the players, the events of 1911-1912 which will drag American industry, along with contemporary political thinking, kicking and screaming into the twentieth century, are only a few short weeks away. To add flavor to the stew, the nation's ready-to-boil over, class war which has simmered beneath the surface for more than a decade, appears to be prepared to play itself out against the background of what undoubtedly will be the pivotal election of the last century!"

"Hey Jimmy, turn that shit off will ya?! I wanted to hear gabbin' all day I'd stay home with the sister!" The disgruntled patron at the end of the twenty foot, dark oak bar nodded towards the large RCA radio standing with pride of place in the center of the back bar.

Unperturbed Jimmy the burley bartender continued leaning against a shelf between the radio and cash register, wiping down the same beer mug he had been for the last ten minutes.

"S'matter Kelsy? Ain't you got no patriotism? Don't give a damn about the good ol' U. S. of A.?" He taunted.

"Fuck you Jimmy! I had patriotism once. No more."

"Yeah, why's that?"

"Left it down in Cuba at Kettle Hill along with his leg, didn't ja Kelsy?" The guy on the stool next to him emphasized his contribution with a slap on the back.

"Fuck you too Frankie!"

"Jimmy, give corporal Kelsy here one on me."

"And easy on the head this time huh?! I don't want a mug

288

full of foam." Jimmy took his time pulling the beer but after setting it in front of Kelsy, Jimmy reached onto the back bar grabbed a bottle of Jameson's and a rocks glass then proceeded to pour Kelsy a healthy shot.

"What the fuck is that?"

"What the fuck does it look like, ya grumpy bastard? Shut up and drink it. Maybe we can get some peace n' quiet around here." Frankie hid his smirk as a humiliated Kelsy shot him a nasty glance before he shot back the whiskey and chased it with a good slug of lager. There was a respectful moment of silence as Kelsy stared down into his beer.

"Frankie, what the hell is happenin' anyway?"

"Jesus Kels, ain't you never had nobody buy you a drink before?" Jimmy complained.

"Fuck you Jimmy and the drinks! I mean in this **fuckin'** country! Fourteen years I'm limpin' around this city! Can't work, wife took off with the kid -"

"Which presumably was yours."

"Fuck you Jimmy! Disqualified from workin' on two counts: missin' a leg and I speak perfect god-damned English! I got no help from good ol' Uncle Sam! Wasn't for this place I'd have no place! No life." Kelsy slid off his stool and hobbled over to the food bar in the far corner.

"If this place is all ya got Kels you're in deeper shit then I thought." Frankie commented. The bartender/owner took offence.

"Fuck you Frankie! Plenty of other bars for you go freeload in!" The barman snapped.

"I'm serious lads! I don't get it! What's happened to our country?!" He asked as he slapped two slices of bologna between a slice of rye bread and folded it over. "Anarchists tryin' ta blow up factories, pandemonium in the streets and fuckin' foreigners floodin' in faster'n we can count them. Is this what I went to war for?!"

"Ya went to war ta fight for what's right! So the people in dem lands could know the truth!" Jimmy shot back more than a little defensively.

"Yeah the truth! Truth, justice and the American way!

That's why there's more fuckin' Italians in New York then there are in all'a fuckin Italy!"

"Kels, relax a little, huh?! Ya givin' me adjita just listin' to ya! Sit back down and take a breath."

"We got a president the size of a gazebo, a star-struck, day dream believer who wants all nations to 'live as one' and my old commander as runners up for the leader of the nation fer Christ's sake!" Frankie nodded at Jimmy who pulled another one just as Kelsy drained his mug.

"And now we got private interests buyin' taxpayer's land sold to 'em by crooked government officials!" Kelsy emphasised his declarative with a mongrel like bite of his half sandwich.

"WAIT, WAIT, WAIT! Private interests buyin' up government land?! You tryin' ta tell me
. . . that there's . . . actually . . . the possibility of . . . crooks in our government?!"

Kelsy and Frankie found themselves staring eye to eye for a full five seconds while Jimmy froze in place, dumfounded by Frankie's apparent ignorance. Frankie was the first to burst out laughing. Kels just shook his head smiled and turned back to his lager.

"Fuck you Frankie." He half swore, half whispered. Frankie nodded at Jimmy for two more. Kelsy finally lightened up.

Of course no American election worth its salt could take place unless there a was a scandal and the scandal the lads were chatting about was no small thing. Although it dragged on for more than a year the Ballinger-Pinchot scandal began when, three years prior *Collier's* had written an editorial accusing U.S. Secretary of the Interior Richard Ballinger of questionable dealings with the expansive, publicly owned Alaskan coalfields. In November of 1909 the publication had charged that Ballinger improperly used his office to aide Roosevelt, the Guggenheims and other Bosses to gain properties otherwise closed to their commercial interests by law.

Gifford Pinchot, Roosevelt's chief forester and a government employee, slung counter accusations charging that Ballinger and Taft were violating the fundamental principles not only of conservation, but the very precepts of democracy and American Capitalism itself by not letting The Bosses exploit the land.

Taft fanned the flames by sacking Pinchot from government service, which didn't help Taft's image, and the smouldering embers remained well into the 1912 election year. Litigation-wise, nothing ever really came of the case, but the P. R. damage was done.

Prophetically, this was to be the last time America would come close to escaping the crippling stranglehold of the two party system. In late Winter of 1912 however, William Howard was still at the helm. Well, at least half the helm.

Bill had a wife.

\* \* \* \* \* \* \*

Earlier that month Taft had been given a report by the Secret Service, compiled by the Head of the Pinkertons and largely founded on the events instigated and fabricated by Agent McParland. The secret report clearly stated that there was a nation-wide conspiracy to over throw the American government. A well organized anarchist's uprising. The prime suspects for leadership of this inevitable nation-wide, sure-to-happen, all out revolution?

William "Big Bill" Haywood and the Wobblies.

Taft had been fully briefed, as he had been throughout the strike, on the dynamite plot details and how the Wobblies intended to blow up the mills to help launch the overthrow of the U.S. government. So even though he had his hands full worrying about the potential nation-wide civil unrest and getting his numbers up in the polls, the flames of hatred for the Industrial Workers of the World burned ever brighter and so he, as did most of the government, turned a blind eye to the use of military force in domestic situations, especially strikes. Additionally, election time was just around the corner so plans were beginning to be formulated on how best to rid the world of those Wobblie bastards once and for all.

That grey morning in late February the weather outside

the Capital Building was blistery cold and bitter. Inside it was just bitter. There was to be a hearing. A hearing on the condition of labor and the workplace in America. The results of which would be predicated on the week long congressional sub-Committee's earlier visit to the mill towns of Greater New England.

The epic confrontation of capital and labor had finally reached the Halls of Congress.

While things were being made ready backstage, out in the corridors and lobby of the Capital building, Representatives casually undulated towards and into the sacred chambers of Congress. All but two.

The forceful speaking Senator Henry Cabot Lodge with his Boston inability to pronounce 'R's' and the soft spoken, Austro-Hungarian born Senator Victor Berger with his thick Germanic accent, representing Wisconsin, were about as comparable as The Book of Genesis and Marx's Manifesto. But it went much deeper than Boston Baked Beans vs. bratwurst and sauerkraut.

Cabot Lodge, who had served four years on The Dillingham Commission, helping compile the report which resulted in the book Hitler would later state was the most influential book he had ever read, *The Passing of the Great* Race, was staunchly in favor of strict immigration control, few if any advancements for unskilled labor and squarely on the side of the industrial bosses such as the Massachusetts based American Woolen Trust.

By contrast Berger was the first and only Socialist in Congress, based the entire constitution of the American Socialist Party, which he founded, on rights for all working men and women and would later be **twice** prevented by The Speaker Of The House from taking his oath and assuming his seat in Congress following his legal and popular election by the people of Wisconsin. The slender thread which only partially brought their moral and political philosophies briefly into parallel was their hatred of Big Bill Haywood and the Industrial Workers of the World.

Huddled close under the massive Corinthian capital of a

marble column they were amongst the last of the stragglers to remain outside of chambers. Both stood perfectly upright as they faced each other. Cursory pleasantries ensued.

"Just what do you expect to achieve by yaw little dog and pony show this maw'nin' Mr. Berger?"

"I realize you have a duty to the industrial barons of your great state Senator Lodge, but perhaps it's time you realized that although the children of the Robber Barons control the purse strings of New England, they are vastly outnumbered by the men and women who in reality are their bread and butter."

"I have studied these situations in great detail Senator -"

"Ah yes! Za famed Dillingham Commission. I am quite sure that that little four year exkurshon at za taxpayer's expense cost far more than za week long investigation of za exploitation of American workers we have just completed." Lodge maintained eye contact but remained stone faced. "Do you truly believe that your Immigration Restriction League will do anything to stem the flow of hard working, honest foreign born workers, skilled or unskilled, from seeking a new life here, in America?"

"More than the Socialist Party will aide them in lowering the cultural and intellectual standard of these United States. Yes." As a page opened a door to exit the chambers the Speaker's gavel could be heard followed by his calling the senators to take their seats. "In point of fact you and I both know that it has little or nothing to do with hard working, honest foreign born workers, skilled or otherwise. It has been scientifically shown that the overwhelming majority of these people are of below average intelligence making it very difficult to assimilate them thereby creating a situation that does not promise well for the standard of civilization in this country."

Lodge was not arguing from a legal standpoint but out of genuine fear. That large numbers of immigrants, primarily from Eastern and Southern Europe, were flooding into the U.S. and flocking to the industrial centers across the country was genuinely believed, by elitists such as himself, to be undermining the national sovereignty of the United States. That the poverty levels of the home countries of these immigrants was being politically perpetuated, crime rates were rapidly rising and as a result dictators were blatantly steering their countries towards war, was never seriously taken into account.

To compound the immigrant issue, Schedule K of the Tariffs Act, to continue ridiculously high tariffs of imported goods in order to protect domestic industries such as the New England woolen mills, was up for renewal through the upcoming vote on the Payne-Aldrich Act. The crippling of industrial imports through the existing law, the virtually limitless supply of human chattel to man the factories combined with the all but non-existence of labor laws was a political stew which the industrialists as well as politicians had been feasting on for years and there was no wish to let anyone close the banquet hall.

"Do you truly hate and fear **all** foreign people Henry?" Undaunted, Cabot Lodge narrowed his eyes, smirked and leaned in towards Berger. He spoke with visibly restrained emotion.

President Taft was fond of speaking in public in support of Labor, but his avid defense of this Act clearly exposed his true colors.

"Let every man honor and love the land of his birth and the race from which he springs and keep their memory green. It is a pious and honorable duty. But let us have done with British-Americans and Irish-Americans and German-Americans, and so on, and all be Americans. If a man is going to be an American at all let him be so without any qualifying adjectives, and if he is going to be something else, let him drop the word American from his personal description." Lodge smiled, lifted his briefcase, took his leave of Berger and headed into the cavernous, dark oak and marble chamber.

A mob of senators still milled through the aisles, around desks and gradually took their seats in chambers and the hub bub eventually lowered into a loud murmur.

As everyone settled in there was a small commotion above in the visitor's box which was quickly quelled as a very special visitor quietly entered and took her seat center front. President Taft may have had no time for the working class stiffs of America, especially those uppity foreigners in the mills, factories and shipyards, however his wife did.

Helen Herron was, as they would say in the mid-West dialectic, no shrinking violet and if she didn't wear the pants in the family, she damn sure had one leg in the trousers. Helen saw the labor struggle as inextricably linked to the Suffragettes' movement as she fully realized women, one day after they rose as the rightful inheritors of the planet, would have those jobs on the production lines as well as in management. She harbored no doubt they would then be poised to move into the public sector and then eventually onto and into the halls of science and technology alongside, if not in the leading ranks of, men.

As soon as they were allowed outside the kitchen.

Today's hearings and debate on renewal of the Payne-Aldrich Bill, a direct result of the Berger committee's investigations of the New England woolen mills, were intended to bring home to The Congress the pathetic conditions all Americans, not just the hyphenates, were forced to endure for the entirety of their adult working life. This, in a nut shell, was geared towards brining about safer working conditions, shorter hours and increased wages. All which would cost something the industrialists guarded more than life itself. Money.

Although pay was the primary impetus to the onset of the strikes, workplace safety was a very close second and it was as a means to painting the dismal and dangerous picture of the U. S. workplaces to which this day would be devoted.

The former clammer of the large room gradually died down to the shuffling of feet, the  sporadic closing of desk tops and the obligatory short cacophony of coughs as the portly Master-At-Arms entered the chamber at the head of a small entourage and took his place in front of the Speaker's dais.

"OY-YEA, OY-YEA, OY-YEA!   THE SIXTY-SECOND CONGRESS, OF THE UNITED STATES, SECOND SESSION IS NOW CALLED TO ORDER! LET ALL WITH BUSINESS BEFORE THIS HOUSE DRAW NEAR AND YE SHALL BE HEARD!" The Speaker, the Secretary and the M.A.A. all took their seats followed by the rest of the House.

Roll call was a mere preliminary and there was 100% attendance. Even to a first time visitor a glance around the room would tell them there wasn't an empty seat. There couldn't afford to be. On that cold day in D. C. this was the big show. Labor was about to have its day in court.

Old business was called and completed and The Speaker asked for any new business. Lodge called for the floor, was recognised and rose from his seat.

"Mr. Speaker, I request, in light of events of the last few days in the Great State of Massachusetts, particularly in the city of Lawrence, we delay the routine of regular business and hear the report to the House of the Special sub-Committee appointed at session herein two weeks since." The senator from New England motioned. A single bang of the gavel resonated through a silent chamber.

"Motion has been made to forego then proceed. Is there a second?" From somewhere in the ovoid chamber a response echoed out.

"I second Mr. Speaker."

"Let the record show motion has been made and seconded. Senator Lodge, you have the floor."

"Thank you Mr. Speaker. " For the required dramatic poise when one is speaking in Comgress, Lodge cleared his throat, stood erect and held onto one lapel. Berger turned in his seat to get a better look at his political nemesis.

"Mr. Speaker, gentlemen and visitors to this most important hearing." On the word 'visitors' Henry made sure to look up and nod towards the gallery. "As I have previously pointed out, within the last decades the character of the immigration to this country has changed materially. The immigration of the people who have settled and built up the nation during the last 250 years, and who have been, with trifling exceptions, kindred either in race or language or both is declining while the immigration of people who are not kindred either in race or language and who represent the most ignorant classes and the lowest labor of Europe, is increasing with frightful rapidity.

The great mass of these ignorant immigrants come here at an age when education is unlikely if not impossible and when the work of Americanizing them is in consequence correspondingly difficult. They also introduce an element of competition in the labor market which must have a disastrous effect upon the rate of American wages.

We here pay but little attention to this vast flood of immigrants. The law passed by the last Congress has improved the organization of the Immigration Department, but it has done very little toward sifting those who come to our shores.

It is with this in mind that I therefore urge the utmost restraint and consideration following these . . . demonstrations which are about to be presented to us here today." Lodge dutifully perused the chamber. "Thank you Mr. Speaker. I yield." Lodge's oration met with enthusiastic applause.

As much as Berger and Lodge were polar opposites in nearly every respect, they were both elected officials and they both harbored a burning hatred of the I. W. W. However Berger, even though Chairman of the sub-Committee to Investigate the Lawrence Strike, hated the I. W. W. with a passion, he and his party couldn't afford to ignore the skeletons the Wobblies had exposed in the national industrial closet. That is the incredible inequities in the political system. And so what would become a staple political tactic, Berger's Socialist Party outlawed anyone even associated with the I. W. W. from entering their party, encouraged other parties to do the same and then adopted the Wobblie's policies towards the poor, claiming them as their own. The American Press dubbed these efforts 'Gas & Water Socialism'.

"The Chair thanks the Senator from the great Commonwealth of Massachusetts." As he took his seat Lodge glanced over at Berger in time to catch a respectful nod. He hesitated but returned the gesture. "The Chair now recognises the Honorable Gentleman from Wisconsin." Berger was already on his way down the aisle to the front of the chamber where a table and five chairs had been set up for the representatives of the committee. The others had all been seated and Berger elected to stand to begin his presentation.

"Mr. Speaker, Honorable Gentlemen of the Chamber. Unlike other days, today an acknowledgement to the visitors' gallery is required. First Lady, welcome." Helen Herron politely nodded to the Senate. "I have here the preliminary report on the

*Hearings on the Strike At Lawrence, Massachusetts, House Document No. 671,* and have requested testimony from several individuals with intimate knowledge of the situation in that city. We would like to first call Miss Camella Teoli, if you please, Mr. Speaker."

"Call Miss Camella Talolli!" He ordered the Master At Arms.

"Miss Carmela Towlowli!"

If the malnourished, young girl holding the bear claw of a hand of the Master-At-Arms leading the petite youngster down the aisle and across the low presidium stage to a seat facing the committee, was nervous she did't show it. The top and one side of her head were horribly scarred and her long beautiful brown hair was missing completely from that side. As was customary, Berger, as Chairman, launched the day's proceedings with the first line of questioning.

"Camella, how old are you?"

"Fourteen years and eight months."

"Fourteen years and eight months?"

"Yes, sir."

"And how many children are there in your family?"

"Five."

The First Lady leaned forward and raised a pair of opera glasses to her eyes.

"What sort of work do you do, in the mills I mean?"

"Twisting."

"How much do you get paid a week?"

"Six dollars and fifty-five cents."

"What is the smallest pay you have recieved?"

"Two dollars and sixty-four cents."

"Do you have to pay anything for water?"

"Yes."

"How much?"

"10 cents every two weeks."

"Have they ever held back any of your pay?"

"One week's pay."

"Why?"

"I don't know."

"Does your father work?"

"Yes."

"And where would that be?"

"My father works in the Washington."

"The Washington Mill?"

"Yes sir."

"How much pay does he get for a week's work?"

"Seven dollars and seventy-cents."

"Does he always work a full week?"

"No."

"Well, how often does it happen that he does not work a full week?"

"He works in the Winter a full week, and usually he don't in the Summer."

Helen Herron sat forward on her chair.

"In the Winter he works a full week, and in the Summer how much?"

"Two or three days a week." A second committee member caught Berger's attention. Berger nodded and Mr. Lenroot assumed the inquiry.

"Now, did you ever get hurt in the mill?"

"Yes."

"Can you tell the committee about that, how it happened and what it was?"

"Yes." The young teen shifted in her seat.

"Tell us about it now, in your own way."

"Well, I used to go to school, and then a man came up to my house and asked my father why I didn't go to work. So my father says I don't know whether she is 13 or 14 years old. So, the man say you give me $4 and I will make the papers come from Italy saying you are 14. So, my father gave to him the four dollars, and in one month came the papers that I was 14. I went to work, and about two week later I got hurt in my head."

"Now, how did you get hurt, and where were you hurt in the head. Explain that to the committee."

"I got hurt in Washington."

"In the Washington Mill?"

"Yes, sir."

"What part of your head?"

"My head." She indicated her scalp around the temple area.

"Well, how were you hurt?"

"The machine pull the scalp off."

At seeing the horrible scar where long flowing hair should be Mrs. Taft involuntarily winced and steadied herself on the balcony railing.

"The machine pulled your scalp off?"

"Yes, sir."

"How long ago was that?"

"A year ago, or about a year ago."

"Were you in the hospital after that?"

"I was in the hospital seven month."

"Seven months?"

"Yes." Berger leaned over from the center chair and addressed another of his colleagues.

"Mr. Hardwick, I believe you had some questions you would like to ask?"

"Yes, thank you Mr. Chairman."

"Miss Teoli, are you one of the strikers?"

"Yes, sir."

"Did you agree to the strike before it was ordered, that is, did they ask you anything about striking before you quit?"

"No."

"But you joined them after they quit?"

"Yes."

"Why did you do that?"

"Because I didn't get enough to eat at home."

Berger looked up at the visitor's gallery in time to see the President's wife leaving the gallery.

"There is a high school in Lawrence, isn't there?" Lenroot continued.

"Yes, sir."

"And some of your friends, boys and girls, go to the high school?"

"I don't know."

"None that you know are going to the high school?"

"No."

\* \* \* \* \* \* \*

The serenity of the snow covered grounds of the White House lawn were deceptive.

One flight up from the lobby, at the end of a long corridor just outside the East Wing dining room a squad of nervous servants loitered with the breakfast cart. The dilemma of their hesitancy to enter arose from the fact that Mrs. Taft had, the night before, left strict orders with the night porter that she and the President weren't to be disturbed in the morning. She would call for breakfast. Word hadn't been passed on and it was an angry White House Staff Manager who now hurriedly made his way down the corridor through the East Wing.

"What are you doing?!" The S. M. hissed through clenched teeth. The terrified Head Servant didn't answer. "Why you don't go in, you idiot? You know he hate cold eggs!" Again stark silence prevailed. The Manager shoved him aside and took the cross bar of the cart.

"Open zee doors."

"She said they were not to be disturbed!" The servant informed him.

"Are they in there?"

"Well . . . yes, of course!"

"Is zis zee breakfast?" The servant became indignant.

"NO. I used the usual double sized cart just for the morning paper! Of course it's the breakfast!" He snapped back.

"THEN . . . then they are at least expecting breakfast, don't you think?! You nincompoop! Open zee doors!" He nodded towards the double doors and two of the staff jumped to.

"Did you meet with that horrible little man last night?" Asked Helen Herron from her end of the table.

"What horrible little man? And where in the hell are my eggs?!" Taft shot back Just as the doors opened.

"The representative of those thugs, the Peep-ington Agency." The Manager entered with the breakfast cart and stopped at Helen's end of the table first. He lifted the lid of the

301

serving tureen as she raised her hand.

"Thank you Jean Paul. The President and I will serve ourselves this morning." Jean Paul's professionalism partially helped him stifle his reaction as he gently replaced the lid.

"Oui Madam." He withdrew and his eyes widened as he closed the doors behind him and chased the others back to work.

"You know how I feel about profanity at the table Will!"

"Yes Nellie. Same way I feel about not getting my breakfast on time! I have a full schedule today. May we please eat?" Helen rose and wheeled the cart to the other end of the table.

"Will, I have something I should like to discuss with you."

"Why do I feel a dose of dyspepsia coming on?" Taft struggled with his enormous girth to reach the cart but managed to serve himself his dozen eggs and 20 ounce porterhouse.

"You once commented to the Press that Roosevelt 'Ought more often to have admitted the legal way of reaching the same ends.'"

"And . . . ?" He dove into his ketchup smothered eggs.

"Do you honestly believe there is some sort of nation-wide conspiracy by the labor leaders of America?"

"Nell, I was much happier when you were just planting cherry trees."

"What do you intend to do about these strikes?"

"I intend to eliminate the anarchists and Bolsheviks attempting to overthrow this country! May we please dine in peace?!" Nell maintained her composure and deliberate manner of speech.

"I'm not referring the Bolsheviks and Anarchists! I mean the women and children."

"Which women and children?!" For the first time that morning he made eye contact with his wife.

"The women and children who are working for starvation wages for the unscrupulous industrialists of this country!" Taft set his fork down and sat back in his seat.

"I'LL APPOINT ANOTHER COMMITTEE! MAY WE NOW EAT IN PEACE?!"

"Yes Will."
Helen returned to her end of the table.
"Thank you Will."

\* \* \* \* \* \* \*

Rocco, Gino and the others, in between out maneuvering the police, militia and managing over 30,000 strikers and family members, had been taking it in turn to visit Giovannetti and Ettor in jail. This afternoon it was Flynn's turn.

The visits were important to update the two, ask advice and, as they were forbidden from associating with their fellow prisoners and were on 'reduced rations', bring them food. At the time, as is still occasionally done, starvation tactics were employed as 'pre-punishment' until the prisoners could be found guilty by a competent court.

With a half dozen books, several news papers and a food basket Flynn passed through the small square in front of the court house and crossed the frozen grass where about a dozen members of the Relief Committee were setting make shift tables to feed the nearly two hundred now in custody.

Official reports such as the Lawrence arrest register claimed that only thirty-six to forty were arrested. However, like most things concerning the Lawrence authorities record keeping abilities, something was lacking, namely the identity of most of those arrested. They were simply never entered into the official arrest record. The men and women were just forcibly taken away, incarcerated, abused and ear-marked for trial and most imprisoned.

But they were never arrested.

By now the authorities' refusal to reveal a court date for Giovannetti and Ettor was receiving some national press. Although a firm foundation of indignation and anger had not yet established itself, sympathy was mounting so, in addition to a dribble of money, food and clothing began to arrive as well as personal gifts for Joe and Arturo. Chief amongst these were books. Both leaders were diligent about answering as much of the correspondence as was practical.

As she waited for the guards to finish searching her parcels Flynn couldn't help but muse there was a touch of surrealism to their situation. They were awaiting trial for the murder of one of their own people, which they obviously didn't commit, in a court which would almost certainly convict them and a penalty which would, in all likelihood, be nothing less than death.

At the same time the warden was being congenial enough to give them their own cells, which were in extremely short supply, he was also being very liberal about correspondence and visitors and allowed the two full access to his personal library. The entirety of which they read within the first three weeks of their incarceration. Both not only read everything in the warden's library but Giovannitti was now holding his own daily matineés, reading Shakespeare to fellow prisoners and any bored guards or staff.

As nearly all trials against the I. W. W. inevitably went against the union, speculation quickly arose that the warden was going the extra mile to distance himself from the court which would condemn the two innocent men to death.

After being searched and signing in Gurley Flynn was escorted to the basement cells where Arturo sat on his bunk propped against the wall wrapped in a blanket, working on a poem. Joe stood on a chair gazing out the small barred window at the relief Committee tables where the other prisoners formed orderly lines and joked with the women serving them food.

"What's on the menu?" Joe asked without turning around.

"Kant, Doystevsky and Nieztche for you and Byron and Shelly for Arturo."

"No Carlyle?" Arturo asked with the disappointment of a child.

"Didn't find it yet but there's a nicely wrapped package from an admirer at Harvard." She passed the package through the flat iron bars. Bread, meat and cheese wrapped in cloth along with hot tea in milk bottles which was wrapped in cloth for insulation was also removed from the baskets and passed into the cells.

Through his cell window Joe watched the police backed by a company of militia, surround the cheering crowd of prisoners being fed as a procession entered the square.

"Gotta give him credit! He knows how to make an entrance!" Big Bill Haywood had come to town.

"Bill tell you?" Joe asked Flynn.

"Tell me what?"

"He got a telegram yesterday. Tresca wants to come out and join in the fight."

"WHAT?!"

"I thought you'd be happy!" Ettor said.

"I don't want him near Lawrence! They'll kill him if they find out who he is!"

"I don't think so. They'll arrest him. But they won't kill him. He survived the entire Italian government, they tried cutting his throat and I hear he's already been through a marriage."

"What's that got to do with anything?" Snapped Flynn.

"Way I see it, not much more anybody can put the guy through."

"They'll arrest him, give him to the Federals and they'll execute him!" She countered.

"Gurley, don't get to upset. He may not even come." His back peddling wasn't working and she suspected that Tresca was probably on his way already.

"But, if they do find out who he is and turn him over to the Federals, to be executed, there is one consolation."

"Yeah? What's that?"

"At least he'll get a fair trial first."

Her eyes narrowed, her mouth opened ever so slightly as she repeatedly clicked her rear teeth together.There was no mistaking the language she now spoke as Elizabeth through the other newspapers threw the bars and left the room. Ettor smirked to himself despite the disappointed experiment at using humor to relieve her anxiety. He glanced over at Arturo who still had his head in a book. A guard wandered over, retrieved the newspaper from the floor and passed it through the Arturo. Giovannitti didn't bother to look up as he commented.

"So, what's'a the title of your next'a book Joe? *How To*

*Win Friends & Influence People?*" Arturo noticed something on his blanket hem and looked more closely.

"How do you suppose Wood and the Bosses would feel if they knew they were aiding and abetting the strike effort?"

"How's that?" Joe asked.

"Look at the label sewn into the hem of your blanket." Joe went to his bunk and examined his blanket. He mused at the label.

'Made in Lawrence, Mass, USA
by
the American Woolen Company.'
* * * * * * *

When he first arrived in Lawrence Haywood insisted on seeing the jailed leaders before going over to the Mason Street hall to speak to the strikers but, given the liberties the authorities had been taking with the law, was advised against it by Rocco.

Outside the jail Flynn caught up with the Haywood circus just as it was undulating up to the intersection of Lebanon and Oak about three blocks away. Flynn scurried along with him as the crowd gradually swelled enveloping the two. They made their way towards Oak Street as they talked.

"How's their spirits?" Haywood asked.

"You kiddin'? You'd think they were in jail for a littering violation instead of facing the death penalty!"

"That's good news at least. They need anything?"

"They're living better than the guards. Food parcels, packages, books, letters, everyday. Arturo's actually a bit embarrassed about all the celebrity."

"Let's hope the bastards don't turn his celebrity into martyrdom!" Flynn's face dropped.

"How long you gonna be here?"

"I gotta get back to New York day after tomorrow."

"You're not staying?"

"No." Flynn was surprised. "I'll stay around for another day, and talk to the workers, but I'll be blunt with you. This place is so well organized there's nothing I can do to improve it.

Besides, I'd be of a lot more use on the road raising money." Bill continually shook hands with workers and well wishers as they conversed. "We gotta win this one. The coffers are empty, Gompers is organizing a concerted campaign to shut us down once and for all and, now that it looks like the Republicans are gonna split, there's a real danger Wilson will get in." Flynn fully realized the implications if the 'Man of Peace', who built a substantial part of his campaign promising to wipe out the Wobblies, got be the top lawyer in America.

By the time they reached the intersection the crowd had swelled to triple its original size and their forward progress stopped.

"What's the atmosphere in New York?" She asked.

"Most have no idea what's happening up here. The presidential race dominates the headlines. The space that's left is carefully crafted not to give us any PR, good or bad. But Reed is doing what he can in the Free Press and Independents. Rest assured the Hearst machine is milking the murders and demanding 'justice be done.'"

"Meaning he wants somebody to be tagged with the death penalty!"

"Exactly! We need something. Something to push this strike over the edge."

"HAYWOOD! HAYWOOD! HAYWOOD!" The crowd began to chant.

"Like what?" The noise level rose until the two were compelled to shout.

"NOT A CLUE, BUT I'LL KNOW IT WHEN IT HAPPENS!" Several burly men lifted Bill into the air. Haywood hastily reached into his coat pocket and tossed Flynn a thick, brown envelope tied closed with multiple strands of string.

"WHAT'S THIS?"

"PLEDGES OF SUPPORT. ABOUT $5,000 WORTH!" Flynn was flabbergasted. "WHAT'D YA THINK WE WERE DOIN' DOWN THERE? SITTIN' ON OUR ASSES DRINKIN' TEA?!"

"HOW DO YOU WANNA USE IT?"

"WHERE IT'LL DO THE MOST DAMAGE TO THAT

BASTARD WOOD. LET HIM KNOW HE'S GOT TERMITES! I'LL BE BACK WHEN I CAN!"

"IN THE MEANTIME?" The short lived discussion became mute when Haywood was suddenly swept away by the crowd, lifted to their shoulders and carried in the direction of Broadway.

"IN THE MEANTIME, PRAY FOR THE DEAD AND . . ."

". . . FIGHT LIKE HELL FOR THE LIVING!" Gurley Flynn could only stand and shake her head as the thousands of ecstatic bodies flowed around her and Big Bill was passed over and around their shoulders riding the waves of the charged masses like a human beach ball.

"He's in his glory." She mumbled as he quickly vanished around the corner.

Haywood had had time to briefly coordinate with Rocco at the train station and was able to survey the situation at the hall before the crowd physically carried him out into the streets and the first impromptu parade ensued. Now, hours later he found himself at the home of the senior Moroccan striker leader.

From Joe's communicés he knew that the Middle Easterners were still not committed to the battle and so thought it would be a critically strategic gesture to accept. He was right.

After many cups of strong, green tea, Big Bill sat on the other side of a thick beaded curtain separating two rooms, his shoes off, in the center of about 20 smaller North Africans. On his right sat the senior elder, both men toking from a massive Hookah pipe.

Two hours later Haywood had their pledge to join the strike.

* * * * * * *

The dozen relief centers scattered around the city were run and supplied by the Central Relief Committee set up in a small store front with a large warehouse in the rear. Most of the branch centers were manned twenty four hours a day and so provided round the clock services.

Each family of the entire workforce were allotted $2-5 per week. There was usually food clothing and a limited supply of fuel to go around but money was the biggest problem. Gompers' efforts against the Wobblies were paying off and cash was in very short supply.

"No matter how full their bellies, they still have to pay the rent." Flynn explained to one of the volunteers as she helped off load the last bundle of clothes from a horse wagon in the rear of the warehouse. As the wagon pulled away from the loading dock a second volunteer approached from the front of the warehouse.

"There are two girls here for bread and vegetables." The volunteer informed Gurley Flynn.

"Do we still have some?"

"Yes, but . . ."

"What?"

"They each have three baskets!" Gurley Flynn smiled.

"Are they young? Fourteen or so? One light, one dark?"

"Yes. You know them?"

"I do. Italians. They collect for most of their tenement."

"That's very Christian of them!"

"It's not Christianity. They come to see Arturo. Give them what's left of the carrots and some extra bread. It's late and the bread won't keep for a third day anyway." The volunteer smiled and turned away.

"And tell them Arturo would like it if they visited him in the jail." Flynn added. She hadn't taken two steps when she saw a small group of women approaching. She recognized the woman in the lead as one of the French/Belgian translators. The women were in control of themselves but visibly upset.

"Es femmes sont inquiétes pour leurs enfants." One of the French women addressed Flynn directly. The lead woman translated.

"These women are worried about their children."

"Are they sick?"

"No. They are concerned for za . . . securité?"

"Safety?" Flynn guessed.

"Yes! The violence is becoming too close for them."

Two Italian women, both mothers, overheard the conversation and wandered over to the group.

"What do you propose we do?" Asked Flynn. There was a quick exchange in French and the women seemed to be definitive as to what they wanted. The translator again addressed Gurley Flynn.

"They say in Marseilles when za riots came they send their children to za country. To the homes of family and friends." Flynn contemplated the idea. A second flurry of French was exchanged. "They say if za soldiers don't try to kill their children maybe comes a stray bullet or somezing on accident."

One of the other French interjected. "Next thing they will come into their homes and attack us there." Flynn certainly admitted to herself they had an argument. "They say perhaps it is possible to do za same here? Send away za children?"

"Tell them . . ."

"You say send the children away?" Asked the eldest of the Italians now standing next to Flynn.

"Yes." The French translator answered.

"We do eet also in Livorno!"

"And my mother do it for us in Naples!" Another chimed in.

Flynn was convinced.

"Well then, let's do eet in Lawrence! But tell them they must understand the Bosses will say we are doing it for propaganda purposes." Immediately following the translation two or three of the women shot back at the translator who relayed to Flynn while they still spewed their anger.

"They can say what they want! We do eet to save za children! She say she don't leave from France with no economy to come to a police state with no regard for the lives of children!"

The Italians began let off steam as well by bantering amongst themselves and this started to draw a crowd as the fifteen or twenty relief station volunteers coalesced into a crowd around Flynn.

"Tell them we will have a committee meeting tomorrow morning at the hall on Mason Street. Tell them to relay the message to all the mothers they can. I will contact the committee members. We'll meet at . . . eleven o'clock. Okay?" All were in agreement.

And so it was that Gurley Flynn had made one of the monumental decisions of the Lawrence strike.

'Give me your tired, your poor,
your hungry. And I shall
fuck them over.'

**- Lou Reed**
*America*

## CHAPTER TWENTY

The three figures made their way across the massive expanse through the slowly gathering crowd with a definite sense of purpose. The two burley men who flanked the smaller man in the blue uniform, cheese-box cap and the thick black book under his arm, respectfully strode a step behind. Despite the fact they had done this many times before they didn't like it and it didn't make it any easier. It was their least favorite part of the job. But it had to be done.

One carried the short length of hemp rope with the brass ringlets attached, which is how they formed the noose. The other carried the ladder. Just long enough to reach the top of the scaffolding.

The small crowd of curious onlookers which had gathered at the base of the scaffolding parted as the two men raised the ladder and climbed the eight or ten feet to the thick, oak planking. The uniformed man waited to give the order. By now a larger crowd had gathered.

After cinching off the short safety rope, the two men firmly grasped the thick, jute hawser rising up to the heavy block and tackle, looked down and waited.

"LET 'ER GO!" Came the order. The big man firmly kicked a lever and the two now bore the full weight of the three hundred pound, twelve foot by six foot schedule board.

After slowly lowering it to the concourse floor, the uniformed man proceeded to post the new arrival and departure times for that day's trains at Grand Central Station in Midtown Manhattan.

Mrs. Bearnice Applebaum, Head of the West Side Ladies Auxiliary, was one of the curious crowd.

With executive-like efficiency, she read the board, annotated the track number and time of a train's arrival and headed straight back to Cafe en Seine over on the East concourse. There she dutifully informed her well intentioned, filthy rich and bored silly group that they had enough time for one more cappuccino or, in the case of Mrs. Jarad David Henrys

III, another cup of Twining's tea.

The former tense atmosphere at the table now dissipated, orders went out to the wait staff and conversation returned to helping select members of the poor, disadvantaged and underprivileged of the world.

This week it happened to be the kids of Lawrence, Massachusetts.

Meanwhile, downstairs on Track 29 the Italian Socialist Federation were well represented. Reinforced by a small battalion of the New York Chapter of the Socialist Party they were at nearly five thousand strong.

Three cappuccinos and one cup of Twining's later Applebaum et al sashayed across the main concourse and down the double wide, marble staircase where they ran smack into thousands of Socialists singing the *Internationale* followed by a robust round of *Le Marseillaise*. Applebaum parked the group off to the side and made her way to the platform gate to find the platform master and just as they carved out a nook for themselves the train pulled into the platform.

The platform manager met the conductor, was handed a sheaf of papers and then approached the opulently dressed Mrs. Applebaum.

"You the head'a the reception committee fer the kids from Massachusetts?"

"Actually I'm . . ." The Socialist Federation President rushed to the platform manager to make her presence known and while the administrative emergency was resolved the conductor had already begun to offload his confused, young cargo and the chain of children, locked hand in hand, streamed out of the train and onto the open platform shepared by several volunteers who had accompanied them from Lawrence.

The P. M. suddenly realized he was talking to the side of Applebaum's head and looked down the platform to see what was distracting her.

Shock and amazement dominated as the stunned Federation members, and bystanders saw their frightened and nervous charges disembarking the train. The singing slowly faded until silence prevailed. It was the state of the children which shocked them.

Given the harshness of the weather, not one of the hundred plus wore what could be construed as adequate outerwear, none wore gloves and virtually every one of them with coats shivered uncontrollably. The committee would later discover that only four of them wore undegarments.

The banter died down and 10,000 eyes and five thousand hearts were frozen by the sight. For children in any scenario to be so shabbily dressed and treated was bad enough, but the children of garment workers in the largest garment production sector of the world to be inadequately clothed was an affront to humanity. That this was the situation in the United States of America, to these people, was inconceivable.

But the thing which pushed it over the edge was the physical condition of the children. There was no other word for it. Only one. Emaciation. On their subsistence wages the workers could hardly feed their children enough to stay healthy. But in the ensuing five weeks since the onset of the strike, even with the little aid they got, the situation had become desperate.

The animosities between Applebaum's do-gooder group and The Socialist Federation quickly dissolved in a lake of compassion and they immediately pulled together to organize the kids and get them upstairs to street level where they could be marched to the Downtown district where for the gala reception which had been put together for them. As they guided the kids upstairs, back across the concourse and out through the large steel and glass doors of the main exit out onto 42$^{nd}$ Street and the South side of the station, the women realized they were not as prepared for the task as they thought. No transportation had been arranged for the group.

The last thing the youngsters needed or wanted was a long walk down a cold avenue of a strange city on empty bellies. But when you're one of the poorest people in the richest country in the world you can develop a strange sort of philosophy. One predicated heavily on the realization that life is a series of contradictions punctuated by strange and bizarre occurrences. Occasionally all coming at you at the same time.

So, although the follow-on events nearly put the kids into

shock as they were paraded down the middle of Broadway to a union hall in Lower Manhattan, with what must have seemed obscene amounts of food, new clothes, parcels and gifts, the resulting elation launched them to new heights of awareness of the inequities of life in America.

Curiosity mixed with anticipation, but was tempered by a healthy amount of fear as, by fours and sixes, the line of kids was led through the front door, across the vestibule of the union hall and into the gaily decorated, turn-of-the-century main meeting room.

Cheering members and volunteers gave thunderous applause, which scared hell out of some of the younger ones, but made the adolescents stand just a little taller. Regardless of their initial reactions every one of the kid's eyes immediately locked onto one of the dozen tables virtually buried in food.

Breads, cakes, meats cheeses, sauces and drinks, enough to feed half the entire striking force. As if that weren't enough, local volunteers circulated the room with lush trays of biscuits and small cakes.

One of the younger members of The Federation, a co-ed from Buffalo, caught sight of a small dark-haired boy sitting alone on the floor in a corner. She squatted down and through an undulating sea of legs she observed him for some minutes then made her way over to where he sat, knees pulled to his chest. She crouched in front of him and held out her tray of biscuits and chocolate cup cakes. The boy shunned eye contact and hesitated to take anything.

"Please." She prodded and held the tray a little closer. He took the smallest biscuit on the tray. "Have another!"

"No grazi."

"Why not?"

"My mother say I must take only one."

"Why?"

"So's can be enough for everyone."

"There's plenty for everyone! Why don't you take one for later. Just in case." The boy was apprehensive.

"I won't tell. Cross my heart!" She teasingly whispered. He half smiled and took another small biscuit.

Dream Big READ! • Dream Big READ!

Dream Big READ! • Dream Big READ!

"How much'a we have to pay?"

"You . . . you don't have to pay. It's all free. You can have all the food you want." The boy stared at her unblinking until his eyes welled up.

She went off to the toilet so no one could see her cry.

\* \* \* \* \* \* \*

Next morning the early editions left no doubt about where the New York Press stood.

The children's plight caused every major New York publication to halt the presses and alter the banners.

## "STARVATION CONDITIONS PREVAIL IN LAWRENCE MASS!"
### 'APPEALS FOR DONATIONS STATEWIDE!'

As was to be expected, Hearst's propaganda vehicles jumped on the bandwagon.

## "EMACIATED TODDLERS ARRIVE AT GRAND CENTRAL WRAPPED IN RAGS!"

Even the newly established *New York Daily Press* with its irresistible pension for cheap alliteration was not to be out done.

## " SCANLON'S SCANDAL!"
### 'Gov. Seeks to Starve Strikers into Submission'

Wood, the mill owners, and no doubt J. P. Morgan himself, never thought the strike would go. Never thought the immigrant rabble would put up a fight, much less gain the upper hand.

The thought of losing their platinum umbrella, the Schedule K tariffs against foreign imports, never even entered into it. Suddenly it had become a real possibility.

The day after John Reed and his New York colleagues broke the story food, clothing and a little more money began to come in and the I.W.W. had cause for celebration. It appeared now, with fresh provisions, the strikers had the strength to hold out little longer.

However, the battle was far from over.

\* \* \* \* \* \* \*

"I'd feel a whole lot better if we'd a met in Boston."

"With all due respect Mr. Mayor, this ain't about your comfort. This is about the future economy and stability of New England!" Wood shot back. "You want a drink?"

"Yeah." From his overstuffed, Queen Anne chair Wood signalled the lone servant in the room who immediately stepped to the wall-to-wall liquor cabinet, retrieved a crystal decanter and poured the drink. "We need to get the Army to put more pressure on 'em! Shut 'em down completely. Get Sweeter to crack down harder!"

"Crack down harder?! He's assumed complete marshal law, banned groups of over three, and issued a 'shoot-to-kill' order! Hell man, whattta ya want him to do next? Start using artillery?"

"If that'll do it!" Scanlon took his drink from the servant.

"You seen the New York headlines?!" Scanlon produced a folded over copy of the *Morning Edition*. "*Every one of the 119 children sent to New York last week was found on physical examination to be suffering from malnutrition. Those children had been starving from birth. They had been starved in their mothers' wombs. And their mothers had been starving before the children were conceived!'* Strike leader William Haywood was quoted as saying." Scanlon downed his scotch. "For Christ's sake Wood! We're already being compared to Russia! And the citizen's of Lawrence are getting tired of living in a city under siege!"

"Don't give me that 'good citizens of Lawrence' horseshit Mister Mayor! Fer years those yookles who elected you had no idea what the hell was going on in them mills and as long as the money was flowing' into town nobody gave a rat's ass and was happy as pigs eatin' shit! But as soon as things get a little bumpy, you come to me whingin', 'talk to the workers'!"

"God Damn it! You made the U.T.W. an offer! Make **the IWW** an offer!" There was a brief stare off and Wood sat back in his chair.

"You think that'll settle it, if I made them an offer?"

"Hell Yeah!" Scanlon sat upright.

"Maybe you're right. How would I get it to 'em?"

"Through me! I'll take it to 'em!" Wood gave a dramatic pause.

"How about this?" He threw back his drink. "They all go back to work, first thing Monday morning and I won't fire all their sorry asses and bring in a whole new crew! Huh? Take that to 'em GOD-DAMN IT!" Wood downed his drink and held his empty glass at arms length towards the servant. Scanlon slid forward on his seat.

"You don't get it, do you?! It's coming apart at the seams! The situation's changed, we aren't at square one anymore!"

"I ain't settlin'!"

"You predicted it would last two weeks. It's goin' on six!"

"Guess it was my fault. I didn't count on your cops givin' 'em an excuse to go on bleedin' heart fund raisers all over the fuckin' country now, did I?"

"Make 'em an offer before it's too late, Wood!"

"You just do your job! Make sure we don't get no more scandals in the press! Think you can handle that, Your Honor?"

"They're talkin' about bringing in more strikers!"

"Just contain it, God-Damn it! Keep it in Lawrence! Give His Honor another drink. Make it a double!" The servant approached with the nearly empty decanter. Scanlon set his glass on the arm of the Queen Ann, stood and walked out of the room.

"Fuck him." Wood swore as he held out his glass. The servant emptied the rest of the decanter into it.

*******

319

The monumental tide of public opinion which had washed over the country in the last twenty-four hours was unstoppable. Reporters from every corner of the country were flocking to Lawrence. Writers, union leaders and clergy nationwide condemned the authorities, and as similes and metaphors with Russia and Bolshevism grew, word reached the White House via Frederick Lehman, Attorney General for President Taft. With the arrival of these reports Taft was having second thoughts concerning his overt backing of the Lawrence industrialists.

With the 'foreign vote' increasing exponentially each year, and his shaky standings in the public eye as of late, a Congressional investigation over campaign contributions underway and nation-wide outrage at the escalation of the lobbying situation Taft, prompted by his close advisers, opted to take action.

Back in the State capital Foss stood at the large window behind his desk and watched as yet another handful of reporters lingered across the street from the State House smoking and joking as they huddled around a fire barrel.

"Dudley! Dud . . .!"

"Yes Governor?" As Dudley entered the office Foss threw a telegram across his desk. Dudley quickly read it.

"Berger's convinced Taft to send a Presidentially Ordered Congressional Investigation committee to Lawrence?!"

"A C. I. C.! In Massachusetts!"

"Yes sir."

"In MY FUCKING STATE!!" The yelling easily permeated the front door to the outer office where a well dressed gentleman stood in front of the secretary's desk.

"The Governor is in a meeting, sir. I suspect he'll be tied up for a while." The secretary politely informed the businessman. Today was not going to be a good day for visits.

"What do you want to do Sir?" Foss walked around and flopped into his chair.

"Get a meeting with the party Heads. This afternoon. We'll need an emergency session to plan for immediate damage control. We'll appoint a committee to start our own investigation."

"I believe somebody did a study a few years ago on wages and conditions in Lawrence, Sir."

"Dig up a copy of it."

"Yes Sir."

"Set the emergency session for day after tomorrow. We need to make damn sure we have something to show Berger and those other clowns when they show up here."

"When are they due sir?"

"What? You think they're gonna give us an engraved notice before they show up on our door step?"

"Well if it's a legitimate fact finding . . . "

"FACT FINDING? This isn't a fact finding mission! This is a we-got-them-on-the-ropes-now-let's-beat-the-shit-out-of-them mission! They're coming up here to score as many points as possible with the goddamned Press! They've already had their dog and pony show with the workers in Congress last week. Now anything they report from up here is gonna be taken as fact!"

Foss had cause to be uncharacteristically irritable. True he had rocketed up the political ladder to seize the governorship of the Commonwealth rising from the ranks of the region's business community with little or no previous professional political background, but he only took the election by about 8,000 votes. Additionally, party plans were already underway to make a bid for the White House in 1916 and was being groomed as the #1 man for the Presidential Candidacy.

To aggravate matters, crosses were already being built and hammers and spikes were being passed out as it gradually became clear that it would be the industrialists who were going to be crucified at this point in the ongoing, national labor wars. Foss' additional headache was that he himself was a major industrialist before and during his tenure in office.

"You got any of those letters of complaints those workers associations used to send us all the time?"

"No sir. Disposed of them all."

"Why for God's sake?!"

"You told me to."

# The American Way

**\* \* \* \* \* \* \***

"'The sending away of children was a new departure in this country, it being a practice followed by continental Syndicalists. It was justified by the strikers as a relief measure which would enable them longer to continue the contest, because relieved of the burden of feeding and caring for their little ones, whose sufferings in such struggles is the cause which often compels a return to work. While that was the ostensible reason, there were others which did not involve solely the creature comforts of the children."

"This ought'a be good." Flynn gave her commentary as she turned the page of the newspaper. In their adjoining cells Giovannitti remained reclined on his bunk and Joe Ettor stood on a stool and continued to watch events outside through his barred window.

"'The persons who arranged for these parties were not in Lawrence or in the State, the active agents being the women Socialist clubs in New York, Philadelphia, and other cities. At a meeting of the Strike Committee on February 5, Chairman William Yates announced that arrangements had been made to send a large number of children to New York, to arouse sympathy and enlist support by parading in the streets of that city. Several days later it was also announced that, in the hope of securing a large number of children of the strikers for the purpose of holding a big demonstration in New York, three members of the New York Women's Socialist Club would reach Lawrence the next day.' So what's their point?" Flynn queried to no one in general. Without turning away from the window Joe answered her.

"That they're crack detectives and that they did their homework." Flynn continued    reading.

"'These statements alone are sufficient to disclose the ulterior motive concealed in this move, ostensibly  intended to promote the safety and comfort of the children. But the manner of conducting them to their temporary homes, in the coldest weather of a bitterly cold month, confirms that impression. The

322

party previously sent to New York, numbering two hundred . . .' That's strange, I counted 119 when I put them on the train." Gurley Flynn commented.

"Maybe they picked up some hitchhikers along the way!" Joe joked.

"'. . . and ranging in age from four to fourteen years, attracted the attention and aroused the indignation of men and women truly solicitous for their real welfare. Wearing thin apparel and marshaled by **well fed**, **well clothed** Socialists, they marched across the city and traveled for twelve hours at a time when the temperature was so low as to disorganize railroad service.' How Dramatic! 'Reaching New York after nightfall, they were greeted by throngs of strangers shouting revolutionary battle cries, and carried to a hall, where they were fed, displayed, and parceled out amongst their stranger hosts.'" She read with a mockingly deep voice.

"'Protests were sent to the Boston Society for the Prevention of Cruelty to Children and to others in authority, against permitting the sending away of other parties. Some of the complaints were based upon the lack of care shown several sent to New York, two of whom were detained as lost children.'" She folded then dropped the paper to the floor. "Well, good to know Yellow Journalism is alive and well. Thank you Mr. Hearst." Flynn concluded.

"Did you get reports of lost children?" Joe asked as he slid down onto his bunk.

"None."

"That article is a good omen." Giovannitti finally spoke.

"How do you see that?" Flynn was puzzled.

"If we have pushed them so far to the wall that they are extending their propaganda to out right lies, maybe they will accommodate us and come up with something really big. Something so ridiculous we can expose it and turn the tide."

"How's their spirit?" Ettor inquired.

"High. The workers have a joke."

"Tell us."

"Who would be stupid enough to plant wooden crates of dynamite with serial numbers on it?"

"I don't know who would?"

"Wood would."

"The Great Lawrence Dynamite Plot!" Joe shook his head.

"What could they have been thinking?"

"That because we speak with an accent we are stupid." Giovannitti offered.

\* \* \* \* \* \* \*

It was now late February and, although it was slightly below freezing, the weather had temporarily broken and the skies had been clear for the last three days.

"Che significa, la vacanza?, mama?" One of the young girls asked.

"**You** are going on a vacation Nina." Her mother slipped the too large coat over her small arms and smiled. "A vacation is'a when you have some time and can'a go someplace nice. Eets where you are going, Bella. To'a someplace nice with some very nice people who will help us."

"Some at school say they will be lot's of food in New York!"

"There will be more food than you can ever eat, Bella!"

"Then you must put on me one more coat mama!"

"Why you want one more coat Bella?"

"So I can fill all my pockets with food from New York and bring it back to you and father!" Fighting back a tear Nina's mother wrapped her small head in a worn woolen scarf, took her hand and led her out to the street.

Although there was no anticipation of any real trouble the assembly point for the children and mothers for the next group to be evacuated had been strategically located away from the previous assembly point. This time they would gather at the Cedar Street Relief Center only four blocks from the Manchester Street train station then move on to a private residence to prepare the kids.

The seventy-nine year old Mrs. Bibou, after clearing out all her cats, volunteered her spacious house to assemble the group out of the weather, and was busy helping dress some of the kids to meet the 9:07 to Philadelphia via New York due in about twenty-five minutes. Gurley Flynn, a half dozen volunteers and a small handful of mothers were making ready another group. When all were prepared she stood at the door and double checked the rooster of 40 kids and their assigned guardians.

The original number of children was set higher but several of the mothers had second thoughts about separating themselves from their kids for an unknown period of time and in a couple of instances the families realized how much the extra pair of hands would be missed around the house.

After assembling outside on the street and forming into four teams of ten kids each with three to four parents or guardians per group, they were off up Broadway in the direction of the station.

The adults were too preoccupied with the children to notice but within a few minutes of leaving Mrs. Bibou's Flynn, walking at the head of the group, picked up on the conspicuous lack of police or militia roaming the streets. She put it down to the authorities finally understanding their limits and finally backing off.

That is until the group rounded the corner on the other side of Broadway.

Up ahead on Acton Street a pair of cops peered around the corner, spotted the small procession and casually withdrew back onto the side street. About ten minutes later, when the group reached Acton, there was again no sign of any authorities.

However, as they turned right at the next corner to move parallel to the tracks and only a couple of hundred yards from the station, a rank of police lined either side of the street. The fear and intimidation were immediate. The entire procession slowed and closed ranks as children hugged closer to their guardians and even Gurley Flynn fell back to a cautious walk. As the family members passed the middle of the uniformed ranks, a rear phalanx of police appeared and closed off the back of the small procession.

Struck with fear, a few of the mothers cradled their children, stopped and fell to the back of the group, uneasily drifted between the police ranks unmolested and headed home.

Unbeknownst to Flynn and the Relief Committee, Scanlon and Sullivan, essentially 'the authorities', infuriated by the favorable publicity in New York and Boston of the strikers first evacuation effort, had decided no more children would leave town. Using such absurd excuses as most of the parents didn't know where the children were going, that it was abusive to send them on a train journey in the middle of Winter or that they were being forcibly made to go by the I.W.W., a Town Council resolution had been quickly passed. No more children would be permitted to leave Lawrence. Of course no parent had been consulted by any member of the police or town council.

Fifty yards from the small Victorian building which was the train station, Sullivan, flanked by a pair of pugnacious cops, stood outside the main doors with an 'official', piece of paper in his hand.

Oddly enough, she thought, they were allowed to enter the depot waiting room which was large enough to allow all fifty or so volunteers and children inside. Then the heavy wooden, green enameled door behind them slowly closed over. Flynn realized what their play was.

Still, nothing seemed inordinately out of place as the ominous echo of Sullivan's boots on the tiled floor resonated through the long room and the cops out side remained outside. Silence prevailed as he mounted one of the wooden slat benches.

Off to the left of the room the ticket clerk, who until now had just been observing through the ticket window, suddenly remembered he had someplace else to be and so closed over the shutters and locked the window.

Sullivan unrolled the official looking piece of paper and read from it.

"By order of His Honor, the  Mayor of the City of Lawrence, in and for the Commonwealth of Massachusetts, you and your co-conspirators are hereby ordered to cease and desist your forceable exiling of any and all under aged minors from this city!"

Flynn stared in disbelief, as an involuntary smirk crept across her face. Every time she thought they couldn't get any dumber, they disappointed her.

"Any acts of disobedience of this order shall be deemed criminal and . . ."

"Are you mad?! You have no authority to tell these parents what they can and can not do with their own children!" Sullivan nonchalantly rolled up the paper as he reiterated the order.

"Any acts of disobedience of this order shall be deemed criminal and punishable by arrest."

Gurley Flynn, holding a child in each hand, pushed past Sullivan's goons and through the door leading out to the platform. With little doubt he would be defied, it was the acting Police Chief's turn to stare in disbelief. Several mothers moved to follow Flynn. He glared at the two cops nearest the group. Just then the train let off a whistle blast as it coasted into the station.

"WHAT ARE YOUSE WAITIN' FOR?!" He yelled.

It was over in a matter of minutes.

The first few women stood stark still in terror as the cops pushed past them knocking several  to the floor in pursuit of the few who had made it out onto the platform. When they had been beaten and dragged back into the waiting room they were kicked to ground and thrown and left moaning in pain. The children they led were roughly dragged away by the arm and handed off to the police waiting outside in the streets. Meanwhile a half dozen Paddy wagons, which had obviously been standing by parked out of sight, backed up to the station entrance, the rear doors flung open and the children thrown in like so much cargo. The women weren't handled quite as gently. None of them escaped the thugs' baton.

The mothers still in the station grabbed their children in panic and tried desperately to escape the attack. The tactics were too well planned and so most couldn't and fell to the ground on top of their children as the police waded into them clubs swinging wildly. Women were beaten indiscriminately as they had their children ripped from their grip. Screaming in terror the young ones were dragged away and manhandled out into the waiting vans as the mothers were beaten, handcuffed, dragged and thrown into separate vehicles.

The entire sordid incident lasted less than ten minutes from the time the attack had begun. Ten minutes of shrieks of terrified women and children were replaced by shrill police sirens screaming through the streets of Lawrence, Massachusetts.

By six o'clock that evening *The New York Times*, *The New York Daily News* and the *Post* were running nearly the same exact banner headline:

## 'HELPLESS WOMEN AND CHILDREN BEATEN BY LAWRENCE POLICE'

Those ten minutes would alter the course of labor history in America.

'Once looking out of Joe Sistrom's window on the United film studios lot I happen to see the big boys strolling back from lunch from the executive dining room in loose groups. I was transfixed with a sinister delight. They looked so exactly like a bunch of topflight Chicago gangsters moving in to read the death sentence on a beaten competitor. It brought home to me in an instant the spiritual kinship between the operations of big money business and the rackets. Same faces, same expressions, same manners. Same way of dressing and same exaggerated leisure of movement.'

**- Raymond Chandler In a letter to Dale Warren**

## CHAPTER TWENTY-ONE

**D**udley Holman sat reading some notes in the vestibule of the Governor's office as Foss was on his way out the door when the secretary caught his attention.

"Governor, there's a call for you Sir."

"Who is it?"

"It's Mr. Wood." Foss didn't hesitate.

"Tell him I'm not in. Then put a call in to Mr. Vagoda from the fund raising Committee. Tell him I won't make our lunch date. I'm . . ."

"Out of state on an emergency." Dudley suggested as he stood up.

"Out of town on an emergency." Foss repeated. "Holman, meet me in the rotunda in ten minutes. Lunch is on me."

"Ye . . . yes sir." As Foss passed in front of them Holman shrugged to the secretary who shrugged back.

Foss and Holman didn't speak for the entire brisk walk through the Capital Building then, once out on the icey sidewalk, Foss stopped at the intersection and glanced up and down the street.

"Carlucci's?"

"Suites me."

Once inside the upscale eatery they were seated immeadiatly.

"Waiter we'll have two Steaks Florintine and a bottle of Chablis."

"Chablis?" Questioned Holman.

"Sorry. A bit distracted. Make it a Cabernet sauvignon."

"Yes sir."

"And some warm bread."

"Right away sir." As soon as the waiter was out of ear shot Foss got right to it.

"How bad are we hurt? Holman hesitated to answer. "That bad huh?" By way of a reply Holman slid a cartoon ripped from the morning's front page across the table. It depicted a giant, pugnacious cop, scooping up people, mostly women and children, off the street and beating them with his club. The below panel caption read: ' The Lawrence Way!' Foss just stared at it.

"What the fuck were they thinking?!"

"Apparently they weren't."

"The candidacy?"

"Too soon to tell but Roosevelt's independents are already going after the immigrant vote and his nephew is kow towing to the Jew industrialists down in New York." The waiter reappeared and Foss declined to sample the wine. They sat silently until the waiter poured and left.

"I guess we'd better see what we have to do to help these, poor defenseless immigrants."

"Governor, may I speak frankly?" Foss stopped midway lifting his glass to drink and shot Dudley that, 'What the hell are you waiting for?' look. "As long as there are troops of the U.S. Militia holding a city of The Commonwealth under siege, the other two parties will have the leverage they need against us."

An hour and a half later the two men finished their lunch, and again in silence, walked back to the Capital Building. Once inside the vestibule Foss stopped and motioned Holman aside.

"Draft a wire to the Commander-in-Chief, State Militia. Tell him to pull out of Lawrence."

"Deadline, Governor?"

"Tell him at his leisure. As long as they're out by the end of the week."

"The Press?"

"I have just been informed . . . no. It has come to the attention of the Governor that there exists . . . that there is a new law which casts doubt on the use of Federal troops to break a strike and that he is withdrawing . . . ordering the withdrawal of The State Militia. Forthwith."

"Got it." Holman turned to leave. "Besides, we've come to the decision that it is not right to use American troops against American citizens?" Foss mulled it over before answering. "Some, the I.W.W., might wonder why it has taken the leadership seven weeks to come to this decision." Dudley prompted.

"Whatt'a you suggest?"

"An investigative committee might go a long way towards . . ." Holman suggested. They exchanged glances.

"You're right. Start the paperwork. Pick the committee first, then make the announcement. Get a hold of Senator Simons. Ask him to head it up. Tell him the Governor would be most appreciative."

"Yes sir. Good idea. Most senior member of the State Senate."

"Dudley." Foss turned a little more serious.

"Yes sir?"

"You got anything, records notes, memos mentioning our late night calls to and from the White House?"

"No idea what you're referring to. Sir."

"Good."

\* \* \* \* \* \* \*

It was six in the evening and already dark outside as the barman served the beer to the dishevelled man in the wooden booth in the sparsely populated, seedy tavern. John Breen looked up from his second pint to see Detective Rooney come through the bar room door. The cop made straight for Breen and took a seat across from him as he gulped his beer.

"There goes the fucking neighborhood." Breen cracked.

"Never figured you for a Mulligan's man, John."

"This place used to have class. Now look at it. They let anybody in the door!" Breen polished off his pint. "I remember back in '99 they wouldn't let cops anywhere near this place." He signalled to the barman for another who immediately began to pull it.

"That was then. This is now." Rooney calmly countered.

"What's eatin' you?"

"Nice job on the lead you gave me, John."

"Hey! I did my civic duty and reported suspected criminal activity to the police. Which is you!" The barman set Breen's lager on the table between them and left with the empty.

"That you did John, that you did. And you shall be

332

rewarded for your efforts." Rooney leaned in, elbows on the table. "Problem is John, you left out a few crucial details."

Breen's puzzled expression melted into surprise as he looked up in time to see two uniformed Staties coming through the front door. He sat with his hand on the handle of his beer mug with his mouth open as the Troopers approached the table.

"Mr. Breen, we have a warrant for your arrest."

Rooney was already on his feet and didn't even flinch when Breen went for him but was restrained by the two Staties.

"I'M NOT THE ONLY ONE IN ON THIS YA KNOW!"

Rooney produced a copy of the *Boston Herald* and held it open to the front page for Breen to see as he was dragged away fruitlessly struggling. The banner was clear.

### "Boston Builder Commits Suicide"

"Yeah, we know." Rooney shot back. Breen turned white.

As he was escorted out he repeatedly cursed Rooney and called him a Judas. Rooney ignored him and stared across the floor to the stunned barman who'd been watching the show.

"This beer paid for?"

"Uh . . . yeah." The barman stuttered back. Rooney took Breen's seat and raised the pint.

"Here's to Mrs. Markowitz, beloved mother of three."

"To Mrs. Markowitz." Echoed the puzzled barman.

'The Victory at Lawrence was the most decisive and far-reaching ever won by organized labor.'

**- Eugene Debs
Presidential candidate
and I.W.W. member**

## CHAPTER TWENTY-TWO

O n the 12th of March, 1912, approximately 62 days after it had started, the strike was essentially over. Following a series of harried meetings by the mill owners and their management, heated arguments and significant fractionalization of the formally iron clad Trust, the owners capitulated to the striker's demands. American Woolen, wholly without Wood's participation, authorized a joint committee to draw up plans for and to enter into negotiations with the committees organized by the I.W.W.

These committees and so the negotiations, were rightfully headed
up by the man who, although depending heavily on the I.W.W. leadership, was directly responsible for the decision and initial organization of the strike. The Lawrence I.W.W. Local President, Angelo Rocco.

\* \* \* \* \* \* \*

It was a grey New England morning and, dressed in an expensive grey suit with brown wingtips and slumped in a chair nursing a brandy, William Wood stared out the window, into the abyss. Home alone in his study Bill waited for the inevitable visitors he was tipped off would arrive that morning. Finally the doorbell rang and he tried to block out the conversation of the servant answering the door as he spoke with the visitors. Heavy footsteps followed the servant into the study.

"Mr. Wood?" Wood continued to stare out the window across the frozen landscape.

"Yeah."

"Apologies for the inconvenience sir, but, we have a warrant for your arrest."

"Yeah. I know all about it." Wood rose, finished his drink and walked ahead of the two policeman. "Where to?" He asked as he donned his grey seal skin coat and matching hat.

"Local station."

"There's a $500 fine as well Mr. Wood." The second cop chimed in. Without hesitation Wood produced his wallet fished out five $100 notes and handed them over his shoulder to the first cop.

"Your office is making arrangements to pay the fine sir." Wood nonchalantly restowed the money.

"This is merely a formality sir. We need to book you in, you can sign the paper work at the station and be on your way."

"Jackson get the driver to meet me at the police station."

"Yes sa."

It was a grey New England afternoon. Dressed in an expensive grey suit with brown wingtips, as he slumped in a chair nursing a brandy, William Wood stared out the window, into the abyss he no doubt at the time failed to realize, was his future.

*******

Campagnone Common was eerily peaceful. The crisp afternoon air was crystal clear. The clean up had begun and city workers scoured the streets to clear the debris which in some cases completely blocked the roads.

In the far corner just off Jackson a two man sanitation crew collected the abandoned picket signs, rubbish and odd bits of clothing which littered the park. Near the corner of Union and Garden Streets, one of the men, the younger of the two, found a spent cartridge casing.

"Hey Bert! Looks like I got me a souvenir!"

"Yea? What's that?"

"A genuine shell casin'!"

"Throw it in the shit can!"

"Why should I?"

"Probably from one'a them damn Comm'nists, that's why!" The junior man pretended to toss it into the oversized garbage bin on wheels then quietly slipped into his waist coat pocket.

Across the street from the Common, in a near empty barber shop, a radio played. It was the morning news program

336

broadcast from New York via Boston.

"The development of new conditions is always resisted by the old. During the nearly nine weeks of the fight in Lawrence, every barbarity known to modern civilization had been perpetrated by police, military, courts and detectives, the willing tools of the bosses. To these should be added press and pulpit, and the craft unions. The defeat of all only serves to reflect the soundness of the strikers' basic organization and their belief in the righteousness of their cause."

"Could be the beginnin' of a new era." Suggested elderly customer.

"Could be. At least Wilson'll keep us outta any European war!"

The barber continued to leisurely clip away.

\* \* \* \* \* \* \*

The ten story Georgian-styled office building just off Massachusetts Avenue in Cambridge was fully rented a year before construction was finished. The avenue side of floor #10 was where Wood had his office with the rear half of that level dedicated to a small hall able to seat fifty or so of the top share holders.

With a solemn sense of occasion, tainted with just enough remorse The Chief Mill Agent entered the small hall and mounted the podium to address the ten or twelve stockholders, representatives and lawyers scattered about the room. It took less than a minute to give them the formal announcement.

"Mr. Wood has agreed to your demands to step down as C.E.O. of the American Woolen Trust. Forthcoming, he will recommend a replacement. Mr. Wood will remain unavailable for comment and any inquiries should be directed to his lawyers. In light of recent events, the quarterly returns report for both the first and second quarters of 1912 will be delayed. Accounting apologise for any inconvenience this may cause." His perusal of the sparsely populated room was another unnessassary formality.

"Thank you for taking time out from your busy schedules." The room immediately began to clear.

The American Way

No bar had been set up.

*******

The Morgan Building on Sixth Avenue, in Manhattan was designed to impress. It was the first loft building with nothing on the ground floor save the lobby. There was nothing on the top floor save J. P. Morgan's office. J. P.'s total wealth in early 1912 was estimated to be greater than that of the entire Gross National Product of the United States of America.

The grey haired, senior exec stepped off the elevator and by-passed the three desks in front of the solid Canadian maple, double doors and cherry panelled walls. He held a memo in his hands. It was from the American Woolen Trust Head Office in Boston by way of The Morgan Trust, Morgan Corporate Headquarters, New York City.

He politely stood still for the required thirty seconds in front of the Head Secretary's desk while her aged but delicate fingers glid effortlessly over the expansive keyboard as she continued to type at a lightning rate. He finally interrupted.

"Is he in?"

"Yep." She answered through the pencil in her mouth without looking up.

"Is he in a bad mood?"

"Yep."

"Is he seeing anyone?"

"Nope." She retrieved another blank sheet of paper from a desk drawer.

"Something's wrong, I can tell by your conversation." The secretary smiled as she pulled the typed sheet from the huge Smith-Corona and fed in another. "Well . . . can I see him?"

"Not unless you're a window washer." She quipped. Screaming and yelling violently erupted from behind the doors. "Still wanna go in?"

"What's he all riled up about?"

"We got a call from Pittsburgh this morning. Since the Lawrence fiasco there's been trouble. The steel mill Shop Stewards at five plants want a meeting with the plant managers

338

or they're threatening to strike, the workers at the Boston and Philly ship yards are looking for a pay raise and there's trouble brewing in the rail yards." She threw him a short sharp smirk then returned to her work. "Other than that all's quiet on the Western front."

"Well, no point me ruining his day." He gently lay the memo on her desk. "Be a doll and slip this in with the afternoon stuff, would'ja?"

"Why not bring it back yourself? Chicken?"

"Nope." He turned and made for the elevators as he answered over his shoulder. "Six weeks from retirement."

\* \* \* \* \* \* \*

Andrew pierce Jr., the son of the man who gave Wood his first job, was named successor to the A. W. C. conglomerate.

Taking his doctor's advice, William Wood retired and relocated.

Wood sat on the edge of his bed in his three bedroom, stucco house in Port St. Lucie, and peered out the window. It was a rainy February day, little more than a month since William Wood and his wife had moved to Florida.

"*Fucking rain!*" He thought to himself. It was about half past three in the afternoon when his wife still hadn't returned from her one o'clock dental appointment. He knew because her bedroom door was still locked. It wasn't logical that somebody would have two dental appointments a week for three weeks. How the hell much work could you do on teeth anyway?!

Wood threw back the last of the scotch, and yelled down stairs for the butler to call his chauffeur to pull the car around. He made ready and went down stairs.

"Where to, Suh? "

"Drive South, James."

"Yes Suh'." James dutifully kept the helm due South on the four lane macadam road as he fell in line behind a flatbed Ford over loaded with wooden caged, squawking chickens. Several cars passed going North. They continued through the moderate traffic then drove some more as the rain began to fade to a moderate but steady drizzle. Propped against the door, in the rear seat Wood stared out the side window.

"Some day these roads will all be lined with factories." Wood predicted to no one in particular.

"Yes'sa. I can see the day Mr. Wood." James affected a cheerful tone.

The mile marker signs and small billboards became fewer and fewer and the side roads and cut offs stopped all together. Ten or fifteen minutes later the shiny wet macadam narrowed to two lanes then vanished altogether underneath a bed of hard packed wet sand. The vehicle slowed.

"Pull over near that thicket of palmetto trees James."

"Yes'sa." They pulled over and rolled to a gentle stop and Wood didn't wait for the driver to open the door as he climbed down the running board onto the hard sand.

"Wait in the car. I'm going for a walk."

"Yes'sa." Once out of sight of the chauffeur Wood stopped and stared out across the low, sweeping sand dunes, beyond the scattered clumps of ice grass and out to sea. The sound of the gently rolling waves lapping at the shore could barely be heard in the distance but produced a calming effect nonetheless. He struggled to hear the mechanical rhythm of the thousands of weaving machines in his old factories, but his ear wasn't so discerning anymore.

From his overcoat pocket he produced a revolver, cocked the hammer and without hesitation wedged the barrel between his teeth.

Sitting in the car, leaning on the large steering wheel, the chauffeur heard the shot, quickly turned towards where Wood had wandered off, stared for a moment then dropped his head onto the over sized wheel.

\* \* \* \* \* \* \*

On March the twenty-fifth, a year to the day of the Triangle Shirtwaist factory fire, there was a general stand down in Lawrence.

Is it too steeped in romanticism to suggest that maybe the 146 didn't die in vain?

**THE END**

# EPILOGUE

On the morning of November 26, 1912 after ten months of illegal imprisonment, potentially facing the death penalty for a crime they didn't commit and draining tens of thousands from the various contributing union kitties, Joe Ettor, Arturo Giovannitti and Joseph Caruso's case went to a jury. For added effect, while in the courtroom, the three defendants were kept in metal cages.

When the trial began in Salem, Massachusetts before Judge Joseph F. Quinn, witnesses testified without contradiction that Ettor and Giovannitti were miles away while Caruso, according to multiple witnesses, was at home eating supper with his family at the time of the murder. Ettor and Giovannitti both delivered moving, closing statements on the fruitlessness of forcible oppression of ideas at the end of the two-month long trial.

For a few seconds following the statements, silence prevailed then the entire gallery began to applaud. Judge Quinn slammed his gavel and yelled for order and several bailiffs wasted no time in selecting individuals to be thrown out of the room. However by the time the entire gallery were engulfed by the catharsis, the Chief Bailiff realized the futility of his men's efforts and called them off.

Five minutes later, the room blanketed in silence, Quinn retired the jury. Not knowing if this was the end of their lives and the last of their struggles in America, Ettor and Giovannitti smiled at each other through the their bars while they waited to be led away back to their cells. Only a few hours later all three defendants were acquitted.

In the wake of the trial, Giovannitti produced his first book of poems, a volume of verse entitled Arrows in the Gale which was internationally published in 1914. In an introduction to the book Helen Keller wrote: "Giovannitti is, like Shelley, a poet of revolt against the cruelty, the poverty, the ignorance which too many of us accept." But Giovannitti, following his ten months in prison, avoided involvement in the following, volatile strikes. Instead, he devoted himself to poetry, editing radical journals, and protesting World War I, which claimed two of his brothers. He also translated and wrote the introduction to the American edition of Emile Pouget's lengthy pamphlet, *Sabotage.*

By the 1920's Arturo had left the I. W. W., and had come to be considered one of the greatest orators and poets of the American labor movement. Through the 1920s and 1930s he appeared at various workers' rallies, charming crowds with his Vandyke beard and flowery Italian and English.

Following WWII his health began to fail and he retired to a life of writing. In 1950, Arturo was stricken by paralysis in both legs. He remained bedridden until his death in 1959, in the Bronx, New York  on New Year's Eve. Giovannitti's papers, including a play called "The Alpha and the Omega; In Memory of a very Rich Holy Man", are housed in the University of Minnesota archives.

Joe Ettor went on to become one of the leaders of the 1913 Waiters' Strike in N.Y.C. and the barbers' strike a year later, also in N.Y.C.  He rose to be a member of the executive council of the I.W.W. and in 1916 was expelled along with Arturo and Flynn after a dispute over how to manage the Mesabi Range Wars defence against the U. S. Justice Department. Joe retired to San Clemente, California where he ran a fruit orchard until his death in 1948.

Elizabeth Gurley Flynn, after the Lawrence strike, moved right on to a strike which was fermented and encouraged by the I. W. W.'s victory at Lawrence, the Patterson New Jersey strike.

As part of Wilson's 1915 rampage against anyone or anything mildly associated with the Left, and with the Justice Department hiding behind the Espionage Act, Flynn was indicted, arrested and tried for High Treason for helping to lead the strike at Lawrence three years after the fact. Owing to the flimsy nature of the Government's case, she was immediately acquitted.

Once while visiting songwriter Joe Hill in prison the evening before he was executed, (again for crime for which there was no evidence he was involved in), Hill composed a song in her honor that would become her trademark, The Rebel Girl, thereby guaranteeing that Flynn would remain a well known force in labor politics for the next 40 years.

A founding member of the American Civil Liberties Union, she was involved in the campaign against the conviction of Sacco and Vanzetti.

In 1936 Flynn joined the Communist Party and wrote a bi-weekly column for women's rights for the Daily Worker. Two years later she was elected to the C. P. U .S .A.'s National Committee. In 1942 Flynn ran for Congress in New York and received 50,000 votes.

Flynn was again arrested in 1951 along with other members of the Communist Party despite the fact the party was legal. Herself and alleged associates such as Sterling Hayden, Lee J. Cobb, Elia Kazan and Edward G. Robinson were taken under the Smith Act. She was convicted after nearly a year in custody and a nine-month trial and served more then two years in the women's penitentiary at Alderson, West Virginia and later published a book detailing her time in prison in The Alderson Story: My Life as a Political Prisoner, 1955.

In September of 1964 Flynn succumbed to a life-long heart disorder and died of heart failure while on a speaking tour of the Soviet Union. She was given a full State funeral through Red Square following which her remains were flown back to the U. S. for burial near the graves of Eugene Debs, Haywood and the Haymarket Market Martyrs in Chicago. Originally scheduled to be buried in the Kremlin Wall a plaque now commemorates her contributions to the International Communist Party.

In 1919 during the infamous Palmer Raids where thousands of Eastern Europeans were arrested, displaced, left destitute and deported by J. Edgar Hoover, despite having been granted asylum and citizenship, Giovannitti , Ettor and Flynn were at the forefront of the fight against the illegal extraditions.

Following the trial the famous triumvirate again endured a series of arrests fighting against  human atrocities, and remained, as they would for the next thirty to forty years, a thorn in many an unscrupulous politician's side.

Much like the leaders of the Russian Communist Party, Truman, Hoover, Thomas, (Chairman of HUAC), McCarthy and

Nixon were all master propagandists and much like the Stalin purges, the Communist Witch Hunts of the forties and fifties in America were led by these same men, all of which no doubt hoped Elizabeth Gurley Flynn would die in prison. To their chagrin she did not and following her 28 months in federal prison she lived to see the deaths of Truman, Thomas and McCarthy followed by the various electoral defeats of Nixon through the early sixties.

Given this, it is also interesting to note how the American leaders who hunted Ettor, Flynn and Giovannitti are remembered.

J. Edgar Hoover, aside from being remembered as a cross dresser and habitual voyeur is chronicled in former F.B.I. agent Marston's book on the agency as ". . . being the best friend organized crime ever had." Additionally his collusion with the New York Mafia by taking tips from gangland insiders to win no small sums of cash at the track, are well documented.

J. Parnell Thomas, as Chairman of HUAC and therefore the most powerful of the anti-Freedom of Speechers, was eventually tried and convicted of payroll fraud and for 'Bringing Congress into disrepute.' He was later imprisoned with the great Hollywood writer John Howard Lawson whom he himself had vigorously prosecuted and convicted a short time earlier.

Richard Nixon persecuted the union organizers of the time as Communists in order to help establish his power base. Whatever good he might have done, he is indelibly scarred by the Watergate scandal and will forever be the U. S. leader saddled with the one who lost the Viet Nam war.

Joe McCarthy, heavily in debt, his falsified military records exposed, died a debilitated alcoholic a few short years after his rampage through the halls of justice, censured by his colleagues also for 'Bringing Congress into disrepute.'

As for Carlo Tresca, Flynn's secret lover for many years, he never abandoned the fight for unionism going on to fight in a half dozen major labor battles into the late twenties when he became increasingly concerned about the Fascists and what they were doing to his home country, Italy. He came to fight them and their attempts to institute Fascism in the substantial Italian-

American community in the United States.

He would eventually be instrumental in preventing Mussolini from gaining a political foothold in America however, his efforts cost him his life.

Starting in 1919 and for the rest of his life Tresca was under constant surveillance by the U. S. government. Mussolini even took time out from his busy agenda of conquering Europe, to officially request the U. S. government suppress Tresca's anti-fascist newspaper, Il Martello, (The Hammer). The Justice Department was only to glad to oblige, and ordered the U. S. Postal Service to stop delivering his papers.

When several 'raids' into his printing office followed by wrecking his machines failed he was finally arrested and charged with sending obscene material through the mail. This based on a two line add for the sales of a book on birth control he had once run. At his trial conviction was a far gone conclusion and he was sentenced to one year and a day, just enough to get him deported as a felon back to Italy where he would likely be executed.

After only four months in the Atlanta Federal Penitentiary public outcry over the contrived persecution forced President Coolidge to commute his sentence to time served, technically negating his deportation order.

A short time later he was attacked from behind and had his throat slit. The assassin botched the attempt and Tresca lived.

On January 9, 1943, in Manhattan, N. Y., Tresca's government surveillance team watched as a speeding car attempted to run him down. Two days later, as Tresca was leaving a meeting with his parole officer he dodged his surveillance officers by jumping into a car that was apparently waiting for him. Two hours later, Tresca was crossing Fifth Avenue on foot when a black Ford pulled up beside him and a "short, squat gunman in a brown coat" jumped out and shot him in the back and head with a handgun, killing him instantly.

The black Ford was later found abandoned nearby with all four doors open. It was believed at the time that Carmine Galante was the suspected assassin, acting on orders from Vito Genovese. Galante was taken in and questioned, but never charged and was released.

Interestingly both Galante and Genovese were heavily involved with Commander Haffenden's Top Secret, U.S. Navy operation, Operation Underworld at the time.

Another interesting story concerns Dashiell Hammett, the famed noir writer who served as an operative for the Pinkerton Agency from 1915 to 1921, with time off to serve in World War I.

However, the agency's brutal and ruthless role in union strike breaking eventually disillusioned him. In Butte, Montana, Hammett was offered $5,000 to murder Frank Little, a friend of Big Bill Haywood's and leading organizer for the I. W. W. Hammett refused to commit the murder and subsequently left the agency. A short time later Little was attacked and abducted then lynched by masked vigilantes known to be Pinkerton agents.

As far as Angelo Rocco's future following the strike, on February 21st, 1984, the UPI ran the following story:

### Angelo G. Rocco Dies at 100; Leader in Mill Strike of 1912

*Angelo G. Rocco, a key figure in the Lawrence mill workers' strike of 1912, one of the earliest walkouts in the American labor movement, died Friday in Fort Lauderdale, Fla., after a heart attack and a fall. He was 100 years old.*

*Mr. Rocco was a lawyer who owned a lumberyard in Methuen, Mass., and worked as a builder until he retired at the age of 96,*

*He was a "chief figure" in the nine- week strike and "skipped school [university] to march with pickets from mill to mill," said Gregory G. Rocco, his son. His father was an organizer for the Industrial Workers of the World, which led the strike.*

*"He had worked as a weaver in mills in Madison, Maine, and in Lawrence before he went to high school," the younger Mr. Rocco said. 'His friends were working in the mill."*

*Angelo Rocco, born Dec. 13, 1883, in Caserta, Italy, came to Lawrence in 1909 and graduated from Boston*

*University Law School in 1916. Beside his son, he leaves his wife of 61 years, the former Antonetta Iacobo, with whom he was vacationing in Florida; a daughter, a second son, a sister, 11 grandchildren and two great-grandchildren.*

Despite delaying the Wobbly leaders' trial to distance themselves from the bad publicity of the Lawrence attacks in order to assure themselves of a conviction, it was at least partially due to the violence of the police in Lawrence that the jury had sympathy for Ettor, Giovannitti and their co-accused, Caruso.

The international publicity of the Lawrence strike and the ham-fisted attempt to use the law to murder Ettor, Giovannitti and Caruso altered the subsequent political history of the country. The Lawrence strike not only destroyed the presidential prospects of Governor Foss but provided Roosevelt with ammunition to form the 'Progressive Party' which he predicated on industrial and social reform.

Politically speaking, starting in August of 1913 during the hops pickers' strikes in California,
things would get progressively worse for the Wobblies. Until these strikes, workers were compelled to work in the open fields, men women and children, in the sun with no water for up to 12 to 14 hours a day, sometimes seven days a week.

On the Durst ranch in Wheatland, following unbelievable physical abuse of the migrant workers, two I. W. W. reps, Ford and Suhr, were preaching to the workers the benefits of unionization. The Durst brothers contacted the authorities, reported an impending riot, and two car loads of heavily armed deputies arrived, led by the District Attorney himself. The cowboy lawmen challenged the two organizers and when the workers banded together to prevent the police from arresting the Wobbly speakers, the deputies open fire on the crowd killing four, including two of their own, and wounding many more including women. This was an exact repetition of at least a half dozen previous events all up and down the West Coast.

Upon realizing what they had done the "deputies", along with the dead D. A. they had shot, who had no business being there in the first place, much less shooting at crowds of unarmed workers, fled. State-wide warrants went out for Ford and Suhr for multiple counts of homicide, they were caught, imprisoned, sent to trial, convicted and executed.

The ensuing strikes that swept the country virtually closed down 75 to 80% of U. S. production and scared the be Jesus out of everyone up the chain of command all the way to the White House.  Newly elected Wilson authorized a federal investigation on Wheatland in order to convict the I. W. W. leadership shut them down and put them away for good.

He couldn't find anything, primarily because they hadn't done anything, but he got his chance again in 1914 when The Great War descended upon Europe.

Much like the fiasco in Iraq, the outbreak of WWI in Europe would polarize American opinion even further and, as would be the situation from 1938 to 1941, an American president would consistently promise the English war aide while promising the Americans to keep them out of war.

So, exactly as the Bush government got the brainstorm for the Patriot Act from the Espionage and Sedition Acts the same way he copied 'Freedom Fries' from Wilson's 'Liberty Cabbage', they used the World Trade Center bombings to solidify and enforce their personal powers and strike against their domestic political enemies the way Wilson's government used World War I as an excuse, through passage of the Espionage & Sedition Acts, to crush the I. W. W. once and for all.

It worked well.

Upon the U. S. declaration of war in 1917 the Wobblies wisely ceased all anti-war activity, but even this did not help. In September of that year Department of Justice agents made simultaneous raids on 48 Wobbly union halls across the country and over 164 of the leadership and an unaccounted for  number of the membership were arrested for conspiracy against the United States. One hundred and one went on trial before cowboy judge Kenesaw Mountain Landis.

All were convicted, even those arrested who were not members of the union. They were convicted without benefit of council or a jury trial and were given sentences of up to twenty years. One of those sentenced to prison by Kenesaw and released on bail was the I. W. W. leader 'Big' Bill Haywood. He was sentenced to thirty years.

As prosecutors conspired to find 'evidence' for a death penalty against Haywood, he fled the U. S. to the Soviet Union where he remained until his death in 1928.

He lies buried at the Kremlin with Jack Reed. Half his ashes are interned in the Wall at the Kremlin the other half are buried at the site of The Haymarket Riots & bombing in Chicago, the tragic incident which galvanized his politicalization and subsequent entrance into labor organization.

Following the1917 raids, police-encouraged vigilante violence swept the country. In Centralia, Washington WWI veteran and decorated war hero Wesley Everest, and I. W. W. member, was also arrested on a false charge and then turned over by the Sheriff to a vigilante mob. After smashing out his teeth with a rifle but, they castrated him, hung him three times in three separate places then riddled his body with bullets. It is believed he was then dismembered and hidden in an unmarked graves. The official coroner's report listed Everest's cause of death as "suicide".

These were by no means 'isolated incidents'. There were dozens of these incidents across the country for nearly the entire life span of the I. W. W.

Joe Ettor, along with Gurley Flynn and Carlo Tresca would be amongst the first to be severed from the dying Wobblies in 1916 amidst relentless government sponsored prosecutions. By 1917 the entire organization, though completely legal under existing law, was eviscerated by prison sentences, prosecutions and government sponsored assassinations.

Following the victory of the 1912 textile strike, the American Woolen Company was forced to increase wages. The increases ranged from five to twenty-five percent and included all the ancillary demands of the workers such as not having to pay for their drinking water any more.

The company reached its apogee in the 1920s, when it controlled 20% of the nation's woolen production. However, its water-powered mills were unable to adapt to produce new fabrics in response to changing consumer demand, and the non-unionized Southern mills were able to produce staple woolen products such as blankets more cheaply. The two World Wars were a boom to the A. W. C., keeping the company prosperous into the mid 1940's.

Following the end of the Korean War, government contracts ended. Virtually bankrupt, the American Woolen Co. was absorbed by the Amerstron Corp. in the mid-1950s.

Like other manufacturing companies in the area, the A.W.C. eventually left Lawrence after World War II. The Wood Mill has had several subsequent uses, including as a facility for the Honeywell Corporation. The mill is, as of this writing, currently used for office and light manufacturing facilities for the Psychological Center, Malden Mills and MassInnovation, LLC.

It is a common misconception by many historians and writers of the period that the Wobblies lost most or all of what they had gained in the Lawrence strike. The I. W. W. Local #20 did diminish membership somewhat in the months following their victory and Wood's replacement, (after Wood was forced to resign, not because of the Great Dynamite Plot, but because of the negative press it garnered), and his cronies were able to whittle away at some of the concessions of the workers.

However, of no little consequence were the follow-on victories in Lowell, New Bedford and Little Falls which gave impetus to the rest of the Eastern Seaboard factory workers to rally behind the concept of labor organization which would eventually take hold and provide the workers of America some protection against the government backed ruthlessness of the industrialists.

At least until organized crime entered into the equation. But, that's another story.

However, after Wood was forced to resign and Congress was forced to pass more, though still pitifully inadequate, minimum wage laws in defiance of the industrialists who owned the politicians, including Taft who forfeited all chances of re-election, things were never the same for the Monopolists.

They had been dragged into the public spotlight by the hated "Big" Bill Haywood and the membership of his hated

Industrial Workers of the World.

For his part in the "Great Lawrence Dynamite Plot", Breen was sentenced to three years in prison but served only 18 months and on release, resumed his life.

Wood was eventually brought to trial for complicity in the dynamite plot, but owing to friends in the courts, escaped jail. He was fined $500. After stepping down as CEO he moved to Shawsheen Village, Massachusetts to work in the Trust's interests there and later moved to Florida with his wife. Perhaps emotionally drained by the stress of the 'Rat Race', perhaps consumed by guilt, on February 2nd, 1926 Wood followed Pittman's lead and blew his brains out with a revolver.

Unknown to most of the stockholders, during his tenure as CEO of the woolen conglomerate Wood had cheated the companies out of additional funds having the companies pay his income tax. Consequently, following his death Wood's vast fortune was tangled in the courts for years after until the battle finally reached the Supreme Court.

Rendering their interpretation of the tax laws of the time the Judges, headed by former President of the United States William H. Taft, held that where a third party pays the tax of an individual, that tax constitutes additional income. Wood's lawyers were therefore compelled to pay well over a million dollars in taxes and interest, now deemed in arrears. Even in death the former woolen mill baron's troubles followed him to his grave.

Possibly in part due to the stress suffered during and after the wave of strikes which swept across the U. S. and which planted the seed of labor rights in his steel mills, railways and factories across the country, in March of 1913, J. P. Morgan, commander of one of the largest fortune's in the world, died of a heart attack, exactly one year after the strike.

As a possible barometer of just how intense the material of this chapter of the unacknowledged class wars in American history can be, there is the case of author Anthony Lukas, Pulitzer prize winner for The Big Trouble, the in-depth story of what the Idaho authorities, with the full support of the White House tried to do to Haywood, Pettibone and Moyer and succeeded in doing to countless other I. W. W. organizers.

Lukas was himself left so physically and emotionally spent after seven years of work on the book that on June 5, 1997, after discussing final revisions with his editor, he hanged himself.

Not long after the strike was settled the Lawrence City Fathers ordered the rail station where the police attacks had occurred torn down. Gurley Flynn later commented in an interview, "I am sure one reason is that they didn't want people to be pointing it out as the place where the police and the soldiers had beaten the women and the children."

It is worthy to note how truly astonishing it is what some authority figures will do when they think no one is looking. It rarely occurs to characters of this caliber that no one has to be looking at the time because somebody sure as hell is going to go looking later.

As a final note, David von Drehle writes in his multi-award winning novel, *Triangle*, that in August of 1943 the Tammany political machine, founded at the birth of America late in the eighteenth century, were in a situation whereby they had to sell the New York hall. The buyer? The International Ladies' Garment Workers' Union.

The phrase "poetic justice" comes to mind.

Thanks for the read.

# The American Way